Shadows of the GREEN SKY

THE OGRES' RING SAGA BOOK ONE

MIGUEL SMITH

This is a work of fiction. Similarities to real people, places, or events are entirely coincidental.

SHADOWS OF THE GREEN SKY

First edition. June 24, 2024.

Copyright © 2024 Miguel Smith.

ISBN: 979-8227415998

Written by Miguel Smith.

Shadows of the
GREEN SKY

For JIMMIE, SMITTY, AND HILTON

CHAPTERS:

Prologue *7*
    Chapter One – The Alley *13*
    Chapter Two – Lay of the Land *61*
    Chapter Three – Gathering of Foxes *97*
    Chapter Four – All Roads *147*
    Chapter Five – With any Luck *213*
    Chapter Six – Some Minutes Ahead *261*
    Chapter Seven – Cacophony *319*
    Chapter Eight – The Days Begin *413*
    Chapter Nine – Forty-Eight Hours *469*
Epilogue *513*

Prologue: Early Hours

March 30th, 1972. The night was still in the Cherry Hill neighborhood of Baltimore, Maryland. Rains had passed though hours before, but lightning still flashed in the clouds above. The air still smelled wet as the calm wind blew. Suddenly a light flashed in the sky like a signal flare drawing attention from the entire neighborhood. From it a ball of rings emerged and descended down. It came to rest in an open field between Joseph Avenue and Round Road. Cars passing by stopped. Soon many eyes were on the object. The rings continued to spin and rotate while the object hovered a foot or so off the ground as a small crowd started to form. Flashes from cell phone cameras illuminated the object briefly. Onlookers could make out that there was something among the rings. Just then the rings began to slow. And then stop. They parted and formed staircase for three figures that stepped down from the center. Each wore a sandy colored robe. As they descended none of them seemed to pay any particular attention to anyone gathering around them. One appeared to be a man with lighter skin and longer curly dark hair. Another was a woman of light hair but an olive complexion. Her hands and forearms were encased in what looked like metal gauntlets. Another man dark of skin had a sword at his hip. They all looked around as their feet touched the ground.

"They were here. Recently. Their sin still carries a stench in the air," the dark skinned one said. The woman walked out holding out her armored hand. She breathed in deeply and exhaled.

"Hezekiah is right Ezekiel. We've missed them by mere hours. We draw closer to their departure windows. They're growing careless," she said. Ezekiel looked around and smelled the air himself. He exhaled and looked back at the other two.

"Perhaps Leah. Perhaps. Or they may be finding out they are not nearly as suited to pursue the quest they have insisted on. In either case their incompetence or inadequacies erode what little lead they had to begin with. They merely delay the inevitable. And poorly at that," he said and kneeled down to the touch the ground. As he did a group of people began approaching their position. The trio ignored them and continued to analyze the scene. A group of five young men walked up behind Hezekiah. The expressions on their faces were a mixture of fear and arrogance. One of them addressed him.

"Yo playa. Is you aliens?" he said. Hezekiah didn't immediately respond which seemed to agitate the young man. After a few moments he turned his head to the youth who seemed offended.

"Alien to you I would gather. But not aliens congruent to your world's popular fiction would depict," he said and then resumed what he was doing. The young man looked back at his friends and then he turned back to Hezekiah.

"Well, what are you 'Not Aliens' doing in my neighborhood?" he said aggressively. Again Hezekiah did not immediately respond, which seemed to agitate the young man even more. He turned to the group of youths again.

"We search for sinners," he said. The young man frowned deeply. Then he laughed.

"Hey brotha. If you looking for sinners. You came to the right place. What kind of sinners you looking for?" he said with an antagonistic smile. Again Hezekiah waited to respond. Then he looked at the smiling young man.

"Not really any of your concern. But since you asked. We are looking those would defy God's natural law. Those with the audacity to spread their stain to multiple worlds against the will of God. He so commanded his Angel of Death to select among his ranks three to end their foolishness. We are this three. Angels of Death commanded with this Holy task. Do you have any further questions?" he said and looked at the young man sternly. Getting no answer he turned and resumed what he'd been doing. By then others had begun to gather. An elderly woman walked up behind the young man.

"Clarence? What is going on? Who are these people?" she said. Clarence, without looking at her, responded.

"Space aliens calling themselves angels Grandma. Ain't that some shit. This brotha keep turning his back on me like he all that. Shit, this ain't nothing but another psy-op targeting the neighborhood. You hear me dawg? Ain't buyin' what you're selling! Look at me when I talk to you!" Clarence said angrily. His grandmother grasped his arm, which he shrugged away. He then pulled a pistol out of his waistband. His grandmother's eyes grew wide.

"Clarence baby please don't!" she yelled. Clarence scowled at Hezekiah and disengaged the safety.

"I said look at me motherfucker! Government Spook! You come in here with Area 58 bullshit? To my neighborhood? Fuck You! Turn your ass around and face me!" he screamed and pointed the pistol at Hezekiah. Ezekiel took a small seed, about the size of a pistachio nut, out of his breast pocket and moved it around with his thumb. Hezekiah again did not respond. Clarence's grandmother was emphatic.

"Please baby! Please my baby, put the gun away!" she pleaded and put her hand on his arm. Clarence shrugged her off again.

"Have it your way G-man!" he screamed and opened fire. The clearing cracked again and again as spent casings twirled away from Clarence. Bullets struck Hezekiah who barely seemed to notice. Clarence's grandmother screamed.

"No Baby No!" she shrieked as she grasped at Clarence's pistol. The air cracked and her coat lit up. Clarence looked at her in horror. His grandmother felt her knees buckle and she sank to the ground. Clarence dropped the gun and caught her.

"No Grandmamma No!" he screamed. Hezekiah seemed to conclude what he'd been doing and looked over at Clarence who was holding his grandmother. She was bleeding profusely from a wound in her chest. Hezekiah began to slowly walk toward them. Clarence saw him out of the corner of his eye and picked up the gun again and pointed it at Hezekiah's face. The seed in Ezekiel's hand began to grow then and extended into a staff-like weapon. Hezekiah kept walking forward. Clarence pulled the trigger again not realizing the slide had already locked back. He dropped the gun and then he pulled a knife from behind his back and pointed the blade at Hezekiah. The angel held out his hands. Tears rolled down Clarence's face.

"Stay away from us motherfucker!" he snarled. Hezekiah knelt down close anyway. So much so the tip of Clarence's blade touched his robe.

"The flesh of Henrietta Finch is broken. I understand your distress Clarence Fillmore. You were named after your great-grandfather. He was a postman in this very neighborhood for thirty-five years after serving in World War I. He was an honorable man who loved his community. You are suffering from great pain right now. Your relationship with Althea Smith has ended as she has taken your daughter to live in another part of the city. You have a deep distrust with the authorities that facilitated this fracture. All authorities for that matter. You distrust me. I am not here to harm you. None of us are. You are not who we are looking for. Henrietta is a beautiful name. I am quite fond of it. This evening is not one for these distresses," he said. Henrietta reached out weakly and touched Hezekiah. His robe was soft and warm to her fingertips. Ezekiel approached and laid a hand on Clarence's shoulder.

"Please if you would, lower the blade." He said. Clarence looked up at him. Ezekiel's dark eyes were kind and showed no anger toward him. The angel looked down at Clarence's knife and looked back at him.

"Your daughter loves you and is looking forward to the day the two of you can decorate your Christmas tree together again. This will take some time, but it will come again," he said. Clarence slowly lowered his blade and looked down at his dying grandmother.

"But I just killed my grandmamma. I ain't never gonna see my baby again," he said as tears continued to roll down his cheeks. Ezekiel shook his head. Hezekiah smiled slightly.

"Destiny is greater than flesh. Her death tonight is not part of the structure," he said and reached into Henrietta's coat pocket and pulled out a deformed bullet and handed it to Clarence.

"Don't lose this again and enjoy the time you still have," he said and looked into Henrietta's eyes. There was an understanding then between them. She smiled and touched her chest. There was no wound now. She looked up at Clarence and embraced him. Hezekiah and Ezekiel rose to their feet and looked around at the other people.

"You should be indoors now. A hailstorm is inbound. Thirty-five minutes out," Ezekiel said and turned toward the craft. Leah turned and held out a hand. The vehicle began to flash as it activated. As Hezekiah began to turn Henrietta looked up at him.

"Thank you," she said. Hezekiah stopped and looked back.

"The thanks don't ultimately go to me. But, as long as things follow the natural order I am satisfied that others appreciate that it is so. Farewell Clarence and Henrietta," he said and turned. The trio entered the spinning wheels of their vehicle, which then lifted off the ground and rose into the sky. With a loud guttural wail, the craft disintegrated into bolt of lightning that filled the sky. Onlookers looked back at their phones to post their pictures and videos, but found nothing.

Chapter One: The Alley

It had been a few hours since the sun was overhead. A dry windy morning had given way to a virtually dead calm. No circulation in this idle stillness that hung in this isolated alley in the middle of this dying city. A city that cried upward and around as it belched smoke, screaming and sirens. The alley walls radiated immense heat stored within from hours of punishing sun beaming down from cloudless skies. The acrid redolence of cooking asphalt made each breath an ordeal. Antonio Salazar could almost hear in his head the sound of an electric range creaking and warping as its expanding element began scream out light.

    He sat there in a heap of exhaustion and pain on a slab of cracking blacktop, gravel and scattered debris. His spot was shaded but it offered him little comfort as the entire alley, and city for that matter, was an oven baking around him and everything else suffering inside it. He also found no assistance from the damaged cooling system of his valiant suit. A gold turmeric hued melding of advanced light tactical armoring and technological enhancements. This would be otherwise a trivial issue repaired or replaced at a later time. This generation of valiant was all but obsolete and the unit Antonio wore was more than well past it's need of replacement. He hated breaking in new gear and valiants were expensive and time consuming to design and manufacture. An inconvenience he very nearly didn't live to regret. His dark hair with flecks of gray glistened with perspiration that dripped from exhausted pores as he looked out ahead of him with reddening dark eyes stinging with sweat dripping into them. Twenty feet away lay a motionless form on top of the shattered remains of an old shipping crate. It was a man who just mere few minutes ago took Antonio down to his last fraction of a second. A man who was absolutely determined to make this dirty alley bear witness to the last of Antonio Salazar. Also a man who, until just 10 minutes before, was a good friend and colleague he'd fought side by side with in many a venue.

    Estrello Nocivo was his name. A good man but also one that Antonio Salazar had good reason to believe was the deadliest creature he would ever come to know. The last six minutes only served to reinforce this belief.

He was doing all he could to fight off shock and dial down the effects of the curse which made even the dripping of water around him lash out at him like a cornered animal. Against other men it could be counted on to give him a needed edge. Today no such advantage was apparent. Nocivo was a completely different fighter. Hard forged technique, precision with a seamless transition to mercurial adaptive improvisation made him a fool's gamble for any opponent who could not adapt as readily. Most could not. It was appallingly effortless for him to diverge on the fly. Knowing what Nocivo was going do a split second before mattered very little. He was no ordinary opponent that made all the same mistakes other men would. The men fighting side-by-side Nocivo knew where Salazar's weaknesses resided. Any true hunter would. Antonio had knowledge as well. Nocivo was an ambush predator. Quick. Close quarters. As few strikes as necessary that lead up to a killing blow was his signature strategy. A prolonged fight did neither man any favor. A quick end to the fight was never going to happen either. Nocivo's blood tally was far longer than his, and Salazar knew it. There was no card Antonio would be allowed to leave aside. All had to be played, or all would come to an end.

The brickwork and even the ground itself bore the open wounds of their clash. If the cuts were into flesh the alley would bleed and awash the scene in a grisly crimson tint. There was plenty of real blood though. As advanced as the materials of Salazar's valiant were, Nocivo's vulcanium blade would not be denied a taste. Antonio groaned as he began to move. From a compartment on his side he took out a pair of aviator sunglasses and put them on. They immediately activated and connected to the tech in his suit. Paltry technology compared to his helmet, but it would have to do. Nothing but bad news popped up on the heads up display screens imbedded into the optics.

"Guess I voided the warranty," he weakly muttered. He didn't need them to know he was in bad shape. Rips and tears meant to be killing strokes to his heart, lungs, and throat bled out and stained the high tech polymer and alloy plating of his armor. Armor that thankfully did its job. But only just. Millimeters separated Salazar from Nocivo from succeeding in putting him in the grave. Millimeters would have to do. Antonio didn't have time or right to ask for more.

The purpose for which himself and his colleague were here in this place still loomed over them like a shadow with eyes gazing down on them unmoved by their violence toward one another, or the wounds they both bore because of it. Hours earlier Antonio was lounging around a tropic themed restaurant called The Cove, which is where the crew of the VCS Natty Bumppo convened most commonly for a good meal, completing crossword puzzles and enjoying a hot cup of cinnamon tea. It's what he normally did between his long stretches in the lab. Every hour he spent there seemed to add another gray to his dark hair. This was the price of peak science, which was his passion. Located at the western end of the ship, The Cove was one of the Bumppo's fifty major on-board restaurants that still had an active kitchen. The others were primarily being used as storage areas or otherwise repurposed, as much of the ship lay unused. The Cove was chosen as the primary common area due to it being relatively close to the west end personal quarters, and it being the most protected and easily defendable should the ship's outer defenses be breached. It was contingency not likely to be utilized, given all the other layers of structure around it, and all the levels of security set up within them, but still a comforting bit of trivia.

There were others here this late morning of the Fifth of September. The morning shift had largely come and gone at this point but there were still a few stragglers that had yet to be anywhere but here. Several booths away from Salazar sat the Chief Engineer. She was a younger woman approaching thirty with a shade blonder than auburn hair. The crew just called her Chief. She had a proper name but didn't like to use it. In fact nobody knew her real name.

Chief was a name she'd chosen for herself. If anyone asked why, she'd say it was a long story she wasn't ready to share. Outside of a handful of people nobody knew what story she could tell. She was the fourth of her name. Three others had come before her, and shared her memories. By going by Chief she distinguished herself from the others. However, unlike the others she was an engineer by design, as well as in training. A fascinating story to be sure. But not one she would tell at the moment even if she felt compelled to. She wasn't a very tall woman. Only standing about five-foot-two. Her hair was tied back and peeked out from under her themed ball cap. She didn't have time to brush it properly this morning. Other things commanded her attention. At present Chief busied herself pouring over all manner of schematics, diagrams, reports trying to solve issues with the ship's engines which were heavily damaged and needed extensive repair. Solutions weren't coming easily. The Ship was drastically modified incorporating a variety of technologies that required some exotic and exceedingly rare materials that were hard to come by and in many cases very difficult to fabricate with. The Bumppo was a formidable asset. And had been missed these last few weeks since a particularly drastic escapade. One of which Chief was still dealing with the considerable consequences from. There was damage all over the ship that seemed to take up most of her time as she put out one proverbial fire after another. Automated repair mechanisms didn't help much either. It was exhausting, but The Cove was a nice place to hang out to unwind from her growing list of tasks.

Commodore Josef Mikko Persson had commissioned the Vacation Cruise Ship Natty Bumppo to be the new flagship for his fleet of merchant ships. The crew knew him as "JP" or "The Commodore". The Bumppo was purposely crafted for operating along the borders some very hostile, but very lucrative, systems. The largest configuration of the model VCS-645981-Rho cruise liner structurally possible with expanded living quarters, amenities, excursion gondola bays, and an additional engine system were ordered stock and delivered to Commodore Persson under the false premise it would be used as intended. A luxury liner used to ferry thousands of wealthy clients from destination to destination.

This is what the public and shipping authority understood to be true. Persson had other plans, which saw the Bumppo diverted from its original course to a dark location. There it would have most of it's outer living quarters and amenities removed and replaced with thickened and vastly over engineered hull plating, as well as heavily reinforced understructure to support the added mass and increased inertial strain from an expanded engine system. What space wasn't taken up by the ship's new armor and skeleton was then taken up with weapon batteries, both projectile and energy based, which were illegally obtained through various underworld channels. The Bumppo's existence was highly illegal, breaking a long list of laws and regulations prohibiting the construction and ownership of what was effectively a warship outside of a military or law enforcement entities. A grand masquerade, but a necessary one for two very important reasons. The first of which was the lax attitudes of the aforementioned structures of military and law enforcement. In the areas of space The Commodore did business in, any law enforcement or military presence was sparse and complacent. Every merchant ship operating in this sector had some form of illegal and unregulated weapon system. The degree of lawlessness there necessitated it. Also The Commodore himself was a dominant figure. Some might describe him as a kind of gangster that attended to his business in an active fashion that would earn him considerable reputation among those who would otherwise have the aims and means of incurring into his territory or threatening any of his assets. The Commodore was not a man to cross. And he had the arms, ships and most importantly the captains to hold his territory with few challengers. The Bumppo was a vessel, in its scale and ambition that set it in another league entirely. One might even describe it as unreasonable. In comparison, its sister ship The VCS Scarlett Pimpernel was far less ambitious. A modification of the VCS-495203-Beta it was no vessel to be underestimated, but its scope was scaled far back from its sister, The Natty Bumppo. Commodore Persson's most trusted captain when completed would helm it. The Commodore sat in a booth adjacent Chief with his teenage daughter Martha as they dined on their breakfasts of chicken and waffles, and strong black tea. He was massive man towering over most on the ship, and dwarfed Martha considerably. His fiery red hair and beard gave him a level of additional intimidation few could ignore. Even if they had never heard him speak and only seen the intensity of his eyes which commanded their owl level of respect from people around him. Martha by contrast was not very intimidating at all with dark hair tied into pigtails. They both read silently as they ate. Their tablets propped up in front of them. The pair shared much in common. Not least of which was their love of literature. While Josef preferred authors such as James Fenimore Cooper, Louis L'amour, Jules Verne, and Mark Twain, his daughter Martha opted for more contemporary authors such as Tom Clancy, Isaac Asimov, Robert Ludlum and J.K. Rowling. They also shared other interests as well. Their love of flying is what truly bonded them together after Martha's mother passed. She was almost eight years old and in the care of her ailing grandfather who was a powerful shaman in his First Nations tribe of Northern Alberta, Canada. She had 'The Eyes of the Red Fox' according to tribal lore, which gave her The Sight. Being young her talents were only beginning to emerge and in need of honing. Antonio Salazar had The Sight as well and had reluctantly agreed to be her tutor as a favor to her father. Martha's grandfather had passed and could no longer be her teacher. Martha would need further guidance. Wesley Two Eagles was one of Josef's dearest and oldest friends. During his stays on Earth Josef and Wesley would spend entire nights talking about old tribal lore. One winter Wesley introduced Josef to his daughter who had just left the army to pursue work in the private sector. The two didn't immediately hit it off, but grew close to each other when Wesley was given a grim diagnosis. It began a seventeen yearlong battle he would ultimately lose. The pair married despite all the difficulties they may face in the future. Josef had long feared marrying given his unique situation.

But at this time, for reasons he would not be able to really understand or articulate, he gave in and followed his heart. Their daughter would be born the following January. Josef's work kept him off planet for long periods of time, but he cherished his time with his family upon his returns home. After a few years his fears felt like they were passing and he began to come to terms with what was, and what would inevitably be. But he wasn't prepared for the news of an electrical fire at the power plant. His wife did not survive. Her actions saved many others though. But this was little consolation. The old fear took back its seat at the table in his mind, and it gorged voraciously.

Over at the restaurant's bar stood Phil Tabaracci sporting his usual big goofy grin peering out from his razor stubble mug. The crew called him Tabs. He was hired on accident by a recruiter working for The Commodore, who wasn't altogether in the loop as far as the nature of the Natty Bumppo, or what types of position actually needed filled. Tabs just showed up at the Armey Angle Space Station, a small planetoid, where the Bumppo was docked after its surreptitious refit. Upon his arrival he was quite taken aback at how small the crew was to man such a massive ship. Most luxury cruise vessels this size carried a crew of tens of thousands to cater to the hundreds of thousands it ferried from place to place. There was, at most, ninety people he could see gathered at the sign-in. Not very many struck him as people he envisioned would work on a vacation cruise vessel either. The few who did were looking around at everyone else like he was. They had much of the same look on their faces. He'd find out later the same recruiter that hired him signed them up. He had a bad feeling about this situation. He half expected the gig to fall through and be thanked for his time as he made his way back to a job listings hell. A fate he was piecing a plan in his head to face. He was taken aback when the cargo bay doors opened and everyone was invited on. He was even more taken aback by what he was seeing in the ship. The Commodore discovered Tabs' presence quickly and took him aside not sure what to do with him. Tabs informed him how he'd gotten hired and who had been his recruiter. After a heated call this was confirmed. Josef still didn't know what to do about it. He then invited Tabs to the last working restaurant on the ship and asked him to make him a lonkero. Tabs did this not knowing why this particular drink was requested. Josef was impressed and decided to keep him on. He wasn't going to bring on a bartender, but a computer couldn't mix a drink the way a man could. The contract Tabs signed gave him ownership of the bar with some very harsh non-disclosure agreements. None of which fazed him much. Just the day prior he'd walked out of his old job in Toronto after one argument too many with a man he liked too little. Now he had job security with a guaranteed regular clientele, dirt cheap rent, and more adventure than he could ever dream of. And The Commodore paid Very well on top of what he'd make tending bar. Hard to pass up with the way the economy was headed.

In the kitchen behind Tab's bar A.J. Tucson, called Deuce by the crew, was helping his sous chef Penny and station chef Seijin clean up his kitchen along with all those who worked under them. He was the grandson of a Black Southern Baptist minister and had grown up cooking in the church kitchen. He had known The Commodore for about ten years after striking up a conversation with him in the little Ft. Worth restaurant he started working in after moving west from his home town. Seeing the young man's potential The Commodore put the idea of Deuce applying for culinary school. He did just that. It took him five long years to save up for it. But he did it, and he did well graduating with honors. Sometime later The Commodore got a call. A day later Deuce got a job on one of Persson's ships. Now he was here with Penny and Seijin. Two of the most disciplined people he'd shared a kitchen with. Deuce had dreamed of being the head chef of a big restaurant on ground, or in space. This gig was beyond anything he could ever imagined, and despite the small clientele this was right where he wanted to be. Commodore Persson paid well and the tastes of the crew were varied enough he never found himself bored. He knew Penny and Seijin felt the same. Harrison Station was a dead end for most. It was an opportunity however for those that fit in nowhere else to find employment. It was one of several stations owned by Josef Persson, and where one his freighters, the FSV Hartdegen, docked most frequently. Deuce worked there for a time before formally joining the crew of The Hartdegen. He never forgot the work ethic of Penny and Seijin. When it came time for Commodore Persson to select a kitchen staff for The Bumppo the only two people Deuce could recommend were Penny and Seijin. Now the trio ran this kitchen.

Aside from the kitchen at the register stood Rick Patterson, the Maître d' and co-owner of The Cove along with Deuce. He wasn't as tall as JP, but he was built as big as The Commodore was. Some people joking referred to him, as 'The Black JP' which he thought was hilarious. He was an imposing but welcoming figure at The Cove. He was tabulating receipts from the breakfast rush and was recording the numbers with E.V.E., which was The Bumppo's onboard AI.

Patterson had been working in one capacity or another for Commodore Persson for the last twenty years. He usually found himself as a head chef for one ship or another. Now he was the Maître d' of The Cove. It was a long ways away from his time in an Army mess hall. Now he was running his own restaurant on a ship in very unique circumstances. When he was told about his promotion, and offered The Cove, the only partner and man for the job as his head chef he could think of was Deuce. Rick met him through The Commodore a few years prior. The young man reminded him of a good friend he had back in the army who went MIA after a mission to a remote outpost in a dangerous part of space called The Graft. It was an area of planetoids, which was dotted with cobalt mines. The official story was their ship broke apart in rough planetary atmosphere. But this story never sat well with Rick because he knew every man in the platoon that was sent. He cooked for them every day and heard every one of their stories. They were his brothers. Rick never got more than the official report no matter whom he asked and how many times he asked. The Graft was an area of space controlled by powerful people who could afford to keep certain matters quiet. After he left the military he took a job with a man who had a dubious reputation but one that paid well and took care of his people. Commodore Persson saw everyone who worked for him as his people. He was also a man who could gain access to information in ways few others could. Even so new revelations in the case of The Graft had been few and slow coming. One key thing had come to light though. Wreckage of the ill-fated army vessel was found on two different worlds in the same system. This was dismissed as simply as case of two different incidents involving two different ships. It didn't take into account the age of the wreckage and that how another ship of that class had been sent to that system in the same time frame. Records identifying this second ship disappeared. This raised considerable suspicion in The Commodore given that the army was meticulous about keeping records of their fleets. Even decommissioned vessels sold to the private sector. Though nobody could account for this mysterious second ship. Josef vowed to continue pursuing this matter, and made good on his promise. The Commodore tried avenues that were legal. This predictably proved fruitless. His new approach was decidedly less legal. Within weeks a cadre of corrupt officials, military personnel, and cobalt industry figures were arrested. The Commodore would not speak of what it took to get this information. Rick has never asked.

On the wall mounted television in the main dining area of The Cove the morning news broadcast droned on about this and that. The weatherman Grant Kale seemed to be artificially enthusiastic about an arctic blast that was headed south into central Texas. It was likely to bring moderate rainfall and gusts up to fifteen miles per hour by the first of October. Late summer had been cooler than usual which suited Martha just fine. She wasn't a fan of the triple digit heat that had graced San Antonio for much of the last four months. Nor was she a fan of Grant Kale and his saccharine delivery. She preferred the people on The Weather Channel. They weren't much more accurate, but at least they didn't have an insufferable demeanor. Thankfully the weather report was over and the camera switched over to the anchorman Trae Dillon. He had a grin spanning ear to ear and tapped his handful of notes on his desk like he could barely stop himself from burying a lead.

"That was super exciting Grant. I'm sure San Antonians are glad to get a break from the heat. Now we go to Amanda Gutierrez live right now at the Alamodome with four members of America's own Civic Protectors in town to promote Get Fit U.S.!" Dillon said with a glint in his eye as the camera changed and new graphics unfolded to set up the field shot. There, wide-eyed and gleeful, was Amanda Gutierrez standing next to Patriot Man, Madam Cardigan, and the detective duo The Night Eagle and Proto Jay. The Civic Protectors looked as enthusiastic to be there, as Amanda appeared to be. With the exception of Night Eagle, whom appeared to want to be anywhere but the parking lot of the Alamodome. Proto Jay seemed to be in far better spirits as the wind wisped around his blonde hair.

"Good morning San Antonio. I'm Amanda Gutierrez reporting live from the Alamodome with The Civic Protectors! They're here to Get US Fit with Get Fit U.S.!" she said almost half chuckling as she tipped her microphone over to Patriot Man all decked out in his blue and red tactical suit with bronze Liberty Bell shoulder patches. He had a big winning smile and a thumb up to greet Amanda.

"Thank you Amanda and the great city of San Antonio for welcoming us here. Admiral Mercury, Full Scale and rest of the gang are awful sorry they couldn't make it out, but I know they're cheering us on. It's such a bright wonderful day in America Amanda, to get focused on building on that great American Spirit and put that good work in," Patriot Man chimed. Amanda seemed to glow at the sound of Patriot Man's voice.

"And how do we do that Patriot Man?" Amanda inquired, almost humming into her mic. Patriot Man snapped his fingers and pointed his blue-gloved finger at the camera.

"By getting fit Amanda. Getting Fit, with Us. Your Civic Protectors," Patriot Man said before winking at the camera. Off to the side Night Eagle's eyes seemed to narrow in a subtle glare. Madam Cardigan and Proto Jay seemed to be more in the spirit of the occasion and pointed at the camera as well.

"I'm kind of disappointed that The Four Men, San Antonio's own team of crime fighters, aren't out here to help everyone Get Fit," Amanda said. Patriot Man didn't hesitate and held up a finger to the camera.

"Now now Amanda, you mustn't fuss. We can help America Get Fit knowing that The Four Men are out there working hard to keep the city safe from those who would seek to harm it's valuable financial institutions and the citizens of this great city that depend on them," Patriot Man said with a wink and a snap of his fingers. Martha looked over at her father who didn't seem to be paying any attention to the television.

"Looks like the Protectors are in town. Why didn't they call any of you downtown to Get Fit U.S.?" she said. Josef looked up at Martha with a plain if dismissive expression. He rolled his eyes and sighed.

"We're more on a 'don't call us, we'll call you' kind of basis. If they need to fill a collaboration quota they can call up The Guardian League on the other side of the pond. We're D-list at best in the grand scheme of things. Also not even capes in the traditional sense. We stop a bank robbery or two on occasion just for appearances sake. What we really do is none of their business. None of us are overjoyed to even be on their radar to begin with, but it's hard to operate the way we do without running into certain people," he replied. Martha laid down her reader and picked up her mug of tea.

"So you've said before. But don't you think it's out of place for them to be here on TV without someone from your team there to represent?" she said before taking a sip. Josef shook his head.

"Not our scene. Even if they did call, I'm with Skip on being aloof. Once you get on a buddy level with these people it gets hard to breathe without them in your business pretty damn quick. Can you imagine Tony hanging out with any of them?" Josef said. Martha thought about it and then glanced over her shoulder at Salazar. Overhearing their conversation, he was sporting a half grimace.

"Leave me out of cape talk thank you. I have enough stress as it is," Antonio grumbled in his deep toned voice before looking back away. Martha turned back to her father who was shutting off his reader and setting it aside.

"Where even is Skip?" she said as Josef pulled out his wallet to pay the check. He answered promptly.

"Dawson's I expect. Black powder competition is a month away and he wants to be ready win back first place. He hates being number two. And I don't think his horse does either. The both of them are bizarrely competitive. It's weird," he said as he pulled out cash for the bill and tip. Martha kind of nodded her head awkwardly.

"Blueskin is a weird horse," she said as Lillian the waitress stopped by their table to attend to the check.

"Can I get you anything else? We have pecan pies fresh out of the oven for the lunch shift," she said. Josef smiled but added a declining shake of his head. Lillian smiled back and walked off with the check.

Antonio raised a hand as she was walking past and as he was finishing his tea. He set down his mug and picked up his book of crosswords as he got up.

"Keep the change. I'll get a slice of pie to go," he said to Lillian before turning toward the register. She nodded in acknowledgment and headed toward the kitchen. Antonio made it as far as the bar before he stopped.

Phil was drying off a glass and watched as an uneasy look wrote itself across Salazar's face. He put down the glass and came from around the bar.

"Hey guy!" he said with some panic in his voice as he approached Antonio who dropped his crossword book and fell to one knee. Phil knew what this was. He'd been part of this crew long enough to know the signs. Josef took notice of this immediately and looked at his daughter. Martha instantly knew what was happening by the look in his eyes and waited for the signs. She couldn't feel them yet, but she knew full well they were coming. Phil grabbed Antonio's shoulder to keep him steady.

"You see the colors eh?" he asked with growing concern. Antonio could barely hear him. The vertigo was kicking in. It was kicking hard. The synapses in his brain were firing like his mind was fragmenting in a strong magnetic field. The colors were coming. He braced himself like he'd done hundreds of times before. But something was very wrong. By now everyone in the restaurant was paying attention to the scene unfolding. Rick looked back at Deuce who rushed over to the comms next to his station. Phil grabbed Antonio's arm and helped him over to a stool at his bar. Salazar awkwardly hunched over onto the bar knocking over some empty metal tumblers which hit the floor behind the bar with a ringing clash.

"Shit is hitting rough! Fucker is close! So Close! Color is all Hell! Mind the kid! She's going to burn up!" Antonio grunted as the world around splintered and fell away.

Then it hit. It was as if all of his nerves became exposed all at once and burst into flames. In the distance he could feel them. It was like anger. Bitter and predatory anger crashing toward him like a swarm of locusts caught in whirlwind screaming hatred. The weight of accusation crushed him under its heel. Then he saw them in the distance. They were here and they brought rage with them. Beads of sweat were already forming on Martha's forehead as she witnessed Antonio falling apart on the other side of the restaurant. This was as bad as she had ever seen. Deuce was shouting for at somebody for assistance over the comms. Rick had rushed over to Antonio and was helping Phil hold him up onto the bar. Lillian and some of the other waiting staff were walking toward

Martha. They appeared to be walking slowly. It looked odd. Martha looked around. Everyone was moving the same. Time was grinding to a halt all around her. Then a sharp pain began in the back of her head like an icepick slowly lodging itself in her brain. It had begun. Her father got up and placed his hands on her shoulders to keep her steady. The waiting staff stood around and watched in horror as The Sight took Martha over.

"Breathe child. Remember what Tony taught you," he said quietly as Martha's state rapidly declined. Chief was standing at this point. Her face was flush with confusion. She looked over at Deuce who pulled the silent alarm to alert ship security and infirmary staff. She then looked up and around at the walls. The dash alert system should have activated by now. She rushed over to Martha's side to keep her from falling out of the booth. She looked back up at the walls. Her eyes were flashing with alarm.

"Why Haven't Alarms Tripped?" she yelled. Martha winced in pain as she braced herself on the table of her booth. The air grew heavier and her breathing became taxed. She bore down as hard as she could. This was nothing like she had ever experienced. Like powerful wind blown nails it struck her. She tried to bear down harder, but it was too much. The wave slapped her down and bowled her over. Her mind tried to grip something. Anything. Everything slipped through her fingers as she tumbled backwards into the darkness.

"Colors are too close" she managed to mutter through desperate gasps.

Antonio gripped the brass pole that ran along the top of the bar so hard his knuckles were a pale white and the pole itself began to twist in its seating. The colors wrapped around him like a circle of accusers striking him and clawing at him.

"Too oggdim kloss____," he wheezed in response. Then he felt himself start passing out. Phil recognized this and prepared himself to catch dead weight. But then the episode stopped and the image became clear in Antonio's mind. Martha's symptoms weren't as quick to subside. A cool calm took over Antonio's mind. He could see the colors. He knew what they meant. As quickly as they arrived, they passed from his eyes. Still very disoriented he looked over in Martha's direction.

"You get the locus this time kid?" he shouted. Martha couldn't hear him. She was curled up in a ball as the darkness howled around her. It picked her up and slammed her down knocking her limp. She was picked up again and thrown high and spun in the air helplessly before hitting the ground. The darkness screamed at her again as she helplessly curled into a ball. It howled at her from all directions. Their screams struck her again and again. Then a light broke the darkness. Martha cracked open an eye and looked upward. There they were. In the distance she could hear Antonio's voice. He kept repeating the same thing over and over again. Slowly the darkness melted away and Martha found herself slumped over the table in front of her. Her face was lying on her tablet. In the corner of her eye she saw her father, Chief, and the waiting staff hovering over her. Then she heard Antonio's voice again. She picked her head up.

"No Tony. I saw the colors. I know there's red somewhere. I didn't get the locus. I could feel it was close though," she replied as loudly as her voice would let her. Antonio threw her a weak thumb up.

"No problem kid. You'll get the hang of the locus. Just takes time," he said and inhaled deeply. Just then the ships alarms began to ring surprising everyone in the room. As the lights flashed around them Phil looked up and raised his hand.

"You kidding me my guy? Now?" he said with exasperation. Projectors kicked on from the restaurant walls and ceiling and the image of E.V.E., the ship's artificial intelligence, came into focus.

"Sensors have detected a disturbance," she announced. All Chief could do is scowl and whip out her tablet. Her fingers furiously danced across the screen. Phil was having none of it.

"No, yeah no kidding," a frustrated Phil remarked. E.V.E. shrugged her shoulders.

"Hey I'm only as quick as the dash interface tech that I have to work with. I didn't get any indication from it until this already started. I do the best I can with the tech at my disposal. Anyway Deuce already put the word out, but I'm still programmed to alert the crew. Settle down man," she said. Phil wasn't happy with this answer at all and was about to retort. Antonio raised his hand and looked up at them both.

"Esta bien. It's okay. Other things to worry about. You get Skip and Strat?" he said as he felt his strength beginning to return.

"Skipper didn't answer his phone and Strat is en route. I wouldn't expect him anytime soon. He had to travel a good distance to fill up. I'll get Terry up to speed," E.V.E. said before the projectors shut off. Antonio looked back up at Phil and flashed two fingers. Phil nodded and went back behind the bar to grab and bottle of Jim Beam.

"You got it guy," Phil said as he picked up a glass and poured one for Salazar. Over at Persson's table Martha had regained some of her composure. Josef picked her up as medical staff rushed into the restaurant. Antonio downed his glass of bourbon and pointed over to Josef and Martha. The medics unfolded a stretcher and helped to lower Martha down. Her body went limp as she came to rest on it. The medics stood up and gently began walking her out of The Cove. She looked up at Antonio as she was carried past him.

"Does this get any easier?" she could only loudly whisper. Antonio looked down at her. He could see in her eyes she was very scared. She had every right to be. The Sight wasn't a pleasant thing by any measure. He didn't want to exacerbate the situation, but he also didn't want to coat it with sugar either.

"Lo siento. Será más difícil a medida que te hagas más fuerte," he replied. Martha just stared at him. This puzzled Antonio for a moment, but then he realized he must have been speaking Spanish to her.

"No," he just said simply. Martha didn't like hearing that but seemed to appreciate Salazar's brevity and honesty nonetheless. Josef laid his hand on Martha's shoulder and held her hand as the medical staff began wheeling towards the exit. Josef looked back at Antonio.

"Get to Skip, ASAP Tony. I'm going with Martha to the infirmary and start her on some fluids and sedatives," he said to Antonio and he walked out of the restaurant.

"I'll do the same," Antonio replied and flashed another two fingers at Phil. A second glass of bourbon was poured and slid over. Antonio swirled the liquor around in the glass to check out its legs and was about to drink. Chief walked up to him with a disgusted look on her face. He turned and looked at her.

"Okay?" he muttered as she glared.

"I am not happy about this. I am not happy about any of this. First you people burn out my engines. Now your stupid dash tech isn't even in synch with Evie. What if the colors like that didn't hit here, but in another part of the ship and Martha was alone? No detection. No med team. Tough luck for her right? What if someone found you at the bottom of the stairs with your head cracked open? Tough luck for Tony! Skipper is going to hear about this!" Chief growled. Antonio was almost at a loss.

"Yeah, well okay I'm about to go find him. I'll pass on your report," he said almost stuttering.

"Oh no. Hell no! I'm handing him this report myself. In Person! Now!!" she shouted. Antonio nodded slowly in agreement.

"Groovy groovy. Have fun," he said and gave her a thumb up. He started to raise his glass again, but Chief snatched it out of his hand and downed it herself startling both Antonio and Phil.

"Saddle up Sport! You're driving!" Chief barked and tossed the glass to Phil. They both looked at each other. Then they looked back at Chief. Rick and Deuce, watching the scene, had the same expression. Antonio and Phil looked back at each other.

"Sport?" Antonio muttered. Phil didn't seem to have an answer and just tilted his head to the side.

"I'm not paying for that one," Antonio said as he pointed to the glass in Phil's hand.

"Yeah, no yeah. I'll put it on her tab," Phil said and set the empty glass into the sink beside him. Pauly, the ship's range master, a taller burly dark bearded man, walked into the bar and sat down.

"Sounds like there was an alarm," he said. Neither Antonio nor Phil could say much.

"You could say that" Antonio replied. As he got up to head down to the garage level he gave Pauly a fist bump.

"But we got this man" he said. Just then seven members of the security team rushed into the restaurant. They looked around like caffeinated meerkats to see what the emergency was. Antonio wiped the sweat from his brow and shook his head.

"Scene Secure! Conformation Salazar Hotel Bravo November 868!" Antonio shouted in their direction. The team lead Hudgens looked over at Antonio who gave them a thumb up before he walked away and disappeared through an exit.

"Acknowledged Security Protocol Victor Charlie Sierra 702!" the team lead yelled back. Rick walked up to the security team and they stood to attention as he approached.

"Sir!" the team lead said respectfully to Rick.

"At ease Hudgens. I expect y'all want a debrief?" Rick replied.

"Affirmative" said the team lead. Rick stepped to the side with an open hand pointing to a nearby booth.

"Step into my office" he said. The effects of The Colors had all but diminished by the time Antonio caught up to Chief a few levels down. She moved quickly for a shorter woman. Particularly if she had a high priority task in the forefront of her mind that was normally the case no matter what time of day it was. She was a little auburn-ish dynamo with a tablet and a schedule to keep. And keep it she would. Salazar wouldn't normally take the trouble to keep pace with anyone but The Colors hadn't hit him this hard in many years. Long before he knew anyone here. He was seventeen and out in the Texas Hill Country with a pair of ex-IDF commandos that his father had hired to train him in self defense. An attack a few years prior on his family by militants at one of his father's overseas facilities had left a number of emotional scars in both Antonio and his younger brother Marcelo. The ex-commandos did what they could to care for Antonio while he endured The Sight. He had had episodes for years starting in early childhood, but they were comparatively mild and he never mentioned their true extent. But all this changed. He was found lying in a heap near camp. His mentors sprung into action and cared for him while an ambulance was in route. He underwent extensive testing that amounted to nothing and took medication after medication with much the same result. Doctors falsely diagnosed his episodes as an extreme and unpredictable form of acute anxiety disorder. No discredit to them or their diagnosis. If it were explained to them what was really going on they would have called it madness. For Salazar this was just part of the package. After six months he threw his medication in the trash and refused to keep taking it.

He'd taken medication in his youth for what turned out to be the same condition. It had been decided then the side effects of the meds were too extreme and they were abandoned then. He saw no sense in trying again.

"Here we go," Antonio said as he turned a corner to see Chief waiting for a lift down the garage level. As expected she was scrolling though various floating menus on her Magnavox Hector 3 tablet. There were too many kinks in the wiring as of late and that didn't sit well with Chief. This was as much her ship in her mind than anyone else's. It was how she was built. She had an affinity for technology and a deep desire to see things working properly, which was a challenge in this place. Everything shifted from operational to less so from mission to mission. Footsteps behind her caught her attention. She looked up as Antonio approached. He still looked awful even if he was capable of walking around. He also had apprehensiveness in his eyes, like he knew exactly what she'd want to talk about. Chief decided to dial back some. Restraint won out over emphasis given what had just happened.

"Evie messaged me. She's having trouble nailing down a locus for the disturbance epicenter. She'd be more efficient if our only dashers would get together and make adjustments to their phantom nonsense tech that I've been asking them to do. A task all of them seem adapt at putting off. You do want to eventually win this right?" She said. Antonio didn't have much of a rebuttal aside from the one he'd become accustomed to giving.

"We've only had a little over a year to study the dash devices. We can't even confidently use language that describes its state of existence. 'State of existence' even feels like strong language to use. We don't know for sure how it's powered. Or even what with. Because it's not with dash, or else it would shut down every time we use it. It collects dash and allows us to use it to travel. That much you know. Even being able to reverse engineer a fraction of it to build probes is nothing short of a small miracle," He replied. Chief was unimpressed.

"I was hoping, after seeing you turn inside out back there, for better explanation. You're a broken record Tony. Same bullshit. Different day.

I don't think I'm alone in feeling uncomfortable knowing how cavalier you guys are with something you don't really understand. If you, Skip, JP and Strat weren't the only ones who could use it, we'd be doing things very differently. I can guarantee you that," she huffed. Again Antonio didn't have much to rebut. She was right. He and the other three were the only ISOs. A nickname of sorts thought up by The Commodore to describe who could interact with the dash tech and the devices it is derived from.

Across the hall from the lift was the security room. There was a security checkpoint just outside of it. Vernon, the guard assigned to it this shift, glanced up at Antonio when he looked in his direction. His blonde hair jutted out like straw from under his beanie. He just shook his head and continued reading his magazine. The door next to the security room was slightly ajar and open just enough that Antonio and Chief could hear a raised voice shouting in Spanish growing in volume. They couldn't make much out, but they could tell there wasn't a spectacular mood in the next room. That didn't seem out of place on this morning. Just then the door swung open slamming the wall it was hinged to sending an echo down the hall. Vernon shook his head again. The ship's security head Angelica Nocivo stormed out. Younger than her brother but could be nonetheless intimidating, her brunette bob bounced slightly as she angrily dialed her phone as she made her way to the middle of the hall. She stopped in a spot not far from Antonio and Chief and began twisting back and forth as her phone rung. She stopped moving when she heard the inbox message begin. From the looks of it she'd heard it quite a bit recently.

"Hermano! No bromees conmigo! Llámame! Soy muy serio!" She yelled before hanging up and pocketing her phone. She stared at the wall for a moment then looked over at Antonio and Chief who stood about twenty feet away. She locked eyes on Antonio, waving a finger at him as she walked up.

"Before you ask, No. I can't get through to him. Tried ten times since the alarms. Nada!" she said with exasperation.

"Well I gathered that. Run a trace on his phone?" He replied. Angelica seemed slightly annoyed with the question.

"I don't need to. I know exactly where he is and why. He's on that horse shooting at stupid balloons because he hates to lose. He's just like mother!" she shouted.

"Well yeah. Big tourney is going down soon. Homie has to up his game," Antonio said. Angelica rolled her eyes. She nodded and then looked back and forth at Salazar and Chief with a look of disapproval.

"What the hell is wrong with you two? It's not even noon," she snapped as she waved her hand. Antonio and Chief looked at each other then they looked back at Angelica. Chief shrugged her shoulders and Antonio's eyes narrowed.

"Well you might say it's been an interesting morning," he said. Angelica just side eyed him and headed off down the hall.

"Whatever. Tell my brother to quit shutting off his phone when he's out!" she yelled.

"When did that work the last twenty times I asked him to do that?" Antonio yelled back. Angelica didn't respond as she rounded the corner. The lift door pinged behind them and with a whoosh, slid open. A group of five warehouse crewmen emerged with a pallet of containers strapped down fast. One grunted as he tugged at the jack positioned under it while the others pushed. It clacked loudly as they exited the lift and proceeded down the hallway. One of them gave the pair a nod as they passed.

"Jack and Hammer have an early Christmas heading their way." Chief muttered as she entered the lift. Antonio followed behind and tapped on the garage button on the console just inside. Another whoosh and the doors were closed.

The wind was steady in The Bracelands just north of The Crown of the Sentinels, a tall range of mountains that bordered the far south that rose high above the landscape and could be seen just above even the tallest trees. To the men of old this was as far south as they dared to venture. It was because of the stories told of what lay beyond the river pass that led past the Sentinels. Most were stories of evil spirits. Other stories told of a madness that would overtake the strongest of minds. Less fantastical stories told of hunting parties caught in the basin beyond the peaks when the Frostfall River overflowed. A time when the river was thrice the span of what it is now and would seasonally flood the pass. Anyone caught there would have to wait out the winter or brave the Frostfall when it raged the hardest. This is how things were thousands of years ago. Other tribes of the world had their own stories that kept them away from the south. Men were not unique in this respect. Life could be difficult here for those inexperienced with the harsh climate. Right now though the frost harvest was in full swing. Early autumn was near. The Bracelands were already growing colder and what should be reaped just north now, was. The snow fell from the gray skies like thick white ash. Atheon, the eldest living son of King Herald the Second, nocked his arrow and drew back. He took aim and let loose with a thwip. His arrow jumped past his grip and sailed out in a subtle arc toward its target. It missed by some feet and buried itself in the snow just to the side. Only the gold fletching was still visible. Stockard, Atheon's squire of twelve years looked on from his chair and examined his master's score thus far. The target at the end of the clearing lay bare just as it had been when Atheon had begun. Thirty arrows in and all there was to show for it were channels dug into the snow on either side of a hay bale that appeared in no danger of being struck.

"Ah," Stockard muttered. Atheon, paying no attention, nocked another arrow and drew back just as before. He took slightly longer to aim this time. Snow casually fell around him and upon him. His warm breath billowed out in a mist around his face. His eye locked on to his goal. A thwip as the arrow loosed and whistled away. It cut through the air just as sure as the last one. Stockard followed the gold fletching's trajectory. With a chiff it dug down in the snow just in front of the target.

"Right," Stockard muttered again. Atheon pulled another arrow from his quiver, which was now almost empty. He nocked same as the last and began to draw. Stockard sat up in his seat and prepared to comment as respectfully as he could manage.

"Begging your pardon Master Lamb. I would not deign to offer up my opinion on your method based on my own skill as a marksman. I cannot boast equivalent merit that would give me any place to comment on today's exercise. I would go so far as say, respectfully, and begging your most pardon my Prince, but shouldn't one of your goals be to strike the target you've set up, at least somewhere?" he said. Attheon considered the query for a moment or two. The Prince sighed, said nothing, and just stared ahead as he had done before. Attheon then took a deep breath and relaxed. He disengaged his arrow and dropped his shoulders. He looked over his shoulder at Stockard who looked like a sugar dusted pastry in the form a clean cut young man of twenty-four. He was an average looking fellow with dark brown hair and cheeks rosy in the crisp air.

"Your pardon is accepted. As is your critique. A fine morning we have here. The air is crisp. The wind is calm. The trees barely sway. More snow than I should expect for this time of year. Our breakfasts were warm enough however. The kitchens did turn out wonderful loaves today. Milk gravy was especially nice. Peppercorns do add so much. Why should such a morning be displeasing in the slightest? Can you smell the crispness in the air Stockard? The hints of pine and the perfume of fragrant logs on the fires bellowing through so many a chimney from the village off in the distance?" Attheon said before turning back to gaze into the snowy clearing again. Stockard was a bit puzzled by the response.

"I can Master Lamb. The fragrance is quite nice. As was the bread and milk gravy. But, respectfully, I do have remaining curiosities," He said. Attheon looked back at Stockard then back at down at the clearing. He raised the arrow itself and pointed it at the target and then looked back at Stockard.

"Curiosity is a good thing. It leads one to ask all the questions one would need to in order to answer a question. Or in this case, questions," He replied. His eyes were like two black jewels polished to a glisten and his long straight black hair just swayed back and forth ever so in the calm wind. With almost a single movement he nocked his arrow, drew, and then fired. The arrow whistled through the air and thunked hard just an inch or two away from the center. He cocked his head to the side slightly then reached for another arrow. Stockard was even more puzzled. He sat back in his chair as Attheon nocked and fired another arrow. It chiffed expertly about 20 feet behind the target with understated precision.

"I should have brought a spade," Stockard said with a tone of defeat in his voice. Attheon looked over at him. Then turned away to draw another arrow from his quiver.

"A miscalculation that has opportunity to educate. Preparation mitigates miscalculation. Squires require education to have an appreciation for preparation. It should be your motivation to pay towards the cessation of miscalculation through the appropriation of preparation," Attheon said before nocking and drawing back.

"Your pardon Master Lamb, but I didn't follow half of that," Stockard replied. Attheon remained silent for a moment then loosed. The arrow cut through the air and chiffed hard to the right of the target. Attheon smiled as he turned to select another arrow.

"Pack better next time, was the general implication," he mused. Stockard frowned slightly and rubbed his forehead. He was a Fletcher, of Hall Fletcher. Archery was in his blood. His forefathers were fletchers to the kings of old. His family took the name Fletcher and built it's own Lordship west of The Bracelands and founded the manor of Gilder's Bend keep. His father sent his first born to ward with the King's brother, but Herald had other plans for the thirteen year old. He entrusted Stockard to Attheon to be his squire instead. Attheon was at first resistant, but took the young man under his wing when he found they had shared respect for the bow.

Now Stockard observed this odd folly unfold before him, and witnessing such a spectacle as this was unsettling. He watched as Attheon missed the target yet again. He'd seen the Prince in moods before, but this was ridiculous. He sighed and looked away. Something caught his attention then.

In the distance a small cavalry of horsemen neared on path leading to the clearing. It was at least forty to fifty men by Stockard's rough estimation. Several of the men displayed standards from Hall Lamb aloft from their mounts. Pennantmen. Near the front of the pack rode a young man in full plate armor, which contrasted greatly from the men around him who wore mostly leather and mail. Their approach caught Attheon's attention as well. But only just. He fired another arrow which chiffed into the snow like the others. Stockard squinted hard to make out a face beyond a raised visor. It was no common knight.

"Your brother approaches Master Lamb. With fifty of your father's guard. Seems like a rather large entourage for a morning jaunt to The Bracelands Range. You'd use a fancy word like 'amiss' for this I would reckon," Stockard said as he rose from his chair. Attheon glanced over at the approaching crowd and grumbled something under his breath that Stockard didn't catch. The prince relaxed his shoulders and set his bow down on the wooden rack his quiver rested against. He then turned toward the road and crossed his arms as he watched as the group drew nearer. The golden standards flapped in the wind as the horsemen approached. The mighty Mountain Anvil displayed proudly as the sigil of his Hall. The clopping of hooves began to fill the air. Attheon mumbled something under breath again. He removed his archer's glove and tossed it back to Stockard.

The party arrived shortly thereafter. A command was given to halt just short of the clearing. The men at the head of the line parted and two emerged. One was Prince Antimony of Hall Lamb. The other was a captain of the royal guard. They rode up to Attheon and Stockard. Prince Antimony removed his helmet and held up his open hand.

"May the hammer fall true," he said. Attheon uncrossed his arms and held his open hand up as well.

"May the anvil bless the steel brother," Attheon responded. Antimony grinned widely and passed his helmet over to the captain. This was the signal to dismount. His feet hit the snow with a familiar crunch, and the plates of his armor clacked together which clashed with soft sound of the snowy forest clearing. He walked over and embraced his older brother. Despite this unusual arrival and disruption Attheon was nonetheless polite in greeting him.

"How does the day treat you brother?" Antimony said. Attheon fought the desire to be frank.

"The day treats me well," he replied. Antimony looked across the clearing to the target that lay in the falling snow with its single arrow.

"The bow it appears is not so kind. Or perhaps the wind which carries it," he said. Attheon smiled and patted Antimony on the shoulder.

"Merely warming up brother," he said. Antimony looked over at Stockard and greeted him as well.

"Fletcher. I'm pleased to see you in a good way as well. Please send my regards to your father," he said with a smile and a nod.

"That I will do Prince Antimony," Stockard replied sheepishly. Attheon wasn't in the greatest of moods for banter. His session was cut short and his peace disturbed. He hoped there was very good reason. His gaze reached over his brother's shoulder at the cadre behind him. They were lightly armored but Attheon knew many of their faces. These were not men one brought for a casual jaunt through the Bracelands to make pleasantries with one's brother and his squire. Stockard was accurate. Something was amiss.

"Who do you ride to fight little brother?" he asked and gestured toward his brother's entourage. Antimony looked back at his escort, and then to his brother. A serious look was in his eyes.

"I would ride to fight anyone trying to harm you brother," Antimony replied intensely without looking back. This caught Attheon a bit off guard. He took a moment to process this.

"Has there been a threat?" he replied. Antimony didn't immediately respond, but the intensity of his eyes grew more so.

"I can't be sure. Father instructed me to collect you. Only you. And to bring along however many men I felt my brother would need, should there be a need. After Mercurian, I felt there was a need," he said after a moment of reflection. Attheon just nodded. Though he understood greatly. His older brother Mercurian was lost. Reports often conflicted but what was commonly agreed on was a murder led to a small rebellion against the group of Lords called The Green Foxes to break out. Vile rumors had emerged that this group of Lords were poised to make peace with one of the islands of the Exiled Kingdoms. A rumor that would eventually be proven false once it's authors were unveiled and tried. It was not in time to prevent bloodshed, and not in time to save Prince Mercurian or his fleet. A victim of pirates in league with rebels the story went. Attheon gestured to Stockard to bring over his horse. The squire immediately jogged over to the post his master's horse was hitched to and loosed it.

"There has been a meeting called. All the lords from the closest Halls will be there. The Foxes I should expect will be among them. This is all I know right now. All I can say is that father is greatly alarmed. Birds and riders set out shortly after you left your breakfast table at North Frostfall to come here I'm told. He wants us back before supper and was highly adamant about that. We should not delay," Antimony said as Stockard brought Attheon's horse to him.

"Then haste is what we will make. The weather will be turning soon. It'll be no small feat to make it back to the Old Hall in time even at a good pace. I'm hopeful regardless. No doubt Carcino will be recalled from patrol in the west. Though I would not expect to see him for several days even if the wind favors a messenger's flight I should suspect," Attheon replied before scaling his mount and gripping the stirrups. Antimony set his boots into his stirrups, loosing compacted snow off them.

"A silver lining in a confounding situation. I just hope for the weather hold enough for us so we make good time." Antimony said as he gestured back toward the Southgate men, who in turn readied themselves to reverse course and head back toward the King's castle.

"It should hold well enough brother. We should be able to keep well enough ahead of the darkening on the horizon," Attheon said pointing east. Antimony glanced at it momentarily before steering his horse back toward the path. The captain followed behind him. Attheon looked down at Stockard.

"Be a good lad and fetch my shots. Then find somewhere to be other than here for the afternoon. Wind is calm now, but it won't stay that way for long. Snow is going to be thick and it'll be hard to see the road afterward. Make your way north to Hopperstown as soon as you can. Too far from North Frostfall now," he said. Stockard nodded.

"Will do Master Lamb. Will do. And I hope your ride is favorable as well," Stockard said. Attheon almost laughed.

"Weather will do as it will. At least I won't be lonely," he replied. Stockard smiled.

"Aye Master Lamb. No you won't." Stockard mused as Attheon kicked his heels and headed off to the road. Stockard walked over to his master's bow and quiver. He took up the bow and unstrung it for travel. The snow that had grown somewhat deeper than it had been only a short while before. Biding time would not be wise.

He made his way to the target at the other end of the clearing. The single arrow protruding from it almost struck him as comical. He did not look forward to digging through the snow for dozens of arrows that should all be in once space, but for whatever reason were not. As Stockard drew nearer and nearer to the target something began to occur to him. The arrows were not just haphazardly placed. The closer he got the more an order to the chaos of gold fletching began to emerge. He stopped about fifteen yards from the target and looked from side to side. There, in the snow around the target was the image of an eagle with wings spread widely from side to side.

With mouth open he glanced back at where his master had stood. Then he looked back at the image of the eagle.

"Confounding artist," he mumbled under his breath and walked over to begin retrieving his master's arrows.

The lift came to a stop on the western garage level and the familiar ring of the destination chime sounded. The doors whooshed open and out of it stepped Salazar and Chief. The garage level was a cavernous structure within the middle tier of the ship and housed a wide variety of vehicles. Most notably the Pathfinder exploration vehicles, which hung in a row off to the side on the first floor in repair restraints. Parts of all the pathfinders lay strewn around in piles according to type, function and serial number. The sight of this cacophony nauseated Chief and she shook her head. Salazar could sense a complaint coming and braced for whatever it was. Oddly enough Chief didn't say anything. She just glared back and forth at the chaos that lay about. The crewmen assigned to this level watched the two of them as they made their way to the automotive section. They knew the expression well and didn't envy Salazar, because they knew what was coming. So did Antonio. He could scarcely blame her for being angry. This wasn't the first brash action the team had taken on mission. And it wouldn't be the last. There was always collateral damage. Much of it was just a consequence of events playing out as they would. Other things though, were regrettably preventable.

Bravado was the symptom. Antonio and the others were guilty of that certain brand of cavalier panache. One might call it hubris. Antonio would call it 'Style' if asked. It contrasted sharply with their otherwise careful and calculating methodology. It was a highly conflicting philosophy to any outside observer. The contradiction was frustrating for Chief. She had no patience for this sort of unpredictability. A wild card in an otherwise sensible deck, which usually meant extensive repairs after a critical mission that, necessitated the Bumppo's usage to begin with. The ship, as impressive as it was, was a patchwork of stolen technologies. Many of which were not easy to repair if damaged. This was the aspect Chief liked least, and this was a conversation that Antonio knew was brewing. Whatever Sword of Damocles was on Chief's tablet, he knew he'd need aspirin to recover from whatever she had to say. This was the effect of the cause.

Their feet clanked down the metal staircase to the automotive section. Dozens of vehicles were here. Magnetic restraints, which prevented them from shifting during flight, were not active at the present and sat retracted to either side. As they neared the center of the lot Antonio glanced over at the row where Nocivo kept his vehicles. A space was empty.

"Looks like Skip took the Indian," He said. Chief looked over at the empty space then away again.

"He always takes the Indian to the arena. It's his alone time. If he took any of his other vehicles he'd run the risk of someone asking if they can go with him. Then he'd have to tell them exactly why he wanted to be alone. That's more truth than most people can handle. Which is why he takes the Indian to the arena," she said. Antonio was a little taken aback at such a concise assessment.

"How do you know any of that?" He inquired. Chief smirked and pointed to her tablet.

"A good chief engineer should always have a good gauge for those she works for, and to be able to sift through the chaos for the amount of work she can likely expect," she said. Antonio nodded but said nothing.

"Looks like he's got Jack on trailer duty again," Chief said while pointing at the empty space where the ship's quartermaster Jack Riggs parked his pickup.

"Looks like Jack will have to wait for his early Christmas," Antonio quipped.

The pair crossed over a few rows of SUVs and Suburbans issued to the hanger crew should the need be to go out into the field. So far no such need had arisen, but these vehicles were kept fueled and optimally maintained nonetheless. Given the nature of all the operations ongoing on the Bumppo there wasn't the luxury of assuming anything as audacious as a need never arising. Antonio took out his keys as they reached his row. His collection was modest, but sporty. His eye locked onto one in particular. Chief could appreciate a fine machine and did thoroughly what she saw before her.

"Oldsmobile 442? What year?" She asked as her eyes followed the classic lines from headlights to tail lights. Antonio smiled.

"She's a 2012. Restored. Oddly enough where I'm from Oldsmobile stopped producing the 442 in 1987. Here the 2012 looks like a '66 but this one came stock in Sebring Yellow, which wasn't an available option until 1970. It looks good on her though. I also ditched the stock flat black wall tires for retro red lines. It just looks better. Had a few sets custom made. Wasn't cheap, but I know a guy," He said as he opened the door and unlocked the passenger side. Chief continued to admire the machine as she walked around to the passenger side. When she sat down in the bucket seat it felt tailor-made.

"These seats are ridiculous." She said. Antonio nodded in agreement.

"They are amazing. And no, she's not for sale. These seats were discontinued after 2015 and it's actually a challenge to find originals in great condition. You're better off getting a 2009 or 2010 and getting aftermarket seats built to similar specs. Those years are still easy to find. I wouldn't try getting anything newer or else you'd be in store for some modifications. I actually asked the CEO of Oldsmobile a few months ago why these style seats were discontinued by GM. He told me the recession of 2015 changed Oldsmobile's game plans and vehicles needed to be cheaper to produce. Total interior design overhaul. Kinda sad.

From 2013 on the engine got Nerfed too to meet new emission standards. On my world that went down all the way back in 70s," he said.

"That's too bad." Chief replied as she took in the well-restored leather interior. Something caught her attention in the corner of her eye.

"Hey Tony. Why aren't we taking the Diablo?" she asked as she pointed to the vehicle in the next space. Antonio looked at what Chief was pointing to. He chuckled.

"I take the Lambo if I want to look like a badass for the people who work for me. Just so they know who is the badass, and who isn't. I take the Olds if I want to go anywhere and be a badass without looking like I want people to know I am the badass. Which I am, but I don't always have to say it. Sometimes I just let the badass speak for itself. Like a badass would," he said as the slid on his gold toned aviator sunglasses. Chief thought this was a peculiar thing to say.

"That makes no sense," she said. Tony put his key in the ignition and fired up the engine. It growled loudly to life and then settled into a steady purr.

"I suppose not," he said and pulled out of the space and drove in the direction to the lift best suited for Antonio's vehicle type.

After passing several rows near the back of the automotive level the pair reached the exit. It was a series of powered lifts circled with caution lights. Attendants stationed here directed them to lift three.

It seemed to be the only one not undergoing repairs that could accommodate the vehicle. Antonio gave them a thumb up as he slowly pulled onto the lift. A green light at the back of the lift indicated there was still enough room to continue pulling ahead. When the light turned red Antonio put the car into park and turned off the engine. Chief seemed to have something on her mind, which wasn't unusual for her, but Antonio thought he'd ask anyway.

"When's the last time you went into town?" He asked as the lift activated and began to rise. Chief rolled her eyes and looked over at Salazar.

"What, between the times you break something and I have to spend weeks fixing it?" She said, giving Antonio a hard stare.

"Well, yeah." He replied. Chief rolled her eyes again and sighed.

"Three weeks ago. I stopped at this great BBQ place just outside of town. Floore's Country Store I think it was called." She replied.

"That's in Helotes. Just past the 1604 Loop. Good place. Great brisket." Antonio said as the lift came to a stop. The light in front of them turned yellow and the wall it was attached to swung up like a hatch. More attendants were here. One carried a tablet, which she monitored closely. Her hand was held up, signaling it was not the right time to proceed. After a few moments she waved them out. On the attendant's tablet several feeds from well-placed cameras were laid out on a grid. Antonio drove forward and toward an exit marked with lights. As the vehicle neared it the light turned from yellow to green and two massive concrete doors separated and slid open.

Antonio drove through and into another parking facility. But this structure was not a direct part of the Bumppo hanger complex. This facility belonged to Antonio Salazar and his chemical company. He had bought the obscure site a year prior. The Commodore and his team discreetly modified the location to fit all of their needs using advanced technology stolen from a deep space mining company.

Great care was taken to ensure that each step in the process was done quietly. Antonio even went so far as to buy all the lots that surrounded this facility as a greater measure. All the right legal documents were signed. All the right state and local politicians' campaigns were funded. Great care was taken. A plausible cover story based on the implied intention for future development was weaved. Antonio even went so far as to hire a firm to create concepts. It was all for appearances. He never intended to follow through. Although, if the situation necessitated it, a contingency was in place to green light these concepts into reality to please all that needed pleasing. It would be costly. But far less expensive than a crucial cover blown by too many of the wrong prying eyes.

Salazar drove out from parking facility and into the city. Off in the distance the Old Pearl Brewery building could be seen peaking over the tops of the surrounding structures. He exited onto highway 281 going north. They would be at the Dawson arena in around thirty-five minutes given favorable traffic. Today they were. In the corner of Antonio's eye he observed that Chief was becoming more and more interested in his vehicle's instrument panel.

"Tuned like a Swiss watch huh?" He quipped. Chief gave out a meager fake laugh and sat back in her seat.

"No, she's not. But I can fix that," She said and opened up a new tab on her tablet to jot down a few notes. Antonio was a little hurt. He'd thought he'd been doing a great job keeping his ride running smooth as glass.

"How about some music?" Antonio said trying to lighten the atmosphere. Chief didn't seem to be too agreeable.

"I'd rather not. I'm still getting used to the quasi-retro pop culture here. And if I hear another campaign ad, I'm going to punch someone in the face." she said. Antonio chuckled.

"Not a fan of President Sanders?" he said. Chief shrugged her shoulders.

"He's not any worse than any other President. They're all about the same. It's just that the Federalists don't seem to understand economics. Senator Brownwell is hard to listen to, but the Whigs at least grasp the concept of money. I'm not a registered voter. No dog in this race. But that's my opinion," she said while waving around her hands. Antonio nodded.

"Okay then," he said. The pair crossed north of the 1604 loop into North San Antonio. Traffic hadn't been that bad. More than a few idiots out today weaving this way and that with no indicators, but it gave some fodder for Antonio to mock along the way. Chief ignored him for the most part. She was more distracted by the car's engine and the desire to pop the hood. They arrived at Dawson's in decent time.

The arena lot was thickly populated with pickups and horse trailers. There was an odd mixture of sporty athletic and western wear in the people milling about. The distinct essence of horse filled the air as Salazar drew close to Nocivo's cell phone tracker. The signal led them to the western end of the lot near a grassy embankment. Most the horse trailers seemed to be parked along it. The signal strength hit on a hundred percent when they sighted their quarry. The pair came to stop next a blue 2016 Mitsubishi Raider. It was adorned with racing stripes, custom rims, custom bumpers, Yosemite Sam mud flaps, and a pair of truck nuts. The crew of the Bumppo understood it to be Jack's curious attempt at blending in. In short, Antonio recognized the vehicle, and the trailer, which actually belonged to Nocivo.

Jack insisted it be painted bright cobalt blue as well. Nocivo didn't care what color it was, as long as it did its job. Antonio and Chief got out and approached Jack's truck. At first it appeared like there was nobody in it, but as they got to the drivers side and looked through the windows Chief laughed. Jack was fast asleep with the seats tilted back. Antonio was less amused. He knocked on the window loudly. Jack jumped up quick and bewilderedly looked around. He turned to see Chief grinning, and Antonio wearing a less cordial expression. Jack set aside his portable AC, adjusted his seat, and turned the key on enough to supply power to the window, which he rolled down.

When it came down he began hearing Chief snicker with a snort. Jack pushed up the brim of his straw cowboy hat he only wore to the arena. When he did his sandy brown hair fell into his eyes. Despite his best efforts he still looked like he rode a desk instead of a horse.

"Hey Jack. How's things?" Antonio inquired not really concerned at all about concealing his displeasure. Jack rubbed his eyes.

"Hey Tony, Chief. Can't complain." He said. Antonio nodded.

"That's great Jack. Glad to hear it. It is a lovely afternoon for a drive. Isn't it Chief? __Chief?" He said and looked over at Chief who was not really paying attention to either of them anymore. An older couple leading their horse, a beautiful painted mustang, had arrived at the trailer a few spaces over. Chief's eyes were filled with joy and she began walking over toward them with her hands clasped. The older couple noticed Jack and waved.

"Hey Jack!" The older man yelled over. Jack waved back.

"That's Tucker and Marge. They're on the senior circuit," Jack said. Antonio looked around and waved as well. He then turned back to look at Jack.

"That's amazing. Say Jack we're looking for Skip," He said. Jack yawned and shook himself awake then looked back at Antonio.

"Oh no, I gathered that Tony. You know the Skipper. He doesn't like to be disturbed when he's training," He replied. Antonio stared for a moment as his eyes narrowed.

"I know that he doesn't like to pick up when he's training. That doesn't explain why your phone is off too," He said intensely. All Jack could do was shrug his shoulders.

"I don't know what to tell ya man. He's pretty serious about not being disturbed," He said. This was not an answer Antonio really wanted to hear.

"Extenuating circumstances seem to have crept up in this equation though Jack. And we're gonna need to talk to Skip," He said. The look in Antonio's eyes was almost haunting. Concern began to form on Jack's face. Antonio glanced over at Chief was patting Tucker and Marge's horse as she talked to them. He looked back at Jack.

"I got hit by the colors a while ago. Hard. Haven't been hit that hard in years. I was swimming in hell. Locus unbelievably close," He said.

"Has it ever been this close?" Jack asked. Antonio shook his head.

"We don't know yet. Alarms went off after the event. We don't know if we dropped the ball, or if we don't have the first clue if the tech can calibrate for an event that close. This makes it kind of important I talk to Skip," He said. Jack knew that the colors trumped anything else but he was still reluctant. Even so, Antonio's insistent stare was making him uncomfortable.

"Okay he's probably in the locker room by now. Number three. It's not easy to get to. You'll have to fight through a crowd to get there. We're better off waiting for him. Unless of course you want to go on in and have to shake hands with everyone that recognizes you," He said. Antonio shot a look at him.

"You and I must have a different definition for extenuating circumstances Jack," Antonio grumbled. Jack held up his hands.

"Hey man I get what you're saying. But I'm taking the safe route," He replied. Antonio cocked his head to the side.

"Is that right?" He asked mockingly. Jack shrugged his shoulders and sat back in his seat. Antonio looked back over at Chief who was still petting Tucker and Marge's horse and making a cooing sound. He sighed and shook his head. He looked over at the Dawson building. The number of people entering and exiting was substantial.

He also considered the possibility that people who worked for his company could be inside. He furthered the line of thought to include the inevitable questions he may have to finesse his way through. He kept his business life separate from his other business life. He thought about sending Chief, but she seeming to be enjoying herself too much. He looked back at Jack who now had his straw cowboy hat covering his face. Antonio sighed again.

"Fine. We wait." He mumbled. The mountains along the eastern Gatherian coast were locked in a veil of mist. For the last several days a warmer air had blown in from the north and now fought a battle over eroded ancient peaks of The Huntsman's Caps. This made some mountain passes far more treacherous than they would otherwise. Misfortune befell many travellers who chose to traverse these ways under these conditions. But the lure of knowledge one could glean from The East Lodge lured many through this land regardless of peril. The structure sat elevated in a mountain gorge at the junction of two melt water rivers that originated farther inland where the icy mountains were taller. The East Lodge was the oldest of all the lodges.

All the others had succumbed to one tragedy or another and had to be rebuilt. Replacing the texts they contained was sometimes impossible due their rarity. Much blame had been cast this way and that. A lodge was a difficult and expensive fact. Maintaining such a structure was quite the undertaking. Older sections were currently under extensive renovations. Work crews from many of the neighboring villages were here. Work like this was some of the only work a man could find now that the opal mines had run dry.

Many gladly traded in their picks for saws and learned a new trade. It was a better prospect than packing up their families and travel far west where mines were still active.

The East Lodge was well funded by many powerful Lords, and thus could pay well for any man who could swing a hammer, or any woman who could sew a straight line. New wings to the structure were being added now.

New books and various records arrived almost daily. Most were copies from other lodges of the realm. Others were originals written by scholars under the employ of one Lord or another. They were sent here to be copied, and then rode out to all the other lodges. Brothers of The East Lodge carried about their day performing their duties. Some enjoyed the activity in and around the structure. The change of atmosphere and pace was a welcome thing. As well as conversations to be had about one thing or another. Some admired the work that was being done. Some had their criticisms. It was all new things to talk about that had nothing to do with the texts or daily chores. Others among the brothers had little appreciation for all the work that was going on. They despised the distraction, changes to their Lodge, and all the strange faces they had to see on a daily basis. These were men who cherished a quiet day of study and resented anything apart from that.

One such man was Brother Pepper. He was a wanderer. A wolf-like creature that walked like a man for the most part but built enough like a lower wolf that he could charge on all fours if the mood struck him. For the most part it did not. He came from a very old pack, The Redflowers, which regularly contributed members to the ranger packs that recruited many wanderers, but men as well.

They protected the trade roads all throughout Gatheria and beyond. A continent so vast not even the forces of all the Lords of the realms were enough to patrol them alone. The ranger packs were a valuable ally to any Lord, and thus were able to operate with a high degree of autonomy. Even going so far as to be granted the legal power to execute a Lord's law on land they owned. Even so bandit parties still attacked traders with some regularity. It was a high risk but also high reward strategy.

Even the ranger packs could not be everywhere at once. Which is why it was unusual to see a high wolf not bear The Leaf. Pepper's cousin Snowbrace Quickwill was a respected Captain of a large chapter of the ranger packs of The Barley Lands located in The East Pines district.

His chapter often operated just west of the East Lodge and he would occasionally pay his younger cousin a visit if a particularly valuable convoy needed a personal escort. Their interactions were brief, but meaningful. Snowbrace never quite understood Pepper or his affection for books over the open road. But he respected it. Pepper's older brother Flint was less understanding but loved his brother nonetheless and represented the Redflower name as High Captain. Many Redflower kin wore The Leaf. No exceptions were Flint's younger brothers Raven, Alpine and Tracker, as well as his younger sister Southstar, whom the rangers referred to as a Greenpaw. It was name given less experienced rangers who held the rank of lieutenant. A rank she'd just earned the previous season. As a pup, her older siblings and cousins teased her for her yellow fur. As was her brother Tracker who had a coat of similar hue. A common stigma held that yellow fur denoted lesser intelligence and was pervasive irritation. Tracker took the jabs in stride. Southstar had a different temperament. She took it more personally. Pepper however never teased her. He instead read to her when she was sad or angry at her pack. It helped her cope until she was old enough to hold her own in the game of verbal sparring. They were all pups sired by Brewster Redflower The High Chieftain of Gatheria. He was a wanderer whose reputation was well earned through many decades of service to the rangers before he took his father's role as High Chieftain. He was known as Brewster The Devastator in banditry circles as well as other Ranger Chapters. To most anyone else he was known as The Red Wolf. A stalwart moniker earned by stalwart ranger. It was also a moniker that cast a broad shadow over all his pups and other relations. For many years the young ones competed to stand just above this shadow and catch some light themselves. Pepper differed from the others in this respect.

Pepper sat alone in his study pouring over old fading texts. He was given stacks of scroll to copy and issue reports to the elder brothers as part of his senior position in the rare texts wing. A tedious chore, but he liked this better than serving in the main galleries where most of the other brothers worked. Few bothered him and he was far enough from the areas under construction that he could barely discern the hammering and yelling. Today had been fairly placid.

He awoke at dawn as he usually did. A few laps around the complex to get the blood flowing and a dip into the frigid river that ran behind his wing to settle him down for a morning of work. This was a good start. Now he sat in his big comfortable chair. His large bushy tail that jutted out from under his tunic flicked back and forth to the side of his chair. The other brothers took to calling it the 'Pepper Fidget' and understood it was best not to disturb him. This was wise especially on a steamed mussels day. This was his favorite dish and a fresh plate sat next to him. Garlic didn't agree with him so he opted for a simple wash of clarified salted butter instead. One after another he would pluck one from the stack and unshelled it, savoring it, and then discarding the empty shell in a sack beside him on the floor. Today had been fairly placid, but that would change.

Pepper was about to reach for another mussel but his ear caught a sound. It rotated slightly to better listen to this new sound. It took a moment to identify it. He growled slightly and shook his head disapprovingly once he surmised the nature of the sound. A few moments later the faint sounds of construction and the East Lodge brotherhood were overtaken by the quick sounds of footsteps on the walkway leading up to Pepper's study. A few moments later a figure stood at his open door. Pepper looked up from his desk to see the small stature of Brother Garrett Grain. A halfwyn. They were a segment of the race of men short in stature like a dwarf, but not of the dwarven tribes. Men, often called staffwyns by other races, were not generally trusted by the dwarven tribes. Even so halfwyns were regarded as more trustworthy by dwarves than taller men and thus were valuable to Lords who regularly dealt with one tribe or another.

A popular myth among the tribes that all halfwyns descended from a prodigious dwarf from lore named Latalec whom laid with many human women many thousands of years ago in an age when men and dwarves could still mix blood. At least according to legend. Thus all halfwyns are referred to as sons or daughters of Latalec. One of these 'sons,' Brother Garrett, was assigned to The East Lodge to train to become a Court Liaison for his homeland's Lord so he could act as the go-between with a large dwarven mining guild.

Despite the prestige such a position would garner him, Brother Garrett was fearful. Dwarves were reputed to be very intimidating people and Garrett was a rather timid young man. His fear was quite apparent at this very moment as he stood in Bother Pepper's doorway looking at Pepper himself who did not appear to very pleased to see him. And he wasn't. Pepper glared at Garrett who was having trouble just speaking to the large salt and pepper coated high wolf.

"Br__Br__Brother Pepper sir?" Garrett could barely manage. Pepper laid down the parchment he was holding and turned his shoulders in Garrett's direction. As he did the chair under him creaked sharply under his shifting weight. It was an unsettling sound that added to the halfwyn's dread.

"I'm sure I'll be enthralled with whatever you've come to bother me and my mussels with. Brother Garrett if I'm not mistaken. One of the liaison trainees?" Pepper replied sarcastically. Garrett nodded slightly.

"Y__ye___yes I am, Brother Pepper sir," He was barely able to reply. Pepper looked the small man up and down for a moment then gestured him forward. Garrett reluctantly entered. He looked around as he did. Pepper's study was neat and organized. Shelves along the walls were lined with dozens books and orderly stacks of scrolls. One end of the study was an open window. Garrett could hear the soft rush of the river below. It was a bit cooler in the room than he cared for. He didn't have a thick coat of fur to keep him warm. On the other side of the room were massive iron doors of a vault that contained many of the most rare of texts that remained enigmatic despite being in the possession of the brothers for generations. The air was a mixture of burned sage, mountain air, and mussels that Pepper was dining on prior to the interruption.

"Go on then. Enthrall me," Pepper said as he pointed a clawed toe to the scroll that was poking out from under Garrett's jacket. Garrett looked down and pulled the scrap of paper free from his pocket and approached Pepper cautiously. Pepper looked at Garrett's eyes as he did this. The young man did not want to look at Pepper directly.

"Did they tell you I was going to bite when they sent you up here?" Pepper said with a sigh before whisking the scrap from Garrett's hand. Garrett looked down at his feet bashfully.

"Well no sir," He said. Pepper shook his head and unrolled the document. Drawn upon it was a glyph, rounded of shape, and vaguely familiar. Pepper stared at it for moment or two then looked at Garrett.

"What is this? Why did you bring me this? I'm not a pictograph expert. Why didn't you take it to him?" Pepper said. Garrett looked up at the wolf.

"He's the one who sent me to you sir. Nobody in his wing can identify it. It's not in any of their catalogs. This was flown in a week ago?" He said as Pepper continued to study the mysterious image.

"He didn't bother with sending feathers or riders out with this to any of the other Lodges? Instead he decides to send you up here like a quivering page to bother me? Why? What is his hurry?" Pepper said as he looked away from the image at Garrett who didn't look particularly prepared to answer any of these questions.

"I don't know sir. He wasn't very specific about anything. He just told me it was important for me to bring this to you," Garrett said. Pepper folded his ears back in annoyance upon hearing this. He said nothing for a moment. But then began to stand up from his desk. The large chair he sat upon scraped loudly backwards as he did making the floor shake. Pepper wasn't large for a wanderer.

Standing only five foot and ten he would not be considered very intimidating in his pack. His coat coloring was exceedingly rare. Most wanderers were of black, brown, gray, white, red, gold or even of a patchy pattern. Very few were salt and pepper. It was considered a throwback to very ancient times and only the very old packs had members with this coat coloration that resembled the fur of the wild lower wolves.

Pepper theorized this is why even many familiar with wanderers approached him with caution. He looked like a wild wolf. Over the years he had come to terms with this and came to expect it from those not expressly familiar with him personally. The look in Garrett's eyes was one Pepper had seen a thousand times. Even from other wanderers.

"Very well then," Pepper muttered and brushed past Garrett who staggered back as the wolf made his way to another desk a few paces away. Pepper pulled open the top right drawer and rifled around in it for a few moments. A second later he produced a ring of iron keys that clanked loudly against each other. Pepper turned his attention to the large iron doors at the other end of the room which he walked toward. The iron keys chimed out a metallic ring like festival bells each step he took. He held the keys up and shuffled through them as he reached the lock. Finding the one he needed he inserted the toothed end and twisted the key a few turns to the right. The lock clacked and clanged loudly as the tumblers inside moved and aligned. A tinny snap signaled the lock was open. Pepper turned the door's handle and began pulling the door open. It groaned as it slowly gave way. The inside of the vault was not lit. Garrett could not see anything beyond the open door. He moved closer to get a better look. Pepper's eyes were better suited for seeing in the dark. He could see things well enough. It didn't occur to him to bring a lamp with him. This was not a move that Garrett mirrored. He promptly lit a lamp that had been sitting on the same desk the keys were in, and walked up behind Pepper. The wolf had pulled out a book from one of the shelves inside and was thumbing through its pages. He wasn't paying much mind to the small man behind him. As the light revealed what was inside the vault Garrett was struck by the size of the collection it contained.

It was almost like a small library unto itself. He had always heard stories of the Iron Room of the far wing. It was built directly atop the bedrock of hill that ran along this side of the East Lodge. Brother Darius Brookshire had it commissioned hundreds of years ago. At the time it was a controversial move and he had many opponents. Texts, particularly rare ones may contain properties that only the natural essence of a wooden structure could properly contain. This is one of the reasons few brothers opted to work in the rare text wing.

Pepper was one of just a handful of brothers with an office on this side of the Lodge. He took the book he was thumbing through and sat down at one of the tables inside the vault. Garrett followed slowly behind him. The lamp he held created shadows all over the room that moved as he moved. This did not put him at ease at all. He fought his imagination that spawned images of creatures in the dark emanating from some dark text improperly contained. All around him sat stacks of books on small tables. It was far less organized in here. It smelled very peculiar. Like Garrett imagined a long undisturbed crypt would smell. It was clear that Pepper rarely spent time in here, if ever. The books that lay about had a myriad of odd pictograms embossed into their leather covers that bore many different languages. There were many images he did not recognize and some even bordered on decorative accent instead of a readable tongue. Pepper continued to examine the book in his paw for short time while Garrett walked around with his mouth agape. Unsatisfied with what he was finding Pepper closed the book and dropped it on the table beside him. The noise made Garrett jump and glace back at Pepper who was looking back and forth at the shelves in front of him.

"Thought it might be an old farmer's land marker. Rounded shape and laurel circling a mountain looked like something I saw years back. A few similar glyphs, but nothing exactly matching," He said then stood up to pick out a different book. He took a book down with a golden hue and sat back down. After a period of thumbing through this one he snapped it closed and set it down.

"Doesn't appear to be sigil from old dead Hall. At least not one documented in that volume there," He said then looked back at the shelf next to him and scanned at the spines. First he looked to the left and then back to the right. Garrett turned back toward Pepper who didn't seem to acknowledge he was even in the room.

"Sir. May I?" He said as he pointed to a stack of books next to him. Pepper glanced over at him, and then down at the books around the halfwyn.

"I don't care," He said and then resumed his scanning. Garrett picked up a book with a black cover. On it was simply the words Hall Lamb embossed into the leather. He opened it and began to read. It was a book about the family Lamb. Most people in these parts knew of Hall Lamb. They were an old family of the far south that controlled the arms industry. Master sword makers whose family land sat on the largest iron deposits in the world. Entire dwarven mining guilds only did business with them. Its patriarch was one of the Lords powerful enough to be declared King of his lands and it not be considered an honorary title bestowed to a powerful Lord. Though Hall Lamb was still under the larger banner of the Exalted Emperor, as were most Lords, it was economically independent. The Emperor needed channels of commerce to Hall Lamb. Hall Lamb needed no such thing from the greater empire.

It was one of the small number families of Gatheria that operated with autonomy for one reason or another. Most autonomous city-states of the realm enjoyed this status largely due to their distance from the Imperial Capital of Frest. Most didn't have a monopoly on the best and most abundant source of iron in the world. Nor did they enjoy the natural defenses of The Sentinels. They did however enjoy political ties to Hall Lamb and it's King Herald. This book about Hall Lamb wasn't very interesting to Garrett, but he could understand the text, unlike so much that was here. Pepper took down another book and flipped through it. Like the others this one didn't yield very satisfying information. He snapped it closed and set it down.

Chapter Two: Lay of the Land

Antonio and Chief had been standing around the arena parking lot for what felt like an hour. Antonio looked down at his watch to look at the time. They had been out there for over three hours. Most of the other trucks and trailers had left by now. The early September daylight was in that position it was normally in before the eye expected early evening to start setting in. He was happy for the cloud cover they had. Cool front that blew in the night before knocked temps back into the 80s. Chief had spent forty minutes or more poking about under the Oldsmobile's hood after the horse she was petting was trailered off like so many others. Marge and Tucker were the chatty types it turned out. Meanwhile Antonio texted Terry back at the Bumppo for updates on the color analysis, which there were none. A lot was going wrong today. Not least obviously of which was having inability to fathom what just happened. Antonio lamented how green their operation still was. He liked having a contingency. How could one have a contingency for this? One had to experience this in order to have a contingency. One couldn't observe others to construct a contingency, because nobody else was doing this. Well, not in the way Antonio and Martha were. He had also been monitoring the chatter from the so-called metaphysical network of psychically gifted personalities The Civic Protectors kept in contact with through their mystic member Madam Cardigan. She was a Romani like Antonio's grandmother on his father's side who sent out the alert to her list of contacts. All of them picked up something to varying degrees. None of them knew what it was or what it meant. None of them were Antonio or Martha. They may have sight, but they could not see. The sound of a hood dropping distracted him. He looked up to see Chief wiping her hands off with towel. She waved a hand at Antonio's car like she was pantomiming a magical incantation. To which Antonio grinned, shook his head, and focused back at monitoring chatter. It was almost 5PM now. Chief stuffed the rag and tool kit she had been using into her bag and walked over to the concrete island that circled the parking lot and served as barrier between rows of spaces. Tall aluminum light poles stood on either side of her. They had begun to sway slightly as the cooler early evening wind began to blow.

She picked up and threw bits of loose gravel sitting around her feet into the spots along the row in front of them. Every few seconds another bit of gravel popped off the surface of the blacktop. Jack was asleep in the truck again despite the hum of his portable air conditioner. He was more accustomed to being up all night working on one mission related task or another. Daytime was when he normally slept. Becoming bored with same droning confusion from the psychic network Antonio clicked back to his inbox to check for new messages. There weren't any. He slid his phone back into his pocket and walked over to where Chief was sitting and sat down next to her. He watched as she hurled another bit of gravel out into the lot. It came down with a pop and bounced this way and that as it tumbled away. Chief picked up another bit and looked at it before tossing it as well.

"Tucker thinks you sound like an idiot in your commercials," She said. Antonio's face took on an expression that was halfway between disgust and confusion.

"Tucker? The guy with the horse?" He replied. Chief picked up another bit of gravel and threw it.

"The guy with the beautiful gorgeous lovely horse, thank you very much. But yeah," She said.

"Maybe Southwest Chemical can afford to have Russell Crowe in their commercials. Salazar Chemical can't. What we can do is lead the country in green technology and save money by having my dumb ass on camera instead of an actual actor. I'll go with innovation instead of pomp thank you very much," Antonio snapped.

"He also said you dress like a drug dealer or a street corner pimp instead of a CEO," Chief said with a grin. Antonio frowned.

"You really want me to like Tucker don't you?" He scoffed.

"Tucker is kind of a grumpy old shit sometimes," A voice behind Antonio and Chief said. The pair of them turned around. Standing behind them was Estrello Nocivo.

He was holding the reigns of his horse. The beast glowered down at them with cold and judging eyes. The parking space was close enough to the grass he didn't have to walk very far over asphalt, but Blueskin was a horse, and that didn't matter. His mood was poor. Salazar and Chief were in the way. He gave them a low guttural whinny in discontent with their impediment.

"How do you handle that thing without it biting you all the time Skipper?" Antonio said. Nocivo smiled.

"Blueskin has always been nice to me. He only bites Jack," he said grinning even more and looked over at the truck. Jack was awake again and glared at Blueskin mouthing obscenities. Blueskin didn't seem phased by his contempt and shook his black mane confidently in the early evening breeze. Jack got out of the truck and a reluctantly walked over and cautiously took the reigns from Nocivo. Blueskin shook his head again. Jack flinched back a step. Blueskin snorted at him almost mockingly. Nocivo patted him on the neck.

"Tranquilo ahora caballito. Se amable con Jack. Por favor no muerdas," he said and patted Blueskin again. The horse seemed to settle some. Jack pulled on the reigns slightly and began leading Blueskin off to the trailer. The ebony equine shot dirty looks at Antonio and Chief as he walked past them. As his horse departed Nocivo turned his attention to Antonio.

"Tu llegada es inusual. Why are you two here? I'd think you'd have much better things to do," he said. Intensity washed over Antonio's face. The air around the lot seemed to get heavy as a response gathered in in his mind. Nocivo knew this expression and had a good idea of what his friend and colleague was going to say, but the signals the man was throwing off were nonetheless unexpected and unsettling. Something was more wrong this time. There was a cold grimness in Antonio's eyes.

"I got hit by the colors man," he said. Nocivo nodded in acknowledgment. Antonio looked off to the side slightly.

"Fue muy malo. Muy, malo." Antonio added in a half whisper. Nocivo glanced over at Chief. Her expression confirmed the seriousness of the situation.

"How close?" Nocivo said. Antonio crossed his arms and looked back at Estrello.

"Damn near next door. Bowled me right the fuck over. Hit the kid harder. She's in your infirmary right now being looked after. The colors walked right in and kicked the shit out us. The crystal balls are having a shit fit on the Walter Mercado cape network. Blowing right the fuck up right now. I figured a kick in my teeth this big would show up on their radar. But, damn Skip, it lit them up like a wet fart in an elevator. As for our side of the coin, Evie is probably having a hell of a time zeroing in on the locus. We're all five fingers into a shit sandwich amigo," he said. A very serious expression took hold on Nocivo's face now. He took his phone out of his pocket and turned it on. He looked back up at Antonio and Chief.

"Mierda. Has she detected any contamination?" He said. Chief shook her head.

"She hadn't by the time we were heading out here. Without a complete picture that's not unusual. Nobody has messaged us with a substantial update. If I had to guess, she's still crunching numbers, and nobody else knows how to compute what just went down. Tony's noggin isn't cooled off enough yet I expect to take a deep dive for more intel." Chief said. This was even more concerning to Nocivo.

"Claro," he muttered as glanced down at his phone to see the progress wheel still spinning. He looked back up at Antonio who seemed to agree with what Chief just said.

"How well did the kid take it?" he said. Antonio shook his head.

"Not well Skip. Like I said before. She's being treated right now. Last message I got she was loopy on meds. It hit me like a fist man. It hit her like a freight train hauling a ton of bricks. Downhill. She's young. It hits harder early on," he said as he stared down at his feet.

"And JP?" Nocivo said. The progress wheel was still spinning.

"He's with the kid in your infirmary, and I don't expect he's going to leave her side. Wouldn't even be right to ask. So it's looking like a duo mission to me. Like the old days," Antonio said. Nocivo shook his head disapprovingly.

"What about Stratum?" he said. Antonio looked like he didn't have anything good to say about it.

"Yeah, he's still out on the San Andreas doing his thing. We messaged him but it's going to take him a while to get back over here. It's not like he can just take a bus," he said. Nocivo rolled his eyes and sighed. He looked over at Chief.

"What is the status of the Pathfinders? Anything flight capable yet?" he said. Chief looked pensive, like she had a lot to say on the subject. She opted for brevity though.

"Squadron is still grounded. N-37B the closest but we're still fabricating replacement parts for her grav-lev stabilization system. All other systems are more or less in the green. But they'll need more work as well. Two weeks is the most optimistic outlook. JP's future tech is hard to replicate in this century. It's been slow going. As soon at N-37B is ready I'll let you know," Chief said as she pulled out her tablet and clicked it on. Nocivo could sense more coming. Chief just began tapping away at the screen though and didn't add anything just yet. A jingle emanated from Nocivo's phone then. He scrolled to his text messages. There were several dozen new messages. He apprehensively clicked on the icon.

"Hijole," he muttered.

"Tu hermana estaba muy enfadada contigo. You might want to start keeping your phone on. It seems like we've had this conversation before. I could be misremembering though," Antonio said. Nocivo glossed over his sarcasm as he scrolled through his sister's texts. Antonio wasn't joking. Angelica was pissed.

"Angel and I are going to have a conversation soon I don't think I'll care much for," Nocivo said.

"I don't expect so," Antonio said as he pulled his keys from his pocket and turned to walk back to his car. Nocivo continued to scroll through the scathing messages from his sister. He almost didn't notice Chief walking up with her tablet. He looked up and saw the expression on her face. He had an idea what she was about to say. He glanced over at Antonio who was unlocking his car. Antonio seeing his look just shrugged his shoulders and opened his door.

"Skip." Chief said. Nocivo prepared himself for a barrage.

"You want this operation running as smooth as I do. I understand that you and the guys have a lot of very important work to accomplish that only the four of you can do. With any sort of ease. But when you guys decide to do crazy shit with the Bumppo or any of the other equipment remember how hard it is to fix, because One, we do not live in the future where most of it comes from, and Two, the rest of it is stolen from elsewhere and that makes it even harder to repair and replace. I have asked for a number of materials that I am just not getting. The indium for example," Chief said sternly. Her eyes were even sterner. Nocivo glanced over at Antonio sitting in the car. He was watching them with a smile. Nocivo looked back at Chief who still glaring sternly.

"What was the indium for?" he said. He didn't know more about this aspect of the operations. His discipline was medicine.

"Indium is for the fabrication of the engine housings. Engine housings which you and the guys busted the hell out of flying through a flipping war. Shielding was shot to shit, but I've managed fix that. Hull plating on the port side still looks like it was kicked by a mule, but her seals are finally back up to snuff. Just be glad the ship is equipped with floating automatic maintenance platforms that can handle large repairs like that. I know I am. When they're actually working that is. That just leaves her engines. She's not going any damn where without those new housings. Unless you like flying her around in a cloud of radiation. That's if, If, the engines don't fail outright and she's dead in the water," Chief said as she furiously tapped away at her tablet. She held the screen up to Nocivo. What he saw displayed he didn't understand. He could hear Antonio laughing in the distance. Nocivo sighed as he continued to look at Chief's tablet and searched for a way to respond.

"I can ask Antonio if he can allocate some via his company," he replied. Chief didn't seem too impressed with this response.

"You know I asked him about that very thing yesterday. Do you know what he told me?" Chief growled.

"What did he say?" Nocivo said. Chief smiled and stuffed her tablet back in her bag.

"He told me that his people were starting to ask questions about why he needed so much indium. And let me tell you Skip, we need a Lot of damn indium. He also said he was running out of secret research and development excuses and he was starting to sound 'bullshitty and implausible' to people. His words, not mine," Chief said. Nocivo was at something of a loss.

"We can try to look for sources of indium when we're out on dash," he said. Chief clapped her hands together.

"See, there. Now that's the spirit Skip," she said. Nocivo was less enthusiastic.

"That's a big if Chief. We don't know what we're in store for here and we know even less if we'll have time to look. Once we cross over we may not know what kind of operating window we're looking at before channel destabilization, or how fast the dash tech is going to charge. Not always clear at the onset," he said. Chief raised a brow and threw her bag over her shoulder.

"I don't expect any miracles. Just keep an eye out," she said and turned to walk away to Antonio's car. Nocivo looked over at Antonio who cocked his head to the side and started up his car. A loud yelp rang out over to Nocivo's left. He could hear Jack cursing loudly.

"Fucking Horse! Stop biting me!" he could hear Jack wail. Nocivo sighed and walked over to help Jack. Chief opened the passenger side door and sat down. She pulled the seat belt over and clicked it secure and shot a glare at Antonio.

"Report go well?" he quipped. Chief set her bag by her feet and scowled at Antonio.

"Went great," she said. Antonio put the car into reverse and began backing out of the space.

"Ah," he muttered.

"Get me my damn indium," Chief snapped as Antonio shifted back into drive.

The sun tried to peer through the flowing veil of cloud cover above the tree canopy. Though as it seemed like light might pass another layer of the veil closed the gap. The smell of campfire, hard tack and tread root hung in the air. Sounds of chatter broiled among the crew sitting around the fire keeping warm as they watched the flat bread cook on the flatirons.

Raltec was awake but reluctant to get up. He was hungry though and the flat bread smelled good. He rolled over off of his bedroll that lay under his lean-to tent. He and his team were up most of the night surveying the damage caused by a recent spate of landslides in the region.

It was critical to remap the area and return with a report of any and all instabilities of the hillside to the guild office. They were short on time. It was not easy to get out here in the first place. It would certainly not be an easy trek back. They had to split into several teams of a few men each to measure the affected areas and compare them to existing maps. Word that more rains would be expected didn't sit well with Raltec or his team. They felt it was a waste of time to survey now when even more damage could be caused by unusually heavy rain loosening up the hillside even more. Even so he went where the guild leaders told him to go and surveyed land he was told to survey. Any lands within their territory that could provide promising mining potential would need accurate measurements. It made for smoother establishment of new operations. Or at least that was the doctrine preached at him by guild leaders. Raltec didn't care either way. The weight of their gold, silver and copper in his pocket was all he really cared about. Company dogma didn't buy mutton, flagons and loaves. Coins did. Right now his pockets were lighter than he'd like them to be, so thus he was here with his team hammering in stakes, peering through searching glass, and sketching out new elevation lines. Hammering things and telling people what to do was the key reason Raltec was here with this team. He was good at keeping things running smoothly and on schedule. Sketching things was largely Balocan's area. He was sitting by the fire eating what remained of the last batch of flatbread the party cooked up while Raltec slept. He noticed Raltec staggering to his feet and instinctively poured him a mug of tread root and held it out. He was a far older dwarf than Raltec, gray had already crept around his dark hair, but he respected the younger dwarf. He was quite good at getting things done, and getting others to get things done. His talents had not gone unnoticed and he continued to get more and more assignments. Some garnered the young dwarf some prestige. Others, like this one, were a walk through the muck and night too many out slapping bugs. It was respectable work though and kept the pockets heavy enough not to want too badly during the winter months. The weather was still fairly hostile this far north. It was a far cry from the icy grip of the far south.

"Hot mug for you young feller. Dreadful night. No sure footing. Biting flies sure loved them torches, and the taste of dwarf," he said. Raltec walked over to the older man and sat down on a rock someone had rolled up to the fire some hours before.

Raltec's back ached on the high right side. He's set up his bedroll in some haste in the night and laid it on some uneven ground. His fatigue put him to sleep and kept him there, but now he paid a price. With a twist he cracked some of the discomfort away, but not all of it. The steaming cup of tread root would help though and he reached out and took the wooden mug from his older teammate.

"I hope they like the taste of tread root from my veins, because I'm going to drink my fill," he said. Balocan smiled and picked up another mug, which he filled from the kettle swinging above the fire.

"In that case, I'll be having a share of my own," Balocan replied. All around them other dwarves in their party were unpacking their gear for a days work. Twenty-seven dwarves prepared for a day of tedious and meticulous measurement and mapping. Some of them whistled old dwarvish tunes. All of them cursed the dark clouds on the horizon because each of them knew if the volume of rain was anything like before, they would get word handed down to report back to this area. Some were even worried the weather would turn their way while they were still here, which would force them to ride out the storm in whatever little shelter they had. Which was nearly none. Even worse, redo all the work they had already done. Every few minutes someone would look west to see if the heavier darker cloud cover was any closer than it was before. The trees made it difficult to see. When a drop of water fell around them they weighed whether it came from a rain cloud that had snuck up overhead, or if it was just older rain that was just now dripping down from the canopy above. Raltec sipped from his mug. The earthy flavor hit him favorably. Much of the mist still in his mind began to clear and he found himself becoming better mentally geared to take on the day. Balocan was a fairly chatty dwarf compared to most other dwarves. It came from his long time in the company of human men his people called staffwyns. It was name given because human men were tall like staffs. A more derogatory variation of this term would be for humans to be called 'staffs' or 'staffies.' Guild guidelines forbade the utterance of either two permutations around staffwyns or on job sites where dwarves would be expected to be representatives of the guild.

Outside of this, the more colorful terminology was bandied about with some frequency. Mistrust of humans largely stemmed from the fact that their relatively small population ten thousand years ago had exploded and now there were humans in most regions of the known world. The last population to be this widespread was the elves. Their civilization collapsed beginning two thousand years before humans began their rise during what has come to be called The Troubled Times. A period of time not well documented. Even to this day all accounts from this time are questioned as gross exaggeration or outright fantasy. Such was the severe distrust of elves. Now elves were exceedingly rare. Most never meet one in their entire lifetime. Raltec's father claimed he had met one once long ago when he was a boy. He described the elven woman as tall like a staffwyn, but her ears came to a slight point near their apex and she always moved with a dancers grace. Her skin was fair and her hair was of an auburn shade. She carried around a small stringed instrument, which she played often while she would walk alone through the forest. One night she just disappeared into the night. Raltec's father never saw her again. Nor had anyone he talked to in the decades since. He would talk often about her and her strange songs to his sons. He even went so far as to learn to play himself to try to replicate the music. He tried his best, but his level of skill was never particularly good. Raltec was not a musician himself but he would often hum what his father was able to produce. He expected he would be doing a lot of that later between yelling out measurements to other members of the party. He took another sip from his mug and looked up at the new mass of mud and rock that would have to be mapped out to the inch over the next several days, or until his party began to run out of food.

This was not a good area for hunting and foraging. It was call the Drylands. Not so much a description of the climate, but rather one should expect to only eat what food they brought with them unless they could stomach the foul tasting creatures that crawled about. Raltec and his crew would be departing well before that was even considered. Nobody travelled here for a very good reason. Deeper into this wood there was a stretch even called The Starving Forest. All sorts of dark tales could be heard from the locals who lived west of this land. Some going back thousands of years. The hillside was dotted with dwarves carrying and placing measuring instruments.

With some frequency one would begin yelling to the others to move from where they were placed as they peered through rings mounted at the tips of their sight staffs. Others would walk along with strings pulled taut between two or more crewmen that would hold it in position while another would observe a plumb bob settle into position. At that point they would declare a line was true and scrawl down the numbers the process reaped. Apart from them were the scouts that would venture ahead of the group and find the safest points at which to conduct their next set of measurements. Raltec's eye gravitated toward this group, which he could barely see from where he was sitting. These dwarves had one of the most dangerous jobs on the crew. He worried most about them. There seemed to be something halting their progress at the top of the hill. Balocan handed Raltec one of the new batch of flatbread fresh off the iron. It burned his fingers slightly but he didn't pay that much attention. He took a bite of it as he continued to watch the dwarves at the top of the hill. They continued to just stand around talking to each other. Balocan noticed Raltec's gaze and looked up over his shoulder. He squinted hard to get a glimpse of what Raltec was looking at. Soon he saw what Raltec saw. A group of about four to five dwarves stood at the top of the hill looking back and forth at each other. One appeared to be crouched down and was looking at something below him while the others talked among themselves. Balocan turned back to Raltec whose gaze was still fixed upward.

"You figure they found a deposit up there? I hope it's copper. Guild has been wanting to find new copper veins the last score of years or more. Be good if we're the team that finds one. I'd even settle for a good nickel deposit. Always good money in nickel. Staffwyns can't get enough of it. Though if the gods are feeling generous we could have the smell of silver or gold. Not likely, but one can hope. Still I would not envy the poor dwarves that would have to operate here. No place for operation. Bad country even for riches," he said. Raltec's sour expression became even more so the longer he looked up at the other dwarves.

"Riches may be on tap. But not for those gossipers up there if they just stand around wagging tongues all day while the rest of us get things done. And if they keep it up I'm docking their pay," Raltec said as he began to scowl. Balocan stretched his shoulders and held up his drink.

"I'll head on up there in a bit and break up their fun. Stick men need to make up good ground today. Weather may not hold," Balocan grumbled and then took a sip from his mug. Raltec rubbed his reddish bearded chin and frowned.

"I'll go up there myself," he said and then finished off his flat bread and took a big gulp from his mug. He set it down and picked up his survey hammer, which also served as a walking stick and tapped it a few times against a rock to shake off the dried mud that had caked on earlier. He then walked away from Balocan who watched his annoyed friend head up the path that led up to the safe route to the scout team. He felt a little bad for the scouts who had to deal with Raltec now, but dawdling about for any reason was not well advised on a dwarven survey crew.

"Keep ironing up the flats. I'll be back down shortly," Raltec yelled back over his shoulder. Balocan acknowledged with a wave. Raltec found the way up easy enough. Plenty of footprints showed the way for him. All the patches of ground, exposed tree roots and firmly set rocks had muddy marks all the way up. Every few steps he would glance up at the scouts above.

They noticed him as well when he was about halfway up the hill. They didn't disperse or move on like Raltec expected them to. They just continued to stand around talking to each other as they did before. This struck him as strange. He was almost offended. It was as if his approach didn't matter to them. It felt like an insult to his authority. The higher he climbed the more and more angry he became. Even as he neared the top of the hill the scouting team continued to just stand around in the exact same spot as they had been standing before when Raltec first spotted them. As he approached the group one of them broke from the circle and walked towards a now very angry Raltec. As the two met he looked the scout up and down. The scout, a dwarf named Caltamec, who held a lead scout position, held up his hands. This was a gesture of appeal and gave Raltec pause.

"I only have time for a Good explanation Caltamec," Raltec snarled. Caltamec didn't immediately respond. He just looked back at the scouts. They all had the same very alarmed and confused expression on their faces. Caltamec turned back to Raltec and pointed to the ground just past the scouts.

"We found something sir," he said nervously. Raltec gave him a long stern look as he continued to point behind. Just past the scouts there was a bare rocky patch. Some of the earth around it had been dug away by the scouts. Raltec focused his attention to this but didn't know what he was looking at or why it was so important to the dwarves who stood around it.

"This something had better glitter," Raltec snapped and pushed past Caltamec. The group parted in half as Raltec walked toward them. The scout who was crouched down stood up as Raltec walked up to him. His hands were muddy as were his clothes.

"Come on Konku, what have you got?" Raltec said.

"It don't glitter sir. I don't know what it is. But it looks old. Older than anything I've ever seen," Konku replied as he pointed down at the ground. Raltec looked at him for a moment. The look in his eyes was almost disturbing. Dwarves were a people who had surveyed and mined in areas no others in recorded history had ever tread. It was rare for anything to be unfamiliar to a dwarf. Raltec walked around Konku and looked down at the stony patch for himself. As he circled the area an image began to appear to him. Cut into the super hard granite bedrock with extreme precision was what appeared to be a two-headed shark. Raltec had heard stories about sharks from fishermen who had travelled inland during off seasons for work. He had never heard them described as having two heads. He looked over at Konku.

"Has anyone ever heard of shark with twin heads?" he said. The group looked around at each other. Nobody seemed to have an answer.

Half of them didn't seem to know what a shark was in the first place. Caltamec stepped forward from the group and stood next to Raltec.

"I know of sharks yes. Enormous beasts that swim in the seas not afraid of any man or ship, and can kill with a single bite. Mouths like handfuls of knives. Eyes like a dead man. Never heard of them having two heads. Never heard anyone talk about them, much less carve up a hillside with them," Caltamec said and pointed behind him. Raltec turned and looked in the direction he was pointing.

"What?" he said. Caltamec stopped pointing and walked several yards in that direction, stopped, and then held out his arms.

"They're all over this hill. Dozens of them. We found the first one as soon as the sun broke dawn. They stop a hundred yards east of here where the hill just shears off. Beyond that one can see the Easterlands." Caltamec said. Raltec walked past Caltamec and scanned the forest floor. Dotting the ground were several semi-circles of disturbed earth. At each of the sites were more gorgeously carved images of sharks. Some images had two heads like before, but most had only a single head.

He noticed a contour that seemed to differ from rest next to one of the images. He bent down and using the wooden end of his hammer dug away at the dirt, which was covering what looked like a straight line. When the dirt was clear what Raltec saw stunned him. The stone looked like it was highly polished like glass here. Almost newly polished like it had been done in the night while he and the others slept. He looked closer at the stone. A very small seam, not even big enough for a sheet of parchment to slide between ran in a straight line back under the soil. He couldn't believe what his mind was considering, but this looked like highly advanced stonework. Its grandeur mapped itself out in his mind the foundation of a palace. Perplexing, this palace sat here of all places, and one that appeared both ancient and new at the same time. He stood back up and walked back to the group.

"Who do we have on the crew who knows old marks?" he said. The scouts looked at each other. Their expressions didn't look promising. Caltamec stepped forward.

"None with any training for this," he said. Raltec shook his head and rubbed his red bearded chin. He looked around at the group and then to Caltamec.

"Who would know these marks?" he said. Caltamec thought about this for a moment.

"The only people that know old marks within a months journey from here would be from The East Lodge. It's a hard walk sir. But there is a river that runs near it that flows north of here," he said. Raltec didn't like this answer. He didn't want to go anywhere near staffwyn country. What was here disturbed him very much. He wasn't the only one. Every dwarf standing around Raltec was having trouble hiding his dread.

"Caltamec, I want you to go back down to Balocan and tell him to go and gather everyone back to camp," Raltec said almost in a hushed tone.

"Everyone sir?" Caltamec replied.

"Yes, everyone," Raltec said. Caltamec seemed to be struggling with something. Raltec picked up on it.

"Out with it," he said sharply. Caltamec looked around at the others and then back at Raltec.

"Board of Antiquities will want to know about this. If we bring in outsiders to our find there will be Bureau reprimands sir," Caltamec said with as muted a tone as he could muster. Raltec's expression told a very turbulent story.

"What about this place makes you think the Board of Antiquities has any business swinging a pick anywhere near here?" he said as he looked Caltamec dead in the eyes.

"Sir, I really__," he tried to say but was cut off.

"There is something very wrong with this place. You know it. I know it. All of them know it. As soon as I touched the rock I could feel it just as sure as hand over flame. This isn't some hole filled with broken pottery and few crudely carved idols. I don't know what this is. Unless you can tell me I suggest you get the men together and be quick about it," Raltec said sternly.

"Aye sir," Caltamec replied and gestured to the rest of the group, which turned and made their way down the hill. Raltec watched as they departed then looked down at carvings again.

"What is this place?" he said to himself as he looked around the surrounding area.

The concourse of The East Lodge was sparse at this hour. Most brothers were in the dining hall taking tea. Pepper didn't want to be part of all this ruckus. His father had always criticized this attitude.

He called it 'Anti-Pack' and unnatural. Unbefitting of a wolf. He endured it for years before he'd had enough of the pressure and sent a feather to The East Lodge. His father initially resisted and forbade him from departing for the eastern coast for a season, but ultimately agreed to let his pup join the Brothers once he'd reached eighteen years. It was another kind of pack after all. It was what he wanted for Pepper. To be a member of a pack as a wolf should. Although this would not ultimately be the trajectory Pepper would take. Even here, even now, he was fairly solitary. As long as the other brothers were minding their own business and not minding his, he was fine. There were a few exceptions. Behind him he picked up a strong aroma of lavender. Only one brother washed his robes in so much lavender salts. Senior Brother Alvin. A hand rested on Pepper's shoulder. The wolf looked up to see Alvin standing behind him.

"Good day to you Brother Alvin," he said warmly. Brother Alvin smiled and sat down next to Pepper and looked at what he was reading.

"And good day to you Brother Pepper. Studying the history of Murty Turner I see. Have you gotten to the part about the horse?" he said jokingly. Pepper smiled and closed the book.

"I have. It seems silly to think that a man's horse could start a war. Or that anyone would ask the right questions that would lead to that very strange fact being uncovered. It seems impossibly remote. But here it is. A fascinating journey," he said. Alvin agreed. It was a book he'd read as a lad.

"Most fascinating journeys begin with the right questions. I have a few myself. Tell me, what do you think of Brother Garrett?" he said. Pepper had an idea or two what may be on Alvin' mind.

"Less tedious and bothersome than most of the brothers. Stays out of one's way for the most part. Not large enough to get in the way that's for sure," he said. Alvin knew he shouldn't laugh at that last remark but couldn't help himself.

"Yes, yes I see. Though how does he strike you in terms of assistance?" he said. Pepper was somewhat relieved at least the old man was upfront about things.

"I don't need anyone's assistance. But since you asked, I could do a lot worse," he said. Alvin was hoping that Pepper would say this.

"Would you object Brother, to having Garrett stay on as your assistant? At least for the time being. Until you find what it is you are looking for," he said. These were the kinds of questions Pepper like the least. If it were any other Brother he would have bid them good day already. But this was Alvin.

"I'm not one for collaboration. But the boy isn't as slow witted and sluggish as some of the slew footed oafs in robes who traipse around these premises," he said. Alvin was disappointed to hear Pepper say these things about the other Brothers, but he was happy to hear he felt differently about Brother Garrett.

"Not an ounce of saccharine as always. Though I have come to trust that you will always give a most blunt and unfiltered perspective on things. Despite how I may disagree with them. I am happy that Brother Garrett does meet with your approval. I was worried he may be received poorly," he said. Pepper understood the importance of this to Bother Alvin. A man who had more than earned his respect many times over the years.

"He'll do," he said. Alvin smiled. Pepper's solitary nature was well known to him by now and he knew what the wolf would have to give up in order to complete his task. The old man patted Pepper on the shoulder and stood up. Pepper looked up at his friend.

"I'll keep the lad on until the job is done. Though it may help inspire me to know why exactly he and I are charged with completing it in the first place. Are you able to shed any light on this Brother Alvin?" he said. Alvin slowly shook his head.

"No Brother. I'm afraid I cannot. This is an official assignment handed down to us from the Delegation of Lodges. Not even I know the nature it," he said. This was not what Pepper wanted to hear. This was an unknown. An intangible. A piece of an equation he could not factor in. It was peeve born from an inquisitive mind.

"Ah, the faceless and nameless monolith. Arbiters of the height of one's leap. So delighted to fulfill another one of their cryptic requests," he said. Alvin almost laughed. He too had his criticisms of the Delegation, but he kept his opinions to himself. Pepper had a far more cavalier regard expressively. Something that Alvin had come to admire about the wolf.

"I don't disagree. But they oversee all The Lodges. Representatives from this very campus sit among them. You must always remember that. There is always a method to what you see as madness, or triviality as the case may be," he said. This was not the first time the subject of The Delegation had come up. He had less restraint in airing his grievances about them than Alvin. He respected him though. He did not hold the position of Senior Brother as Alvin did. He was much freer to state his opinion about certain things.

"Respectful disagreement it is then," he said. Alvin looked to the side for a moment.

"I suppose that will continue to suffice. I suppose I will go and visit the other Brothers now. Take care Brother Pepper. A colorful conversation as always," he said and began walking away. Most of their conversations ended like this. Pepper always felt bad that he should always talk more with the man. His need for solitude often hindered relationships that should be closer and cut short conversations that should be longer. But this was a difficult aspect of himself to combat. He stared off into space for a few moments then opened his book again and began to read.

Neither man wanted to be here. Neither man really wanted to know what such an episode of The Sight might mean. At any rate Nocivo and Salazar walked down the corridor not saying much to each other to the Records Room, which sat near the heart of the ship. It was manned almost twenty-four-seven by Terry Nikolaou. This area of the ship was kept colder to keep the supercomputers in this area cool. It had it's own independent climate control, life support, living amenities and power apart from the rest of the ship. It could in extreme emergencies be a refuge should power be lost to the rest of the ship. It was one of a handful of areas on the ship like this. But it was by far the largest given what resided here, which was functionally the brain of the entire ship secondary only to the central kernel. The men walked down a short flight of stairs to the first of the security checkpoints that led to the records room. The security personnel must have been expecting them because they were already standing at their posts to greet them. One was already activating the scan pad, which lay just a few feet from the first security door. The guard gave Nocivo a thumb up and he and Salazar stepped forward onto it. The familiar scent of ozone hit them both as the deep scanning instruments did their work. Each security door had it's own set of deep scans which alternated randomly creating a different set of scanning configurations every time anyone passed through the gates.

Any way in or out of the Synapse Level had gates like this. Each of them was equipped with unforgiving anti-personnel measures. In short, it was a very good idea to have a valid reason to pass through. Ignoring a rebuff for entry was inadvisable and would be dealt with harshly. Just then an alarm sounded as the last scan type ran over Salazar. Strips of lighting along the wall began to glow red. A targeting system had been activated and locked onto Antonio.

"Standby sir," the guard at the controls said. Antonio shot an annoyed look his way.

"I always fail this one Dougie. You know that," Antonio groaned.

"Sorry sir. Your rules. Standby," Dougie, a tall slender man with curl relaxed hair, replied without looking up. On the screen in front of him a digital rendering of Antonio Salazar was displayed. His head was glowing red. This was not unusual. Salazar was right. This particular scan was one he always failed. Dougie pulled up another screen, which was a log of all of Antonio's previous scans. This latest scan was then meticulously compared to all previous logins. This usually took a few moments. But they felt like minutes to Antonio every time. He just stood there and rolled his eyes. Nocivo chuckled.

"Yeah, laugh it up pendejo," Antonio muttered. On Dougie's screen one check after another came up green. A nominal result came up and passage was granted. Dougie looked up from his console. Antonio's face was riddled with disgust, but Dougie McBain and Chandler Moon, an auburn headed man in his late 40s, and was the other guard stationed at this checkpoint, just shrugged. They'd grown accustomed to seeing this. It hardly registered with them anymore. Nocivo turned to Antonio.

"What new blood do you have in mind for this week's thing?" he said. Antonio thought a bit as the machines around him scrutinized his very existence.

"I'm thinking Sully. Good dude. Whole ship loves him. He's really good at communicating. People really listen to him. Adventurous enough dude. Can't think of a better guy right now. If we get him, then other people maybe later. Math looks good in my head," he said. Nocivo nodded and then raised his brow.

"He may not appreciate the initiation. It's tradition, but he might not understand," he said. Antonio shrugged his shoulders, which elicited a dirty look from Dougie.

"Can you hold still Doctor Salazar please?" he said. Antonio narrowed his eyes for a moment, and then continued.

"All newbies go through the same thing. It's tradition. He's got enough of a sense of humor I think. It'll be fine. Even Jack got over it," He said. Nocivo sighed.

"We're assholes," he said. Antonio smiled.

"Yeah, we're assholes," he said. Dougie looked back up at them.

"Good to go." He said. Mechanical whirring filled the hallway as the first massive set of doors unlocked and slid open. Nocivo and Antonio walked through and headed to the end of the hall to a lift that would take them down to the next set of security doors.

Terry sat back in his chair with a game controller in hand. On the screen in front of him Spyro the Dragon flew through an adventurous 3D game world. He paused for a second to reach over and grab a chicken tender from the basket on the desk beside him. He took a big bite and laid it back down in the basket. Then he resumed playing. The Records Room was next to one of the transit pathways so every so often a pod would go by carrying crewmembers to another part of The Synapse level. It happened so often Terry didn't even notice anymore. The doors off to his left opened up.

"Hey guys," Terry cheerfully said without looking up from his game. Standing in the doorway was Nocivo and Salazar. Visits here were always interesting. Even though mission related for the most part, Terry and his personality made trips here a unique experience. Terry, a slight dirty blonde haired man with southern Australian accent and higher pitched voice, paused his game and initiated all the functions related to dash analysis and mapping. Several panels opened up on two of the other walls exposing screens that lit up with many different types of graphics related to the latest bout of colors that hit Antonio and Martha hours earlier. One screen was devoted to the dash analysis for Antonio and the other was one for Martha. Even now E.V.E. was still running through processes comparing the two readings from both seers. On the screen between the other two were the results of these comparisons.

It was painting a picture that would be useful in the next steps of planning out the mission, which usually started here in the records room. Nocivo and Salazar entered the room, which brightened as per the preset. Terry squinted a bit and slid on a pair of shades. He preferred it darker and kept it that way much of the time, but now other matters needed tending to. He activated the interactive projection system. Holographic emitters along the walls activated and E.V.E. materialized in the middle of the room.

"Hola," she said as she typically greeted Estrello.

"Hola Evie," he responded. Terry turned in his chair away from his station.

"Hey Eve," he said in his cheerful Melbourne accent. E.V.E. turned and smiled at Terry who tapped a button sequence on his game controller. A large rectangular table began to rise from the floor beside E.V.E. that sprouted a holographic wireframe of an urban setting along its surface. It was the Gary Default Map or GDM of the approximate locus. Nocivo walked up to it and examined the rendering.

"That's Sky Harbor airport. This is Phoenix, Arizona. How old are these numbers?" he said and turned to his holographic friend.

"This is near real time Skipper from Tony's satellites. Albeit an unfocused approximation without new locus data. All we got right now without more intel. Like looking through foggy lenses. As for the epicenter, signal is coming from a universal locus directly adjacent in the .3857 Bravo Papa Golf pathway. Even with difficulties translating the dash language this hit was simple to identify. The fastest on record," E.V.E. said. A look of deep concern washed across everyone else in the room.

"Damn, it felt close. I never would have thought .3857 pathway close. That is right next door," Salazar said reservedly.

"Is there any blowback contamination here? If so how bad?" Nocivo said. E.V.E. smiled.

"None. Exactly 0.0%. Gary's World is positioned in such a way that it sits independent of any other multiversal system pathway. Neutral Locus. No dash fallout damage detected. All damage isolated to universe BPG.385704183-Alpha Echo Romeo pattern group. Unsurprisingly it carries a Gamma Nu designation. No cheating in the timeline. Further analysis will be needed to determine if this is the primary fallout epicenter, or if this disturbance originated elsewhere. No more speculative data is available at this time. Sorry Skip. A silver lining though is that selection of Gary's World as a home base continues reap benefits," she said. Nocivo's expression changed to one of guarded relief.

"Curious. We keep running into 0.0% on these hits on our general neighborhood. Anyhow Neutral Locus appears as effective as JP first theorized. Remind me to apologize to him for taking as long as he did to work out a way to get here without a prefix. As shots in the dark go, this one has been beneficial. I don't like his theory of blowback. Let's hope we never encounter a contamination that large." He said and looked over as Antonio pointed to him.

"A fuck yeah to that," Antonio exclaimed. Nocivo looked back at E.V.E. who hovered just away from the table.

"How big is the signature?" he said.

"Small. At least according to what I was able to extrapolate from the initial data. Given the proximity of the hit there are a lot of weeds to work through that would otherwise have worked themselves out by the time my instruments picked up the disturbance. This is the first time both seers have reacted prior to any of my systems tripping. I was hoping Tony could bring a fresh perspective," E.V.E. said and looked over at

Antonio. He wasn't happy to hear this request. He'd have go deeper back down the rabbit hole than he would otherwise. But they needed to know a great deal more than what they already did and peripheral analysis wasn't cutting it this time.

"Can you give us an idea what sort of window we're looking at before dash pattern degradation and shear danger?" he said. E.V.E. looked at Nocivo and them back at Antonio.

"Projected? T-minus four point eight hours." She said. Antonio's eyes widened. Terry rubbed his short bearded chin.

"Oh man that's bad," he said understatedly. Almost deadpan with an upward inflection. The others looked at him a moment not really knowing how to respond to his tone. Nocivo leaned over the map and looked it over carefully. Then he looked up at E.V.E. who was looking back and forth at different graphics.

"I don't expect Martha's condition to stabilize sufficiently in time for us to be on the ground. Her last recovery time from a big hit was eleven hours and that was with a color hit locus much farther away. JP isn't going to leave her side until she's far enough out of the woods. Stratum left San Andreas, but even at his top speed we won't see him until morning. Four and change hours means exactly what Tony said earlier. We're not fielding a full squad this time. We go in old school," Nocivo said. Terry laughed.

"Vaquero and El Gitano back to save the day," he mused cheerfully. Antonio grinned. Estrello was less entertained.

"Don't call me Vaquero man. I hate that name," he said. Terry laughed again. Nocivo shook his head and turned to Antonio who was still grinning.

"What can you see now?" Nocivo said. Antonio's grin left his face.

"Can't make any promises. My head is still in knots. But I'll see what I can do. I hope the interface tech is thirsty today. It's about to get a shit ton of data. Get ready for the word salad Evie," Antonio said. He turned and sat down in an office chair that was a few feet away. He closed his eyes and began focusing on a single memory.

It was a vivid memory he called his calibration. The moment he learned that his daughter was born. His marriage to her mother was a brief but complicated bit of business that lasted only as long as divorce proceedings lingered. He wasn't with her when their child was born. He received a call from her brother who gave him the news. It is this phone call that Antonio focused on every time he wanted to read the profile of the colors. It brought him to a state to allow them to flow freely to the forefront. He would then cycle through a few other important memories to form a structure around the colors to adjust their clarity and observe their proportions more accurately. A snap like the crack of the whip broke his serenity. This time was different. There was no delay. It flooded to the front quickly like a dam breaching. Far faster than he could have anticipated. He braced himself in his chair. The others had not seen a reaction like this. Terry began to get up from his chair. Nocivo held up his hand.

"No. Let him steady," he said. Antonio gripped the chair's armrests tightly and opened his eyes, which seemed to gaze off into nothingness.

"Being a real piece of shit this time. Throwing me around, hard. Got this though," he said and began to refocus. Again he latched onto the memory of his daughter. This time he was prepared for the flood. He alternated from memory to memory instead of leaning into the structure collectively as a whole.

This allowed him to slowly navigate through the power of the currents along their grain. After a few moments he was able to find his footing. A picture of the profile then began to map itself out in front of his mind. The others watched as Antonio began to relax and sit back in his chair. A calm seemed to come over him. The tension that had gripped the room seemed to settle. Antonio opened his eyes and looked up at E.V.E. who had an understandably concerned expression.

"We have encroaching blue. Some green to work with. But not a lot. Red is very small. Hard to see. You'll want to highlight Scottsdale. Just east of the city proper. You'll get an interface data package from the dash tech in a moment," he said as he pointed at the map, and then buried his face in his hands.

E.V.E. recalibrated her instruments to receive the transmission. It arrived just then. Translation activated. Models based on the new information began building. She looked down at the table map and shifted it east. Suddenly the color of the buildings shifted to red indicating that the new data flooding in began detecting a higher level of disturbance through the cacophony of dissonance. A grouping of blocks around and area called Fashion Square on the Gary Default map began to flash. Nocivo looked at this area closely.

"Epicenter identified. Launching dash probes." He said and turned. Terry and E.V.E. looked on as Estrello began to manipulate something that neither of them could perceive. It was like watching a strange pantomime of a man operating non-existent machinery. When he had done what he needed to, he looked back at E.V.E.

"Probes launched. Monitoring dash usage. Get ready for comparative mapping overlay," he said.

"Acknowledged," E.V.E. replied. She waited for a few moments. At first there was nothing. Then a flood of new data hit her translation matrix. On Terry's main screen a new map began to draw itself. On the side of the screen a set of percentages allowed the group to know how much BPG.385704183-Alpha Echo Romeo-GN differed from Gary's World.

The number changed constantly as data was received and translated. Finally after a minute or two the number remained static holding steady at 38% difference. The new map overly was complete. But this wasn't all. Additional sensor data was now available. Including accurate live video feeds which began loading up on auxiliary holographic screens that popped up above the table map. They updated to reflect the new data coming from the dash probes. Antonio watched as progress bars below the screen extended their way to 100%. He looked over at Nocivo who was watching something closely on a piece of exotic machinery floating in front of him. It was dash tech Antonio could see and manipulate as well.

"How bad is the dash drain Skipper?" he said.

"Modest. If the pattern holds we won't lose much prep time. An hour or two at most. We shouldn't have significant degradation before departure," Nocivo replied without turning away from the machine's readout. Antonio didn't like this answer.

"That's if, If, the gig turns out to be as small as the math is making it out to be. We could be wrong about this one like we've been wrong before, and we'll wish we had more prep time," Antonio muttered. Nocivo glanced over at him.

"In that case we're gong to need to bring our 'A' game. We'll get the job done however the dice fall," he said.

"Orale," Antonio replied. He stood up fighting a slight head rush and looked at the holo-screen with the highest level of completion. Just then the video feed activated. Then the other screens finished loading just after that. Antonio looked back and forth at them. What he saw disturbed him. He looked over at Terry. His mouth was wide open as he was trying to come to terms with what he was seeing.

"Is that some kind of riot?" he said. Antonio looked over at E.V.E. who looked distracted like she was crunching enormous numbers. Antonio looked back at the screens. People were running through the streets attacking other people. Cars were flipped over and burning. Businesses were being ransacked. No law enforcement was anywhere on any of the dash probe cameras.

"Evie, what the hell are we looking at here? It has a riot veneer, but I see no Five-O. I know this may be wrong way to put it, but this looks messy. It looks like a fustercluck everywhere all at once," he said. E.V.E. pointed to the video feeds.

"My pattern analysis eliminates traditional riot as a possibility. Resource scramble is also eliminated. Post-Event panic has a very low probability. Highest probability is that we have zomb zombs. Movement and damage analysis is at 84%," she said. Antonio and Terry looked up at E.V.E.

"Oh no," Terry said in a Terry like way. Antonio was much less subdued.

"Oh For Fuck's Sake. 84%? How strong are those numbers?" he lamented. E.V.E. paused for a moment.

"I've made a miscalculation. I apologize," she said. Antonio relaxed his shoulders some.

"Well, okay then. I should hope so." He said. E.V.E. looked right at him.

"Further analysis confirms a pattern match of 87%." she replied. The color began to run from Antonio's face. Nocivo had been studying the movement pattern of the madness unfolding on the screens. A few things stood out him. He looked over at E.V.E.

"Eve, according to sensors of the dash probes, are we dealing with a zombie outbreak that is chemical, biological, technological, subliminal, or supernatural?" he said. Antonio looked over at him.

"Supernatural? Is that even a serious question?" he said. Nocivo nodded.

"I know you don't subscribe to the concept of metaphysical, which as I have pointed out many times in the past strikes me as odd given all I know about you, but we can't overlook the possibility we are dealing something science may not have complete answers for," he said. Antonio frowned at him and looked back at E.V.E. who appeared to be having trouble with what the dash probes were telling her. She seemed to be able to decipher the new data enough though.

"The probes have observed an anomalous frequency. It has a limited range. The affected area seems to be localized to the urban center of Phoenix. Police chatter indicates they have been pulled back and have formed a perimeter starting at North and South Mountain Village, Maryvale Village in the west, and Scottsdale in the East. National Guard has been called in. Estimated Time of Arrival is one hour and forty five minutes," she said. Antonio looked back at Estrello.

"If it's a signal we can block with tech you should be fine. No way to know if you have enough physiological differences to be immune," Salazar said.

"What differences I may have that are most relevant do not largely extend to how my brain functions. I would still be vulnerable to an invasive signal. Tech would be smart in this case. I don't have your, whatever it is you don't want to call it," Nocivo said.

"Skip. Dude," Antonio replied as he narrowed his brow. Terry snapped his fingers.

"Hey guys, I think I found something," He chimed. The others looked over at Terry who had brought something up on his screen.

"The probe you have deep diving their internet turned a few things up. I looked up what I could about behavioral control using high frequencies. A heap of articles about a nutter named Hanson Barnes popped up. He also shows up A Lot on the deep web. All connected to high-energy research, brainwave frequencies, and behavioral control in animals. He also shows up in law enforcement and intelligence circles as well. A ten-year prison sentence for kidnapping. Other charges didn't seem to stick. Looks like the only smart thing he did, was get a good attorney," he said. Nocivo looked at the picture of Barnes up on the screen as well and glanced at some of the other things posted.

"Does he have a more substantial connection to the current matter further than an interest in high energy behavioral control?" he said. Terry turned back to his keyboard and typed away for a few moments. Then he picked up his mouse and clicked away at a few of his desktop tools. They ran for a few moments and then one after another windows began opening up all over the giant screen. Terry stood up and looked back and forth at these results. Then he turned to the others.

"Damn good chance. His transaction patterns before his arrest in Bangor, Maine match transactions from an unknown party over the last five months here in Phoenix, Arizona. Facial recognition is over 76% all over the city. Oh and he has an aunt that lives just past Superstition Springs," he said. Antonio smiled. Estrello grinned as well.

"Good work Terry," he said. Terry chuckled.

"Well it's the best I could do in five minutes. I'm sure I'll find more before you leave." he replied. Nocivo gave him a thumb up.

"Keep at it. As complete a report as you can muster in the next 45 minutes," he said.

"Will do," Terry replied and sat back down to get to work.

The ship infirmary was chilly and sterile environment. A low rolling roar of air to and from the filtration venting coupled with the ambient drone of the mishmash coming from the television screen mounted near Martha's bed made for a room temperature experience. If that room was warmer and her head didn't feel like a child's oil and water toy, it would be a better time here. Though better times weren't really on the menu here in the infirmary. A few the other dozen or so beds in the room were occupied by crewmembers in here for injuries sustained in other parts of the ship. Two ship's nurses went about their duties patching them up. A medication drip hung above Martha on her left. It seemed to be helping for the most part. Antonio had often described really bad episodes of sight with her in the past. She was not prepared for this even given her own experience up to this point. She had only been seeing for a few years now. Antonio had been living with this for decades. Just thinking how many times he was in her situation, with nobody really knowing what was going on or how to really help him, truly saddened her. Her new mentor was by no means a perfect man, but even he deserved some sympathy. Whatever complacency she had for listening to him when he tried to instruct her now felt very childish to her. Whatever she thought she knew about sight seemed like a game in comparison.

Her father told her stories of what Antonio Salazar discussed with him about the sight when he first started working with him. She didn't really understand her father's alarm or concern for her as she grew stronger. She had never been this close to an epicenter. The whole process was something of a novelty to her. An ability that set her in a position of some esteem among the people of her tribe and an identity that made her feel special and unique. Her universe was comparatively distant to much of the action going on elsewhere. She had no idea what sort of burden and responsibility having the sight might have in the thick of it. It was a game she played with her grandfather. Seeing colors in her head and advising those who came to her for guidance about things they were terribly uncertain about. Here on Gary's World, this was the very unmitigated real battlefield her game was based on.

The smoke and fire were close enough to smell here. It had been a reality creeping up in the back of her mind for some months. Months after her first sight in this new place. A sight that felt more real. It was a day where the insulation wasn't there. It was small sight not any more severe than the ones she had at home, but also somehow different. Like falling onto pavement instead of grass for the first time. At this point she had only known Salazar a short time. She was upset that her father was trying to push this stranger into a role she only cast her grandfather in. The look in Salazar's eyes when he would describe the sight only held meaning on a superficial level. She thought he was rude and boastful when he explained his home being closer to a contaminated prefix meant his bouts with the sight were generally more severe, and that she should pay close attention to what he had to say. To her he was just another one of her father's friends who would waste few opportunities to talk at length about all of their great travels, insights and accolades. Martha dismissed Salazar outright and his instruction largely disregarded. He was not the warm, kind and generous man her grandfather was. Salazar's flaws made it easy for her discount him. Whatever he had to say about anything meant little. She felt she had a firmer grasp on it all and didn't really need him. She was after all destined to be shaman to her tribe and he was, well, he was Antonio Salazar. He was an issue that up until this point had been driving a wedge between her and her father. She was unable to see what he saw and understand what he understood. She understood now. Seeing more. Dismissing less. She looked over at her father who was sitting in a chair beside her bed. He was a massive muscled man, with a dirty reddish beard, that for most people was intimidating to deal with. But he was her father. He was reading a book called "Common Sense" by someone named Thomas Paine. A real physical book and not a file saved on a tablet. She never heard of the author, but her father read intently. Every so often he would highlight a passage, and then continue reading.

Martha didn't enjoy television so much here on Gary's World. Entertainment of this century didn't resonate with her for the most part, apart from the music. She enjoyed documentary films and sports here, but not much else. Her father was a more complicated case. He found things to be fascinating and entertaining no matter what year it was. An attribute no doubt developed over time as a necessity. She'd celebrate her sixteenth birthday in a few months.

A fraction of the time her father had already lived. She had often wondered what her future would be like. Would it be like her father's future, or would it be like her mother's future.

A tale only time would tell at this point. She only knew what time told of her present. At this point the only one she could compare herself to was Antonio Salazar. But only just. Despite having the sight as she did, his came from a different source.

Salazar described the nature and source of her sight as "Etherity." Although he took a decidedly agnostic view of spirituality and metaphysics he was hard pressed, even being the "man of science" as he often described himself as, to come up with a better description for how her sight worked. He frequently described his sight coming from something he referred to, as "Chronosis" and he tended not to elaborate much further. What Martha had gathered it had something to do with time. Not as an abstract concept, but as tangible entity like photons or electrons. But regardless of the differences in the nature of their sight they both were sensitive to what was going on that brought her father together with Salazar, Stratum, and The Skipper. Her father closed his book and looked over at her. The deep look of concern was still very much in his eyes.

"How ya doing kiddo?" he said trying very hard to mask the worry in his voice. Martha smiled.

"I'd be doing better if 2020's comedy was actually funny," she said and weakly pointed up at the television. Josef laughed.

"I guess it could be better. Trust me, the comedy of our world during this time was a lot worse," he said as he changed the channel over to a weather station.

"You actually looked it up?" Martha quipped. Josef smiled and sat back in his chair.

"Well I wanted to catch up on what I missed. I didn't miss much. It isn't going to be funny if people are too afraid to laugh," Josef joked. The concern took over his eyes again.

"Seriously though, how ya feeling?" he said. Martha sighed.

"Like I was hit by a car. A few times. How is Salazar still walking around? This sucks. I hate how he makes this look so easy," she said as she watched weather graphics dance across the screen on the wall in front of her.

"It only looks easy because he's been through this so much longer than you have. I have seen what happens to him. More than you have. There is so much damage he hides from us. So much he doesn't say. I have a feeling in time he'll tell you about it. If you'll listen. I know he isn't Papa. But he's the only one we have that goes through what you do," Josef said. Martha couldn't help but roll her eyes a bit. It was a force of habit at this point.

"I know. But he is kind of an asshole," she said. Josef frowned. He didn't like Martha using that kind of language, but it was hard for not to pick up given her environment.

"Yeah, he kind of is. Some people just are. But that doesn't discount what they have to say just because they are. They just don't package what we need to hear in the way we'd like. Corroborate if you feel like you're not being played straight though," he said. Martha looked at him.

"What does corroborate mean?" She asked. Josef thought about this for a second and then held up his book.

"It means to confirm. It means to not take anything your read, what you hear, and even half of what you see, at face value. Take this book for example. Or any book for that matter. Usually what you get is a mixture of fact and opinion in varying proportions. I could take everything in this book at absolute face value. I'd be a fool for doing it. I have however read enough additional material peripherally related to it, authored by others, to have the context I need to know what sort ratio of opinion to fact I'll be dealing with. This book is a great example of opinion informed by fact. I now give it to you," Josef said. He handed it over to Martha.

She took and opened it up. On the page she did was a highlighted quote. She read it out loud.

"I draw my idea of the form of government from a principle in nature which no art can overturn – that the more simple any thing is, the less liable it is to be disordered, and the easier repaired when disordered," She read. She looked over at her father who nodded.

"What Thomas Paine means by this is that simple systems have the advantage of having fewer points of failure to fix once they're broken. It's something Salazar says a lot. I once asked him where he heard that. At the time he just smiled and said 'somewhere.' He then bought me a copy of this book. Now it is yours," he said.

Chapter Three: Gathering of Foxes

The snow poured on as Attheon and his younger brother Antimony neared the walls of Southgate. It was the last significant kingdom of men before the land drifted from mountains into vast tundra called The Old Lands by the few people that lived there. Beyond these Old Lands the land finally gave way to the Southern Sea that no sane man would ever sail. Southgate was also the home of The Old Hall. The oldest keep in the south. It stood on an elevated area roughly twenty miles in diameter in a basin circled by mountains. Ten miles out from this formation in every direction was the narrow ring of treacherously steep rocky peaks that reached up into the sky like the teeth of some great beast. It formed a natural barrier that was easy to defend and made any attack on Southgate a foolhardy suggestion. This mountain formation was called The Crown of the Sentinels by the local inhabitants. It was also referred to as the Ring of Blood by those foolish enough to try to invade. If not for Southgate, but certainly a name earned by those who had been foolish enough challenge the Dwarf King and the Dwarf Lords who resided in these mountains. The land in between is where the family Lamb took root and built a kingdom of it's own three thousand years ago when the only settlements of men in the south were small villages doing their best to live in this unforgiving land. King Darrell the First discovered vast deposits of iron ore here and in the surrounding mountains. Significant deposits of silver as well. They contained more ore for steel than in any other kingdom in the known lands. It was of greater concentration and quality as well. House Lamb became renowned for their skill at forging steel. Other families rose to power at the point of blades forged on Lamb anvils. An empire now thrives on weapons and armor that come from Lamb smiths. Despite Hall Lamb's renegade reputation the throne of the Emperor has never risked warfare in the south, as it would like.

As a result it has never effectively enforced Imperial Law in the south. It was law which most in the lands consider overreaching at best, and cruel at worst. Its reach was weak in the Borderlands as well. Lands where Southgate has some overlapping influence. Thus even the throne of the Emperor regarded Southgate as a sister state, grudgingly. Living in the south came with a price though. Autonomy didn't come without cost. Winters were harsh. One had to know how to live here. Dwarves preferred the warmer climates of The Midlands but found that adapting to life here was fruitful in comparison to doing business with Midlanders who had become increasingly corrupt and hostile in recent times. Imperial attitudes towards dwarves had never been friendly. King Darrell's family was one of the first major Halls to forge an alliance with a Dwarven kingdom. His middle son was a halfwyn, which went far in gaining the trust of King Chutal. In exchange for their prowess for mining Hall Lamb provided protection from the line of Exalted Emperors and their disdain for dwarves. Few dwarves lived in The Midlands now. All major families have been driven to either the far north to the continent of Pasaria across the Vorshal Sea, or to the south away from their ancestral desert homelands on the north end of Gatheria, known as The Midlands, where gemstones were plentiful. Now they turned their focus to mining metal ores. Metal that was on full display adorning Antimony and his entourage of swordsmen led by the flapping colors held aloft by pennantmen. Attheon stood out in plain leather and fur. He was an archer by heart and preferred freedom of the forests. He had planned to join one of the larger ranger packs at one time. His father King Herald disapproved of this and did his best to dissuade his son from leaving Southgate for the Barley Lands. After his brother Mercurian's death the King outright forbade it. He would not have his heir parted from Southgate and the duties it demanded. The people needed him. As did Southgate's fighting men. Some of which rode behind him as they approached the outer walls of the city on a road that led through the Outer District. The walls stood high on the deep and sturdy bedrock. Ramparts were well engineered to withstand long periods of siege.

 Merlons jutted up from the crenels like the teeth of a great saw. Ever thirty-third merlon had the hall sigil carved upon it. There were usually a few of these sigils between the giant turrets that loomed over the ground below. Each installation could man several dozen archers.

Touring them when he was a small child inspired Attheon to pick up and learn the bow. As a result he never attained the feel for plate armor. That was for other fighting men following him in that clanking mass of metal that crawled its way like a steel serpent through the first of three gatehouses on their way to The Old Hall. The path took them by members of the local peasantry who milled about here in the Outer District peddling whatever wares they may have to incoming travellers to the city. Fresh produce, eggs, meat and other goods poured in from the north where the weather was fairer. These lands were controlled by The King's brothers and cousins in an area referred to as The Silver Arc which included The Bracelands. These were all formidable Princes and Lords in their own right who all lived in great keeps, and enjoyed the protection and the support of wealth and influence of King Herald and Southgate. The best these lands produced went directly to the Royal Keep at the heart of Southgate. The rest was sold in the city surrounding it, and in the many small villages that dotted the floor of the basin within the mountains. Mostly fishing villages that worked the Frostfall River that flowed from a massive lake farther south that bordered The Old Lands. The multi-storied slope roofed houses that resided past the first gatehouse in The Far Ward were mostly occupied by carpenters, stonemasons, cobblers, weavers, tailors and other craftspeople. A city unto itself, like the Outer District, with it's own governing minister who resided in The Far Keep who answered directly to The King. A subterranean tributary that broke off from the main Frostfall River fed a series of springs within the city. Low lying areas quarried from bedrock, which circled each portion of the city created enormous moats that separated the wards of the city from each other. At this time of year it was still too warm for them to be frozen over. Overflow posterns were built in several places along the outer wall in which flowed out of the city into the surrounding stream system. They could be adjusted by the men manning them in times of heavy precipitation. Two wooden bridges on the north and south connected The Far Ward with the inner parts of the city. The second gatehouses were much more substantial. It led to the Decuman Ward. This layer was in itself a garrison complex incorporated into the battlement all along it's perimeter. It was well manned. Horns sounded and the enormous portcullis of the second gate clanked and groaned upward as Attheon and Antimony approached. Passing through it Attheon glanced up to see the gaping and ominous murder holes installed on either side of the gap. They were ringed by the anvil sigil of his Hall in an older style of carving. They were put there by one of his ancestors at a time when the city was expanding. The wind made an odd whistling sound through them. Upon passing through the second gate the entourage was greeted by the sights of armored men training in the bailey while others sat around fires and laughed heartily as others told tales. Barracks resided here instead of civilian homes. Between them were training areas and stables for war horses. The turrets of Decuman Keep where the High General resided were painted the gold of Hall Lamb. Attheon and his brothers spent a lot of time in The Decuman being trained by his father's guard. Many of which along the path to the third gate stood to attention as Attheon and his brother rode by. This was not the civilian route, which resided on the south end of Southgate. This was a route travelled almost exclusively by military and the ministry.

"Fancy a shooting match brother?" Attheon said and pointed at a nearby range. Antimony looked to his side and chuckled.

"Honestly Attheon. Would a kitten accept a challenge from a cat in a game of smacking yarn?" he said. Attheon smiled.

"Such modesty brother. Or just an attempt at improving my spirits?" he said and grinned at his younger brother. Antimony raised a brow.

"No false modesty here. I do recall seeing you take down a game bird through heavy tree cover. Any marksman who can lead a moving target he can't see though thick branches is not one a challenger would expect to best when the target does not move," Antimony said and laughed. He got a chuckle out of Attheon as well.

Another round of horns sounded at the third gatehouse. A much stouter portcullis groaned its way open. It like most of the others would otherwise be open at this time of day but annual maintenance necessitated they be closed while crews tended to them.

Crews that could be seen up on the battlements huddled by fires to keep warm in the winds that blew over them. Attheon and his brother passed through this gate and its gap into the third layer known as The

Brewers Ward. It served three purposes. One of which was the university run by the Salvers and other learned men along the western end. The Quilled Keep housed a very large library. Warehouses along the northern end served the second purpose. It's said that a decades worth of grain and preserved meats were stored here. It was protected by the soldiers who manned The Larder Keep. The eastern end was home of the great brewers of Southgate. Attheon could smell the boilers as the wind shifted. Depending on how quickly whatever it was his father summoned him for concluded, he would be making his way back there to sample some of it's product.

"Dark ales filling barrels scarcely strong enough to hold them waft through this crisp air. I'd think Father would always fear I'd become a drunkard given how delicious that aroma is," Attheon muttered. Antimony turned to him with a questioning look.

"A jest brother surely. You'd never take up a habit that would foul your aim," he said. Attheon smiled and pondered this as he rode over the wooden bridge that crossed the narrow dry moat that connected the Brewers Ward to the fourth gatehouse. This one dwarfed the previous three. Beyond it was The Kings Ward. At the center of it was the Kings' Keep surrounded by the estates of the various nobility and their servants. Attheon knew this would not be their destination.

When his father hosted The Green Foxes they always met in the traditional venue of The Old Hall at the southern end of The Kings Ward. The King's own house in The King's Keep was a far newer edifice he didn't even like to dine in, much less meet with anyone he respected. It was a palace built five hundred years ago by King Vincent The Fifth. He was also known as Vincent the Vain.

He was certainly not an ancestor spoken about warmly. The closest Southgate had ever come to being invaded was under the watch of Vincent the Fifth. An irony given that Vincent the Fourth was nicknamed Vincent the Victorious who won some of the most legendary battles in the history of Southgate.

Vincent the Vain's gift to himself was the King's Keep with it's tower and don jon that King Herald kept all Vincent's tapestries, busts, and other finery dedicated to his conceit. Attheon's mother Queen Viccaria had a more positive opinion of it. She was the youngest daughter of Lord Lirs Barter of Hall Barter. He ruled over a keep in the lake town of Icescape. The Barters were one of the other oldest families of the south. Icescape resided between the great Barter's Bay, which was more like an inland fresh water sea, and The Old Lands, which gave way to the fierce Southern Sea. This was the first marriage between a Lamb and a Barter in over a thousand years. The last union came with King Darrell The Seventeenth's nephew Aluman and the cousin of Lord Gortan Barter. Aluman was not well liked. He was a drunk and a gossiper. He was another Lamb not spoken about highly in Southgate.

The bailey of The Kings Ward seemed rather empty this evening. One could usually expect to see various ministers, academics, generals, business people, and foreign ambassadors in the midst of whatever official matters concerned them the most. It was almost inviting in a way. A far cry from what he had become accustomed to spending time here in the last ten years. So many greeting him with one face and then lamenting that he was not his brother Mercurian with the other.

He didn't need their approval, nor did he need their company. He expected a fair number would be in the Old Hall talking out of both faces. He would do his best to remain cordial. Attheon and his younger brother's entourage reached The King's square at the very center of King's Ward. Attheon held up his hand to signal to the procession to halt. He then dismounted. Antimony followed suit as well as the captains among them. Attheon looked back at the next highest ranked man in the entourage.

"Stable our horses lieutenant and feed them well. Then return to your posts. We'll walk the rest of the way," he said attempting to sound like Mercurian did when he issued orders. It felt false to him. Forced even. Like he was using borrowed words. But it was convincing enough. The lieutenant saluted just the same.

"Aye my Prince. It will be done," he said then began directing the other men toward the rider less mounts. Attheon turned and began walking in the direction of The Old Hall. Antimony caught up to him with the captains following behind.

"You're getting better at that," Antimony leaned in and whispered to his brother. Attheon just sighed as he walked.

The sun was getting low. Debate had taken up much of the day. Opinions ran deep in the survey camp. For much of the day as the dwarves packed up their gear and stored their measurement records carefully while others argued back and forth what should be done. It was up to either following The Board of Antiquities Bureau guidelines and report back to the guild office with their findings, or act unilaterally and trek to the East Lodge to find assistance from the Brothers there. The back and forth had lasted for hours until Raltec step forward, looked each holdout in the eyes and challenged them to view the find for themselves. Each did. Each returned singing a different song. Dwarves had a very good sense for these kinds of things. Although typically a stubborn people, dwarves trusted two things outright.

One was a new vein of ore, which they preferred. The other was a bad feeling when they ran across it. Rubbings of some of the carvings were made as well as drawings of the hillside site itself that had the survey measurements scrawled upon them as reference. All the art was then stored in beeswax saturated leather tube-like containers. Raltec and Balocan elected to set out on their own to the East Lodge leaving Raltec's second men Totitl and Caltamec in charge of the larger group. The weather was turning and a thus gave them a plausible cover story for ceasing operations and heading back home.

Partial measurements were still valuable and would help when the crew would be sent back out. A harder story to sell was that Raltec and Balocan had opted to stay at the site rather than return. Raltec was a good man, but not one known for doing such a thing, especially in rough weather.

The ruse all hinged on how well Totitl and Caltamec performed under scrutiny. The home office was usually fairly thorough in these matters, so they had to keep things tight and to the point. They were reliable and a hard workers, but ordinary. This would be a test. If they failed the next thing to worry about is how quickly The Antiquities Bureau would mobilize to send an excavation team to the site. They were hit-or-miss in terms organization. Raltec and company had to hope it was the latter. That meant they needed to make as much haste as possible to The East Lodge. That would not be easy to do. This was rough country, and would continue to be until they reached the river. That was a three-week journey at best. Whatever sparsely populated areas there were on the way, had to be strictly avoided. This meant keeping east. Prying eyes belonged to men who asked too many questions. Discretion had to be maintained and they must reach The East Lodge as soon as possible. The brothers had the advantage of owning ships that could be sailed down the coast quickly in just a matter of days. The challenge then would become convincing them this was an important enough find to persuade them to invest in ships and an expedition crew. A bad feeling and some rubbings may not be enough to convince them to even bother, and they'd reap the ire of The Antiquities Bureau for nothing. This was a thought banging around in Raltec's mind as he bid his fellow dwarves farewell and good journey.

"I'd reckon we have half a night before the weather makes a turn our way," Balocan said as he looked up at the trees. The tips of the top branches whipped around in circles in the wind, which was picking up. The others would fare better. They would reach an abandoned cabin on their journey back to the guild. Raltec and the others would not be so fortunate. They needed to make good time north before the weather overtook them. Finding or building shelter then became a matter of what they found when it did. Raltec turned to Balocan as he tightened the leather straps on his pack.

"We can only hope that we don't get caught out in the open, but we can't hold back even if we have better cover. We need to push hard and if we end up in a field with the sky falling down on us like we stole its silver, than so be it. That sick feeling in your heart is as strong as mine Balocan. I know it. I can see it in your eyes," Raltec said.

"I got that sick all right," Balocan replied. Behind him two other dwarves walked up. Pulcan and Manati. They were very young but had a good strong work ethic. Pulcan patted Balocan on the shoulder and looked at Raltec.

"Pardon us sir, but if you're going to need some extra hands, we got 'em. Two dwarves may be able to make the journey, but four can set up camp faster and you've more feet to forage. Manati and me volunteer to venture," Pulcan said with and encouraging smile.

"Aye," Manati concurred. Raltec looked at them both in the eyes. He looked at Balocan. He shrugged his shoulders. This wasn't a no. Raltec looked back at the two young dwarves then nodded.

"You boys have signed up for a slog and a kick in the teeth, but the help is welcome. Pick up your packs and your tools. We're setting off," Raltec said. Pulcan and Manati nodded to each other and turned to fetch their gear. The group set off shortly after. Each of them turned back to look at the hill one last time before heading off. The pit of their stomachs still ached from whatever pall the place emanated.

One of the most heavily armored levels of the VCS Natty Bumppo was not just the hull, but rather it's shooting range. It was designed to contain the fire of all manner of small arms. Like many sections of the ship it had it's own independent ventilation system engineered specifically to scrub any residue from the hot gasses produced from live fire. Which on any given day was considerable. Skip insisted that a minimum of forty five percent of the crew be firearms capable, and the other fifty five percent to be at least firearms literate.

That's where Pauly came in. Paul Maxwell Oettinger was the head range master, gunsmith, and firearms instructor. People just called him Pauly or The Otter. He was a well studied erudite in many areas apart from firearms. Many of the crew stopped by for the weekly competency exercises just to talk to the man. He had a striking radio voice and was always receptive to talk about things in which he was not as well versed.

Antonio sat in the lobby outside the range eating chili cheese corn chips with a spicy bean dip. People thought of him as stress eater. They could be right. He had no idea one way, or the other. He was far from rare on this ship. For now he had to cool his heels here in the lobby. A light outside the entrance to the range was glowing red indicating the range was still declared hot. That meant shooters were still on the firing line and it would be unsafe for anyone to enter. Every few minutes a round of Thump Thump Thump percussion pounded the air within the lobby. Antonio reasoned there were at least two shooters being tutored by either Pauly himself or his assistant range master Mike Lund who was another interesting fellow to talk to. On the other side of the lobby was the magazine manager Quentin Ibiza. People called him Quiz. Good guy. Loved tabletop role-playing games. He sat at his station painting minis, which were figurines used in these games as game pieces. He wasn't paying Antonio much mind because he was too busy painting a tank-like vehicle while the radio played Donny Paige next to him. Antonio already knew what caliber he was going to ask for and what brand he typically used for practice. Of course it would be TMJ ammunition. No other ammunition was permitted on the range. Total Metal Jacket was not his first choice in the field. That would of course be hollow point expanding tip ammunition. That ammunition would mushroom out after initial penetration causing a larger damage cavity. TMJ didn't do that and thus fed differently to Antonio, even if only very slightly. Pauly and Mike didn't think it was a significant issue, but Antonio felt differently. He'd be requesting a box of a brand local to Gary's World called Brent Wilderness. It was a closer match to the feel he preferred in the field.

Antonio looked up at the clock on the wall next to the range door. He needed to be in the dash staging room in thirty-eight minutes. If he lollygagged any longer he'd be risking dashing into an unstable pattern. He'd done that before and wasn't enthusiastic about doing it again any time soon. The higher the instability the more severe damage to the dasher and any people or equipment the dashers brought with them. This came to be quickly understood in the early days over a year ago. The group called it 'Shear.'

Lessons were learned then neither Antonio, nor anyone else felt eager to relearn. He would be in the staging room on time. But first he would need to pick up side arms he brought to Pauly for some work after the last mission. He'd need to run a box of ammo thorough them to make any adjustment to the sights that need to be made before dashing out again. The firing had stopped by this point. Antonio reasoned the session was over and Pauly was going make whatever final points he needed to make before dismissing whoever he was instructing. The light on the wall turned a bright blue. That didn't take long. The session was still technically going on until the door actually opened. Antonio took this time to get what he needed from Quiz. He set aside his snacks and stood up. Quiz looked up as Antonio approached his desk. He put down his figurine and instinctively reached behind him and pulled a box of Brent .40 Smith& Wesson down from the shelf. A snappy round he didn't care much for, but for whatever reason Antonio liked. He set the box on the desk in front of him.

"Good thing you're stopping by now. In about ten minutes a newbie class is coming through here from the forest level," Quiz grumbled. Antonio picked up the box of cartridges and looked over at the class schedule screen displayed on the monitor on the desk next to Quiz.

"Twelve of them. Damn man. Gonna sound like a popcorn bag in here," He said. Quiz picked up his tank figurine with a dour look on his face. Just then the door to the range slid open. Two of Rick's kitchen staff walked out. They waved at Antonio and Quiz before heading out the lobby talking amongst themselves. Behind him Antonio could hear a familiar voice.

"File in Salazar. Burning daylight," Pauly's deep inflection rang out. Quiz snickered and held up a fist. Antonio bumped it before turning toward the door. Inside the range he saw Pauly sitting on a stool about ten feet from the door. He had his electronic earmuffs hanging around his neck. He looked up and greeted Antonio with a wave.

"Hey Tony!" he said boisterously. Antonio grinned.

"Hey Pauly. How the noobs treating you today?" he said. Pauly laughed.

"Life is a shipwreck, but we must not forget to sing in the lifeboats," he mused. This sounded familiar to Antonio but he wasn't sure where he heard it.

"Jefferson?" he asked. Pauly shook his head.

"Nah man. Voltaire," he said slyly. In the game of quotes he had with Antonio, it was satisfying to utter one he couldn't identify.

"I like that line. Looks I need to read more Voltaire," Antonio said as he set his box of cartridges down on the desk next to Pauly.

"I would recommend that. Interesting guy," Pauly replied as he reached over and grabbed the handle of bright yellow plastic gun case. He slid it over to Antonio who spun it around and unclasped the latches with a snap. He opened it to see resting inside the foam inserts two Walther P99 AS semi-auto pistols freshly oiled. The Hoppes aroma hit his nose. Antonio threw Pauly a thumb up.

"New springs and barrels. Gave the feed ramps a polish just for shits and grins and replaced that cracked back strap. Didn't touch your sights. But you may wanna sight them in anyway," Pauly said.

"Orale," Antonio replied as he snapped the case closed and reached up for some hearing protection that hung from the wall next to him.

"I've always wondered man. How come you haven't moved over to the PPQ or even the PDP yet?" Pauly said. Antonio thought about that for a second.

"Used them both. Great pistols. Always run well. Still prefer the P99. We just vibe. Know what I mean? Also neither the PPQ or the PDP come chambered in forty. It's not everyone's cup of tea, I know, but I like it," he said. Pauly nodded.

"Fair enough. Those things which I may be saying now may be obscure, yet they will be made clearer in their proper place," he replied as Antonio carried his yellow case over to one of the lanes. Again, Antonio thought this sounded familiar. He set down the case and turned toward Pauly.

"Copernicus?" he said. Pauly clapped his hands together.

"Correct!" he exclaimed. Antonio smiled and put on his ear protection. Pauly reached over and pressed a button on a console near him. The door to the range slid closed and the blue lights outside the door came on. He then pressed the button connected to the intercom.

"Range is Hot!" he said. The blue lights switched back to red. Antonio seeing the light go red hit a switch next to him sending a paper target backwards. Once it had reached twenty or so feet away he released the switch. He then opened his case up again and pulled out his pistols, which he laid on the table in front of him with barrels facing out to the target.

Tass Clayton entered his small bedroom at the back of his family's cabin. The harvest had been good this year. His belly was full of the barley stew his mother had cooked for dinner that evening. The mutton was a little tough for his liking but that is what meat they had. His family wasn't wealthy. They lived in a small farming community called Bell Store at the northeastern end of land ruled over by Hall Tolliver and it's lord Craig. A smaller Hall but one well respected in the lands. Tass's family had lived here for over a century once the land had had been cleared and soil made suitable for farming. Land north of the rivers that cut through The Barley Lands had only been recently settled after newly named Lord Trent Tolliver built his new Keep here two hundred years prior. The cabin the Claytons lived in was built by Tass's great grandfather Gable when he married. It was a modest cottage but it suited the family just fine. Tass set the small candle he carried on the small table next to his bed. He lay down and pulled the covers over him. The coming spring would see his thirteenth birthday.

After which he would be expected to carry more duties in the household and in the community. These things did not bother him so much. But he still thought about them. And that had been the case for much of the summer. He'd already been harvesting the barley crop with his father and older brother in the fields for three years now. Hard work wasn't unfamiliar to him. He wasn't looking forward to the expectation to deal with other farmers in the small community. He was not particularly outgoing. Tass wasn't even his proper name. It was Vernon. Tass was short for "taciturn" which was a nickname his grandfather gave him after noticing that his young grandson didn't talk very much. The name caught on. Tass didn't object very much. He loved his grandfather and recognized the spirit behind it. The door of his small room cracked open. It was Tass's father Vill. He had a big smile on his face as he entered and sat down on a small wooden stool near Tass's bed.

"Laying down early I see. Well after today I should expect as much. Sun is starting to go down earlier. I appreciate the extra hard work from you and your brother. With what we harvested today I should say we might be able to sell enough to buy another horse to help us out in the field. You and your brother would like that. Wouldn't have to push the plough as much by hand," he said. Tass sat himself up and smiled.

"Old Bess does her best papa, and we do try to help her, but a friend would be a good thing for her," he said. His father reached over and laid his hand on Tass's shoulder.

"It should be a good thing boy. A good thing. I hope we can get one before there is too much chill in the air. Not like last year. Even with my leg still strong and pushing along with you lads so much crop got lost under the snows. No boy. Things will be different. You'll see. Better," Vill said. Tass was comforted by his father's optimism, but he was still troubled.

"What about the Shadow Tides papa?" Tass said trying not to sound to his father the way he sounded to himself.

"The Shadow Tides? The Shadow Tides have you worried boy?" Vill said with a brow raised. Tass reluctantly nodded. He didn't want to bring it up but that's what was talked about in town. His father was having none of it.

"People that have a rough spot of luck and go blaming their misfortunes on one bad omen, or that bad omen, or whatever bad omen. People keep talking about bad omens a soon enough misfortune is all they get. It's all they see boy. Do you think I blame my leg on a bunch of old wives tales?" he said. Tass slowly shook his head.

"Well there you go son. There you go. I make my own way. Just as you. Just as everybody. Some of our family's biggest harvests came during a time of so-called Shadow Tides. The only people who still believe Shadow Tides are the fanatics that roam the forests singing to trees, and men who trip over their own feet because someone told them a scary story once. Now they got it in their head phantoms lurk behind every rock making them sow their fields too late. Or too early. It's just stories son. There ain't no Shadow Tides. No matter what those sour characters may say," Vill said then chuckled and patted Tass on the head. Tass smiled and then settled back down.

"You get your rest boy. We have a lot of hard work until the end of the month. Then we'll see if you lads and good Old Bess get a new friend in the fields," Vill said as he stood up and stood in the doorway. He smiled again and closed the door behind him. Tass leaned over and blew out his candle and then lay back down. A bit of wind whistled by his window. He rolled over just in time to see a bit of cloud roll in front of the moon that was just over the horizon. He watched for a while to see it if the moon would return. It never did. His eyes were soon closed.

Attheon stood on the cobblestones at the edge of a span of grassy area. He looked out across it remembering the times when he was a child and ran around it with his brothers Mercurian and Carcino. The others had not yet been born. These were good and happy times. Antimony and the captains looked at Attheon. They wondered why he'd stopped here.

"The Kings Courtyard. It does look pleasant this time of night," Antimony said. Attheon wasn't paying much attention. But he turned to his brother.

"Aye little brother. It does. No ordinary bailey. Once you pass by the Old Wall there's no sight like it anywhere else in the realm. The history here runs deep. There may be other places in this city that are bigger with stone more perfectly carved, but this place beats them all," he said. Antimony folded his arms and looked at his brother.

"Oh aye. Agreed. But are you sure you're not just standing around here because you don't really want to go into the Old Hall?" Antimony asked. Attheon turned back around to take the scene in again.

"That could be it," he said. Antimony laughed.

"I know father can be a bore sometimes. Overbearing other times. But he did have something very important to discuss. And if the Green Foxes are here, it must truly be," Antimony said and pointed at the men standing about near what remained of the old barbican gate. They were all adorned with sigils, pennants, and armor themed for their respective Halls. Some of them represented the Halls of the Green Foxes.

"Why are they called The Green Foxes? I've always wondered. I've never really asked anyone for the answer," Antimony answered. This was something Attheon knew. He grinned and looked back at his brother.

"It's a corruption of Granf Hawks," he said. Confusion ran across Antimony's face. The name didn't seem to resonate with him. The captains looked equally puzzled.

"Who or what is Granf Hawks?" he asked. Attheon turned back around and began walking toward the old barbican.

"Remind me to tell you sometime. Right now, we shouldn't keep father waiting," he yelled over his shoulder. Antimony looked back and forth at the captains. They just shrugged their shoulders. Antimony shook his head and jogged up behind his brother. As Attheon neared the group of pennantmen in front of the old barbican they stopped talking amongst themselves and paid both he and his brother attention by correcting their postures. Each nodded and acknowledged with a slight bow as they passed.

"My Prince," each of the dozen or more pennantmen said in succession as the two Lambs walked by. Most of the men Attheon knew by face and many of them by name. A few were new to him. But all were duly respectful. It was a rare thing to meet a pennantman who stood out unfamiliar apart from the standard he carried. Dignitaries from other lands ware far less familiar to him. Good thing he had Stockard to tell him whose hand he was about to shake when he was called away from the forests by The King. He didn't care to remember their faces or names. A humble pennantman was another story. These were men he could look in the eye and not see the wheels of scheming behind them. They were men who were always surprised such a highly born noble like Attheon would look them in the eye. He didn't desire their awe. He just wanted good conversation.

The beams of the old drawbridge that no longer functioned thunked under the solid leather heels of the brothers as they walked along it to the inner bailey by The Old Hall. Men standing on either side of the door snapped to attention as Attheon approached.

"My Prince," they said in succession as the brothers entered the inner bailey. It didn't have a name like the other. Standing here were Attheon's cousins Freegale, and Brey. This meant his uncle Persal was here as well. This was unusual. Persal's keep was eight hundred miles away near the shores of the lake of Proseous. Beyond it was the Westlands. Beyond, which was the western sea that separated the Westlands from the great sands of the continent of Hastonera. It had the reputation for being wild land. It is said the Cyclops tribes rule the western coast of that land that overlooked the unknown waters, but nobody had seen one pass the western sea in almost two thousand years.

For reasons unknown the Cyclops retreated to the western most edge of Hastonera according to Lodge scholars. Those that travelled past the sands that at the heart of Hastonera and lived to return, were broken men. Stories of sky serpents, giants, sand shadows and all other manner of scary stories were told about these lands to frightened children by those eager to see fear creep across their little faces before bedtime. Attheon heard theses stories and more from his uncle Persal and others during his stays there when he was younger. His cousins took notice of the Princes as they emerged into the inner bailey. Freegale simply nodded. The light of the torches reflected off his bald head. What was left of his golden locks now hung from his beard. Brey on the other hand was far less bald and more friendly. His golden coif, a gift from his mother, shimmered in the torchlight. He was far less dour than his older brother. Charisma ran through his veins like blood. Attheon had seen Brey shower many a strumpet with silver and gold on his visits to Southgate and other cities. He was an outgoing soul with appetite for wine, women, and war. His tousled yellow hair wisped in the moonlight. By contrast Freegale, a year younger than his cousin Mercurian, was far less sociable. He had the same taste for wine and war, but his marriage was not a warm one. He married his third cousin Hallie Yesterward ten years back. She gave him two daughters so far. He was a good father, but did not get along well with his wife, whom he described as cold and duplicitous. These things could be true. Attheon did not know her well. She came from the Yesterwards, which was a small noble family from northern marshes southwest of the Canyon Lands, and cousins of the Lambs. For generations they traded in spices from the Midlands. Cale Yesterward also maintained a network of spies who reported to him the goings on in the cities in the north that made up The Warlord Alliance. The four lords who made up this alliance were said to practice dark magic to maintain control of the Midlands and protect the capital from a southern invasion. This was one of the key reasons the Emperor turned a blind eye to their practices. It was a mutually beneficial arrangement and one that made it necessary for all the keeps in the south, west and east to keep a watchful eye on the Midland north.

"I hope the evening treats you well my Princes," Brey said as he greeted Attheon and Antimony.

"My Prince," simply muttered Freegale. Attheon took no offense. He'd known Freegale since they were boys. It was always his manner.

"I'd have better prospects for the evening if I weren't being summoned to a meeting with The Foxes," Attheon said as he looked back in the direction of the gathering of pennantmen. Brey knew enough about them. Any gathering of The Green Foxes never led to anything good. A gathering of The Foxes eleven years ago in response to the killing of the son of one of the high born families of the east most opposed to communication with the Exiled Isles, was one of the events that led Attheon's brother Mercurian to travel to the coast to root out the ones responsible. Mercurian never returned. His ship was lost in a storm while on the hunt. He was the first Lamb in centuries to be lost at sea.

"I feel the same cousin. Which is why Freegale and I find ourselves out here taking our time. It appears you and Antimony are of the same spirit," Brey said. Attheon smiled.

"I have a feeling no matter what I hear when I go in there, blood will follow," Attheon lamented.

"Oh naturally. Such is the way of this cruel world. But that doesn't mean we can't enjoy the riches such a journey should bring. And a whole new set of names to forget and bosoms to remember for a lifetime. There's always a candle lit on the darkest night eh cousin?" Brey mused. Attheon smiled and shook his head.

"I'll keep my eye on the war maps. I'll leave the riches to you," Attheon replied. Brey laughed.

"Suit yourself cousin. I'm a giving generous man. Enough of me for the whole of Gatheria," he said. Attheon looked over at Freegale. He was a far away from this conversation as he could be and still be standing so close to it.

"Blood is also another subject I predict will be brought up sooner or later. Ten years since I was named heir. Ten years I have been expected to marry. The subject will come up. And I know what my father The King, will say," Attheon said.

"Oh aye. The Lady Pallas Brian. That's a name well travelled at this point. Well cousin there are worse fields to sow. Not terrible on the eyes. Could not say the same for the ears. Would she be an acquired taste? I would imagine so. Won't be the warmest of beds I would reckon, but the Brian Hall is an old one and her brother Banathir is a formidable sword to wield in the defense of Southgate. I suggest you wed The Lady Brian and plant those fields deep. When The Foxes are out of their dens, an ill wind blows. A belly full of Lamb babes is a good way to gain more ground in The Canyon Lands. I'm assuming your tool is up to task?" Brey mused.

"Oh good. I didn't need to talk to father after all. I've gotten the speech already from you," Attheon grumbled. Brey grinned widely and patted Attheon on the shoulder.

"Ha Ha cousin! Just softening the blow. But look on the bright side. The deeper you plant the Lady Brian's fields, the less time she'll have to file grievances. Moans all sound the same regardless if they're accolades, or complaints. Other men foolishly believe the way to silence a woman is with the back of their hand. I'll tell you plainly the secret of a woman's silence is at the back of her side. I'm sure your quiver has enough arrows. Keen archer eh?" Brey quipped. Attheon was at loss for words and just stared at Brey. But his cousin's wit found it's way past his resolve. Attheon relented and laughed loudly. Brey raised a hand triumphantly in the air.

"See there, now that's the spirit. Take that vigor, a gift from an ever-humble Brey, and hear my uncle's lecture with the wind in your hair. Gods know you have enough of it man," Brey added.

"Thank you for the inspirational reinforcement," Attheon said. Brey bowed sarcastically.

"My pleasure. Now lets go in there and meet this gathering of gloom," he said. Attheon nodded. He then turned to head into the Old Hall. Brey stopped him though.

"My Prince. Assuredly you wouldn't walk into such a gathering dressed like you've been out trudging among the trees cousin?" he said. Attheon looked down at his plain leather jacket. Brey grimaced and shook his head.

"No this won't do at all," Brey said and snapped his fingers at his squire who was sitting just away minding Brey's horse.

"Foster! Fetch me my spare tunic!" he yelled. The boy turned and unbuckled one of the saddlebags. He pulled out a bundle of fine golden fabric and ran it over to his master.

"Here Master Brey," Foster said as he handed the bundle to Brey. He unfurled the golden roll and passed it over to Attheon.

"It should fit well enough," Brey said. Attheon held up the tunic. On it's chest was ornately embroidered the sigil of Hall Lamb.

Estrello Nocivo stood in the staging room aboard The VCS Natty Bumppo as Slow Dancing in the Dark by Joji played. It was by far the most isolated room on the ship. The number safeguards installed here were enormous and being added to after missions. Thankfully they haven't needed using extensively. The group had been reasonably careful in prior missions. Having seen what they had already seen, the kind of amateurism that would necessitate these sorts of countermeasures was paramount for them to avoid. Even so nobody was perfect, and nobody could anticipate every eventuality. This is where the countermeasures played their part. At that moment E.V.E. was running checks on this system. Nocivo took this time to equip himself. Unlike Salazar and his battle suits Nocivo preferred lighter tactical attire. Some armoring. But more lighter weight materials that would allow him greater freedom of movement to use his natural agility.

"How we looking Evie?" he said. E.V.E. took a moment but chimed in.

"Five by five. Looking green so far Skip," she said. Nocivo smiled slightly. For twenty years of his life he was an elite assassin who commanded top dollar from clients across the globe. His preferred method of killing was with bladed instruments, but he carried a Ruger Single Action Army revolver. As a child he was fan of western movies and cowboy culture. He often wore a blue western style shirt over his light armoring as he was now. The nickname Vaquero had become associated with him, but he did not call himself this. He didn't care for nicknames, but did understand their marketing utility. If someone truly needed someone or many people dead, and could afford his hefty price, they would contract Vaquero. It was a catchy name that could be bandied about. And they would pay.

His record was flawless. But nothing was meant to last. New clients betrayed him. It was an elaborate plot years in planning and cunningly executed. It would not be enough to kill the man. The woodwork would erupt with those who loved him, respected him, or owed him ferociously zeroed on one goal. Killing every conspirator with extreme and absolute prejudice. So they tarnished his name instead. A complete deconstruction of his life, engineered like a fine Swiss watch, came together in the shadows. It was such an elaborate and meticulous superstructure of lies that truth alone could not dismantle it. The plot crushed his reputation, and he became a pariah, even among his own people. He became the hunted then. His wife, along with most of his family was forced to distance themselves from him. Those who didn't were forced to disavow Estrello in front of witnesses. One who did not was his younger sister Angelica. She went on the run with her brother. Estrello returned to his world for her after meeting the other travellers.

He knew that if he did not she would eventually be tracked down and killed. It would be the last time he would be back home. There was something much greater at stake than avenging himself. It was a mission critical to protecting all he loved. He looked over toward the doors. His keen hearing picked up footsteps outside in the hall.

A few moments later, the doors to the staging room activated and announced new arrivals. Salazar walked through after they slid open. Speakers called out his ID as he entered. He was already wearing his Generation Five valiant battle armor. His helmet was already on with its smooth featureless copper alloy finished face shield. In one hand was a long case, which he set on a table near the back wall of the staging room. In his other hand was his pistol case. He set that down as well and popped it open. He removed a few of the magazines inside it and set them down next to the case.

"Ammunition release protocol Salazar Zulu Romeo Victor Tango 8106," he said. A chime rang out and then a compartment in the wall slid open revealing a drawer filled with cartridges. He pulled out a box each for himself and Nocivo. The door chimed again. When it slid open Jack and Hammer walked in wheeling a cart of equipment and crates. They stopped near Antonio and began switching their equipment on.

"Hey guys," Hammer said as Jack pulled out a black plastic case and walked over to Nocivo. Hammer was an older man in his early 60s with an exoskeletal support on his left leg to help him walk. Illness and injury working decades for the zinc mining guilds had left him with a few reminders. Deep space zinc mining was some of the more dangerous work. It was the industry with the fewest regulations. Hammer was one of the luckier ones. Many he'd worked with lost their lives due to one mishap or another. Jack was at the top of his list of people to bring along when JP set his recruiting eyes his way. He was also of the few people he knew well that were still around by the time he met JP.

"Hey Hammer," Nocivo said as he took the case from Jack. Antonio seemed to be talking to himself under his helmet. He often did this when he was dictating thoughts on research. Something he was notoriously paranoid about. It was something of a throwback to an earlier time. He was still intensely protective of his science. The others had grown to accept it. The crew still found it annoying though. Regardless, it was a fact of the matter working with him.

Nocivo opened the case that Jack had brought him. Inside was a brain-scanning device, which it looked like a pair of thick-armed sunglasses without lenses. He slid them on. Green LEDs mounted on them blinked on to indicated the device was activated and operating nominally. Jack looked back at Hammer and gave him the thumbs up.

"Confirmed Green!" he said. Hammer flipped a switch on a device on the cart in front of him. It synched with his tablet, which he used to monitor the progress of the two devices.

"Scan is active Skip. Cycle should complete in just a few minutes. You don't have to stand still. Scan will complete no matter what," Hammer said.

"Bueno," Nocivo replied. As he did the graphic rendering displayed on Hammer's screen began changing colors. Estrello looked over at Antonio who was snapping cartridges into his magazines. He walked over to and picked up the box of .45 Long Colt ammunition Antonio had retrieved for him. He slid open the box. Inside were gleaming brass casings. He reached over and picked up his gun case and flipped it open. Inside was a blued Ruger Vaquero. He lifted it out of the case and opened the cylinder gate. One by one he pulled cartridges from the box and slid each one into the next chamber in succession. When the cylinder was full he snapped the gate closed and laid the wheel gun back into the case. Antonio had recently fired his pistols. Nocivo could smell the traces of GSR still clinging to them even now. His eye then shifted over to Antonio's other case. He pointed to it. This caught Antonio's attention. He switched off his helmet's internal sound proofing and looked over at Nocivo.

"I know what you're going to ask. It's not that one. Unless you want to spend hours or even days waiting for it to do what it's going to. I know I don't. We don't have that kind of time. I'm bringing one of my vulcanium blades instead," Antonio said as he popped open the long case he had brought with him. Inside was a highly polished Ulfberht-style one-handed sword commonly used by Vikings.

It was his preferred style of grip that allowed for his duel wielding style of combat that employed the use of a pistol in his off hand. This served him well given he was a dominant left hand shooter anyway. Even so the blade had a three quarter inch extension, which allowed for a half-hand grip if he needed to adapt to two hand techniques. Otherwise it resembled a period accurate sword.

"That looks brand new. Named it yet?" Nocivo said as he examined the sword.

"Pointy Boy is what I call this one. Forged it last week. New resin formulation for the handle you saw me whipping up last month. It should tough out the stresses. First field test though. We'll see if the formula needs adjustments," Antonio replied. Nocivo laughed.

"You and your chemistry set," he mused. Antonio spent a considerable amount of time in his lab which he had all to himself and tolerated few visitors. Estrello was one of the handful of people permitted in the lab. After his career as an assassin ended Nocivo took a different approach to his training and pursued medicine. He leaned on all the medical knowledge he had attained to kill with the highest degree of precision and efficiency. A dark origin to be sure, but he'd become quite the healer in the last few years. Upon arriving in Gary's World, with a little finesse on the part of Antonio and JP, Estrello earned a bona fide medical degree. Some on the ship even called him Doctor Skip. He owned a small practice in town with people hand picked by him to staff it. He rarely spent any time there. Instead, entrusting the medicine to the doctors he hired to heal in his stead. Behind him Hammer's work had finished.

"Good to go. You're up Jack," he said. Jack unplugged a small rectangular peripheral from the larger scanning device, which looked like a small box. He walked over and handed it to Nocivo. He opened it up to reveal a crescent like apparatus, which he removed and placed behind his left ear and handed the box back to Jack. He then looked over at Hammer who watched his screen. Liking what he saw he snapped his fingers and looked back at Estrello.

"Calibration Green. Synchronization Green. Levels holding steady Skip," he said. Nocivo grinned.

"Bueno," he replied simply.

"When you're in the broadcast field the earpiece will let you know with a tone. It's activated already. It's just that when it intercepts the control signal it'll let you know the broadcast field is there," Jack said.

"I gathered that," Nocivo said as he picked up his revolver and holstered it at the small of his back. He then picked up his vulcanium katana and fixed it to his belt. After tying on his mask he was essentially ready. He looked over at Antonio who holstered his pistols and picked up his sword out of its case and slid it into its sheath. He too was ready to go. Jack and Hammer began shutting down and storing their equipment back on their cart. Antonio walked forward and stood in the center of the staging room. He appeared to be getting a communication.

"Okay Terry go ahead," he said. Nocivo picked up his med pack and slung it over his shoulder.

"Tony, display interactive GUI," Nocivo said. Antonio activated his helmet's holographic projection system.

"Understood," Antonio said. Just then beams of light shot out of ports concealed behind his face shield. The image of Hanson Barnes materialized in front of them. Beside him was a map image with a set of buildings flashing.

"Hey guys," Terry said cheerfully through the external speaker system in Antonio's helmet. Skip simply waved where he knew Antonio's external cameras were mounted.

"Hey Terry," both Jack and Hammer said almost in unison. Nocivo walked up to the projected image and held out both his hands. With a gesture he zoomed into the map to get a better look at the flashing building images.

"Terry, tell me what you just told Tony," he said.

"Glad to Skip. This is the most recent photo of Hanson Barnes I could dig up. The buildings indicated on the map are the nearest I could come up with by cross-referencing everything I could find from spending to movement habits. It led me to the only buildings in the Fashion Square area connected to enough juice to power a device capable of producing a signal strong enough to cover the affected area," Terry said in his upbeat manner. Nocivo and Salazar looked at each other and nodded.

"He's being very careful. I wasn't just able to pinpoint using the signal itself. Evie was able to map out what I suspected to be a heap of points he's been bouncing the signal off of. Even if Phoenix PD had a way of scanning for the signal it would have taken them a long time to nail just where it was coming from. Map uploaded to Tony," he added.

"Good thing we have Terry and Evie," Nocivo said. Terry chuckled. Then the projectors cut off. Jack and Hammer took it as a cue to exit the staging room.

"Guess we'll go work on our tans," Jack mused. Hammer shook his head.

"We'd both burn to death," he said as they walked off through the door. Nocivo laughed slightly and looked over at Salazar.

"We do this quick and we do this quiet. Minimal casualties. These people are just puppets on strings. You know exactly how I'm going to play this. Kill only if you have no other recourse. We go in. We neutralize Barnes. Rain on his parade. We get out," he said. Antonio nodded.

"Understood Skip. Paint by numbers," he said. Nocivo glanced to his right and began manipulating something nobody monitoring the rooms cameras could see. Antonio could. Once Estrello finished what he was doing he flashed a thumbs up toward the cameras. Just then the light around the two men began to distort. Then they were gone.

Attheon entered the old throne room to the sounds of shouting and cursing. Antimony and his cousins followed behind. There were about thirty men packed around a large table that had been built were the throne room gallery once stood. This is the most he had ever seen fit into this place. Something must truly be going on to warrant such a gathering. Normally his father's Prime Minister would sit and consult with the other ministers appointed to oversee the various needs of the Kingdom. They were all here. None of them seemed to be overly delighted to be either. Especially Treasury Minister Willem Hatterly. His large cheeks were flushed as if he'd just endured a barrage of insults. Which may be true given the spirit of this gathering. Sitting next to him was the willowy Minister of Candor Linus Emory. He likely had very little to say the gathering wanted to hear. A man with so many ears across the Gatheria was guaranteed to come across something provocative. Beside Emory was the Minister of Grain Hal Woodley. He was the oldest of all the Court Ministry. He used to be the youngest. Appointed at only the age of eighteen by King Herald's great grandfather King Robin the Ninth. Sitting next to Woodley was the Minister of War Francis Keep. He was a veteran of four Bandit uprisings, The War of the Step Sons, and the Battle of Victor's Pass. He earned the nickname "Judgment" by those who fought beside him, and those who fought against him. He was also Attheon's distant cousin and a man he expected he'd be seeing quite a bit of in the next days. He rested his elbows on the great table in front of him listening to the growling and snarling around him. Gray had replaced most of his once coal black mane. Beside Keep was the tall but awkwardly built High Priest of the Mountain Errol Travis.

He would not have been King Herald's first choice to recommend The Priesthood to promote and appoint to the position among The King's Ministers. Travis was a childhood friend of his father, the previous King. And it was his father's wish to have Errol Travis appointed to the Ministry. The fact that Travis was notorious gambler was a poorly kept secret. Southgate was not without it's murkier districts. Despite the shadow the man walked about in, The King felt compelled to tolerate High Priest Travis and all of his mischief. By stark contrast the man sitting next to Travis was Arch Salver Gavon Wedmore.

He was a Midlander by birth and upbringing, but he'd acclimated well to life in the far south and the culture of Southgate. He stood out with his olive complexion, but more so with his merit. An honor graduate of the Salvernium he was the first Midlander to wear the White Mockingbird in a position of esteem. A mockingbird was the sigil worn by Salvers assigned to southern keeps by the Salvernium, which was neutral in all the lands. Arch Salver Wedmore was a kind man with a great knowledge of the healing arts. Next to him was Minister of Sail Klara Upson. Southgate was a largely a landlocked Kingdom. Only a very small part of it actually touched the salt water. Hence Southgate's ocean going navy was small and not regarded as formidable by most other sea powers. It operated from a small island port south of a much larger sea power friendly to the throne. River ships were another matter however. River systems in Gatheria were numerous especially in the south. Southgate was very active in river going commerce and thus floated a considerable number of river vessels involved in trade. Of course vessels transporting soldiers fell under the purview of the Minister of War, however the funding for their construction was a matter for the Minister of Sail. The two often sat far from each other over many past disagreements of how much funding was set aside for these matters.

"I will commission new ships when I am confident there will be competent captains to helm them. I will not lecture you in terms of a marching army Minister Keep, if you will not insist lecturing me on matters of seafaring. The sea is in my blood. I know when a man is too green to take command," she said. Keep of course disagreed with her. Their quarrels however seemed trivial compared to their apprehensions with the men sitting across from them on the other side of the table. These Men were The Green Foxes. These were lords and regional wardens from prominent Halls who resided in major keeps of the Southlands. Aside from Hall Lamb, who was clearly represented by King Herald himself, there was western warden lord Marten Ivy of the Hall Ivy who resided in Westbreak Keep, which lay just west of the Sentinels. The Ivy Hall sigil consisted of a white owl facing right while perched upon a brass trumpet. Their dominant color was black. They were active in the timber market given their soil was perfect for farming timber which would grow to harvest in only ten years time. Many of these tree farms lay active in the lands controlled by the Ivys.

West of his lands was the beginning of what was regarded as the true west controlled largely by Hall Redflower. Sitting next to him was eastern warden lord Sardis Falco who resided in Seastorm Keep, which lay on the far eastern edge of The Kingdom. Sardis Falco was the uncle of Klara Upson and controlled the Port of Seastorm. A small but important port, operating from a central port and a chain of islands, in the southeast of Gatheria just far enough north that the weather was fairly warm throughout the year. A great deal of money and goods flowed into and from it from the entire span of the eastern coast. The entirety of Southgate's ocean navy made sail from here south of the Falco Naval Garrison on the nearby Seastorm Isle. The sigil of Hall Falco was the Seabird of Prey surrounded by ocean blue on their pennant. Seated next to him was northern warden lord Parnell Haddock of Swiftriver Keep that lay north of Southgate at a place where four major rivers intersected called The Swifts. They had a major influence over river trade in the southlands. As a boy King Herald was a ward of lord Parnell's father Miles. The sigil of Hall Haddock was the Swift Fish, which swam across an indigo pennant. The final member of The Green Foxes was lord Kastor Brian of High Canyon Keep, which lay in the canyons northwest of Southgate simply called The Canyon Lands.

Hall Lamb had the least influence here than in all of the southlands. In fact Hall Brian would not even be here if it weren't for the fact is was virtually impossible to do business in the south completely independent from Hall Lamb. Decades of being involved with campaigns in the west had effectively cut Hall Brian off from the west coast. As result Hall Brian begrudgingly allied themselves with Southgate and Hall Lamb despite still controlling much of the land in the northwest of The Sentinels. It was no secret that the Brians envied Hall Lamb's close associations with dwarves as well. Standing behind lord Kastor was his eldest son Banathir. Draped across his chest was a shawl with the Hall sigil of the Fire Serpent poised for strike on a bright red background. For years Attheon's father had promoted a marriage to Pallas Brian. It was offer presented first to Mercurian, and then later to Attheon. A woman a year older and he had never met. Attheon only knew anything about her through stories told to him by those who had.

None of which inspired him to take an active role in courtship. His disinterest was notable. Each time old lord Kastor sat in The Old Hall the last ten years he expected Attheon, or any of his brothers of age to approach him about the hand of Pallas. None ever did. Kastor had mixed feelings about this. He didn't care for Southgate or it's culture, but he did covet the prestige of its court. This Attheon carried himself differently than most in the room though and he stood out to Kastor. He looked like an outsider in his own family's venue. This was the first time that lord Kastor had recalled ever being in the same room as Attheon Lamb. He would have remembered. King Herald also noticed his son's arrival through all the shouting. He raised a hand in the air, which brought a dead silence in the great stone room. A court bellman standing near the throne stepped forward and announced the new arrival.

"Prince Attheon The Eleventh, Heart of The Sentinels and heir to the Throne of Southgate! And Prince Antimony The Fourth, Vice General and commander of the Northern Guard at Northpeak!" the court bellman shouted. King Herald gestured to his sons to come forth.

"My Sons! Come hither," he said gleefully. Attheon proceeded forth. He could feel every eye in the room fixed on him as he did. He'd never become accustomed to that. Most in this room still remembered his brother Mercurian's face. Most in this room were seeing his for the first time. More were familiar with the faces of his other siblings than his own. The Reclusive Prince some called him far from the ears of The King. Attheon sat down in the chair just to the right of his father that he had sat in only one time before when he was thirteen. A flowing pattern had been cut in all the chairs right and left of the throne itself carrying a common mountain motif meant to symbolize The Sentinels. Attheon's chair sitting disused left in some back room of the Old Hall had preserved some of the sheen the others had largely lost at this point. The King had it brought out and placed at his right hand just for this occasion. Attheon sat down next to his father. His brother sat down in the chair his older brother Carcino usually sat in. A chair that many in the room had grown accustomed to see sit at the right hand of The King.

Some even entertained the thought that at some point Carcino would be declared heir over his brother whom even a few doubted existed at all. But there he was. A cacophony of whispers washed over the old throne room as soon as Attheon sat down. Most of the King's children were here. His younger sons Gallian and Lucian sat to his left. Their sister Vanadia sat to the far left. Carcino was in the north aiding the lord of a minor Hall end a rash of banditry that had plagued his lands for much of the last year. His chair is the one his younger brother sat in now. The finish was well worn from its arms. Whoever the eldest brother was at these gatherings typically sat at the right of the King. Typically it was Carcino. A fact that troubled The King who leaned over to Attheon as the shouting resumed.

"Good to see you decided not come dressed as a forest brigand," The King said just loud enough for Attheon to hear. He could hear the retort in his mind, but said nothing, and decided to take the barb in stride.

"The room appears to be a shade on the cold side father. And I do like to dress warmly," Attheon replied. This was wit The Kings was not expecting. He let out a modest guffaw and patted his son's hand. The room was indeed full of cold stares that blasted like winter fronts back and forth across the table. Lord Haddock, large in stature, stood up from his chair and pointed directly at the Minister of Grain. It was a gesture that drew many a gasp from the room.

"Minister Woodley! With the upmost respect to you, your record, and your station, but how can you so flippantly dismiss the greater peril these atrocities place not just the farmlands n, but also the entire south? These villages reside in your purview! Men you appointed yourself to coordinate these lands now lay dead on the very fields under your care! I'll say his name since nobody else will! Addar Marsh!" Lord Haddock yelled. His long graying black beard shook as he did. Minister Woodley looked across the table at him with a fair but firm expression. Lord Falco looked at lord Haddock with a side-glance.

"So you admit your disdain for lord Addar now after all this time," he scoffed. Lord Haddock shot a scowl his way.

"Hush You! I don't want to hear a single criticism from you or anyone in your Hall safe from all this blood on your coast with your cozy little harbor!" Haddock snapped at Falco, who smiled. Minister Upson glared at Haddock while her uncle gave retort.

"A Swiftman so readily given to gossip and rumor. These truly are dark days," Falco replied. Haddock glared at the man with heat that could burn paper. Minister Woodley sat forward in his chair. Haddock refocused his attention back at the Minister of Grain.

"Lord Haddock. My response is neither flippant, nor dismissive. It is one of care," Minister Woodley replied. Lord Haddock recoiled upon hearing this and looked around at the others in the room to gauge their feelings about what Woodley just said.

"Care? Care, Minister Woodley? Care! I can tell you and everyone in this room about care! Care rests at the feet of lord Addar Marsh and his Entire Bloody Hall in a pool of blood seeping through the cracks of Buckler's Bend Keep! We can all stop dancing around what All Of Us have wanted to say For Years! Adder Marsh is a fiend, and so are his progeny. In his pockets are freshly minted Golden Crowns from his Warlord kin and their vile patron. Our So-Called Exalted Emperor! A man who has no claim outside the Midlands but pretends to think so. He has designs on the North continent. Why do you think he is so obsessed at controlling every northern port? Invasion! And yes his eyes look elsewhere. The South. Our South! And the sovereign seat in which Our King sits! All of his agents in Our Lands must be exposed and held to account! The more we mewl. The more we bargain. The more we compromise. The more We Ignore. The More They Will Encroach! I, nor my Hall will stand for this complacency or ambivalence! Call the man OUT! Or so help me I will march my pennants north and drag Lord Marsh back in chains myself!" Lord Haddock screamed so even the ghosts of the Old Hall could hear. Minister Woodley calmly sat back in his chair and folded his arms.

"Lord Haddock. I too mourn for the loss of my colleagues and their families. I too would like to see whoever is responsible for these attacks in the Barley Lands rooted out and brought to justice. But l, like others in this room, would like to see proof that Lord Addar Marsh, or anyone of Buckler's Bend, had anything to do with these attacks. Or anything with the rise in banditry in the last year for that matter. I want justice. But I also want the right men facing the hangman's noose. I do not oppose your passion. Your direction is another matter. Besides, military action is not within my purview," Minister Woodley said and then glanced over at Minister Keep. Lord Haddock looked at him as well then sat back down. Minister Keep's eyes were steeled and stern.

"If lord Marsh is truly a Warlord asset I will spare the hangman the trouble and cut the man in half myself. Until I see evidence of his complicity I will not advise our King our to engage in any campaign north. Is this clear lord Haddock?" he said. Lord Haddock didn't respond but simply glanced at Prime Minister Dane Ford who stood behind The King. Soon others were looking his way. The King gestured his Prime Minister forth. Ford did so and walked to the head of the table with his hands folded in front of him. He was a slight man in his mid fifties with narrow shoulders and graying curly brown hair. He first looked at lord Haddock. Then at the other faces in the crowd.

"His majesty and I spoke long into the night about everything spoken here. And some of what hasn't. I cannot stand here and bellow like our lord Haddock, nor do I have the placidity of Minister Woodley. I may carry a sword by my side, but as you have all very well remarked in the past, it is mostly ceremonial. I cannot therefore credibly offer an imposing presence or the recreate the determination and dedication it took to forge a man like Minister Keep. I will attempt to follow the example set by Minister Woodley and present myself measuredly and rationally. I will attempt to speak loudly enough in this Old Hall so that I have everyone's full and undivided attention, as lord Haddock has impressed upon us as important. And I will try to do so from a source of honor as strong as Minister Keep. I will do this all by telling you precisely what his majesty told me in the darkest hours of the night," Prime Minister Ford said almost meekly to those in attendance. He then arced up his shoulder and brought down his fist hard on the table in front of him.

He stopped just short though, and merely gently patted the wooden surface. A glint from his ruby pinky ring flashed as he did. He raised his head up and looked at the crowd.

"There will be NO action taken against lord Marsh or Buckler's Bend!" he said loudly. Not so much in a shout, but projecting the meaning of his words to every corner of the room with raw and forceful explicit spirit. It took a few moments for the room process what had just been said. Lord Haddock looked down.

"What are we supposed to do then? Do we sit by and watch this keep happening? What happens when the farmers abandon their farms and leave the grain to rot in the fields? Where does our bread come from then? How do we feed our livestock? Spring is far away. Are we to bend the knee to the Midlanders so we can eat? Do we fish our rivers until they die? Do we hunt our forest to death? What would you have us do my Liege?" Haddock said far more calmly as he turned his head toward The Throne, still keeping his gaze down. The Prime Minister looked back at The King. The monarch rubbed his chin then stood up and looked around the room.

"I made up my mind in the night. But I wanted my sons to hear what you all had to say from your own mouths. I wanted to hear all that you had to say as well. Perhaps, in hopes of changing my mind. Alas no. There will be no action taken against Buckler's Bend or it's Lord. This does not mean of course inaction will be our only recourse. The winds are favorable for a message flight to my son Prince Carcino. He is already on horseback. He will be diverted from his current activity and will take personal charge of the investigation into the farm attacks in the West Barley Lands. He will uncover the culprits and bring them to trial. If they have the wisdom to surrender. This is my will as your King. And this is what will be done," King Herald projected into the room. Following his words was silence in which no one dared speak up.

"Good evening to you all. My dearest thanks to you for making this journey. I know it was not an easy one for some of you. Please enjoy the tastes and sights of Southgate, and send my warmest regards with you back to your keeps," The King said. He then began walking out of the old throne room gesturing to Attheon and the others to follow him, which they did. The King followed by his children and some of the Royal Guard took a hallway to the Old King's Study behind the throne room. Upon reaching the study he gestured to his guard to wait outside. He and the others entered and sat down. Prime Minister Ford entered as well and closed the door behind him.

In the old throne room some visual daggers were still being thrown around but the shouting had ceased. Lord Haddock sat silently with his thoughts. Falco joked with his advisors about their forthcoming jaunt through Southgate's taverns. Joviality did not digest well for Brian. He stood up and left with his son Banathir and their advisors and headed toward the King's Palace. Minister Keep did the same. One by one most of the people in the room filed out and headed off in the direction of their overnight lodgings, carriages, or the delights of the city. Lord Ivy got up and sat down in Brian's vacated seat and turned to Haddock.

"Parnell, while we may not have the closest of relationships I do believe we have much common ground," he said discreetly. Lord Haddock turned and looked at lord Ivy.

"What common ground would that be Marten?" he said. Lord Ivy leaned in a bit closer.

"This travesty must not go unpunished. Both you and I know we cannot unilaterally counter The Kings decree. This would appear rebellious and neither would like the outcome that would bring," he said. Haddock leaned over closer himself.

"Agreed. What is it you are proposing?" he said. Ivy grinned slightly.

"Taking action ourselves would be observed as provocative, yes. But nothing much would be said for us giving aid to the young Prince Carcino and his investigations. Though assistance from the other lords and ministers was not specifically requested, it was not expressly forbidden either. I'm sure that between the two of us we can help ease Our Prince's efforts should he encounter any friction from those not so eager to allow for his progress. They could be anyone from a tavern wench to some Noble who may, for whatever reason, find it profitable to hinder Our Prince," he said he said with conspicuous emphasis. Haddock sat back up in his chair and clasped his hands together.

"What is it that you mean by 'Our Prince' Lord Ivy?" he said. Ivy smiled and glanced around the room for a moment then turned back to Haddock.

"What I mean by 'Our Prince' is that I do believe that it would be beneficial for both of us to start showing our support to Our Prince, because he could very well become Our King, and the earlier we start paying him favor the better position our Halls will be in when he does sit in The Kings Palace," Ivy said. Haddock narrowed his brow.

"What about Prince Attheon? He is the eldest son and heir?" Haddock said. Ivy held back a chuckle.

"Oh Parnell, are you honestly gambling on Attheon the Absent? The Reclusive Prince? Our King may love his son and wish him to take his place when he is gone, but you and I both know he will be traipsing around playing at being a ranger in some deep dark forest thwipping his little bow when his father leaves this world. The people will see this. Who do you think they will support? A son who has always sat at his father's side and carried out his duties as Prince? Or a vagabond shooting at shadows in the trees in muddy boots for most his life? A real Prince, or mock ranger?" Ivy said. Haddock looked down for a few moments as he pondered this. Then he looked back up at Ivy.

"We back Carcino now. We give him any assistance he needs. We do not conspire to supplant Attheon. Not just yet. In time others will see the advantage Prince Carcino presents to the future of our Kingdom, and The Throne. His success is crucial," Haddock replied. Ivy smiled widely.

"Yes Parnell. That is all that need be done. For now," Ivy said. Haddock nodded.

The Old Study was The King's home away from home. The study in the King's Palace was often used, but for nothing particularly important. Foreign dignitaries had expectations of Southgate from stories of the Age of Vanity. They always wanted to see as much of what The Vain King built. The current monarch had little taste for such things. He favored the old and traditional of Southgate. This study was by far the most traditional room in the city. It harkened back to a time when the Lamb's oldest ancestors emerged from The Midlands wearing nothing but animal skins and gold face paint. They carried only crude bronze weapons. Eleven thousand years since the earliest members of what would become Hall Lamb walked away from the ruins of a collapsing Elven civilization. The tribe of man was thought of as nothing but a small unremarkable and primitive race only good for cheap labor. Those times echoed in the tribal décor of this Old Study and The Old Hall itself. King Herald sat in a big chair by the fire. Around him sat his sons and daughter. As always, behind him stood his Prime Minister. The King drank deeply from a flagon of dark ale and sat it on a table next to his chair. He looked deeply into the fire beside him, as if The Kings mind flickered with it. He then turned and looked directly at Attheon. He said nothing. Then he looked at his two youngest sons.

"Gallian. Lucian. Both of you are young still and not yet of age, but what I will discuss here will still be important to you. You are Princes of Southgate. You will be expected to take up leadership roles in support of your brother. The future King. In turn he must form the kind of bond a King must have with his Generals and other leaders of esteem. Roles all of you my children will fill. Carcino and Antimony are already well on this path," The King said. He paused for a moment as if to collect his thoughts. He looked at Attheon again.

"Before some of you were born, and when the rest of you were still small I began my mission to prepare my eldest Mercurian to take my place on the throne of Southgate. Fate however decided to take cruel path and lead your brother to his doom. His duties then fell on the shoulders of Attheon. A young man who had only just come of age a few years before. He wasn't ready to take on this burden then. Alas, this has not changed even now," said the King. His other children held back gasps upon hearing this. The King was not easing into criticism. Attheon felt anger toward his father like he had not in many years, but again held back. The King was right. Attheon had no argument. He bit his tongue and kept silent. The King continued.

"Even so. He is my heir, and your future King. While it is true we all grow at our own pace, life and duty gives us no quarter and will test us when it sees fit. Not when we are ready to be tested. Many feathers have brought me messages in the last few months that make me fear war may be looming in the east. When I hear whispers from my Minister of Candor that all but confirm what I have also read, I evaluate Southgate and weigh if she is at all prepared. Her outlook appears grim to me," The King added, as he looked each of his children in the face. The heir broke his silence then.

"Father, if war is coming from the east, Seastorm could be in danger," Attheon said. The King looked over at him. An ashen expression came over his face.

"A vast understatement my boy. Vast. Indeed lord Falco and Seastorm are in grave danger. He has booked lodging in Southgate for the night. It's something he has never done. He and his entourage have always departed hastily. I don't figure being away from the sea agrees with him. He remains to talk to me. He doesn't know now that I am as equally interested in talking to him," The King said. Attheon looked over at Antimony then back at The King.

"Did you want me to be there with you when you do talk to Sardis Falco?" he said. The King shook his head.

"No my son. Your testing begins with you travelling with a battalion of some of my finest swords. Not a host. Merely an escort. You will take Antimony with you. He too will be tested. As will your squire. He has been summoned east to Vashoth village beyond The Sentinels where he will meet you and your party. From then you will journey to Seastorm. It is time for the realm to start seeing my sons in the way my heart knows they are. Southgate's future," The King said. Attheon had not heard his father speak about him with optimism before. Not the way he had always spoken about Mercurian. A brother he loved dearly, but existed under his substantial shadow. The King clapped his hands together.

"My children. Would you please give your brother Attheon and I the room," he said. The younger Lambs looked around at each other then got up. Antimony patted his brother on the shoulder as he departed through the door. When all of his siblings had left the room Prime Minister Ford closed the door behind them. From the look in his eyes Attheon could tell what The King had in store. The King rotated his chair slightly toward Attheon. The thick wooden legs ground upon the stony floor.

"My son. You are now thirty and one years of age. You are heir to the greatest power in the south. Your people and this throne need to know this Hall's legacy will continue after you follow me into the ancestral crypt. This means you must wed," The King said. Atheon sat back in his chair and smiled.

"Cousin Brey has already given me this lecture tonight. Albeit more colorfully than I expect you will," Attheon mused. The King was not in the mood for humor.

"Your cousin is absolutely right. Despite his tone, he has the same concern as I do. As does all of Southgate. Regard this as a lecture if you will my son. But also regard it as your people do. An assurance of stability, security and strength. This is why I will be entering into negotiations with Lord Sardis Falco for the hand of his oldest daughter Lady Marea," The King said. Attheon was stunned. This name wasn't what he was expecting at all.

"Lady Marea Falco? I was sure the name you were going to say was Lady Pallas Brian," he said. The King nodded.

"Aye my son. Lady Pallas Brian would make a favorable wife for you and produce many sons. The climate however has changed to favor a union between you and the Lady Marea. The Lambs and Falcos must form that critical bond now to ensure the security of the eastern coast. A uniting of our navies. Officially. If you are concerned about the Brians and their considerable assets, calm yourself. This avenue will not be lost to us. I have also entered into negotiations for the hand of your sister to go to young lord Banathir," The King said. This time Attheon could not so easily conceal his objection.

"Vanadia? She is not yet of age for marriage! Would you honestly marry her to a man almost twice her years father?" Attheon huffed. Prime Minister Ford looked like he wanted to say something but The King held up his hand and looked back at Attheon.

"I do my son. Although your sister may not be old enough to consummate, she will be betrothed nonetheless. In time they will wed and your nephews will be Lords of High Canyon Keep. Should Sardis Falco's son Denato fail to produce any male heirs, your second son will be named Lord of Seastorm. You haven't lived in times where standing alone is a fools gamble. You don't know the histories my boy. You don't know how much we need Both Hall Brian and Hall Falco for the coming time," The King said. Attheon looked away.

"Is it your wish to marry all of us away to your Green Fox friends father?" he muttered. The King did not take the statement lightly.

"Yes boy. If need be, yes. There is a pall looming. Bandits we know. Organized or nay. Brigands, vagabonds, highwaymen, or whatever you want to call them have always been thorn so long as the Empire and it's Warlord cohorts' permissiveness in the north continues, they will always be a problem. But the slayings in the north and the attacks occurring on the eastern coast are any indication, something else is growing," The King said. Attheon looked back at him. He didn't see anger or disdain in his father's eyes. He couldn't ascertain the look he saw.

"Farmers who refused to pay protection to bandit clans? Salty cutthroats? Why would this elicit these kinds of moves? We have Lords' guards, Stone Lodge swords, and rangers to deal with bandits. Coastal lords, even yes my future father in law Sardis Falco are there to deal with pirates and their ilk. Why does this concern us Father?" Attheon said. The King looked back at Prime Minister Ford. Ford walked to the other side of the room to a table piled high with message scrolls. Ford turned and looked at Prince Attheon.

"You see my Prince. Right here is what has feathered in for weeks. Read them yourself if your father's concern is insufficient to persuade you to take these matters seriously," Ford said then looked over at The King. King Herald then turned to his son.

"What we are inferring my son is something I didn't want to mention in front of the younger ones. You may inform Antimony of what I am about to tell you. Read the messages if you feel you must. But hear me now boy. When I hear that bandits sending envoys to rangers claiming innocence and pirates parlaying for asylum to protected waters I am left to conclude a great deal Concerns Us. I ask you the question Prince Attheon, heir to Southgate. What do we do about those who we fear, Fear?" The King said. Attheon considered this statement for a moment. Then a sick feeling in his stomach began welling up.

"Surely you don't imply that the Exiled Kings are rising up for invasion. Why would they dare? Raiding small fishing ports, backing the odd cutthroat, and even attacking some vessels that sail too close their waters yes, but what you suggest is an invasion. The Exiled Kings may be formidable forces in their corner of the Eastern Sea, but they stack up poorly to either the Midlands or The South in terms of land forces. Again father, why would they dare?" Attheon replied. The look in The Kings Eyes intensified.

"I don't know son. I intend for you to find out. Just as I intend your brother Carcino to uncover the mystery surrounding their mainland collaborators. If it should be true that lord Addar Marsh is indeed involved. Buckler's Bend will have to be dealt with," The King said. Attheon's eyes widened.

"Surely Father__," Attheon began to say before his father waved his hand.

"This conversation is at an end boy! You know my wishes. You will depart before dawn breaks with your brother for Seastorm. Feather me news when you get it. I will retire for the evening now. I will give your mother the good news," The King said and stood up from his chair and walked out of the room. His guard crowded around him to escort him to the King's Palace. Prime Minister Ford looked back at Attheon. Then he leaned over and picked up a scroll.

"You'll want to read this one first," He said then set the small roll of paper back on the table it had been sitting on. Attheon looked at it as the Prime Minister walked out of the room and closed the door.

Antonio Salazar materialized in the staging room aboard the VCS Natty Bumppo. He was far more worse for the wear than before. In one hand he carried his badly damaged helmet. In the other he held his vulcanium sword. His grip loosened and he dropped the blade on the floor. It hit with a clang that echoed off the walls. Then he dropped his helmet, which landed with a thunk. He looked down to his waist. He then disengaged his belt buckle. He reached behind his back and pulled his belt free sending both his holsters to the ground. Antonio took a deep breath and wearily staggered to a chair sitting by the wall and sat down. A moment later red lights in the room began flashing and an alarm began to sound.

"Foreign Technology Detected! Containment Protocols Initiated!" an automated recording blared.

"No shit!" Antonio shouted back as he pulled off his gloves.

The river was calmer north of The East Lodge. The land was level for a good distance until it began to tip downward. Ropes with bright streamers hung from trees on either side of the river well ahead of where the current picked up. Brothers swimming or fishing this stretch would know when it was wise not to swim ahead. Pepper was nowhere near this boundary. He walked out of the water, shook himself off and wrapped himself in his robe. The wet did not bother him but he preferred to dry off quickly nonetheless. He wasn't alone here. Other brothers were around with their poles a ways away with lines in the water hoping to catch a meal they didn't have to wait in the dining hall for. They weren't the only company. Out of the corner of his eye he saw Brother Alvin approaching with his escort. It was two other Brothers from the sound of it. This meant he was here on official business. He was happy to see Alvin himself be the one to ask him questions he had no answers to yet. Other Senior Brothers he found lacking. He stood up and greeted the old man.

"Brother Alvin. I hope the day treats you well. I don't have anything to add since yesterday. If Brother Mandy was displeased with my tone, I offer my apologies." He said. The old man shook the wolf's still damp paw.

"I hope the day has been favorable to you as well. Mandy was apologetic when last we spoke. Sometimes his temperament is not well suited for the types of the requests made of him. We all work with whatever our weaknesses happen to be. These things are as they are. You may be relieved I am not here about any Delegation business. There is another matter," he said and pulled a small rolled message from his pocket and handed it to Pepper. It had the sigil of the Red Flower. Pepper snapped it open and read it.

"A message from my sister," he said and stuffed the paper into his pocket. Pepper's abruptness stood out to Alvin.

"Oh?" he said. Pepper expected some curiosity but this was not a matter he wished to share.

"My sister and I are not close. We haven't been for many years now," he said. Pepper would not elaborate. Alvin pressed.

"I see. What did she have to say?" he said. Pepper said nothing but instead looked away. Sensing his resistance Alvin dialed back his tone.

"A matter better to stay between siblings. This I understand. This reminds me of my two daughters," he said. Pepper looked back at Alvin. He was quite surprised to hear this.

"You had a family Brother Alvin?" he said. Alvin smiled. This was not something he brought up often with his Brothers, but not a secret either. He preferred to keep the subject on those he wanted to mentor and let them talk about themselves.

"Oh aye. A wife and four babes. Two boys and two girls. The boys got on quite well and still do to this day. My girls are a different story. To this day their families are not close. A saddening thing for a father and grandfather. Walk with me a bit Pepper," Alvin said and began walking down the path that ran by the river. Pepper followed next to him.

"My girls are close in age but very different from each other. Their mother passed when they were still very young. I suppose had she been a bigger part of their lives they may have followed a better path. Hard to say though. I often think about that. Regardless after marrying they moved far away from each other. I don't think their children have even met each other. Altogether very sad. I cannot speak to your situation. But I can speak as a father who has seen his children grow distant. The advice I offer is consider, if only consider at this point, in being open to your sister. You may not take one old man's advice, but I don't want you to have to tell a sad story to someone else in the future," he said. Although it was true that Brother Alvin was outside the situation. His words were nonetheless appreciated.

"I thank you for your wisdom Brother Alvin. Perhaps some day I will be more open to talk about my family," he said. Alvin was happy to hear him say that.

"I look forward to that day lad. I do hope though when the time comes the wisdom I impart will become useful to you when a young brother is in need of your counsel. I do wish that very much. Sometimes I don't feel like I am as useful as I can be," he said. Pepper vehemently disagreed.

"Nonsense Brother Alvin. I won't hear you say such things. Your words have helped steer me in more, better, directions than I can count. I'm sure plenty of Brothers can say the same. You sell yourself so very short. It bothers me that you don't see that," he said. Alvin patted Pepper on the shoulder.

"Thank you lad. It's encouraging to hear you say that. It bothers me that I have to be reminded so often. Even the wisest of all can falter in this respect. You have a wisdom of your own. In time I hope you are better able than I to keep more in its proper perspective," he said. Pepper hoped that one day Brother Alvin could appreciate himself like he did, and other Brothers did as well.

"I will do my best Brother Alvin. Until then I will continue to learn from you," he said. Alvin laughed.

"And my boy I will continue to do my best to tender lessons worth learning," he said and laughed again.

Late afternoon was setting in over Hells Kitchen, New York. The sound of several men running echoed off the walls of an alley. Five finely dressed members of the Ace of Clubs gang ducked behind a wooden fence and looked out between slats out into the alley behind them. They didn't see anything. They were sure they had been seen. They all carried sacks filled with jewelry they'd just stolen from a smash and grab operation they'd been planning for weeks. They stayed very still and continued to look. Still nothing. A few of them began to relax, but then the alley lit up brightly. Up above them on a fire escape was a flashing figure.

"Well, looks like bad guys hiding in the shadows again. Good thing Jafus Powers has his electric justice to shine a light on the situation," yelled a costumed hero decked out in purple and yellow lightning bolts. He descended down to the alley floor on his crackling electricity. His platform shoes gently hovered just above the ground.

"If my lightning ain't enough to brighten up your attitudes, my super strength is gonna lift you up my brothers, to a higher place!" he yelled. The gang took off running again. Jafus used his lighting to propel himself forward at amazing speed and caught up to one of the men. He screamed making his cohorts run faster. As they neared the end of the alley a young Latino man in a purple satin jacket, blue jeans and a pair of bright white sneakers stepped out into the middle of the alley. He pulled guitar over his shoulder and played a chord. A burst of energy pulsed out in front of him rattling the windows of the units above.

"Callate Evil Doers!" he yelled in a singing voice. The Aces stopped dead in their tracks. They knew who this was too. The young man continued to play as he began to dance.

"I am Kaepa Jaime, and I will stymie your advance. Drop the stolen jewels or face my dance!" he said and played another chord, which knocked one of the Aces down. A loud crackling sound made them turn around. Jafus Powers dropped the man he caught who he'd zip-tied up. Jafus looked at all their faces.

"Oh my brothers, the NYPD will love meeting y'all!" he said. One of the Aces reached behind his back and grabbed hold of some gas grenades. In one move he yanked them out, flipped the pins out with his thumbs and tossed them both at the heroes. Jafus and Jaime didn't have time to react as the grenades exploded at their feet. Suddenly choking gas erupted up at them causing them to falter. The Aces took out masks and put them on.

"Get em' boys!" one of them yelled. The Aces rushed the heroes and began pummeling them. Fighting through the haze Jafus fought back knocking one Ace out cold.

Another Ace retaliated by hitting him in the back with a board. Jafus fell to one knee. Jaime sprayed chords back and forth blindly hitting the alley walls around him. A few of the aces attacking him fell back as the sound hit them. Another Ace threw a bottle that caught him on the side of the face and he fell back. He picked up another bottle and smashed it on the ground and then charged Jaime with the jagged end. Jaime called upon the power of his magic shoes and reached for his strings. The Ace made it two steps before something hit his arm causing him to drop the bottle, which shattered on the ground. He looked up to see where the object came from only to see and shadow falling down at him. A fist caught him clean on the side of the face. The other Aces turned to look. Their eyes widened as they saw the epic visage of The Night Eagle. Objects came out nowhere and struck the men attacking Jafus. They fell down around him yelping in pain. Jafus looked up to see the grin of Proto Jay as he walked up. What Aces still stood took off running down a side path between buildings. They got to the street but were met by flashing lights and dozens of NYPD officers with weapons drawn. They gave up immediately. Back in the alley one Ace dared to square up with The Night Eagle. He swung at the hero who casually dodged every punch before leveling the crook with a solidly placed elbow. The Ace looked up at him in disbelief. Another one raised his hands in surrender.

"Long way from National ain't ya?" he grumbled. The Night Eagle stared at him. Jafus walked up to him.

"Come on man. We had this," he said. Proto Jay walked up behind him and slapped him on the back.

"Then why did you guys put out the distress beacon? Now you owe me a slice of pizza," he said. Jafus looked confused and glanced over at Jaime. His sidekick looked equally confused. The Night Eagle shook his head.

"We got the distress beacon thirty minutes ago and Admiral Mercury flew us over. Right now he's rallying the NYPD to converge on this very alley, right now," he said. Jaime then let out a loud groan. He shook his head.

"Lo siento amigos. I'm so sorry. I must have butt-dialed you when we got the alert the jewelry store was being hit. Still working out the kinks in our new system. My bad homes," he said apologetically. Proto Jay laughed. Jafus couldn't help but grin himself. The Night Eagle nodded.

"I guess Full Scale didn't send the patch updates he told me about. Regardless, excellent response time to the incident. However a butt-dial is a butt-dial. My young feathered friend is right. Somebody owes us pizza," he said and grinned slightly. Jafus laughed and then shook The Night Eagle's hand.

"So how's that Get Fit U.S. thing going?" he said. The Night Eagle grimaced.

"I'd rather not discuss that in front of the criminals," he said and whipped out a few pairs of Eagle Clawffs.

Chapter Four: All Roads

Antonio sat alone in the staging room alone in a cloud of flashing red lights. The alarms had shut off by now so he didn't have to contend with those anymore. He watched as deep-scanning devices emerged from compartments in the ceiling and the floor and began their task of determining what sort of threat the foreign technology may be. In the mean time Antonio slowly and painfully started to remove sections of his blood stained valiant suit. A holographic image appeared in front of him. Angelica Nocivo's face materialized.

"Where is my brother?" Angelica asked loudly. One arriving without the other was unusual so Antonio understood her alarm.

"Had to dose him. He'll be showing up after a while," Antonio said as he removed a section of bloody valiant and dropped it on the floor. This answer didn't sit well with Angelica.

"What do you mean you had to dose him? Who's blood is that?" she replied. Antonio's brow narrowed and then he continued to remove his armor.

"Mine. That's why I had to dose him. He went buggy on me. Figured he needed a nap, and I didn't need to be dead. A pragmatic approach wouldn't you say?" Antonio said.

"Did his earpiece fail?" she asked. Antonio stopped for a moment, and then he continued what he was doing.

"I can't say for sure. If a failure isn't logged in my helmet's memory I would say no. You should have that information in front you right now. Look for yourself. If I had to guess though, Skip's little flight of fancy may be related to whatever Foreign Tech all this lovely equipment is having a fit about right now," Antonio replied and weakly waved at all the mechanisms at work around him.

Angelica looked at the logs Antonio's helmet uploaded as soon as he arrived. She opened the tab relating to her brother's earpiece. No failure was indicated. She then looked back the camera display.

"And he just let you dose him?" she said. Antonio grunted as he turned painfully to look directly into the room's camera. He held up a section of his armor. Angelica could see light shining through a hole that had been pierced through it. Antonio raised an eyebrow.

"I would say he 'Let' me exactly," he said and then dropped the section on the floor with the rest. Having removed enough of his suit to reach his wounds Antonio tapped on a keypad near him. A compartment in the wall opened up and a shelf containing first aid supplies slid out. He then began dressing his still partially bleeding wounds. Angelica surveyed the flood of new data popping up on her monitors.

"Standby. Scan is 50% complete. Medical team is ready once we get the All Clear," Angelica said. Antonio just sighed and applied an antiseptic bandage.

"Fair enough. Understood. I'll just keep sitting here bleeding, and enjoying the company of my new robotic friends. Glad you're not dead Antonio. I'd be real torn up if my brother turned you into cocktail onion," Antonio groaned sarcastically amid the chaos and machines moving around him.

The sky was large here. So large and blue like a bright shining ocean looming above. The air was dry and hot despite the earlier time of day. The late summer was coming to a close. It allowed one to move about more freely. The sun didn't seem to sting as much though despite the heat. The water was cool enough. Genesis floated around near the bank of the calmly flowing river that ran by her small village of Scanna. The sun was getting higher in the sky. Soon the comparatively cooler morning would give way to the scorching afternoon.

It would be bad to be out at that time. Even this late in the year. It's as things were here in the eastern Borderland plateaus. What settlements there were here in the sandy landscape found their homes next to the Starfair, which flowed up from the south. Genesis feeling hungry swam to the shore and walked up onto the bank. Beads of water glistened on her olive skin. She picked up her shawl and wrapped it around herself and began making the walk to her father's cabin. The area was relatively safe. It was too far out from any major roads so venturing this far into the dusty landscape would not be very appealing to bandits. It was also near enough to a Warlord controlled city anyone seeking to do harm to any of the villages along this stretch of the Starfair feared reprisals from a Warlord's sheriff and his men. Even so, one still needed to be careful. Genesis picked up her spear that lay against a nearby boulder. It was a weapon she was taught how to use and respect by her father who was the highest druid mystic in these parts. He was man of peace, but one who understood the value of preparedness. There was another reason bandits didn't venture here. They were greed-fueled opportunists. But they were also highly superstitious and feared the magic of Vincent Payne and other mystics like him who inhabited these lands. It was a name known far from this humble little desert hamlet. As she walked along the path to town she passed by goat herders out with their trips to feed off the grasses that grew along the river. They waved as she passed. Her face was well known in this area as many made pilgrimages for the autumn and spring solstices to receive readings from her father. Her house was situated at the end of a small herders road that ran through the center of town. The curls symbolizing the god of Winds were painted on the front wall of the mud brick home. As she walked through the door she was greeted by the cool air that the thick walls of the home kept in. Her father sat in the middle of wisps of smoke rising in ribbons off of incense burning all around him making the home fragrant and inviting. He opened his eyes and took up bits of bone which had runes carved in them. He rolled them around in his hands as he chanted prayers under his breath. He tossed them in the air just higher than his head and watched as they descended down landing on the soft rug that he sat upon. He looked over the runes carefully and then sat back against the wall behind them. He looked up at his daughter who sat down in front of him. He seemed uneasy about something but was happy to see his child.

"Genni my girl, how was the river on this bright and sunny day?" he said as he picked up the runes. Genesis had glanced at them before he did. They meant nothing to her without knowing what he'd asked, but it struck her as a peculiar pattern. She didn't think much of it. Her mind had been elsewhere for much of the day.

"As cool as always father," she said as she picked up and lit another stick of incense and buried it in the clay pot of sand the others stood in.

"That's good to hear. I may have a dip in it's embrace later myself. Best to get in as many quiet moments as I can before autumn arrives. Then I throw the runes for others. I just hope that our father on the winds has more to say than he says to me on this bright and sunny day," he said as he placed his set of runes into a small wooden box that set next to him.

"The winds can twist and turn as our father wills it. You taught me this. Are the runes so unfavorable today as to ruin your good mood father?" she said smiling. Vincent picked up his fragrant cup of herbal tea, brewed from local flowers, and finished it off.

"Your mother's smile every time girl. It can remind an old man there is much to be thankful for in this world. A good cheering up is worth its weight in silver, gold, and fine spices." he said. Genesis laughed.

"How would one know how much cheer would weigh?" she asked. Her father thought about this for a moment. Then he smiled.

"Cheer weighs as much as the wind our father provides. Wind itself may not weigh very much, but it can carry the scent of these sticks. It can also carry things much heavier than itself, like the bees to flowers to make our honey. It can also destroy things much harder than itself like stone over time. Cheer can carry joy from place to place. Cheer can feed our souls. And cheer can destroy even the mightiest doubt. It's all a matter of how it moves. And who moves it. You have my thanks daughter for bringing me this cheer. Now as for the runes__," her father musingly trailed off then laughed.

"I'm happy that I can help make your day better. What could those runes possibly tell you that you'd need my cheer to brighten your mood?" Genesis replied. Vincent thought about this for a moment. Then he reached into the small wooden box that contained his runes and pulled one out. He sat it down on the rug in front of him blank side down. He then looked up at Genesis.

"One of two things could be read from what my study today. Either my powers are truly leaving me. Or something very odd is occurring in the wind our father wants me to see," he said. Genesis looked at the blank rune then up at her father.

"I don't understand. What does this mean?" she said. Her father picked the rune back up and held it up in his hand. Genesis took it from him and looked at it. First she examined the runic side, then the blank side, and then she handed it back.

"I've consulted the bones many times this morning. I have asked many different questions about The Days. Even the same question worded different ways. But the 4th Day position is always the same," Genesis was at a loss.

"I ask the winds as I always do before the Autumn Solstice about The Days. This year the 4th Day there is nothing. As if the day itself won't happen or maybe even that the future is still undecided about how it should. A truly very puzzling thing my child. I shouldn't bother you with such things. I don't want to spoil your day," he added. Genesis sat up and took her father by the hand and helped him to his feet.

"Now don't you go getting a sour stomach. I want to take you to down to the baker for some fresh bread. After a full belly if you are still feeling uneasy we'll visit a scribe so you can send feathers to your fellow Men of the Sands," she said. Her father smiled.

"Thank you child. Fresh bread sounds delightful," he said the bent down to place the rune back in the box.

"I wonder if the palm dates will be sweeter on the 4th Day this year than the last?" Genesis mused as she and her father walked out the front door. A moment later the small rune box shook slightly then the top rune flipped over onto its blank side. The lid then snapped shut.

Despite the mid day sun the small goat road was busy. Many that had collected their wages the day before patronized those who had goods to sell. Fishmongers, butchers, tanners, candle makers, and grocers all had their shops and carts open for business. Many in the small town worked for this land's minor noble. A man named Baron Natan Portaro. The Portaro Hall was of lesser standing among the nobility who settled this remote area. Even so, the Portaros were the last southern Hall with relations from the south living this far north. Old Baron Portaro had often made pilgrimages to Scanna to consult with its prominent bone reader Vincent Payne. The last year he did not, being too ill of health to make the journey. Payne instead sent his daughter to read for him. Vincent had been teaching her the art for many years since she was small. The old Baron was quite struck by the young woman's beauty when she arrived. He lamented that he had already married off all his sons by this point. Or else he would have assuredly negotiated with her father to marry her to one of them. Vincent Payne had no plans to negotiate with anyone for her hand. Her brother River had rejected the runic arts to go join with the desert rangers of The Red Clay and had not been seen for many seasons. Not since the last time the banks of the Starfair flooded over thirteen years ago. Genesis was still very much a child then. It broke her heart to see her brother leave. It was one of the reasons she remained so close her father. He was the only family she still had in this world. And he loved fresh bread straight from the stone ovens of the downtown bakery. Beside the bakers house was the wine seller.

"The canyon grapes have yielded some of the best barrels in recent years. My father wishes I impart his gratitude for having it in stock," Genesis said warmly handed him southern silver, which was still acceptable currency even in the Borderlands. Its value in comparison to Imperial gold was considered lesser the farther north one was. The opposite was true in the south. Southerners regarded northern gold paltry given how many trace metals were alloyed with it.

Even so one could buy a good horse with just a handful of Imperial Crowns. Genesis picked a short cask of light red from The Canyonlands vineyards in the southwest operated by the family Brian. It was their least expensive product. Other higher-grade wines fetched a far higher price. The cask would be delivered to the Payne home by one of the boys worked for the wine seller. Meanwhile Genesis and her father sat down on a bench in front of the baker and enjoyed fresh bread dipped into honey from the one of the local beekeepers. The flavor of the golden elixir was exquisite because of the richness of the late summer desert flowers. Genesis was happy to see how much this outing was affecting her father's mood. He'd not been the same since illness had taken her mother ten years prior. He often fell into spells of depression that would last for months. Only deep prayer out in the sands to the Father of Winds and study of the bones seemed to be his solace. A once strong and imposing man, he could now barely walk without a shoulder to lean on. Their neighbors would help him while Genesis was away giving readings to the peoples of the plateau. The time of the Autumn Solstice and The Days were always good times for her father. It truly lifted him to help so many others. For a brief time in the Week of The Days he seemed to regain some of his old strength. It would not last as the autumn would go by. When the frosts came to the sands in the winter none of that strength would remain. This cycle had repeated year after year over the last decade. She knew how important it was for him pass on the art to her and see her faith in the Father Wind be strong. Their next stop would be the Stone of the Winds at the center of town where they would offer their prayers on the wind of their breath to the father. Genesis helped Vincent up. He pushed up on his other side using his cane and grunted under the strain. Once he was up he smiled at his daughter and began walking with her to the Stone. A few other people were kneeling beside the Stone when they got there. Its sides had grown polished over the years with many hands laid on its surface. Soft prayers were muffled by the wind that blew around them. Genesis and her father knelt down and laid their hands upon the stone, which had been carved to represent the curls of the sacred winds. Genesis and her father fell deep into prayer. Her words flowed out of her and wisped around to join the wind. Something caught her ear though. She opened her eyes and looked over her shoulder. A man arrived on horseback wearing southern style garb trotted by.

The hoof beats on the ground sounded more aggressive to her for some reason. The horseman headed toward the wine seller and dismounted. He walked around the back of his horse giving it little pats as he did and approached the seller. A man named Carturas who was a transplant from Seastorm. They talked for about a minute and then the horseman dropped silver into Carturas' hand. The wine seller then turned and walked back into his shop. He emerged a few moments later with a few full wine skins draped over his shoulder. Large ones. Carturas thanked the horseman for his business and handed over the skins. The horseman shook the man's hand and then walked back to his horse. He tucked the skins into his saddlebag and mounted the horse again. Taking up the reigns the horsemen turned west and proceeded forth. The scene struck Genesis as strange. She contemplated this for a moment, but then turned and resumed her prayers.

Nocivo materialized in the staging rom of the Bumppo. He was off balance. Try as he might he could not focus on anything. Suddenly red lights flashed and alarms began to sound around him. That's when he lost consciousness and collapsed on the floor. He awoke later, with what could have been minutes or even years later. He couldn't know for sure. The first thing he saw was a metal ceiling painted robins egg blue. As his head began to clear he recognized where he was. This was an angle he was not accustomed to though. The familiar aroma of rubbing alcohol hit his nose chasing away a bit of the fog in his head. He tried to sit up but then the terrible ache hit him. He felt like he was made of deeply injured lead. The room seemed to move along with him, but it wasn't nearly as bad as before. He turned his head to the right. He could see IVs had been installed in his right arm. He looked up to see a few bags dangling above him. One was the customary mix to replenish lost fluids. He squinted to see what was written on the others. These were detoxifying drips, and not weak ones either. He turned his head forward to see a TV monitor that was off. Below it was a digital clock. It read 2:42 PM. Below it was the date. It read September 8th. He left for the mission on the 5th. It had been three days.

He tried to remember what had happened but images were fuzzy, murky and muddled. The last thing he could be sure about was reading frequency strength levels. Then he was under a pile of wood in an alley. Next he was activating a dashback, then red lights, and then here. Nothing else lay between. He glanced back at the drips hanging above him. Hanging there was a cocktail he called Big Blue. It was not a subtle concoction and would explain the gaps in memory. This would only be temporary. Piece by piece most of what he wasn't recalling now would rebuild after he was off the drip. At this time he couldn't reason why he needed it. It would be something he'd have to ascertain later. He tried to pull himself up again. This time he took hold of the infirmary bed frame and braced himself against it. Gathering some strength he pushed up hard and lay back against his pillow. He could see the room better now. To his right was one of his nurses named Chuck examining a crewman wearing a plumbing level uniform. His arm was injured with what looked like burns. Estrello felt like saying something but saw that Chuck was using the right spray. It was comforting to know that he could rely in his staff if he were in the state he was in now.

He looked over to his left. A few beds down lay Martha. She looked much better than she did a few days ago. Very near what he would regard as discharge worthy. She was watching some kind of comedy show. A man was yelling at a bowl of salad sitting in front of him. The show was called The Lester, and every episode was like this. Martha didn't really seem to be enjoying it very much. Nocivo wondered why she was even watching it to begin with. Chuck walked into another room. He may have run out of the spray he was using and went to get more. He heard a voice then and turned back to Martha.

"I said hey Skip," she said with a smile. Nocivo held up a hand in acknowledgment. He then braced himself again and pushed himself up further. Speaking was difficult it would appear, as he tried to form words. Now mostly sitting up and truly feeling like he was made lead.

"You look like I did a few days ago Skip," Martha said. Estrello grimaced and weakly shook his head.

"I've had worse. Mas mucho malo," he said through a dry and crackly throat. Martha muted her television and looked back at Nocivo.

"It looks like you just lost a fight," she mused. It took a moment to register, but when it did a very sick feeling well up in his stomach over the uneasiness that was already there because of the drips.

"I said it looks you just lost a fight," she said again. Nocivo was finding it hard to articulate. Martha cocked her head to the side and watched him for a few moments as he struggled to respond.

"You've never lost a fight before?" she said. Nocivo looked to the side.

"Not since I was very young," he responded hoarsely. Martha didn't quite know how to respond. Nocivo looked back at her.

"Tony?" he said weakly. Martha rolled her eyes.

"Being annoying as ever. He was in here a couple of days ago getting patched up. The things coming out of that man's mouth. Holy biscuits. Before that they had him in a machine I can't remember the name of. He was not happy about that. Last I heard my dad and a few others where debriefing him," she said. Estrello looked off in the distance. Her tone was flippant. She didn't quite understand. Some memory began to return to him. He remembered the sound of gunfire and clashing of blades. He remembered his focused motions when his intention was to kill. He then remembered why.

"He lives? This should not be possible," he said. Martha's brow furrowed somewhat puzzled by what she just heard.

The waves were calmer today than the day before. The waters this far from the port of Seastorm could be rough given the right conditions. Today the weather was fair. Lady Marea Falco of Hall Falco was used to the sea in most weather. Her family had settled Seastorm Isle almost a thousand years ago.

The garrison there had stood for almost eight hundred years built around the remnants of the old Falco keep. Now it was home to five thousand men and nearly a hundred ships of the Falco fleet. Dwarfing the Southgate fleet of only forty ships docked farther south around Shale Isle, which was the home of The King's youngest brother Prince Harlo Lamb's keep. The Island Prince wished for a larger fleet but funding was always an issue with Southgate being more concerned with land power. Not an issue shared north of Shale Isle. Almost fifty more Falco ships were anchored around the Port of Seastorm where Lady Marea was sailing now. One could just see the port from Seastorm Isle. A great tower stood at the edge of the city. It was there to provide a beacon to sailors during rough weather or thick mists. In times of danger, copper dust was thrown into the fire pit atop the tower. Its green glow would alert the garrison to launch ships to defend the harbor. Lady Marea could already see the tower looming in the distance. She had spent the morning with her brother consulting with Falco fleet captains. It was a task that would normally be assigned to lord Falco's Minister of Harbors. At this moment Sir Enso Pallti was a thousand miles away in Southgate with the lord of Seastorm. They'd departed in the night a month prior in some haste after receiving a rider carrying a message from The King. Time well spent in his eyes. He was content to be away from Marea's grandmother City Minister Lady Terosa. She was a difficult woman in most matters. The port of Seastorm had been in a sate of heightened security for the past several months. Dozens of known pirates had been sailing here flying under white flags requesting parlay since the middle of the previous year. At first this was an odd curiosity. Most were sent to the prison keep of Tidebreak Island south of Seastorm Isle. For months the smaller fish that sailed into port were sent there. After some time the cells there were running few. But the pirates kept coming and didn't seem bothered at all to be within a stone cage. Then the names flowing in became more familiar. Pirates Lord Falco's fleet had tried to capture for many years were now sailing white and offering their spoils in exchange for asylum. Some even taking oaths to become deputized privateers in the Sea Guard. From the lowliest scallywag to the most notorious cutthroat, they all told the same tale. A phantom fleet had emerged from the north in the area of ocean call The Ecliptiss.

It was a treacherous area where no fish were said to swim or birds flew Fishermen had avoided this area for thousands of years. It's outer borders only offered catches of crab, squid, and prawns. It was foolhardy to sail east into it. Few ships returned. Entire armadas had been lost to its waters in the past. Even the bloodiest cutthroats knew to stay away from The Ecliptiss. So despite the riches, ships and recruits that Seastorm was gaining in recent months its lord Falco had become increasingly alarmed after hearing hundreds of testimonies that varied little in their accounts. These tales told of a phantom fleet that darkened the waters of the east. The coasts had always had trouble with raiders flying the colors of one Exiled Kingdom or another. They were generally few in number and easily fended off despite having superior vessels. Conquest never seemed to be their aim. Accounts were seldom where an exiled captain stood and fought. In these cases the prize would be the ship itself, which were built of teak only found in the Exiled Isles. For centuries design methods had been copied from captured exiled ships. Pirates fleeing into Seastorm controlled waters dismissed the possibility the origin of the phantom fleet residing in the Exiled Isles.

They cited the lack of sigil colors being flown and a radically different design of their ships compared to what sailed out of the Exiled Kingdoms. The also cited the levels of brutality were beyond anything they had ever heard Exiled Raiders inflicting. An unruly situation was rapidly building that even the resources of Seastorm could not handle alone. Being the northernmost Lordship of the Kingdom of Southgate, the lord of Seastorm had little choice but to turn to King Herald and the might of Southgate itself. They were the only seaport allied with Southgate and the last great Lordship lying north of the independent coastal forestlands. Lady Marea's escort back to the mainland was ten ships strong with her private vessel sailing the center. Five years ago an escort this large was uncommon. Now it was regarded as rather modest. The Silver Pier had a large military presence upon it to receive Lady Marea. As she stepped off the gangplank she was greeted by the Captain of her personal guard Sir Alpredo Annense. He was an old friend of her father and one of his former generals he promoted to protect his oldest daughter. Sir Annense had contemplated retirement, but his Lord called him back into service. He was still strong.

"Good day to you Sir Annense. If you would be so kind as to have your men escort my secretaries to the keep," she said as she gestured to a small group of men carrying wooden boxes filled with scrolls who followed behind her on the gang plank.

"At once m'Lady. And how fares the young Lord? I trust his day of meetings and minutia wasn't too bothersome," Sir Annense said and signaled to his men to carry out the Lady's wishes.

"Enchanted as ever to set aside training to hear hours of accounts of things he already knows. Except now it's all part of official proceedings, and we all know how much pleasure he takes in such matters," Lady Marea mused as she walked with Sir Annense down the pier to her carriage waiting for her at the end.

"Delighted to hear. I will no doubt hear about it later, but it's good to know he's keeping on top of the paper tasks. His father will be happy to know he's shown such zeal," Sir Annense said. Lady Marea laughed as they reached her carriage.

"Seastorm Keep will be his responsibility one day. I should hope he'd show some enthusiasm. But alas I know my brother. He's more at home on the sea than he's ever been on dry land. I fear that responsibility may pass to little Lord Salbator," Lady Marea said as she stepped up into the cab. Her response surprised Sir Annense. He followed her into the cab with a somewhat puzzled expression. He sat down across from the Lady Marea.

"Oh, but what about the Lady of Seastorm. You would give up succession as well and hand it to young Lord Salbator?" he said. Lady Marea didn't say anything. She instead smiled slightly.

"Unless the rumor is true, and Lord Falco is at this very moment in Southgate amid negotiations for your hand to none other than Prince Attheon," he said. A wider smile spread over Lady Marea's face.

"I too have heard this rumor," she said. Her smile grew ever wider.

"I have to start getting used to calling you Princess my Lady," Sir Annense said with a grin. Lady Marea laughed.

"The King hasn't said yes that I am aware of," she said. Sir Annense brushed this off.

"M'Lady I'll hear no such malarkey. Of course the King will say yes. He wouldn't possibly marry Prince Attheon to a self-important gossiper like Lady Clora Jasper, a gallivanting trollop like Lady Blia Ivy, or a cold fish like Lady Pallas Brian. You are the clear choice," he said. Lady Marea laughed.

"Now Sir Annense you forget yourself. It's poor form to disparage Ladies of such high esteem," she said. Sir Annense couldn't hold in a laugh.

"Seriously though I will get to growing accustomed to calling you Princess. A title that would seem to suit you more that it would for your sister," he said. Lady Marea smiled.

"Alas I must agree. Fabi takes nothing seriously. She's just as likely to wed the first knight that has courage to approach father, as she would ride off with one in the night. Fabi's antics aside I shall wait for father to deliver a message before I entertain calling myself Princess, thank you Sir," she said.

"Suit yourself, my Princess," Sir Annense mused as the carriage left the port and entered the city with its mounted escort.

Estrello Nocivo sat in the records room in the early morning hours of the 12th of September. He had been discharged by his nursing staff from the infirmary just an hour prior which gave him time to collect himself, dress and grab a cocoa from The Cove. Behind him Terry was fully invested in playing his game. He'd chosen Oni this time. The game controller clicking was distracting but Nocivo had thought to bring his headphones for what he was about to do.

Salazar had been concerning himself with his chemical company the last few days while observing the mandatory sequester time that initiated in the wake of the mission. A protocol that nobody ever expected would ever be needed. But the group felt was important if conflict were to occur among them. Nocivo imagined that Antonio was being dragged around by his attorney, and right hand man, for his company through it's various particulars. This would be Anderson Banner. He was a former British barrister from South Yorkshire that came to America to study and practice American law. He was a good man and one he would hire if he were in Salazar's position. Nocivo flipped open the laptop sitting on the desk in front of him and logged onto the server where debriefing records were stored. Scrolling through the many files that had already accumulated in the year and change since they started formal operations he tracked down the most recent file. Estrello plugged in his headphones and slid them on. Then he clicked on the file and the first video started playing.

The room was small and cramped. Salazar sat behind a table that seemed to take up half the room that been a maintenance closet before the machine it was meant for was removed and relocated to another floor. In front of Antonio a can of mango Venom energy drink and a handful of available senior Bumppo crew sat. They were JP, Chief, Rick, Angelica and Hammer. Angelica had originally opted not to be present, due to there being a conflict of interest in this case but Salazar did not object to her being there. After which she changed her mind. Antonio took a sip and waved his finger in a rolling motion expressing his desire for filming to begin.

"I turned the camera on a minute ago Tony," Hammer said as he jotted notes down on his legal pad in front of him.

"Bueno. Lets get this ball rolling," Tony replied. JP clicked his pen and moved his microphone closer.

"Acting Commander Josef Persson. 1:52 pm Central Time. September 8th, 2024. Mission 72, Codename 'Falling Phoenix' debriefing of Dr. Antonio Salazar aka Tony. I will open questioning. Go ahead and summarize the event after boots down Tony," JP said. Antonio took another sip and set his drink down.

The numbers of scrutinizing eyes around him were never anything he was fond of, but he respected the necessity to collect accurate accounts.

"We dashed in at 5:15 pm on July 17th, 2014 Local Setting Time and Date. Our location was four blocks east from what we had best estimation to be the epicenter of the disturbance we observed from the records room. Our Materialization Site was a convenience store. A 7-11 if I remember right. It was the safest mat site we could surmise with the best shot at a route with decent cover," Antonio said. Angelica moved forward in her seat and pulled her microphone closer.

"Security Head Alpha Angelica Nocivo. Were there any hostiles in your immediate vicinity once boots were on mat site?" she said. Antonio raised his brow.

"Thousands. The whole city was going insane. Eve's assessment of Zombie Type SL was right on the money. There was a mixture of converted and squares all around us. Converted were attacking the squares with anything they could get their hands on. Some brutal shit. No fatalities from where we stood. Skip could smell the blood in the air though, so draw your own conclusions about that. Scene was new most likely, but also in a progressive state of conversion. We observed the Zets break off their attacks once a square had begun undergoing conversion. Once converted they folded into the horde. Standard Zet behavior. There were relatively few converted around the 7-11 where we were. We waited about ten minutes for a lane to clear. It didn't. Skip made to call to bait a hook so I pulled the pin on a flash bang and threw it as hard as I could. It landed under some late 90s piece of crap Jeep Cherokee. It went up like a Christmas tree. Tank must have already been ruptured. Noise and fire predictably drew the converted like flies to shit. We got a clear lane in just under a minute," Antonio said. Nobody said anything for a moment. Then Hammer moved his mic closer.

"Tech Specialist Winton Hammer. Okay Tony can you tell me at what point Skip's earpiece failed and his conversion process began, by your estimation?" he said and began jotting more notes down.

"I can't put a finger on the exact moment Skip's conversion began. As far as my helmet could tell his earpiece never actually failed. But this is some muddy water to work though. Tech isn't my area. Once we got a clear lane we proceeded to follow a short concrete barrier that ran along the parking lot below. The street had cleared so we hauled ass across it to an alley on the other side. From there we got back up top on some kind of ladies shoe store. Once we were up we could see a good lane across a few rooftops to the next block. That's when Skip started to complain about difficulty breathing. There was a lot of smoke in there air where we were. Nothing out of place about that. Even so I went to check his vitals, but my valiant helmet electronics were getting buggy. Voice activated reboot wasn't working so I removed it to reset it manually," Antonio said. This seemed to distress Chief. She tapped her mic.

"Chief Engineer. So Tony, you removed your helmet in a conversion zone exposing yourself? What possessed you to do that?" she said disapprovingly. Antonio waited a moment for her to settle back down. He took another sip of his drink, then set it down.

"We didn't know that we were dealing with a Compound Zombie Type at that moment. The nanoparticles in the air were emitting a harmony similar to the signal itself. Eve didn't even pick it up. Her detection methods have been updated now to look for it. On scene our intel told us we were up against Type SL, and not Type SL/TC. We didn't even have a category for that until this mission. So as far I knew I was in the clear. By now most of you know my body and mind are not temporally synced. I can't be controlled. I wasn't worried about myself. But yeah, it was rookie move nonetheless. Once I had rebooted my helmet's systems I did a vitals check on Skip. The scan interpreted his discomfort as damage from smoke inhalation. It didn't detect any malfunction in his earpiece. The scan was wrong," Antonio said. Rick moved his mic closer.

"Cove Maitre'd and Operations Trainer Richard Patterson. Tony, okay man I wanna know right here what went on when you had to engage Skip at the incident point. He give off any signals he was gonna go off? Did you do anything to provoke him? Help me to understand what went down," Rick said then sat back with his massive arms folded. All eyes were on Tony. He could feel a harder stare coming from Angelica. He was prepared for this and collected his thoughts before answering.

"We found an alley behind the building we suspected to be the epicenter of the signal. It was powerful enough where we were, we could not remotely access any passing birds in orbit. All attempts to get an outside signal failed. We didn't realize at the time much of the city was like this. The broadcast was wrecking everything. Cell signals. Wi-Fi. Radio. Everything. If we didn't have the gear we had, we would have never been able to pinpoint it. Anyhow, I walked ahead to use my helmet's echo loc to map out the scene and pick up any hostiles. I was giving Skip the sit rep when I noticed he wasn't talking back. That's when my echo loc picked up a sharp click," Antonio said. He paused and looked down at the table, then back up at Rick. There was some trauma behind Salazar's eyes. Subtle, but Rick could see it. Antonio continued.

"All at once it felt like someone was hitting me in the back of the head with a baseball bat. Again and again and again and again. My helmet alarm was screaming at me. I don't know if I ever hit the ground or if I just started reacting. I have never shifted into Chronosia that fast or that violently before. The next thing I truly remember happening was watching Skip drop his wheel gun in slow motion and begin to draw his sword. The next memory I have is me reaching for my own sword. By the time I was back in Chronos, which felt like an eternity, I was blocking away his first strike. It got considerably more intense after that," he said. The panel was silent for a few moments. They had already had a chance to examine the damage to Salazar's valiant. But this account made things far more real to them.

"How many shots would you estimated struck the back of your helmet," Hammer asked. Antonio looked over at him.

"Six. Six shots. He emptied the cylinder," Antonio said. Again the panel fell silent for a few moments. Hammer had assumed that Skip had taken more shots later that for whatever reason missed. He could have never imagined all six shots would have been fired in succession in such a small grouping. JP was taken aback. He thought he had some familiarity with the specs of Salazar's valiant suit. Apparently he was behind the times.

"Your helmet stopped all six shots of .45 Colt in a space the size of a silver dollar?" he said. Antonio looked over at him.

"Skip is a good shot. I thought we both knew this by now," Antonio mused. His head began to hurt again then. He picked up a small bottle in front of him and shook out a few acetaminophens. He downed them as JP was struggling with something in his mind. Angelica set her pen down and leaned forward.

"I guess it's good you could precog my brother's moves," she said trying hard to hide the emotion building up behind her eyes. But like her brother, she was inescapably honest. Antonio understood this was coming from love and concern she had for her brother.

"No. Not really. If you ask me did it matter at all, I would tell you straight up not a whole hell of a lot. You think it's some great advantage that I can see someone's actions before they do them. It only goes so far. Skip has a technique. I've seen it. JP has seen it. It's scary to watch sometimes. I have trained with some damn good fighters in my time, but holy shit. This was something else though," he said. Angelica looked puzzled.

"Something else, how?" she asked. Antonio looked to the side for a second.

"Angel, it was like someone had just handed him a picture of me and held up a bag of money and told him 'Kill this fucking guy and the money is yours.' None of us have seen this Skip. There are gears to this man I didn't know could exist. His transition from one Skip to another Skip was so seamless. The improvisation was like nothing I have ever seen. He was getting through defenses I had already set up to counter his moves. Like I was standing still. I could see all his moves before he did them. Didn't fucking matter one damn bit. I would have pissed myself as he killed me if I hadn't taken a leak before we left," Antonio said. Angelica looked back and forth at the others in the panel. Then back at Antonio.

"But you're still alive Tony. How?" she said. Antonio gave this a few moments thought.

"I installed an instantaneous emergency rapid osmotic for immediate pacification in the handle of my sword. I deployed it when I knew I was done. He wasn't close enough until that last split second. It killed most of my valiant's systems power just filtering the agent out," Antonio said then took another sip of his drink. Hammer wrote something down and looked up at Antonio.

"How did you know your serum would be effective?" he said. Antonio began to grin slightly and put his drink down. He then looked around the room and then at Hammer.

"How did I know it was going to work? Well Hammer, this is where this debrief get's interesting," Antonio said. Chief raised a brow.

"Interesting how?" she said. Antonio looked over at her.

"The serum in the grip of my sword was a unique challenge. It wasn't just a great knockout gas I concocted in the lab one day Hurrah," he said. Chief tipped her head to the side.

"Oh?" she said. Antonio continued.

"It was quite a thing. What I had to create was something specifically geared toward Skip's biology. Neither he, nor Angel, is human in quite the same way we are. There were some challenges. With that and at the same time producing something chemically similar enough to the polymer the rest of the handle was made of for Skip not to sniff it out. Which we all know he would have. Angel could tell me what flavor pie I got out of the machine down the hall from my lab this morning," Antonio said and looked at Angelica. She glared at him then rolled her eyes.

"Lemon," she muttered. JP looked at Antonio with deadly seriousness.

"You had a serum you made specifically to take down Skip. Why did you have serum specifically made to take down Skip? Also how did your helmet survive six close range shots?" he said almost angrily. This was a moment where Antonio chose his words very carefully.

"These are the real questions though aren't they? How did my helmet survive? The answer to that, really answers both questions. It survived because I designed it to. I knew Skip's caliber of choice. I knew the specs of his custom reloads. He loads up the same every mission. I knew I had to design with materials that could not only withstand one shot, but all six if he decided to use them. The armor plating of my Generation Five valiant suit had to be lightweight but able to resist repeated attack with a vulcanium blade. It did reasonably well, but Generation Six will be better," Antonio said. JP could not hide his disgust.

"Generation Six?" he growled. There was some fire in his eyes then. Angelica was looking equally distressed.

"But why have it Tony? What threat was he to you? He is your friend!" she yelled. JP held up his hand. Angelica collected herself and sat back in her chair. Antonio tried again to explain.

"Not just Skip," Antonio said and looked directly at JP. He and Antonio looked at each other's eyes for a few moments. The fire started burning hotter behind JP's eyes.

"You have countermeasures for me too?" JP snapped. Antonio nodded.

"I do. Double tap with your Mark 82 Gauss Pistol center mass and a third once the tango is down to make sure. That's your MO isn't it JP?" Antonio said. JP just stared at him. Antonio continued.

"Glock 17 is your conventional backup. I needed my valiant to stop at least three shots from a Mark 82 and a full magazine from a Glock 17 if need be. Stratum's Mark 12 Gauss Rifle is a tougher nut to crack. Can't contend with the wallop. The best I can do right now is be alerted when he puts it into battery so I can at least duck." Antonio couldn't help to muse a bit. JP stood up and leaned over the table with enormous arms tensing as he did.

"You joke about this? Why shouldn't I just grab your head and put your face through this table right now?" JP shouted. Antonio leaned back in his chair and just looked at JP for a few moments until the muscles in his friend's arms began to relax.

"This is a debrief and I am under oath during this proceeding, so I guess I'm going to answer this question, truthfully. Here's the truth man. The honest and plain truth. Of all the people I have met in all the strange places I have ever been, one fact has stood out over all others in my mind. And that fact, that out of everyone else, everywhere else, we, We, remain the most dangerous people I have ever met. And we operate with no more checks or contingencies than our own senses of self-control, respect for each other, and respect for the mission. What happens when all of that is removed?" Antonio asked. JP continued to glare at him for a moment. Then he sat back down. He pointed a finger at Antonio.

"Okay Tony. What protects us from you? You said so yourself. You. You are one of the most dangerous people you've ever met. What protects us from you?" JP growled. Antonio took a long sip from his drink and then set down the can.

"You already have it," he said. A mixture of puzzlement and disgust washed over JP's face.

"Come again?" he said. Antonio tapped the table with his finger a few times and then leaned forward. He didn't answer for a few moments. The number of thoughts he had to collect were many. Then he looked up at JP.

"Ever since the Generation Two valiant. Countermeasures to prevent me from un-holstering or drawing my sword were added with that generation of the valiant suit," Antonio said. Rick who had been quiet the last few minutes chimed in.

"Why would you need something like that Tony?" he asked. Antonio looked over at Rick.

"For something you may have heard about but have never seen for yourself. Dashing over long distances affects me in a way it doesn't for the others. My mind is a fraction of a second ahead of my body. I exist in both the present and future simultaneously. And I always have. The more distant a universe is in relation to point of origin, the more severely something I call The Bends hits me. Until right now the others have just known it to be the source of a good laugh or two watching me babble on about lemon meringue recipes to the nearest tree," he said then slowly looked back at JP. A kind of sadness began to take Antonio's eyes.

"Mission 3 JP. The mountain road. Do you remember that one? Early days. Arrival calibration was fucked. You and the others arrived hours after I did. The Bends had cleared up by then. Skip knew something was up the moment he dashed in. Sniffed out that I had discharged my sidearm. I lied and told him I saw a shadow that caught me off guard," he said. He paused for a moment and looked away.

"It wasn't a shadow JP," he said and slumped a bit in his chair. JP studied his face for a moment.

"What was it Tony?" he said. Antonio's gaze drifted away for a few moments. Antonio's demeanor seemed to start fracturing then. He took a deep breath and refocused on JP.

"It was just some guy walking by that got curious about some dude that just appeared out of nowhere. It was a long dash man. I didn't know which end was up. The rain was agitating me. He took a few steps toward me. I drew. He staggered back and over the railing. He was probably already dead before he hit the bottom of the ravine," Antonio said. Nobody in the room said anything for several moments. Antonio continued.

"He didn't steal anything from me. He wasn't a threat to me. He was just some guy minding his own business. Probably walking home from a hard day's work to spend time with his kids. We'd never dashed that far out before. The rain may have washed the blood off that mountain road, but I still had it on my hands. All I could think about when I got back was what would have happened if you or Skip had arrived the same time I did. Would I have killed either or both of you the same as I did that guy? Starting with Generation Two I made sure all of you were protected from me. Holster snap locks and my visor would cloud if I tried to draw. With Generations Three and Four I added neutralizing electrodes that would trigger when my suit's systems detected internal hostile action in the presence of friendlies. Generation Five has an added sedative injection system. There will never be another mountain road guy," Antonio said then sat back in his chair. The room was quiet for what felt like an eternity. Antonio just kept looking away. JP leaned forward.

"I'm sorry Tony. I didn't know. Why didn't you tell me about this before?" he said. Antonio looked back at him. There was redness in his eyes.

"Yeeting a couple of dozen mercs. I couldn't give a shit. Fuck em' and the douchebags paying them. This guy. Yeah, this guy didn't do anything to me. He was just some guy. There is a video file I scrubbed from my helmet cam memory when I got back. Blamed water damage. File mp4.818355. There's a backup on one of my private servers," Antonio said slowly and looked down at the table. Nocivo paused the video and clicked open the source folder the debrief file was located in. Aside from the debrief file itself someone had already located mp4.818355.

He paused for a moment, and then clicked on the video file. He watched on as everything Antonio had said in the debrief played out in front of his eyes. He saw the man he shot clutch his chest as he staggered backward. His ears picked up something then. Amidst Antonio's babbling incoherence there was an agony. A horror. He fast-forwarded past the time lapse to see himself asking Antonio if he was good. He could hear that same agony again in Salazar's voice. He didn't pick up on it then. Then he stopped the video as the camera pointed directly at his face. He'd seen enough of that and clicked it off. He then maximized the debrief video again and resumed watching. Behind him a door opened up. The ground began to shake slightly as large heavy footsteps thumped louder and louder. Nocivo paused the video again and looked up. High up. Towering above him some nine feet or so was Stratum's giant dark metallic frame. His yellow eyes glowed in the dark room. He'd contracted himself so he could walk through the hallways of the Bumppo. This was by no means as large as he could get. Stratum glanced down at the debrief video that was paused on Nocivo's screen. Estrello closed the laptop and folded his arms.

"Hola Stratum. How was San Andreas?" he said. It wasn't the first thing that Stratum thought Skip would say.

"It was filling. Glad to see neither of you two knuckleheads are dead. JP told me about the debrief. Damn clever of him to focus on my rifle.

I'll give him that. Dude really has studied us. Any good tactician would," he said in usual warm voice. Terry paused his game and looked back and waved.

"Hey General," he said cheerfully. Stratum waved back.

"Hey Terry. You gaming hard man?" he said. Terry chuckled.

"As always," he said and then turned back to his game. Stratum looked back down at Nocivo who seemed to have a lot on his mind.

"Did JP tell you about Mission 3? The third one we started numbering after we'd all started working together?" he said and looked back up at Stratum who nodded.

"Tony shot a guy. Couldn't control himself. Hit him hard. Damn shame." he said. Nocivo was quiet for a few moments. Then he stood up and looked up at his giant metal friend.

"That was almost me Strat. Tony could have been the Mountain Road Man. Whatever tech took me over it had me convinced I had taken a contract on Salazar and I was going to kill him to collect. It was full on Strat. Full On," he said. Stratum nodded and put laid his enormous hand on Nocivo's shoulder.

"Shit went SNAFU Skip. We plan for all kinds of things. We dash here and we dash there. Kick what ass needs kicking and get the fuck out. Most of the time shit is cool as a cucumber. Sometimes shit SNAFUs. This was one of those times. Everybody lived though. As SNAFUs go. It could have been worse," Stratum said. Nocivo nodded. General Stratum was ancient and had experience and wisdom he didn't. In times like this he was glad to have the metal giant around. He knew Stratum was trying to cheer him up, but his head was in the weeds. It was a mixed bag to be sure. Guilt most of all sat at the forefront. A thought struck him then. He looked up at Stratum.

"Hijole. I haven't watched the end of the debrief. I wanted to know if he iced Barnes. Spoilers man!" Nocivo said sounding slightly annoyed. Stratum chuckled.

"Sorry Skipper. I didn't know. But yeah Barnes is alive. You told him to go quiet. He followed orders. He didn't even kill any zombies. Used up most of his bag of tricks to pull that one off. Real pro," Stratum said.

Nocivo unplugged his headphones from his laptop and wrapped it up neatly.

"Tony fucking Salazar. That fucking guy," Nocivo said then sighed as he shook his head. Stratum shrugged his shoulders.

"He's our Tony though. Fucked up as he is. Owns his shit. Maybe not all at once. But eventually," he said. Nocivo got what he was saying.

"Having a grasp on nuance is handy for what we do," he said as he began walking to the door. Stratum followed behind.

"Shit has to be kept in perspective Skip. Got to shake it all out sooner or later. For The mission. Better to learn it slowly, then not at all," he said as he followed. The door swooshed open for Nocivo as he neared it.

"For the mission," he said as he passed through the doorway. Stratum ducked in behind him.

Sullivan Trevor and Ray Marcos pushed carts with tablets out of a hanger storage bay on their way a seminar. Sullivan, or Sully as the crew called him, was hampered by an injury that had him pull light duty in inventory. He was an older man in his 60's with grayed hair that used to be red when he was a younger man. He was well liked by everyone on the ship and especially the hanger crews. He was from around the area but from the 25th century like so many people who worked on The Bumppo. As was Ray who was also well liked by the crew. He was experienced ship man and an even older man in his 70s. He was slightly built with a mustache that had grayed over time. He was a naval man who was stationed on ships that floated on water as well as those that floated in space. He had a bulldog tattoo that earned him that nickname from some of the guys. He worked mostly in inventory. Both men met JP about a decade back when he'd just started envisioning what would become The Bumppo. The men entered a room near the back of the hanger that had a classroom of sorts. Sitting in chairs were a number of hanger personnel, as well as several members of the crew from different areas of he ship. Many of them turned around to see what the clatter was. Many smiled and greeted the men as soon as they discovered who was here now.

"Hey y'all. How's everybody doing tonight? Got y'all a tablet," Sully said. Nick Chelios, one of the hanger crew in his mid 30s sporting a beard with a few gray strands, pushed back the frames of his glasses and took a big sip from his Dr Pepper.

He got up from his chair to pick up a tablet and stretched some of the fatigue out of his shoulders. He didn't especially want to be up this late. He'd need to be up early to resume work he'd been at for several days now. He had a good spirit though. He smiled at both Sully and Ray as he picked up a tablet. He sat back down and turned the tablet on. Others soon did the same. It was some time after that the one they were waiting for walked into the room. She was younger woman with strawberry blonde hair, wearing a security uniform, and had a sugary perky demeanor that shined through as she began clapping her hands like she was part of a Sea World show with sea lions broadly re-interpreting classic fictional tales of high seas adventure. Coincidently that's what she did at one time. The room's attention gravitated toward her. She smiled widely.

"Good evening ladies and gentlemen. I am your host and safety officer Chelsea Towers. It's that time of the month gang. The one you all look forward to. The Safety Briefing! And tonight is a special night, because we get to review the Safety Data Sheets!" she chirped. Many groans erupted from the room. Chelsea started clapping again and pointed to the back of the room.

"What's that back there? I can see an Otter approaching. I wonder what he has in store for us!" she said. Some looked back to see Pauly arriving fashionably late as usual carrying his own tablet. He switched on his mic and flooded the room with his dulcet tones.

"Well Chelsea they're in luck, because tonight we're also going over firearm safety!" he said as he walked up to the front of the room. Chelsea pointed to the back of the room a second time.

"Oh, and what do I see now. Why it's Director Clark from the Foreign Technology Research lab. What to you have for all great people tonight Director?" she bubbly said. Director Clark just stood there silently in his lab coat. He was perhaps rolling his eyes behind his goggles. His handlebar mustache seemed to twitch and bit, but he kept whatever agitation he had to himself and merely walked to the front of the room carrying his coffee mug. He was not accustomed to being up at this hour. Chelsea picked up a ringed binder and ginned widely.

"Now let's have some fun!" she said loudly. The Director raised a brow. Pauly chuckled. Chelsea popped the cap off her dry erase marker and wrote something on the board behind her. She then turned to a grimacing Director.

"Say Director, what can you tell everyone about the Globally Harmonized System and all the warning pictograms that keep everyone safe?" she said cheerfully. The Director seemed a bit confused.

"I thought you asked me here to explain Lockout/Tagout procedures. I see. Very well then, I can pull up my GHS notes instead," he said and grumbled something under his breath as he opened a different file on his tablet. Honore, another member of the hanger crew raised his hand.

"Will there be a quiz after the course?" he said in his thick Senegalese accent. The Director shook his head. Honore smiled and put his hand down. Chelsea pressed a button on her tablet that brought a screen down from the ceiling. A video about Safety Data Sheets started to play. A glum look began forming on the faces in the room then. It was going to be a long evening. Ward Wilkinson, a thick bearded man in his 30s who worked with Nick, passed him another Dr Pepper.

For whatever reason, morning air still felt like morning air. Even on The Bumppo. Martha took out the aspirin blister pack that the infirmary nurses gave her and snapped out two. She then filled a cup at the water tower in the fabrication room where she had been waiting for new pilot wheel grips to finish building. Her father was perfectly fine leaving the steering controls in the Pathfinder bare metal but if she was going to spend as much time as she was recalibrating it's damaged controls she was going make things work for her. The grips were the same design as ones in the flight simulator. After swallowing down her meds she sat back down and watched the machines do their work. If it was a simple injection mold without all the other mechanisms she'd have already finished up here and been on her way to the hanger. But her hands were far smaller than her father's so entirely new grips needed constructing. She imagined

Chief sitting here or in one of the other fabrication rooms getting upset that more couldn't be built.

It all came down to raw materials. Resources, that were critical for smooth operation in many key areas of he operation, and which they had run out of for the most part. The repairs to the ship meant supplies were low and slow to replenish. Indium was the word she heard most often, and probably would again when she saw Chief later. She'd be taking a break from engines to address a number of things on her list that had been neglected in recent weeks since the Bumppo returned from Mission 71. Martha looked up at the clock. It read 6:35 AM. She sighed deeply. She heard a familiar voice behind her then and turned around. It was Chief.

"I said, you need to get a grip," she said and smiled. Martha was still too asleep for the joke to register so the humor went over her head for the most part. Then Chief pointed to the fabricator. Martha sleepily looked over at it and smiled. Chief smiled as well and sat down next to her.

"How you been doing? Still feeling uneasy from The Sight?" she said. Martha shook her head. Then she kind of nodded. Chief gave her a hug.

"You're gonna be fine. You're a tough kid. I can't imagine what you saw, but I know it was horrible. There's reading a debrief about it, and there's actually seeing it. I'm sorry so much of this is so intense for you. It breaks my heart. I wish our tech had been better but we still understand so little about it. It made me very angry that the detection network didn't pick up on either of you before it had actually started. I have to keep reminding myself that we're blazing new trails every day. Hard to keep things in perspective when you want things around you to work exactly as you think they should. In this place, that's a lot to ask. From people and from tech. I'm happy to see you looking better though," she said and stood up to get a better look at the fabrication progress. Martha looked up at the progress meter. Her grips were still far from complete. Chief looked back at Martha who seemed to be sulking. There was a rhythm in the fabricator that made her think of something. She reached into her bag and pulled out her tablet and searched through some files. Then she connected the tablet to the room's audio system, adjusted the volume, and pressed play.

A moment later a song that both of them knew well started playing. It was 'Larger than Life' by The Backstreet Boys. Martha had become quite a fan of them back home, and even more since being here on Gary's world. Of course she preferred the version of their music in the ships archives, but she did have an appreciation of their more retro sound here. Chief began to dance to the music. She gestured to Martha to get up off her stool and join her. Martha just sat there a smiled. Chief started to dance more goofily and gestured again. Martha grinned sheepishly and got up.

"Whoo!" Chief yelled. JP was passing by on his way to the hanger when he saw the revelry unfolding in the fabrication room. By now Chief was dancing around wearing a pair of oversized novelty sunglasses that had been sitting around on one of the desks. It made him happy to see Martha up and about, and enjoying herself at the same time. He was thankful for Chief. If he had had another daughter he could see Chief being her. He couldn't think of a better big sister to Martha.

The garage level was abuzz and the hanger area particularly so. The crew had been testing the grav lev propulsion systems all morning long since midnight. Chief had been up since 4 AM running through her checklist inside Pathfinder N-37B. Only taking a break to run to the fabrication room to pick up parts she'd programmed the machines to build for her earlier. After a bit of dancing Martha had joined her on the N-37B running diagnostics. The N-37B's flight controls were at the forefront of her mind. It was a bit easier after she'd installed the new grips. Around them were binders filled with particulars relevant to the vehicle they worked in. Chief sipped coffee as she looked at her tablet. She shook her head watching as one test after another failed. Then came the last one on the list. Test passed. Chief flipped the tablet around and showed Martha.

"Progress," she said and took a bite of the bagel siting on a plate next to her. Chief laid the tablet and coffee down and dragged herself up and pulled on a handle that sat flush to the floor paneling and opened up a compartment underneath. Using a flashlight clipped to her belt she looked around a bit. She then reached down and unclasped a latch.

Upon matching serial numbers she pulled out a square like object and examined it. Outwardly it didn't look whompy, but she suspected otherwise.

"I don't care what the tablet says. This FBH32 unit is bad. It has to be bad. It's like a bad bulb on a string of Christmas lights. If one is bad half the string won't light up. I'll make some modifications so that isn't so in the future," she said. Martha looked up from her station and at the object in Chief's hand.

"Didn't you run diagnostics on that an hour ago?" she said. Chief looked back at Martha.

"I did as a matter of fact. And wouldn't you just diggity know? Bank Test failed now. Just like that. Don't get it," she said. Martha looked over at Chief's tablet.

"Didn't it check out?" she said. Chief stood up and walked back to her tablet. She plugged the data cable in the unit's side port.

"It did, then," she said. Martha took another bite of bagel then set back down. With her mouth still full she expressed the thought on her mind.

"Either your tablet is bugging out, or the unit is really bad. Only way to make sure is plug in a new FBH32," she said. Chief watched closely as her tablet checked the unit again. This time the result was different. She unplugged the unit and looked over at Martha.

"See, I told you. Bad FBH. Don't know why it passed the last time. Loose connection in the unit itself maybe. Won't know until I crack it open. Gonna have to assume all the FBH32s and 36s in that compartment are the same. Only explanation I have right now," Chief said and began looking around for her tools. Martha began running a simulation on her tablet for atmospheric flight. She was not liking what she saw at all.

"I'm thinking N-37B took a bigger tumble than we thought. Her x-axis is off by 12 degrees." Martha said. Chief looked over.

"I don't know what that means, but it sounds bad," she said then pulled a precision toolkit from under a binder sitting next to her. Martha laughed.

"Yeah it's bad. Even when the grav lev is repaired she'd still fly straight into the wall. It's not something that can be fixed on this end. Passing the message on," Martha said as she texted the message out. Chief had removed the housing from the FBH32 unit and lit it up with her flashlight. She laughed.

"I hate being right sometimes. Now I'm going to have to pull all them. Won't that be fun?" she said sarcastically. Martha smiled and texted out something else.

"Coffee and bagels inbound," she said. Chief gave a thumb up.

"Hot diggity," she said and then snapped the loose connection back into place.

Outside the N-37B The Commodore wiped grease off his hands and sat back in the rolling chair under the forward landing gear undergoing repairs. He'd thrown on a speed suit when one of the other guys working here injured his hand. The guys appreciated when The Commodore was around in the trenches. JP would not ask anyone to do a dirty job he wouldn't be willing to do himself. Nick Chelios and Ward Wilkinson were the other two guys working on this task. Nick turned over the oleo cylinder for the Pathfinder's forward landing gear with a hydraulic wench and looked at it closely. He picked his head up and looked over at JP.

"Hey Joe could you pass me a 5/8ths ring spanner. One of the trunnion links is reading red," He said. JP tossed his rag aside and swiveled around to the tool chest behind him. He opened a few drawers until he found it. He took out the spanner and rolled over to Nick.

"Thanks man," he said and flipped on the headlamp he was wearing. Ward stood up and laid the handful of hex head screwdrivers he had been using on a rolling cart near him.

"Just want to thank you again for subbing in for Amadou," Ward said as he began putting the tools back into their case. JP smiled.

"Glad to. I own these Pathfinders. Might as well get my hands dirty to help get them back off the ground," he said as he looked around at the half dozen other small crews working around the N-37B. Nick worked to unscrew the bolts to the housing he was working on, and then he pulled it open. Something had broken inside. He held a sheared off component in his hand and looked at it under his light. He then switched it off and looked over at JP.

"Guess that's why the trunnion was shot heh heh. Any idea when we'll get new stuff dashed in? It's been months man," Nick said. JP understood. He took out his phone and switched it on. After scrolling for a moment he showed it to Nick and Ward.

"It's up to 51% on stability right now. Earliest estimate is middle of next month. It needs to be 75% or higher to dash in that much non-Iso," he said. Nick deflated a little.

"Aw man. We're running out of things we can fix with 21st century components," he said. JP agreed. The limitations of this century were constant headache. Only so much could be fabricated in-house. Only so much could be replaced with older technology. The avenue to The Commodore's universe had been damaged during the last transit and needed time to heal. This slowed things down considerably.

"We'll see what we run across next mission," JP said. Nick dug through a pile of parts from one of the Pathfinders too badly damaged to be repaired. He found a replacement for the part that had been sheared off and held it up with a smile. Ward pulled another hex head driver from a different case and looked over at JP.

"Rough thing that happened with Skip and Tony," he said. Word had apparently made its way around the ship. JP preferred that not to be the case, but The Bumppo crew was a team. A team had interconnecting parts.

"Rough gig we have. Not just for Isos. But everybody," JP said as he looked around the hanger again. Nick chuckled uneasily.

"Damn man I heard that," Nick said. JP smiled. He was happy to have them here. They were locals to this world. They were both friends of Gary. He was the man whom the Isos knew and named this world after. Gary was an amateur scientist working on the theory of multi-versal travel. With his group of friends he built a machine that in theory could detect the energies created when barriers between universes were breached. He'd discovered a form of ultra low-level radiation with an extremely short half-life generated at the moment a dash field decayed inside a destination. He didn't know what that was when he was building it. Like not understanding what water was but building something that could detect and measure ripples on its surface. Gary and his group of friends didn't realize how cutting edge and revolutionary their machine was. They just thought of themselves as a group of social rejects who loved science and engineering. They had no idea their research would help them meet a group of travellers. But that is what happened. Now Nick and Ward were here. Along with their other friends from the neighborhood involved with Gary's passion project.

The sound of rattling wheels caught the group's attention. Walking toward them was Ernie Suarez and Ian Kostopoulos. They were wheeling a cart with a bright orange water jug on top.

"We got the hookup! Who's thirsty?" Ernie said boisterously. Nick grinned.

"Oh shit, here they are," he said. Nick and Ward had known Ernie and Ian for years now. They had owned and operated their own auto garage for years until harder times forced them to close it up. Many of Gary's friends met through this garage in the neighborhood. Some of them worked there, some came there to get their cars fixed and just stuck around to talk to Ernie and Ian. Ernie was a burly built guy who complained the Bumppo's speed suits were too snug in the shoulders.

He removed the sleeves to make the garment more comfortable. Ian was a long and lanky guy with slicked back brown hair who always wore bright yellow safety shoes. Ernie took to calling him Banana Feet. Nick and Ward got up and picked up cups. Nick turned and looked over at JP.

"Hey JP want one?" he said. The water in his jug was warm by now and something ice cold sounded great.

"Hell yeah man," he said. Nick threw him a thumb up.

Up in the N-37B Chief had extracted and repaired several of the FBH32s by now. One after the other showed the same kind of damage. She didn't even want to know what was wrong with the FBH36s. But they needed to come out and get a look as well. The command room door opened up. A woman with dark hair tucked under a crew beanie walked in carrying a tray of coffee and bagels. Alannah Kypreos was a local and had started dating Gary when the travellers arrived. Now she worked in the hanger with the others. Martha was surprised to see her.

"What happened to Sheila?" she said. Alannah laughed.

"She's on lunch break right now and taking a shower. Wing crawlspace was disgusting. Re-check that 12 degrees now to see if it's fixed. I brought tasty goodies from the back kitchenette Chief," she said with her deep southern drawl. Martha was a bit out of sorts.

"Lunch?" she said. Chief looked up from her work at her tablet she had propped up at her station.

"Yeah it's noon," she said then returned to plugging repaired FBH32s back in. Martha stood up and unplugged her tablet from the jack it had been attached to. Alannah just smiled.

"Yeah I'm also here to finish up with the flight diagnostics. You're late for history class with Eve," she said as Martha stuffed her tablet in her satchel and threw it over her shoulder.

"Thanks," Martha said as she snatched a bagel off of the tray Alannah was carrying and jogged out of the command room. Chief watched her as she disappeared down the hall to the rear compartments and snickered.

"Sometimes that kid is too much," she said. Alannah set the tray down and handed Chief a fresh coffee.

"Yeah, but she puts a lot of pressure on herself. I guess we all do here," Alannah said. Chief removed the top and took in the aroma of fresh bean juice and nodded.

"At least we get the good stuff for when we do," she said and cautiously sipped at the hot beverage.

The campus around the main offices of Salazar Chemical was a far cry from when this used to be the headquarters of Gephardt Chemical just two years prior. It was a failing company ranking 3505th in the nation limping along with old attitudes and even older ideas. Under Antonio Salazar they were now a strong 64th and holding. Dale Gephardt didn't have much support when Antonio made his bid to buy him out. He agreed to Salazar's sum and handed over the 60-year-old company without much of a fight. He laughed that day as he left the premises for the last time thinking that by the end of that year the company he couldn't make profitable would go tits up. It didn't. Antonio didn't even particularly like business, but he was good at it. He inherited this from his father who owned the original Salazar Chemical in Antonio's home universe. He took more after his grandfather Enrique who was the first of his Spanish gypsy family to enroll in university to study chemistry. Antonio had the same love for science. His daughter Codi took after her grandfather and started studying business at university, much to Antonio's chagrin. He had hoped she would follow in his footsteps. This was not to be. Antonio pulled up to the front gate in his white 2006 Lamborghini Diablo with the windows down and blaring Kelly Rowland. She sounded closer to a 70's Diana Ross though, given that the culture of Gary's World more closely resembled and amalgamation of the 1970s and 80s happening all at once. It was as if like the planet was decades out of synch. It was both groovy and radical all at the same time.

Technologically speaking it was still 2024, but a very different place as well. The guard who greeted him was sporting a thick mustache like he came from a 1970s cop movie. When he saw the car he waved Antonio on by without even batting an eye. The white Diablo was here. And everyone knew it. Antonio drove through the lot to his own reserved spot. He parked his beast and stepped out wearing a striped silk earth tone button down shirt with a flayed out Barrymore collar, a pair of gold toned aviators, and eating a giant cheeseburger. The riding heels of his boots clicked loudly on the walk as he headed toward the front entrance. His medallion, silver watch, and pinky ring sparkled in the sun. The people he passed whispered to each other about the bruises and bandages he was sporting as well. That didn't stop him from smiling at them and even high fiving a researcher that was on his way back to his car. Heads turned when he walked through the front doors. Waiting there was Antonio's attorney Anderson Banner. His mouth was agape when Antonio walked up. His eyes were widened as well. It was a challenge given his pronounced brow. But the expression of dismay was nonetheless effectively conveyed. It almost made Antonio laugh. Anderson looked at all his injures and held up his hands.

"I don't want to know Dr. Salazar," he said. His deep South Yorkshire accent contrasted greatly with the mostly American accents in the room. It's one of the reasons Antonio hired him. He thought the accent sounded cool.

"Relax Andy. I wasn't going to say anything in the first place," Antonio mused. Anderson was less entertained.

"I thank you very much for that Doctor. I see you're eating a cheeseburger. Why don't we talk about that while we walk," he said. Antonio was a little curious why Anderson appeared so uptight.

"In a rush to get to work? I can respect that. This is a Number Two with jalapeños from Whataburger. I already ate the fries or else I'd share," he mused as he followed Anderson.

They stepped into the only elevator that went to the 13th floor, which is where the main offices for the top executives of the company were. Antonio's corner office was there. Antonio's assumption was that was where they were heading. Anderson had other ideas. He pulled a folded sheet of paper from his jacket pocket and handed it to Antonio who flipped it open. He took a big bite out of his burger as he read what was printed on it. Anderson sighed and looked down.

"I must admit when I'm wrong. I insisted that you were overthinking things. I double-checked. Just to be thorough. You were right about everything," he said. Antonio handed the paper back to Anderson and continued eating his burger. The elevator slid open and Antonio walked out of it and headed right instead of left like he would otherwise. He flipped off his aviators and hung them just above his top button as he walked down the hall. It was clear nobody expected to see the boss today. Those that didn't quickly duck into their offices greeted him with a smile as he walked past them to the end of the hall.

He finished off his burger as he took another right and walked about twenty feet. He turned to his left and then opened the office door of Randy Troy, the company's marketing director. He was sitting back with his feet on the desk talking on the phone. His eyes opened wide when

Salazar walked in. Antonio held out a finger and waved it around as a gesture to wrap up the call.

"Hey Karl I gotta call you back. Give Andreas my best. Boss just walked in. Auf Wiedersehen," Randy said and then hung up the phone. He stood up from his chair and straightened his suit jacket and walked around the desk to greet Antonio with a giant toothy grin. His polished white teeth glinted in the sun as he shook Antonio's hand. He was a shorter well-dressed man with auburn hair. He shook Anderson's hand as well and took a step back.

His large gold pinky ring glinted in the sun as brightly as his teeth as he clapped his hands together. Antonio couldn't help but notice Randy's pinkie ring was larger than his. There was an implied competitiveness, or perhaps imitation there he found almost entertaining. The room smelled faintly of Axe Body Spray, which neither Antonio or Anderson cared much for.

"Dr. Salazar I must say this is a pleasant mid-week surprise. I am so glad that you seem to be healing well from, what was it? I'm sorry I forgot what happened," Randy said. Antonio grinned.

"No worries Randall. Motocross. Hit a bad patch of dirt. Took a tumble. No worse for the wear," he said. Randy smiled widely.

"Hey that's great. Good to hear it. Say, what do I owe the pleasure today?" Randy said with a hint of confusion in his voice. Antonio felt a bit of glee admittedly.

"Oh nothing really. I just wanted to swing by and see the new desk. Heard all about it. Wanted to see for myself," Antonio said. Randy's teeth glinted in the sun again and he took a few steps back and waved his hands like he was in a commercial selling the desk.

"Oh this desk is amazing. When I heard your were updating the look of the 13th floor I couldn't help myself. Put in a word with the decorator when he was by. Great guy. Thick accent. Serge I think his name was. Anyhow she's a beauty. It's all birch. Not an ounce of processed garbage. Sanded smoother than a baby's face. Check out how quiet the bearings are on this drawer," he said and pulled open a drawer.

"Did you hear anything? No you didn't. Completely silent. Swedes can't make quality like this," he added. Antonio was truly impressed. It was a magnificent desk.

"Outstanding construction there Randy. Please sit. We won't be here long. I just wanted to go over 95.12b. with you," Antonio said. Randy looked confused as he sat down. Antonio looked back at Anderson. Banner could see a sparkle in Antonio's eye that was both inspiring and unsettling at the same time. Antonio turned back to Randy who looked a bit lost.

"95.12b? I'm sorry I'm not sure what that is," Randy said. Antonio nodded and took a pen that was clipped in his breast pocket and smiled.

"95.12b? That would be page 95. Sub section 12. Item b. It's the page that outlines the company's drug policy," Antonio said. Randy's face contorted a bit.

"Okay__. I'm not sure where you're going with__," Randy said but what was cut off by Salazar.

"Look Troy. I can appreciate hookers and blow as much as the next guy. In fact I don't really care how much nose candy you do or how much tail you pin to the wall. Not my business. Not my problem," he said. Randy leaned to the side on the armrest of his chair.

"Okay?" He muttered. Antonio waved his hands at the desk in mimicry of what Randy had done a minute earlier.

"As long as you do it at home. Or anywhere else. I don't give much of a shit where that is. My problem is when you do that here," he said. Randy managed a half grin.

"I'm not sure I know what you're talking about," he said. Antonio clicked the pen he was holding.

"You'd like to see a visual presentation? Okay, can do champ," he said and popped the cap off the pen revealing a purple glowing lamp. Anderson twisted the knob on the wall that controlled the mechanical blinds darkening the room some. Antonio then mimed a few moves one might see at a magic show and shined the light on the desk. Glowing patches of discoloration emerged.

"Alakazaam!" Antonio chirped. Randy looked at the light show erupting all over his desk. A sickly look inched across his face. Antonio moved the light around looking at all the wispy white patterns that resembled scrapes on the surface. Randy looked up at Antonio who had an eyebrow raised as he beamed a look at Randy.

"Magical I know. You're director of marketing for a chemical company owned and run, by a chemist. We're a fascinating people. All chemically and peoplelly. We think about chemistry like others, well, think about other things," Antonio said as he continued to shine the light around on the desk running across one new patch after the other.

"Damn son!" he said. Randy looked like he was about to say something. But Antonio shot a look at him.

"Looks like you have been into the booger sugar up in here. Up in here. Spectacular thing. Ultraviolet light. Don't know if marketing people quite understand ultraviolet light. Too much science to it I suppose. Let me educate you. Ultraviolet light has a shorter wavelength than visible light, but that doesn't mean it can't do lot of very interesting things. For instance did you know on very hot summer days it really isn't the heat or humidity that drains all the energy out of you? It's the UV index that does that. The same UV index that's no less potent even with heavy cloud cover. That's why you need to wear your sunscreen Randy. Especially with your complexion. Oh, and UV light does other things too. Like showing me how much Columbia I have in my building. They should really set up an embassy here. And well look at that__," Antonio said as he found some yellowish stains near the edge of the desk.

"This must be the brunette from down the hall. Can't brew a pot of coffee to save her life. Penelope I believe her name is. No idea what she actually does here. Uses those little pink paper clips. Not judging. A man who can afford this much freezy freeze can surely pay for the inevitable paternity suit that's in store for him. Virility is nothing to be ashamed of. You're a Mountain Lion. I like mountain lions. They know what they want and go for it. Ambitious! Ambition is good. Sink that three from half court. A killer! My kind of guy. Well funded guy from the looks of it," Antonio said and then looked back at Anderson who smirked. Randy started to get up to say something. Without looking back Antonio snapped his fingers loudly and pointed down. Randy slinked back into his chair.

"Trips to Marseilles. Nice. Trips to Angel Fire. Holy shit bro. Got that panache. That gravitas. Penelope never stood a chance my dude. Respect. I mean the amount of Cocaine Hydrochloride sticking to this desk ups its value, like what Andy, three fold? Do you know what the current street value of flake is right now ace? Of course you do killer. My man! That roll is F-A-T, FAT! But I have to ask myself. How did your roll get so fat? I mean you don't come from money. And I know the guy who does payroll. Bruce. Good guy. I know because I hired him. So I know how much you 'Should' be making. I also know the street value of toot. And I most certainly know how expensive it is to keep a woman this happy. Damn!" Antonio said as he ran the light all around the edge of Randy's desk.

One yellowish patch after another showed up. He then gestured to Anderson who pulled out the sheet of paper he'd shown Antonio earlier. Antonio sailed it over to Randy. It landed on the center of his desk. Randy slowly leaned forward and picked it up. He looked over it for a moment. His face grew paler than it already was.

"Doctor I can__," Randy began to say then Antonio snapped his fingers loudly again and shook his head.

"Now is when you shut up Randall. I was a little sore when Southwest Chemical booked Russell Crowe for spots and we didn't. Okay fine, I got over it. We got Pauly Shore for the gig next quarter instead. Fucking loved him in Bio-dome. Sure as shit better than doing it myself. Turns out I dress like a drug dealer. I don't see it, but anyhow I couldn't help but be a little curious about our marketing budget. I was sure our pitch to Russell would have been substantial enough. Guess he didn't like the number we put in front of him. Why would that be I wonder? Well, I'm a curious guy. Science! So, I called up my homie Bruce and we had a good long chat about things. Fun guy. Loves cars. I mentioned our little chat to my bro Anderson here. Got his almonds rolling too. Guess what Rando?" Antonio said. Randy was sweating at this point.

"What?" he managed to say. Antonio put away the pen and cracked his knuckles. He looked Randy dead in the eye.

"You're fucking Fired! Get your shit and get the fuck out! You have thirty minutes before I have security drag you out of here by your short and curlys. I'll even specify they do so," Antonio yelled. Randy lost his composure.

"You can't do that, my contract!" he whined. Antonio eyes narrowed.

"Oh yeah about that. Had a chat with HR. Three strikes and you're out. First strike, drug policy violation. Naughty boy. Second strike, embezzling company funds. Really got my gypsy blood boiling there. I hate when people steal from me. Like you wouldn't believe man. And third strike, selling company secrets to rival chemical companies. Companies, that are good and lawyered up. Unlike you big dawg," Antonio said. Anderson looked at Antonio with mouth open. He didn't know this. Antonio snickered.

"I have a few friends in low places that are good for a little 'Water Cooler Chat.' So, Randerino you have two choices. Start packing your things now. Like Right Now. Or getting dragged out of here by your pubic hair will be the very least of your worries. Have I made myself crystal clear?" he said through an expression like a steel mask. Randy weakly nodded and then hung his head like a pickpocket sitting in the back of a squad car after tripping over his own feet. Antonio flipped a pair of thumbs up.

"Good, get the fuck out. And take your yeyo with you," Antonio said then he turned Anderson.

"Let's roll Cochise." Antonio said then slipped his aviators back on.

The trip east would be a long one. A couple of weeks ride in fair weather. Had this been a ride to the west coast the journey would have taken up to a year. Anyone travelling from Southgate to there was far better off going by boat along one river or another until one met the sea. Provided of course one travelled in force.

Even through territory controlled by River Lords, bandits were still a danger. It helped to know when the ranger packs would be out conducting maneuvers. Bandits rarely had much of a presence during these times of training. Forests would be thick with young men and wanderers wearing a Junior Leaf looking to prove themselves. Capturing or even killing a bandit while out training was boost in reputation hard to earn otherwise.

Attheon and the battalion of 650 men that travelled as his escort had no such river system to take advantage of. It would all be horseback from Hogs Hoof until Seastorm. The village was down the road from the one The King sent him to. Attheon regarded the ale in Hogs Hoof to be superior and kept better on the road. Stockard handed an innkeeper a bag of silver and coppers to pay for all the casks of ale being walked out of his larder along with a good portion of his salt pork. The same process would be repeated for the next several villages. Attheon had coin to spread around and his men would be well fed.

It looked good politically as well for common folk to see even those of high standing paying fair price for goods. Hall Lamb was well regarded for this reason and the Warlords of the Midlands were not. They were known to pay poorly and expect more. The common folk of the Midlands to the Northern Borderlands got into a habit of hiding away their best when northerners rode into town. This ruse would fail from time to time. Their best was simply taken and the inn keeps and merchants were severely beaten in the streets in front of onlookers. The Midlanders referred to it as 'A Good Trouncing' as the practice was called up north when an example needed to be made that a highborn Midlander could sit upon his horse and enjoy watching. When time was an issue the phrase 'Lace The Wretch' was expected to be heard. Those unfortunate enough to hear those words would make lasting company with the nearest sturdy tree. Even so common folk still resisted. Those communities that have suffered this Midland aggression in the past tended to welcome the gold wrapped anvil of Hall Lamb and other Lords' pennants that flew for Southgate.

By now villages all along this stretch of roads called The Eastward Bands were abuzz with talk of Southgate. And word was spreading. Even among the bandit gangs that were rife along The Bands. Even those with the largest number and strongest reputations feared The Anvil. The Bands would be relatively quiet as the Southgate force rode through. Those normally too timid to travel were making travel plans to coincide with the movement of Attheon Lamb. The Prince whistled to his captains. The march had begun. Antimony heard the call and quickly rode up beside his brother. Attheon looked over at him. The younger Prince was eating a large chunk of dark bread. Attheon chuckled.

"I was wondering what was keeping you. I should have known you'd be thinking of your stomach," he mused. Antimony finished chewing and swallowed.

"It's going to be a long journey brother. One must keep his strength. They bake up a magnificent dark rye here in Hogs Head. I shall miss it when we are farther down the road," he said. This was area for a great loaf of rye. Attheon did have to admit that.

"And you didn't think to share?" He said. Antimony smiled and reached down and pulled the flap up from his saddlebag. Inside it were more loaves of rye. Attheon laughed. Antimony pulled a loaf out and handed it to his brother. Attheon took it and stuffed it inside his own bag. He laughed again and shook his head.

"Always prepared. Father would be proud," he said. The statement struck Antimony as conspicuously modest.

"As it so happens, father is not the Lamb I learned this most from. I have spent quite a long time observing my brothers. Your example has guided me most," he said. This compliment caught Attheon off guard.

"You were able to learn this from 'The Absent Prince' in all the time haven't spent being an older brother to you? Even in my negligence I have still somehow succeeded in positively influencing my younger brother. I must admit I am surprised to hear this," he said. Praise seldom came Attheon's way. But this is how Antimony regarded him.

"I should say that you and Carcino are as different as two brothers can be. Whereas he tends to think ahead in terms coordinating many others and managing them to evade our enemies' watchful eyes. You think ahead in terms of yourself and how well you can evade father's watchful eyes. A curious study it has been. But the both of you are masters of this art. I am just a student. Tucking away a few loaves of bread may be a small thing, but it is evidence I have been paying attention,"

Antimony said with a big grin. Attheon gave him a side-glance and laughed.

"This is the sense of humor I have always told people you have but am not believed," he said. His brother wasn't wrong, but Antimony felt compelled to clarify.

"My humor errs on the side on subtlety. I find it to be a card seldom played having the most effect when it is," he said. His brother tendered an unusual response, but reasonable in Attheon's mind as they rode along.

"I suppose you're right. Repetition breeds familiarity. A good quip should be as entertaining as possible, or else why quip in the first place?" Attheon said. Antimony nodded as he took another bite of his bread. He chewed and swallowed as they rode. He was curious about something.

"What do you know of Lady Marea Falco anyway? A curious choice by father wouldn't you say?" he said. Attheon was wondering when Antimony would bring this up. Now was as good a time as any.

"We met once many years ago. She was an annoying child running around with her dolls then. Difficult to project where she's gone from then. If we have any daughters I hope for both our sanities the child isn't half as obnoxious as she was. You'll never see black hair turn gray so quickly," he said. Antimony almost laughed.

"A glowing endorsement of your future bride I see. What do you suppose her notion of you as her husband would be," he said. Attheon had preferred not to think about that, but Antimony was asking.

"I should guess not unlike what most outside Southgate think of us behind our mountains. Glad to have our swords protecting their lands. Overjoyed at the silver, which pours from our mines. Giddy at the prestige the name Southgate being uttered in the same breath as whatever their name happens to be. But then the other side of the face starts talking and all that's uttered is brute, savage, uncultured, unrefined, proud, and arrogant. Try as you might brother, once you are away from The Sentinels these are the words you hear uttered from lips drunk from ale Southgate helped the speaker buy. Regard it a cynicism if you will. You will hear these words just the same. Will these words be the ones preoccupying my bride's mind as she is walked up to me by Lord Sardis?"

Attheon said. The heir to the throne could not mask his dissatisfaction with the situation before him. Antimony's ears heard all of this and more.

"I should think you do all you can to persuade her otherwise in the time you have after you make your formal proposal. If she has no reason to think these things about you, then she won't," he said. Attheon could see that his brother was trying to help.

"This I understand brother. But how does one convince a high born woman accustomed to finery and flattery that I don't spend most nights sleeping under a tree, when I do in fact spend most nights sleeping under a tree," he said. Counseling his brother would be a greater challenge than Antimony anticipated.

"I do imagine Seastorm has trees. Many of which grow near Falco's keep. It's not as though she does not sleep beneath a tree herself. That a roof hangs between should not be relevant," Antimony said. Attheon gave him another side-glance.

"I think the Lady Falco would deem that relevant. Could you perhaps suggest I charm her with poetry, political critique, military strategy, or even a wheel of cheese?" he said with some frustration. Antimony was almost entertained. But he would not mock his brother.

"The cheese may be your best plan. But seriously brother, speak to her as yourself. Not as role you cast yourself in as a glittering vindication of your homeland or even eloquent but insufferable ponce. Be Attheon Lamb, the Absent Prince who sleeps beneath trees, but has somehow managed to become a role model to not just one brother, but many. Criticisms notwithstanding," he said. This was becoming a useful conversation Attheon wished he'd had a day earlier when he was sulking even more.

"I am pleased to hear that. And I will take that advice to heart. What criticisms would those be by the way?" he said and turned to his brother. Antimony smiled.

"A perfect role model? No. I would like you to have a better relationship with father. You don't see him when you're not around. He doesn't have the same joy as when you're around. He's not the best at showing it. But I see it," Antimony said. This hit Attheon harder than he expected it to.

"I reckon it's easy to pass by these things whilst sleeping under a tree," he said. Antimony turned to his brother.

"Put these things out of your mind. You have time now to make amends with father. This wedding will be a start. Build on that," he said. This advice was sound.

"Thank you Antimony," Attheon said. The younger Prince nodded and took another bite of bread.

Waves smashed against the rocky eastern coastline as a lone rider trotted on a road high above the surf. He was a dark skinned man wearing the blue highlighted armor of Hall Falco. Winged accents curved around every bend and contour of the plate. A determined look adorned his face still young looking despite being nearly forty. His destination was a small shack on a cliff overlooking the water. The man passed travellers on his way. They all stopped to watch him as he rode by. An odd face to see here, but the Falco armor commanded respect and tongues were held. Any comments uttered would wait until much later when no Falco ears were around to hear. The rider himself commanded respect. Despite his young face, his eyes burned through the eye slits of his maned helm with the kind of intensity only years of combat could fuel. A look was all it took to repel even the most scornful malcontent that crossed his path. It was a path that had come to an end for the time being. The shack was within sight. The man rode up to it and dismounted his horse, which he hitched to a nearby tree. He walked up the dilapidated structure and knocked on what passed for a door. He waited until someone finally answered. The door opened some. It was just enough for the man to see an old man's face peer around the corner. The old man was surprised to see a face such as his. The sigil of Hall Falco hastened whatever pause he may have had.

"Who might I ask has Lord Falco sent all this way to see a very tired old man?" he said. The young man did not seem to care for the question.

"I'm not here to socialize. I am here at the behest of Lord Falco because it's come to his attention you have a story to tell me. We can set aside all gaming of words. You know exactly what story I have rode here for. We can sit down and have a nice little chat, or I can come back here with some friends who will be upset they had to come all the way out here to deal with you when all you had to do is entertain me for a short while about what sorts of scary things you may have seen. I leave the choice to you," the man said sternly. The old man stepped back and gestured the man in.

The Falco man removed his helm and tucked it under his arm. They sat down at the old man's table. The shack was very sparse. He appeared to live alone. The old man studied the young man's face. Boyish and youthful but eyes aged. The young man set his helm on the table. The blue mane resembling the flared head feathers of the harpy eagle sea raptor native to Seastorm and the olive lands shuddered as the metal rested on wood. It was the style officers wore. Lower ranking soldiers had the mane oriented from front to back.

"I won't waste your time young man. Nor will I waste Lord Falco's time. I seen them seven months ago. I was down by the water catching my dinner near dusk. It was cold as a witch's arse and the wind was blowing strong from the north. That's when I seen them. A hundred or more ships. Black as night. Moved across the water silent like. Didn't even know they were there until I looked up from my pole. Watched them sail for a good while before they all seemed to turn away from land back out to sea. They were gone from sight not long after. Didn't tell my story to many. I suppose I know now who I can't trust to keep things to themselves. But that's all my story," the old man said. The young man looked him over. He seemed to be telling the truth.

"This was the only time you saw them? What I've been hearing is that these ships pass by here all the time and that you're the man who always seems to see them. Have I been misled?" the young man asked. He looked at the old man's eyes closely. The old man got up and walked to a shelf behind him picked up a bottle sitting on it. He sat back down with a pair of cups and popped the cork stopper. Out flowed cheap wine into the cups made from hammered tin. The old man quickly downed his and sat back. The young picked up his cup and sniffed at it. He couldn't tell what fruit this wine was actually made of. He took a sip of it. It was reminiscent of wildflowers. The old man poured another cup and downed that one as quickly as the last and sat back in his chair.

"When I was a small child is when I saw them first. I couldn't have been older than eight years. My father was a fisherman, back when this area was good for fishing. A wind just like the one from earlier in the year came from the north. A fleet of ten or fifteen ships. Silently they sailed. Bright and sunny that day. Darkness just seemed to follow them around. I saw him as I sat on my father's boat. He told me not to move or make a sound. I never saw a shred of fear in my old man before or since. At that moment all of that was gone. On the bow of the flagship I saw The Black Admiral. Giant of a man that looked like he was carved from the shoulder of death itself. They passed right by without taking notice. Who would notice a humble fisherman and his boy? My father never spoke of it after we made shore. He forbade me to speak of it as well," the old man poured another cup and downed it quickly. The young man took another sip and set his cup down.

"Is that the only other time you saw them old man?" the young man said. The old man poured yet another cup, finishing the bottle. He took a light sip of the last cup and set it down. His hand shook as he did. He looked up at the young man. Sorrow in his eyes.

"Must have been almost twelve years now. Whole coast was burning. Pirates, people said. It had been a good thirty or so years for the coast. Shipping was good. Lord Destor Birros had an estate up north of here. His own private navy. Arse of a man. Part of lot people called Green Foxes. Met him once. Did not like the man or any of his wretched sons. They didn't deserve what came though. People told of pirates. Black sails. No sigils. I knew who it was that came for them. In a single night Birros's navy fell. Experienced captains. Their ships and their crews cut down by sword and eaten by fire. Birros and his sons soon followed. Didn't even know the 'Pirates' were coming. They came ashore and went right for the keep. The lot of them. Put to the sword. Right back out to sea with all of Birros's silver and gold. Tried to tell people. Nobody was listening to an old man and his ghost stories. They knew better. That Prince of Southgate thought he knew better too.

Mercurian his name was. Bought up a fleet of ships of his own. Falco volunteers, hirelings, men hard on their luck, and even pirates. The boy was throwing around silver like he had any sense. Went after The Black

Admiral he did. Now men sing of the Prince and his pride sitting at the bottom of the sea. Some say he was cut down by The Black Admiral himself. Others say the sea demon outsmarted that Southgate boy and drove him into a storm. Still more name one pirate or another that done it. Just the same. He sleeps beneath the waves just as every other fool who's arse-headed enough to test The Goddess and her perils," the old man said and then fell silent. The young man watched him for a while.

"Is this all you have to say old man?" he said. The old man looked up at him.

"No lad. Southgate and Lord Falco sent ships out to find The Shadows and The Black Admiral after that. Not a trace. Strung up plenty of pirates though. They were out there for over a year looking. Nothing. Not a peep about The Shadows ever again. Not until about two years ago. Then the stories started up again. But you know that. That's why you're here talking to a crippled old man," the old man said and then threw back his cup of wine. The young man studied him for a few moments and then drank the rest of his wine. Then he stood up.

"Thank you for your time old man. And the wine. You tell a fascinating tale. I wish you well," he said. The old man shook his head.

"You'll burn lad. If Falco seeks The Shadows he'll burn, and you will burn. When it comes time and you're under a Shadow's sword, remember. I tried to save you," the old man said and then looked away. The young man looked at him for a few moments and then walked out of the shack.

Ranger camps were typically Spartan with few amenities save for a warm fire and a tent to block the wind. Captain Snowbrace Quickwill of the East Pines Ranger pack stood next to one of these fires with spear clutched in paw watching his rangers prepare themselves for maneuvers.

And for his fish to finish cooking above the fire he stood next to. It was time to season up some of the Seedlings, which was the name they gave new recruits. He stood an imposing six feet and six inches and his coat was as white as his name implied. The warm months may seem like a challenge to a snow white high wolf but years of experience had taught him use the sun and treetops to his advantage in stalking bandits and other criminal ilk in his territory. In autumn and winter he was even more effective. He was related to the Redflower Pack and eldest son of Ravera Quickwill. She was the living legend Brewster Redflower's youngest sister. Around Snowbrace was a circle of Lieutenants. There was Vadom Bluestone, a wanderer, with black fur collared by spots of yellow fur, from a river pack and the first of his family to not take up a fisherman's net. Sitting next to him was Kase Windfeather, a wanderer from the far west of Gatheria, of dusty golden fur, from a pack not connected to any of the southern Packs. Sitting next to him was a human named Kitt Corson, veteran ranger from an old forest family. Next to him were three kobold clutchlings. They were Reemboog, Ves and their oldest cousin Feyiyak.

Kobolds were known as low dragons. A generally small race like Dwarves they are ironically called low despite having far greater intelligence than their far larger cousins called high dragons. Scaled skin and ability to breathe fire were the only things these cousin species had in common. Feyiyak was the son of Chieftain Aepleraq and High Mountain Priestess Maechtalore. Kobolds were considered a magical race being so closely related to dragons. In the distant past they were hunted for their skins, which were said to imbue wearers with the stamina of dragons. Cyclops were the most infamous in this regard. Adorning their spears with Kobold skins. The hunting all but ceased after the Time Of Great Troubles, yet Kobolds remained a reclusive and untrusting race. Seeing Kobolds outside their caves was uncommon unless with a pack. When one did they could assume they were of high status of their Clutch and were undergoing a time of testing. Ranger packs were a common destination for those being tested. Once a clutchling had proven their merit they were allowed to marry and hold titles. Feyiyak wanted to learn all he could from his Captain. Wolves were held in high regard, as were Dwarves. Neither had ever hunted Kobolds in the old days.

They were one of the few races that did not. Humans were known to, so were not fully trusted, but Kobolds never made war with them, unlike the cyclops. Like their close dwarven allies they believed that all staffwyns carried within them the lineage of Latalec the Voyager. He was an adventurous dwarf that was said to have lain with tens of thousands of staffwyn women from all across the known world in very ancient times. Kitt Corson's daughter was a halfwyn who often visited her father when his camp was near her village. It's doubtful that Feyiyak would regard Corson as cordially as he did if it weren't for this fact. Despite this challenge Corson had gradually earned the Kobold's respect. Even saving his life on more than one occasion. Both of them could also agree that this year's maneuvers would be a hard one for the Seedlings. Bandit activity was always a problem.

The ranger packs blamed the Warlords and their activity for creating the problem. The instability of the Borderlands north of the areas controlled by Southgate had been going on for more generations than most could count. This year though seemed different. Something wasn't right about much that was already wrong. Feyiyak had feathered his mother the High Priestess of her Clutch for guidance with what the earth could tell her. She said the humors in the soil and rock were in distress and the autumn would bring a pall. Mystics among the dwarves said much the same he was told. The son of the Chieftain heeded warnings from the mystics. He kept his sword close and his fire hot. One of the junior rangers that had earned his merits a few seasons ago ran up to Captain Quickwill and handed him a message. Snowbrace held it up. It was sealed in his Pack's sigil the Red Flower. It could only have come from his uncle High Chieftain Brewster Redflower. Snowbrace cracked open the seal and read the message. He took a deep breath then rolled it back up. He looked down at his lieutenants.

"Early reports were true. Southgate is on the march. The Prince Attheon himself is said to be leading a host over 600 men east," he said. Feyiyak swallowed the bite of chicken he'd just taken and looked up at the wolf.

"What lies east that would interest them Captain?" he said in the hissing tone all Kobolds spoke in. Snowbrace tucked the note into his jacket and looked down at Feyiyak.

"Could not be certain Fey. I would say they are bound to Seastorm. Reports have been coming in for months from the coastal packs. Trouble is brewing. Training our new blood may be more important now than ever. The Stone Lodges are probably on higher alert as well. I expect we'll be hearing from one soon. If Attheon himself is compelled out from trees, an ill wind must be truly blowing in from the east. 600 men may not be much, but it will be enough to scare up some bandits from their holes. This may bode well for us. We should not waste such an opportunity." He said as he looked up at the point of his spear to see if its edge needed any attention. A junior ranger of light brown fur smirked when he heard the name the Prince's name uttered.

"There really is a Prince Attheon of Southgate?" he mused. Snowbrace looked down at the young ranger.

"Listen good pup and remember well. Prince Attheon has a truer shot than most to ever wear the Leaf. I'd wager his sword is no less formidable. Some respect would be due." Snowbrace said. The junior ranger hung his head upon hearing this. Behind him approached Snowbrace's younger brother Proudwinter, another white wolf but shorter with light gray patches on his shoulders. He was a Lieutenant quickly earning respect in the East Pines Pack.

"A report has just arrived Captain. Horses stolen from a farm near where the river splits upstream from Paltry Bridge," he said. Snowbrace nodded.

"Understood brother. Feather our cousin Flint and our Barley Lands brothers. We're mobilizing. The Seeds are getting their taste," Snowbrace said. His lieutenants took this cue, picked up their weapons, and doused their fire. Proudwinter turned toward the rest of the camp.

"The Captain issues the challenge! Time for some Seedlings to earn The Leaf! Greet The Trees!" he barked. Rangers from around the camp answered this call.

"Greet The Trees!"

Antonio pulled into the front drive of the home he owned outside of Boerne, a town just northwest of San Antonio. The property was in a fairly secluded hilly area surrounded by trees. In the year he owned it he'd probably stayed in it a handful of times. But he liked the land it was on. Antonio clicked the garage door opener and drove inside and came to a stop by a red Lamborghini Jalpa. Anderson had never been here before. The sight of a second Lambo only deepened the mystery of his employer. A mystery he often had trouble coming to terms with. Antonio stepped out of the Diablo and shut the door. Anderson followed suit and followed Antonio into the house.

It was more spacious on the inside than the exterior gave away. Antonio's heels clicked on the warm terra cotta Spanish tile flooring. It looked and smelled too clean in here to Anderson. It was like a model home that nobody lived in. Antonio pointed to the kitchen as he walked toward the den.

"Help yourself to whatever is in the fridge," he said. He honestly didn't remember what he left in it. Anderson walked over and opened it up. Inside was a single six-pack of Shiner Bock. It was the only thing. He rolled his eyes and sighed. Instinctively he took out two bottles instead of one and joined Antonio in the den. When he got there Salazar was already sitting down in a metal chair next to a glass top table. He set the second bottle down near his boss and the looked around the room. Antonio grinned, picked up the bottle and cracked it open. Anderson looked back at Antonio who took out a plastic bottle and shook out a few pills. He took them with a swig of beer. Anderson looked at the bottle and then at Antonio.

"What's that?" he asked. Antonio turned the bottle around so Anderson could see the label.

"Acetaminophen. Want a few? Looks like you need it," he said.

"No thanks. I don't think that bottle is big enough for the headache you've given me," Anderson replied. Antonio found that to be a little entertaining.

"I don't like to half-ass anything. I am a professional after all," Antonio said with snark and took another sip of beer. Anderson was less entertained.

"Ah yes, but professional of what? Of being a scientist? A man who is barely a presence in his own labs and shows up out of the blue with orders for all manner of odd things that myself and others have to explain away. What did you with 3000 pounds of indium by the way? That's an eight hundred thousand dollar elephant in the room. Do I even want to know?" he said. Antonio nodded and grinned.

"Deep R&D." he said. Anderson's eyes narrowed.

"Of course. The Salazar bottled explanation. Coming from a professional of business? Your business? The one you never seemed to grace with your presence. And when you do, you show up like you've been in fights. Motocross was it? Do you even own a dirt bike?" he said. Antonio didn't seem phased much by the question.

"I don't know. Maybe." he said. Anderson didn't seem to like the response.

"Right, well you can't very well participate in motocross without a motor bike now can you? So what does Doctor Antonio Salazar do in order to get cut up and beaten? I'm not sure I should know. I'll ask the question anyway out of concern, to show that I care what becomes of you but I don't think I actually want an answer," he said. Antonio didn't disagree with his attorney's assessment.

"That makes things easier for me," he said. Anderson became a bit more agitated.

"I'm sure it does. You sit there behind your smiles and your nods and your handfuls of pills. How's the head by the way? Have you actually seen a doctor about that?" Anderson asked. Antonio didn't have a bullshit answer for that one.

"Yes I did actually consult my doctor. He's actually the one responsible for all of, this," Antonio said as he waved his finger around in a circle to point out all of his injuries. Anderson looked puzzled.

"I'm sorry, what?" he said. Antonio tried not to enjoy Anderson's increasing consternation.

"He shot me in the back of the head. Six times," Antonio said and took a big sip of beer. Anderson grimaced.

"In paint ball. In paint ball right?" he said. Antonio swallowed and looked to the side for a moment.

"Sure, in paint ball," he said. Anderson stared at him for a few moments then took a deep breath and turned to the side with his hands on his hips. Then he turned back to Antonio.

"I want to make it very clear Doctor. Attorney-Client privilege only goes so far. If you are actively pursuing criminal activity, even if you call yourself a crime fighter, that endangers your life or the lives of others I am obligated to alert the authorities," he said. Again Antonio could not argue with his reasoning. He was curious though.

"Crime fighter? Going wild with the speculations there Anderson. Seems like a distance to jump to that conclusion. Let's back things up a bit. Awfully sour outlook on costumed community activity. Would you call the cops on The Night Eagle?" he asked. Anderson grit his teeth.

"You're not The Bloody Night Eagle! You're a 47-year-old scientist, a father, a horrible driver, and an immense pain in my arse! My own sons don't even make the vein on my forehead scream like you do," Anderson yelled. Antonio saw an opportunity and took it.

"Quite the forehead too," he mused. Anderson looked like he was going to explode. But he stopped himself and laughed it off instead.

"Bloody hell Salazar. I don't know what you're actually doing. I hope to all that is Holy it's for something good. I really do. You're not a kid anymore. I'm almost 70. I know what I'm talking about. You think you're in your prime. But you'll hit that wall. Sooner or later you always do. And when it happens you'll fall down hard and you'll wish you'd listened to me. Legal advice is not the only valuable advice I can give," he said. Antonio stood up from his chair and took a big drink of beer and looked Anderson in the eye.

"The less you know about what it is I do the better perhaps. I can't truly impress on you the importance of it. But it is important. Very. I also want to assure you that I'm not in this alone. I have a lot of other people helping me out. Like my doctor for instance," Antonio said. Anderson wanted to find all this helpful.

"Your doctor? The one who shot you?" he said with dour exasperation in his voice. Antonio genuinely understood.

"The very same," Antonio replied. Anderson planted his face in his palms.

"Bloody hell Salazar," he groaned.

"Is what it is," Antonio said. Anderson could only shake his head.

"I know it. In my bones I know it. One day I will get that call. Either Doctor Salazar is in handcuffs, or I need to come identify what's left of him," Anderson said and buried his face in his hands again and turned away to groan. Antonio picked up the bottle and finished off his beer, then stood.

"I'd have to tip my hat to SAPD if they were ever able to catch me. As far a identifying my remains, that'll be my doctor's job. Which reminds me, I have an appointment with him for a follow up on his masterpiece. Head feels a little whomperjaw. Well, more than usual," he said and patted Anderson on the shoulder.

"Stiff upper lip man. Lets go get some chicken," he added. Anderson was hungry but he also wanted to be alone to process the day.

"Didn't you just have a cheeseburger?" he said. Antonio laughed.

"I did didn't I. Breasts and biscuits help me think though. Let's roll," he quipped. Anderson just gave him a look of exhaustion.

"Fine. Shouldn't I drive?" Anderson said. Antonio considered this an audacious suggestion.

"Oh hell no. Nobody drives my girl but me. I will let you hold the bucket after we hit up the chicken shack. Can I get a fist bump my dude?" Antonio said and held out a fist. Anderson sighed and reluctantly held up a fist. Antonio bumped. He turned and snapped his fingers. The door to the garage opened for him automatically and he walked to it. Anderson took a deep breath and followed. Antonio shut the door to his Diablo and clicked his belt. He looked over at Anderson who looked like he'd been in far better moods.

"Pop open the glove box man," Antonio said. Anderson looked at him for a moment and then opened the glove box in front of him. He half expected to see a gun or a severed human hand at this point, but the only thing in there aside from the owner's manual was small file folder. He took it out opened it. He looked over at Antonio.

"What is this?" he said. Antonio took a deep breath.

"Updates for the coming quarter. You might say I have been keeping a very close eye on my company and more importantly the people who work for it. I know that's not what people think of when they think of me. Observant that is. But I have been watching. Furthermore I have been listening. There is a long chain of communication between the Joe Blows and the people I pay to manage things. That chain isn't in such good shape. That is going to change Andy. These are my people. Except for Randy. Fuck that guy," he said. Anderson didn't know how to respond. Antonio turned the key and the Diablo roared to life. Anderson read some of what was in the folder as the car pulled back out of the garage.

"Am I reading this right Tony?" Anderson said. Antonio figured that would get his attention.

"Damn right you are," he said as he looked back while in reverse. Anderson was amazed by what he was seeing.

The late evening air was crisp and fragrant in Creendea. The last of the summer festivals was in full swing. Vendors sold their wares as musicians played. Revelers came from miles around to visit the second largest city in the lands controlled by Lord Sardis Falco. One attraction of particular interest was that of a travelling troupe of performers called The Opal Cranes. Their name was known throughout Eastern Gatheria. They were part of a greater organization of actors, acrobats and musicians called The Opal Birds. All regions of Gatheria had a branch. Their membership was exceedingly exclusive, and the audition process was a lengthy one and probationary membership had immense turnover. None who never made it to the grand stage ever knew of the troupe's true nature. Those outside The Opal Birds, who did know, were dead. Birds were masters at enforcing discretion. The Barker was the one in charge of each branch's operations. Fadis Frodare was such a Barker. Flamboyant and charismatic, his voice and manner commanded attention from many a paying audience. A man of style gifted with gab and eclectic tastes. He rapped his cane against a barrel in front of the Opal tent with gusto and waved his hands at the entrance of the tent. Two large men stepped out from it and held the front flaps open. Fadis leered at the crowd of people gathering before him with wide and almost unsettling grin.

"People of Creendea and the surrounding lands I do beg your absolute pardon! You see there is crime being committed right now this very moment! Yes good people a crime most heinous and most foul. To speak of it would turn your tongue white and sprout tails from your arse!

I speak of course the crime of not stopping in to see The Magnificent Minly!" Fadis shouted to all who could hear. Behind him a woman stepped forward onto the stage set up inside. A fierce look was upon her face as she drew blades from behind her back. Fadis waved his hand in her direction.

"What makes Minly so magnificent you may ask? Well it just so happens she is the only woman alive who has juggled the razor sharp Blades of Doom without losing a single finger, or an eye! But tonight could be your lucky night to see some blood. Now tell me good people, isn't that worth a watch?" Fadis yelled. Grins started to appear on faces and one by one the audience began to build. Soon the tent was filled with curious eyes. Minly stood there with multiple blades in each hand looking back and forth at the crowd. Onlookers from outside the tent craned their necks and children sat upon shoulders to see. A loud trumpet sounded quieting the chattering throng. Fadis walked from behind a fabric barrier behind the stage and onto the platform with that same unbroken grin.

"Oh good people you have arrived on a special night! This is our last show of the summer. But before we depart we have many sights to share. Thrills! Dance! Music! Spectacle! And maybe a finger to one lucky member of the audience should Minly not prove to be so Magnificent!" Fadis shouted to the crowd who laughed and pointed. Fadis held up his hand quieting the rabble. The he waved his hand at Minly. She spread the blades in her hands like they were feathers. Then her arms began to move. The metal began the glint and sparkle in the light of the lanterns that hung in the tent. They left her grasp and shimmered upward into the air. The crowd stood in awe as the dancing steel fluttered around her like a silver fountain. Her feet arced gracefully around and she began to twirl her body. The subtle sound of steel hitting her palms lulled the crowd. Back and forth she moved from one end of the stage to the other. The crowd began to back away as she drew near them.

Her smile never left her face as she caught the blades. Steel clinking on steel. Then at one end she stopped and like a spinning cloud of death she threw up all the blades and then spun around onto her knees. The crowd gasped. Her hand swooped up into the air and plucked each one from the cloud as it fell. Then she knelt there like a metal bird with wings of polished death spreading out in the wind. The crowd erupted into applause. Fadis jumped back on stage.

"Oh but that's not all my good people! Oh no! There is much yet to see! We do of course accept tips but would not ask of them. Our assistants will be around with their hats should you feel like helping us keep the show going. We would so much very like to perform here again for all you good people," he shouted.

"Praise be to the gods! You have seen good people! Your own Eyes have told you! She is Minly, the Magnificent!" he continued to shout. The crowd cheered and clapped for Minly as she stood and bowed. Giving the crowd another smile she pranced off the stage. Fadis waved his arms around. Hours later the performers sat at a table at the back of their tent around a table. A few hats partly filled with coins sat around on it. A disappointing haul for any troupe that actually had to live on such a pittance. The Opal Cranes were no such troupe. Fadis entered still sporting his grin and sat down among his performers and looked around at them and then at the hats.

"Guess ale is on the hats tonight," he mused and slapped his knee. Some of the others who still had the energy laughed. The grin left the Barker's face and the circle quieted. Fadis looked around at all his people.

"I have some distressing news," he said. All those around stayed silent as Fadis gathered his thoughts. He continued.

"It seems the rumors are true. Wilter Gallow has gone rogue. He's been disavowed by The Opal Swans. That means he's disavowed by us and every other branch," he said. The others took a few moments to process this news. Minly leaned forward.

"Is he stamped?" she said. Fadis' eyes seemed to catch fire.

"Oh the bastard is stamped all right. Big money to the one who brings in his head. Swans got first dibs. But any branch can take a crack at his stamp if he should happen to find himself in a city we rolled into. Loose wheels squeal. If you catch my meaning," he said.

"We got the grease boss," a large burly stagehand name Porj grumbled. Fadis pointed up at him.

"You're damn right we have the grease. We'll drown the fucker in it. That's why we need eyes open, and ears sharp. Off-season shows are about the start. Time to rehearse new material, and listen for any squeaky wheels. Plenty of gold and silver for finders fee in case we can't do the deed ourselves. So keep sharp you lot. Gallow knows our ways. He ain't gonna make it easy. Don't get stupid. Don't get dead. I hate auditioning new talent," he said while giving the others a burning stare.

Chapter Five: With Any Luck

For the last week Estrello spent most of his time in the infirmary tending to the revolving door of crewmembers that arrived with one injury or another, when he wasn't in the arena training off the stress that is. The pressure to get at least one of the Pathfinders flying again was immense. Immense pressure made people work faster. Faster work was fertile ground for injury. And Murphy's Law would not be denied. Despite the frequency of new cases many who stopped by to get patched up commented to Nocivo they suspected he was avoiding contact with Antonio. Estrello didn't hesitate to agree. It had been awkward since the last mission. That it had been the longest stretch of time between seeing the colors on record since they began operations. It only exacerbated what was already a negative situation. The fear of the trail going cold was always present. But again here he was in the infirmary in the middle of the night bandaging up Sully who'd reinjured himself. Familiar footsteps made him turn around. A few moments later the doors of the infirmary slid open. Standing there at the doorway was Antonio Salazar. He was wearing a long gray bathrobe. Peeking out from under it were yellow rabbit slippers. Sully looked up. Suddenly his lacerated hand didn't seem like such a big deal. Nocivo and Salazar locked glances. The background noise in the room seemed to grow several magnitudes louder. Even the condensation rolling down the side of a nearby glass suddenly took on a role in the tension. Sully half expected a tumbleweed to roll between them in the wind. He began to get up but Nocivo gestured for him to sit back down without turning his head away from Salazar. They eyes continued to stay locked on each other like two snipers in each other's crosshairs waiting to see who death would take away first. A smile then ran across Antonio's face.

"You're up late," he said. Nocivo relaxed some. Sully didn't so much.

"He's here a lot lately," Sully mumbled. Antonio walked forward into the infirmary. As he did the doors slid closed.

"That right?" he said, not taking his eyes off of Nocivo. Estrello didn't respond. Antonio shook his head and looked down at his bathrobe pocket. Sully's eyes watched as he did. A chill suddenly inched up his spine. Antonio only pulled out a slip of paper and unfolded it.

"Your nurse Vanessa asked me to come back if my symptoms were persistent. Well, my symptoms were persistent. Which is why I'm awake. Trouble sleeping. Why are you awake Skip? You're not a night owl," Antonio mused with a smirk and held out to Nocivo the slip of paper. He took it and looked it over.

"Claro. If this diagnosis was right, and you're still having symptoms, my first guess would be early signs of post concussion syndrome__Sorry about that," he said and handed the paper back over. Antonio smiled.

"That wasn't so hard was it? I swear with you sometimes it's like pulling teeth. I'm glad you're not a dentist," he said trying to get his friend to smile. Nocivo didn't smile. Instead he just looked down.

"Lo siento Antonio. I am truly very sorry," he said and looked up at Salazar. He didn't see any disdain or contempt. Nor did he detect that he'd be greeted again by sarcasm.

"Seriously man aside from the concussion I'm good. You act you like you're the first guy that has ever tried to kill me. I was going to retire Valiant 5.988 anyway. But our encounter got my almonds working on some new great ideas I'm putting in all my 6.0s I got fabricating right now," he said. Nocivo nodded and pulled a pen light from his front breast pocket and clicked it on to check its battery life. He then glanced at Sully.

"Scoot over Trevor," he said. Sully did what he was asked to and moved over farther down the bed. When he sat down the paper lining the top crinkled. Nocivo then looked back at Salazar and gestured for him to sit down. Antonio did so. The paper crinkled for him as well. Nocivo clicked his light on again and began shining it in Antonio eyes to observe how the dilation contracted.

"No apparent sensitivity to light it seems. Cuéntame sobre tus otros síntomas," He said and clicked off the light. Antonio blinked a few times. He hated those bright light blotches.

"Síntomas. Okay I got over the fine motor control issues early. Fue difícil escribir las cosas por un tiempo. But I got a handle on that," he said. Estrello looked down again for a moment.

"Sorry man," he said. Antonio just sighed.

"You're forgiven Skipper. Any landing you can walk away from and whatnot. Anyhow light and sound aren't a big deal. Headaches, bits of vertigo every now and then, and bad sleep seem to be the only things that are taking their time to fuck off. I think what really fucked me over was being inside that damn Vantolotron," he said. Nocivo didn't say anything and just kept looking down for a moment. Then took a remote control device and clicked a few buttons. A screen dropped down from a compartment in the ceiling beside the bed Antonio and Sully were sitting on. It flickered on. Nocivo held the remote up.

"I had to sit in the Vantolotron too. The nanomachines had to come out somehow. I didn't have a concussion though. I did have whatever you dosed me with. Didn't make my time in there any less pleasant for me. Sit still," Nocivo said as a laser grid painted Antonio in a green light. He then clicked a button on his remote.

"Patient VCS Natty Bumppo crewmember Salazar, Antonio, doctor of chemistry and ISO operative," he said. The screen flickered again and then two images appeared. Two x-ray images rotated side by side. Sully looked at the screen and scooted farther down the bed. Estrello studied both images.

"Bueno," he said. Antonio gave him a side-glance.

"How bueno are we talking about here Skip?" he said. Nocivo pointed at the images.

"The left image is from when Vanessa first scanned you. It shows significant damage to the back of your head. More specifically to your cerebellum and occipital lobe. Your symptoms are consistent to damage to this area. The second image is of you now. The damage is greatly lessened, but not gone. Hence the persistent symptoms," he said, and then looked back at Antonio who grimaced upon seeing it.

"Great. What would you recommend I do about that?" Antonio said. Nocivo clicked on his remote and the screen shut off and retracted back up into the ceiling. He then walked over to a machine with a touch screen mounted next to it. After some prolonged tapping at items on the touch screen a plastic glass elevated up from a compartment in the machine then a thick green liquid began pouring into it. When it was done Estrello picked up the glass and walked back over to Antonio. Antonio narrowed his eyes as Nocivo held the glass over to him.

"Time Tony. And a lot of this," Nocivo said. Antonio took the glass and looked at the green concoction inside it.

"¿Qué?" he said and looked up at Estrello. He smiled.

"It's chlorella, mostly. Bottoms up," he said. Antonio sniffed at the glass.

"Is there ginger in this?" he said. Nocivo just gestured for Antonio to drink it. Salazar reluctantly did so. It wasn't awful, but not great either.

"Has a grit to it," he said. Just then the doors to the back area of the infirmary opened up and Nurse Forsander walked into the room carrying a paper bag with a receipt stapled to it. He handed it to Salazar.

"Lovely," he said. Nocivo folded his arms and gave Antonio a stern look.

"You're going keep drinking the mix over the next few days to remove toxins from the injured tissue and whatever heavy metal residue the nanotech left behind. I've sent the recipe to Deuce. No getting away from it. There's also a refill of the painkillers you're already taking, and please avoid taking any more knocks to the head for a while," he said. Antonio raised an eyebrow.

"You do remember what we do right?" he said. Nocivo nodded.

"I do. Keep your helmet on and learn to duck. Also, quit telegraphing every third move in your attack and defense combinations. You made it too easy for me plot out how to shake your resolve and strike through your blocks and lay traps for you," Nocivo said. Antonio smirked.

"Noted. You still lost. Sounds like you'd like a rematch vato. I'm game jefe if you want to throw down again. Schedule is light," Antonio quipped. Estrello wasn't amused.

"What did I tell you about taking it easy? Relájate," he said. Antonio kept at it.

"Oh you get all critical and shit. I think we need to settle this like men in the way real men settle this shit," Antonio said. Nocivo gave him a stern look.

"Oh?" he said as he began rolling up his sleeve. Sully did not like how this situation was starting to unfold and began to get up. Estrello shot a curt look his way.

"Siéntate!" Nocivo hissed as he pointed at Sully. Sully plopped back down. Nocivo looked back at Antonio.

"Okay man. Challenge accepted. We bring Sully. There needs to be a witness," he said. Antonio nodded in agreement. He then looked back at Sully.

"Orale carnal. You ready to roll ese?" he said. Sully just sat there dumbfounded.

Shadows chased around the forest as thunder clashed and lighting streaked across the sky. Dwarves pushed ahead as best they could through the constant sheets of rain that seemed to drag them back a step for every two they took. Raltec and Balocan, older but far more experienced in travelling through harsh weather, walked in front of the group. Pulcan and Manati worked hard to keep up. Not being as seasoned their footing was unsure and every slip and slide cost them strength and energy as the wind howled around them. The group had to keep aware of falling debris hitting the forest floor as the storm above them tore at the treetops. Every clap of thunder felt like a kick to the chest. Dwarves were fairly resistant to cold but only when they were dry. Every mile they walked felt like ten or more. Soon they hoped they would come across Gamblers Crest. It was a rocky outcropping that would provide some shelter from the weather. Their map said it would be near, but none of them could see anything other then sheets of rain and the looming trees around them. Every few minutes Raltec and Balocan looked over their shoulders to Pulcan and Manati. It seemed that each passing hour saw the two young ones drifting farther and farther back. Someone had to reach Gamblers Crest, but Raltec would not leave the young ones behind. He took the rope he had slung around his shoulder and unraveled it some. He then gathered up the coiled end and hurled it back to the young ones. Pulcan saw it land near him picked it up. He handed the other end of the rope back to Manati. Holding onto the rope helped balance the two young ones as they walked. Raltec trudged ahead pulling the rope over his shoulder. Balocan saw what Raltec was trying to do and took hold of the rope as well. Together the group forged ahead working better as a team. The wind was picking up again though. As if it wasn't strong enough already. It was almost as if the wind felt challenged by the dwarves and dealt out it's rage like a guttural scream through the pines. Raltec pivoted around a tree to wrap the rope around its trunk and hunkered down behind it. Balocan braced himself behind another nearby tree as the angle the rain hit them changed from above their heads to right in their faces. Behind them Pulcan and Manati found a tree of their own. It was large with a thick trunk. The thunder began crashing harder above them. The rain hitting them felt less like water and more like shards of ice tearing at their faces and hair.

Lightning covered the sky like a spiders web woven by the hatred, fear, and spite this storm spat out in contempt for all that dare catch it's light. Manati could barely keep his eyes open. The wind tore at him and pushed him to the ground. Holding the rope he pulled himself up and forced his eyes open to see were Pulcan was. As he did he saw a shadow in the corner of his eye. He turned to the direction he saw it and forced his eyes open and kept them open as best he could. The lightning flashed brightly and he caught a glimpse of it again. It was moving. He nudged Pulcan who looked back at Manati who pointed out at the forest behind them. He didn't understand what Manati was trying to show him. But then he saw it too. A shadow was there moving among the trees quickly enough to be hard to follow. He watched it as best he could for a few moments. Then he felt a tug. Raltec was on the move. Pulcan reached down and pulled Manati up and urged him forward. Manati looked back at the forest behind them several more times. He did not see the shadow again.

The VCS Natty Bumppo was an eerie place this time of night. Anyone who was up would be working at their assigned station, which at the this time of night would not be anywhere near where Nocivo, Salazar and Sully were. The empty corridors were only filled with the low hum of whatever machinery lay behind them. Sully wasn't paying much attention to that but rather the two men who walked just in front of him. Neither of them said anything to each other, or to him. They just kept walking like men on a pilgrimage to meet their fate. He watched the angled heels of Estrello's cowboy boots knocking against the metal floor. They had polished metal decorations in the shape of scorpions fixed onto them. He couldn't see Antonio's yellow rabbit slippers, but he knew they were there. And he could hear their rubber soles squeaking against the floor. Neither appeared to be paying much attention to him. Surreptitiously he triggered the silent alarm on his phone. Someone had to stop them. He knew he could not. These were very dangerous men to antagonize. Their hostility could easily shift to him. He wanted to avoid this. When others arrived he would do what he could. Right now the best option would be to stall for time. He would have to be careful though.

"Skip, Tony, you don't have to do this," he said. Both men stopped and looked back at Sully. His face was flushed and he looked greatly distressed. Nocivo looked him in the eyes.

"It's a matter of honor Sully," he said. Sully's stomach was in knots. He wanted to stall for more time for a security team to arrive but he didn't want to make it look obvious. He looked over at Antonio who also gave him a steely-eyed stare.

"Every man must meet fate Sully. Every man must walk that walk. No man can escape it. Fate always waits at the end of the line," Antonio said. Estrello looked at Salazar and then back at Sully.

"You will come to know what it means to walk your own journey. The time grows near. We mustn't delay any further. Fate grows restless," he said then continued walking. Antonio did the same. Sully followed behind. After walking the length of this hallway the trio came to a lift and boarded it. It took them down another level where they exited and continued to walk a good distance. Sully hung back as much as he could so he could trigger the silent alarm again. Nocivo and Salazar walked ahead a bit faster. A corner came up just ahead. Sully waited for them to turn it. He whipped out his phone and triggered the silent alarm again. What could be taking security so long to respond? Would he be the last to see one or both of these men alive? Would they kill each other before his eyes? He feared what they would do to each other. He feared what they would do to him if he did not follow. He feared what the others would say and do to him before their blood was dry. Would they look at him like he was a coward unwilling to stand between them? Would they look at him like he was a failure that could not find a way to stall them until others could intervene? Upon triggering the alarm again he put away his phone and hurried around the corner. When he did he saw both men standing there looking at him. They said nothing. They only stared at him. Several moments went by. Neither of them spoke. Neither of them moved. They just stared at Sully. Then Nocivo took a few steps back and turned to a closed door. He reached out and placed his palm on it ever so. Then he looked back at Sully. His eyes were intense and burned right through the crewman. He then looked over at Antonio. Salazar flashed an equally intense look and then he turned his gaze over at Sully. Nocivo backed away from the door a few steps. Sully took a few steps to the side and positioned himself with his back to the opposite wall.

Antonio stared right into his eyes with every step he took. For a few moments they all just stood silent and looked back and forth at one another. Sully could hear his heart thumping. Almost in tune with the undulating hum from the wall behind him. Antonio took a few steps back and placed his hand on the door then looked back at Sully. Nocivo looked at Antonio and then back at Sully.

"Fate stands behind this door Sully. You may see me die behind this door. You may see Salazar die behind this door. You will do so because fate demands a witness. It's a matter of honor Sully. Behind this door honor will be upheld and you will be left to tell the tale. This is what awaits you," he said then turned his steely gaze over to Antonio. Salazar then looked back at Sully. Without looking away he reached back and tapped a touch screen mounted next the door. A hollow muted tone sounded as the panel turned a pale sickly green. Antonio took his hand way from the panel slowly never taking his eyes off of Sully. Nocivo did the same. Then another tone sounded.

"Passcode," a voice said. Without looking away Antonio touched the panel again.

"The passcode is, open the door fuckface. Quit being a little shit," Antonio said. The tone sounded again.

"Fine. You fuckers are always so pushy," the voice said again. Sully recognized the voice this time. The door slid open. Standing in the doorway was Jack Riggs. He was wearing a bathrobe and his fuzzy hat. He looked at both Nocivo and Salazar and then at Sully.

"Ah, I see you have brought a witness. Come forth. Fate awaits," Jack said then backed up into the room and waved his hand behind him. Sitting at a table in the middle of the room a stocky bearded fair-haired man looked on.

"No pussies may enter my inner sanctum! Leave your weakness behind you. Second Edition Rules Only!! Is this understood?" the man growled intensely. Nocivo looked at Antonio. Then he looked back at Sully and then back at the man sitting at the table.

"Your terms are acceptable," he said. The man grinned slyly and then laughed a deep laugh.

"Well then, enter brave souls. Fate awaits," he hissed. Nocivo and Salazar looked at each other and then back at Sully. Nocivo entered the room and Antonio followed.

"I hope you have the Cheetos and Mountain Dew," Nocivo said to the man. The man smiled.

"Of course. What do I look like? A chump?" the man said. His voice changed from a gravelly growl to an almost cheerful tone. He looked back into the hall at Sully.

"What's with him?" he said Nocivo and Antonio looked back into the hall. Sully just stood there, flabbergasted.

"That's Sullivan Trevor from the garage level," Nocivo said. Sully didn't know what to do. Antonio snapped his fingers at Sully.

"Venaca!" He said. Sully was still reluctant to move. Then he heard footsteps. Two members of security rounded the corner. Both of them carried a few boxes of pizza. One of them was Louie who was usually stationed in the garage level. He smiled when he saw Sully.

"Hey man you want some pizza?" he said. Inside the room Nocivo sniffed at the air.

"Took you guys long enough!" he yelled. Louie looked through the door.

"Sorry Skip. Someone kept tripping the silent alarm. We had to check that out first," Louie said. Nocivo shook his head and waved him in. The fair-haired man looked back at Sully in the hall. He pulled a small bag out of his pocket and turned it over. A handful of clear red multi-sided dice fell out and onto the table.

"Fate is ready to roll. Get your ass in here!" he yelled. Just then Nick walked by behind the fair-haired man carrying a bottle of Mountain Dew. He noticed Sully and waved.

"Hey man," he said with a smile and continued on. Sully sighed and walked into the room. Nelson, the other security guy had a big grin on his face. He set his stack of pizza down onto the table and danced over to the cooler for a Mountain Dew.

"Sweet caffeine," he said before he yawned and cracked the bottle open with a hiss. Jack looked over at fair-haired man.

"He hasn't sat down with his character sheet. Snack rule man," he said as he pointed back at Nelson. The fair-haired man looked up at Jack with a raised brow. Then he tapped on his tome of etiquette, which sat beside him.

"Rule 14, Subsection B. A visitor not active in gameplay may partake in snacks, if said visitor brings other snacks. Snack exchange clause," he said and grinned. Jack adjusted his fuzzy hat and refocused on his character sheet.

The sun was not up yet but Tass was awake. He knew someone would be around to fetch him soon, but he wanted to stay in bed a little while longer. He turned over and looked out the window. The sky was still black, but there was a lighter shade of blue beginning to encroach as night surrendered to morning. The smell of the sun's warmth already crept into the room. He had another full day of harvest ahead of him. Over the last few weeks he and his brother had made a lot of progress. From what his father said the market for their crop was getting better. He didn't understand what that meant. The crop was the same as the year before. But his father insisted that the price had for it had gone up for reasons he did not elaborate on. His priority had gone from obtaining an additional horse to buying a few more and letting Old Bess retire out to pasture. The town farrier who also sold horses for his cousin who lived farther down the river would not be back in town until the beginning of the following month. It was then that his father planned to go into town and bring back at least three young horses.

He hadn't seen his father this high in spirits in a good long while. It was good to see him moving around with vigor again even if his leg was lame. The way he tapped his cane when he was feeling particularly jovial was comforting. Tass still could not shake his worry over The Tides. Perhaps it was not a story young ears should hear. Much to be made of nothing, but maybe there was more. It was still a thought that spent more than it's share of time in the places of his mind that should be filled with daily tasks. He could hear activity outside. Farmers and other townspeople were already up and about. There was a path not far from their house that was frequented by people walking into town. It's when this activity started he most expected to hear... There was a knock at the door. It opened and a candle lit face appeared. It was his older brother Elmer.

"Small fry. It's time to get up. Mother has breakfast made," he said. Tass rolled over to face his brother.

"I can smell beets. Are we having beets?" Tass said. Elmer was not very patient.

"Yes, if you don't get up I'm going to eat your share," he said. Tass sighed and threw off his covers. The chill of the room hit him, as he knew it would. He picked up his robe, which was rolled up at the foot of his bed. He would not let Elmer eat his beets. It was a rare thing to get them. Most breakfasts were just a bit of bread and maybe some cheese if his mother had been down by the market. She must have been and not mentioned it. At any rate Tass had on his robe and slippers. He trotted down the stairs to the kitchen where he was greeted the aroma of beets cooking over fire. His mother tended the cauldron suspended over the fire by iron hooks. His father was nearby cutting a wheel of cheese into wedges. His brother was already slicing a loaf of rye and serving out portions out to everyone's plate. Tass's mother waved him over. He headed toward her but she pointed to the table.

"Grab the bowls you silly boy," she mused. Tass smiled and turned back around. He fetched the old wooden bowls sitting in a stack on the table. He was eager to eat. Tass set the bowls on a small stool near his mother and handed her one. She scooped up from the cauldron with her wooden ladle and poured a good portion into the bowl.

"I'll never wash this color off. It'll look like beets forever," she said. Tass smiled and he walked back to the table. Then he returned for the next bowl. Tass's father had finished slicing cheese and tapped his cane on the floor. Elmer set down his knife and walked over to collect the large wooden plate and bring it back to the table.

"Do you think the weather will hold today papa?" Elmer said. Vill looked over at his son. He gave the question a bit of thought as he sat down on a stool behind him.

"Well boy I have heard the banter. Old man Rame says the wet grass in the morning means more sun. Mr. Gloss down at the notary seems to think we'll have rain before the week is out. Something to do with the number of flies he's seen. The cobbler's boy says the clouds tell him we may get some chill soon. Hard to say. Depends on who you ask. We'll be working hard anyhow. Ain't no difference of opinion on that," he said. Tass set another full bowl on the table. He turned to his father.

"What do they say of the winter papa?" he said. Vill liked to hear his boys asking good questions instead bantering about the jousting tourney coming up in a month's time. Carrying on about such things didn't sow a field or harvest it. Asking about the weather is something a good farmer would do.

"I tell you what boy. Ask them yourself. We'll be going into town this evening if you and your brother finish up what you started yesterday. I may even be tempted to give you both a copper for some mint bread," he said Tass looked back at his brother who smiled widely. Vill tapped his cane on the floor again getting the boys' attention. He raised a finger.

"But, but only if you boys finish up nice and early. The days are growing shorter now," he said and looked and smiled at his wife. She smiled back.

"Eat up boys. You'll need your strength. Mustn't waste the day," she said. The boys' pace seemed to pick up a bit.

"Yes mother," they said in unison.

The was a blue-blackness called the eastern sea. Some called it The Great Devourer. Some called it a living. Such was the feelings of the fishing boat crew who'd sailed out farther than they'd been before to set themselves out from the crowd closer to shore. It was breaking day but the mists still hung low over the water. Such banks of fog were not a bother to them. By mid-day they'd lift and they'd regain their bearings. In the meantime there were nets to cast and lines to haul up. Money to be made from the deep if a fisherman knew what he was doing. Good enough money to get them out this far in the mists while the entire coast was uneasy. Captain Mortimer wasn't a man easily shaken. He'd dealt with pirate stories all his life. He'd even run from a few himself. They were a determined lot, but nothing like the stories of shadows rising from the sea to claim one captain after another.

The Black Admiral they called him. He was a creature from the depths that commanded a fleet of darkness that claimed no cargo or silver. Just lives. Dead men are all he craved. Tales conflicted on this point however. What they all agreed on was the sea ran red they said. The air smelled of fear they said. So thick it would chase away the sea birds themselves. Beheadings. Drowning. Disembowelment. Keelhauling. Hanging from the rigging. All manner of gruesome tales of gruesome fates visited upon men he knew of by name. Some he knew personally. Scallywags most of them were that found a poor end out on the waves. Others were just sailors like him earning a living on the sea. All of them were fools for letting themselves get run down by salty fiends who took what they would and weave malarkey to everyone who'll listen just to save face. Those that pirates let sail away that is.

"You there, look lively. I want to be hauling up fish before mid day," he said to a crewman he thought was moving too slow. He descended back into thought then. Mortimer could see the looks on every fool's face that bought their rubbish. Skittish men addled by rumor. Dull wits would be. The truth was easier. Taxes from the Midland capital were getting harsher. Made men more desperate. No men more desperate than pirates. Desperate men made more mistakes.

Boldness only favored the savvy. Savvy men like Captain Mortimer. Savvy men like his crew who were pulling up nets full of fish. He smiled to his first mate. It was as if his men hauled chests of silver from the depths. It would be a good day. The fishmongers would greet them cheerfully and offer a more than fair price. The markets would be thick with their catch and their name carried along the coast as other names once were. The way his men strained with the mass ensnared in their net began the cascade of falling coins in his mind. The goddess of the seas was generous to this small vessel and her captain. Mortimer smiled widely and turned to sit on a bench next to the rudder. When he turned back his men had stopped pulling.

He began to get up but one of his men held a finger to his lips and urged him to sit back down. Then he glanced at the others who looked around in horror. It was then he noticed the sky had grown darker again. He looked around. A blackness was moving around them in the mists. They made no sound. All Mortimer could hear was the water lapping up against his ship's hull. To his left a great black shadow rolled through the mist. The silhouette looked to be veering in their direction. Any word in Mortimer's throat dried out and crumbled before he could utter a single sound. The giant shadow passed close. Close enough for him to see the outline of ship. As it drew closer he could make out the outline of man who stood at the bow like dark specter. The blackness seemed to swirl around him like malevolent ribbons floating in the air. The figure didn't move as the massive dark shape pulled along side them. The air the phantom displaced washed over the fishing boat that seemed to drain the warmth right out of his bones. His crew couldn't move. His men held onto the nets for dear life for fear if they let them go the shadows would hear them. The large shadow passed them by, but as Mortimer looked around him more and more shadows rose from the veil and passed by. He sat there motionless for an amount of time. He couldn't be sure how long. All he knew was that the stories were true. Darkness had come for them all.

Sully sat at the other end of the table across from the fair-haired man the others were calling Fate. For almost an hour he watched the others around the table build what they called character sheets.

He knew what Role Playing Games were; he'd just never had the interest in playing them before. Classical games weren't among his interests. Although he had never really been exposed to them. Especially those games played in the classical way with physical dice, small metal figurines, sheets of lined paper, and graphite pencils. People hundreds of years ago played this way. No technology. It was just a circle of friends in a single room participating in a story being guided by a storyteller. Here and now that storyteller was Fate. Sitting to Sully's right was Deuce who was playing as something called a Cleric. It was a type of healer. Sitting next to him was Rick. His chosen class was an Enchanter that Sully reasoned was some sort of charismatic wizard. Sitting next Rick was Nick. He'd never seen him outside the hanger. He seemed to live there.

His chosen class was a Fighter. The others called him a tank for some reason. To Sully's left was Salazar. His chosen class was a Magician. Sully didn't need that one explained. Next to him interestingly enough was Skip. Just an hour ago he was terrified these men were going kill each other in the infirmary. Then he thought they were going to kill each other in whatever Fate called this room. Sully didn't remember. He did enjoy the pizza, Cheetos, and Mountain Dew everyone gave him. He didn't even care to know what a Paladin was that Skip was playing as. Despite not even asking they explained that they were tanks like fighters but had limited healing abilities and adhered to a strict moral code. None of this meant anything to him and he was quite fed up with the morning. He'd re-injured his hand and just needed some patching up before he went back to the hanger to finish his shift. Now he was watching grown men roll dice at each other pretending they were sorcerers fighting things he didn't care to know the names of. Fate looked around intently. The character sheets were complete and now the game could begin. He picked up a remote device and started clicking buttons. Just then different colored lights came on with the hiss off a fog device activating. The mist augmented the effect of the lights and curled around the assortment of props Fate had set up around the gaming table. Medieval style music began to play at low volume as he grinned widely. Fate then he picked up a flashlight and held it at his chest below his chin. Then came the voice.

"Are you fuckers ready to attack some darkness? The Skullmoor awaits!" Fate snarled. Everyone looked around at each other.

"HUZZAH!!" they all yelled. Sully said nothing and just glared at Skip and Salazar as he ate his Cheetos. Fate cackled in his gravelly voice.

"Well let's get it on then!! And I swear Salazar if you cast Magic Missile before the first dungeon I swear to fucking Gorgoth I will summon ogres. Do not test me!" Fate said. Antonio smirked.

"My name is Sparklefinger, Jeremy. Address me properly or I will cast nothing but Magic Missile and the entire party dies," he said slyly. Fate sat back and frowned. Then he threw up his hands.

"Fine! But Skip gets to roll first now. How about that Mr. Sparkly Fingers?" Fate growled. Antonio rolled his eyes and passed the dice to the side. Deuce seemed to have a question.

"Hey Fate, what is the policy on saving throws this game?" he said. Fate backed up and pulled something out of his desk. It was a folder, which he set down and opened.

"I'm glad you asked Herbarian. I printed out tables. Forgot I had them. Thanks for reminding me," Fate said in his regular voice and handed a stack to Deuce. Deuce took a sheet and passed it to the side.

"No problem man," he said and began studying the tables. The stack had been passed all around the table back to Fate and everyone was familiarizing themselves with the tables to the sounds of crunching Cheetos and sharpening of pencils, but Sully was really having a hard time keeping something to himself.

"Okay What In Billy Blue Blazes Guys!!" he yelled. Everyone looked up from their copies and stared at Sully.

"Seriously! What in The Amber Waves Of Grain!!" he yelled again. Nocivo looked around at everyone else then back at Sully.

"What the amber grains about what?" he said. This just seemed to agitate Sully.

"That's what I want to know!" Sully yelled. Antonio slid a narrowed look at him.

"Can you stop yelling? Only Fate gets to do that here," he said. Sully closed his eyes and sighed. Then he opened them again and looked at Salazar.

"Okay. I'll do that. If you can tell me what the hell is gong on with you two," Sully said much more softly. Antonio took a moment to formulate an answer.

"Well, Skip and I came to an understanding," Antonio said. Sully scowled at him.

"Oh really? How? When? In the infirmary? In the hall? Just now rolling dice around? When?" Sully asked. Nocivo rolled the dice around in his hand while he looked at Sully.

"My apologies Sully. There is a lot going on here you weren't privy to," he said. Sully tilted his head to the side as he looked at Nocivo.

"Really? No kidding. How silly of me to have missed that. Could y'all explain?" he said. Nocivo stopped roiling the dice and set them down on the table under his hand.

"Over a year ago before we met Commodore Persson and General Stratum, and before all of this, it was just Salazar and I. Two people from different universes looking for answers to a lot of questions. One thing we had an answer for is that we both understood each other to be very dangerous people. Between the both of us we've killed a lot of men," Nocivo said. Antonio turned his chair slightly to face Sully.

"Skip and I talked a lot about what would happen if we ever really fought. Like a serious to the death kind of fight. And if somehow both of us lived, how would we know if everything was copacetic and we should just let shit slide. Because, you know, at the end of the day we're just two dudes who have to contend with something much bigger than us. And we can't afford to sweat the small stuff. That's just the name of the game. Shit or get off the pot. So I came up with a way to let Skip know it was all good from my end," Antonio said. This only confused Sully more.

"Small stuff? Okay ignoring all the rest of that insane whackadoodle you just said, what was the way you came up with?" Sully said while to trying to maintain his cool. Antonio nodded and slid his chair back and picked up his feet.

"Yellow rabbit slippers," Antonio said. Sully just looked at him for a moment. Then he looked down at the yellow bunny slippers. They had ridiculous eyes and whiskers. Each had a pink tongue that jutted out from under goofy looking bucked teeth. He looked at them for a good long moment. Then something happened that Sully did not expect. He just burst out laughing. The sheer absurdity of everything was just too much. Everyone began laughing with him.

"You crazy sons of guns. This is the craziest damn place I have ever worked. You rum tum tuggers. Holy smokes! Y'all are weird as all get out," he said amidst his rolling guffaw. Antonio held his sides and settled himself just enough.

"Yeah, we're complete assholes man," he said and continued laughing. Sully pointed and nodded as he coughed.

"No kidding hoss. But hey man, why mess with me? You gotta whole ship of people," he said trying not to choke. Sully had a point and Antonio had an answer.

"Well we gave it some thought. We wouldn't have invited over just anyone. Both Skip and I know that you're a no bullshit guy. Or else we would have just left you there in the infirmary. Right now we need a no bullshit guy that people listen to," he said. This sounded vague to Sully so he looked over at Nocivo.

"Just like Tony said. We need a no bullshit guy. When guys like us in ops like this fight, things tend to get dramatic. Drama divides teams. Much drama we can't control. Other drama, we can try. This is where we need a guy who isn't going to bullshit. We also needed some fresh blood for the game. So we fucked with you. It's our way. We can be assholes. My apologies for that. All these guys went through it. Especially Jack. He was pissed at us for days," Nocivo said. Antonio concurred. Fate held the flashlight at his chest again.

"These guys are pieces of shit. I love em' but they're pieces of shit," he said in the voice. Sully pointed over at him.

"You get no argument from me," he said and started laughing again. Nick got up and pointed at Sully.

"You get another Mountain Dew!" he yelled and reached in the cooler behind him. Fate stopped laughing and wiped a tear from his eye then pointed at Nocivo.

"Okay man what was your roll?" he said. Nocivo looked over at him and lifted his hand. Fate looked over at the dice. He grimaced and sat back with the flashlight at his chest.

"Okay Sparklefinger, I won't summon the ogres. Yet!" Fate said in the voice. Sully still found the humor of Salazar and Nocivo peculiar, and mean to those who didn't understand them. He didn't care for initiations either. But what was done, was done. Now came the game. Nick handed him another Mountain Dew and went back to his chair. Sully cracked open the drink and looked over at the table.

"So how do you play this?" he said. The group looked over at him. Rick opened up the folder in front of him and pulled out a piece of paper.

"Tell you what my man. If you want to play, you can use a character I didn't play with yet. A Ranger. Pull on up I can show you how it's done," he said. Sully scooted his chair over closer to Rick and looked at his new character sheet.

The sun had just risen over the horizon and lit up the early morning mists with warm yellow glow. Flint Redflower sat silently near Widow's Pass near the southern edge of the Barley Lands. Drops of morning dew had collected in his thick solid blue gray fur. He could hear the distant sound of hoof falls approaching from the south in the distance. Behind him his rangers sat around as well with all of their eyes looking down the road the same as their High Captain. As the sounds of hooves grew closer Flint stood and walked to the side of the road leaving his captain's spear behind set against the tree he sat under. His gaze stayed fixed down the road. He could see the glint of armor now. Pennants flapped in the wind as well. Gold ones. Flint remained standing where he was until the horsemen in the front of the procession caught sight of him. A hand went up and the procession stopped. A handful of riders rode forth and approached Flint who didn't budge an inch. One of the riders who rode closer to him had one hand on the hilt of his sword. The rider looked Flint over then trotted back to the others. He leaned over and spoke to one of the riders wearing a traditional simple helm with visor. However adorned in more elegantly forged armor with polished bronze accents. Their crenulation-like pattern mirrored to imposing image of Southgate battlements. This man held up a hand and then approached Flint. He stopped near him and dismounted. The clank of his plates and thump of his weight on the road broke the calm of the morning. He walked toward Flint and removed his helmet. His hair was short and jet-black, as where his eyes. He had no mustache and just a patch of beard on his chin. His expression was plain. Almost like stone.

"Good morn Captain. Do you know who I am?" the man said. Flint knew exactly who he was.

"Prince Carcino of Southgate. Welcome to the Barley Lands. What brings you out so far from home?" Flint said. Carcino didn't receive the question well.

"I am here on official business from his Majesty, my father, The King. Who might I ask are you?" Carcino asked bluntly. His expression remained the same. Flint was also unrelenting.

"I am High Captain Flint Redflower of the Barley Lands Rangers and of all ranger packs," Flint said. This gave Carcino some pause. His expression considerably softened.

"Redflower? You're a pup of Brewster Redflower?" Carcino said. His expression did not change. But there was a hint of reverence in voice. Flint had heard this reverence in many voices and from many faces. The name Brewster Redflower carried substantial weight no matter where he went.

"I am his eldest," he said. Carcino held out his hand.

"Your father knew my brother Mercurian. May I shake the paw of the son Brewster Redflower?" Carcino said. Flint was a little taken aback, but did not refuse such a gesture. He met Carcino's hand respectfully. As he did his medallion slipped from under his tunic. Carcino caught sight of the four petal red flower. Only the children of Brewster Redflower wore them. Created by the High King of the Dwarves on his wedding day for one of his oldest and dearest friends who had been named High Chieftain by unanimous vote a year earlier following the death of his father Wolfsdire Redflower. It was a solemn day where all wolves howled in his memory. Flint was very young then, keeping an eye on the younger pups while his father was busy assuming his new role.

"With respect Prince Carcino, would this official business involve the recent killings in this area?" Flint said. Carcino said nothing for a moment then looked down. He looked up at Flint again.

"That is not inaccurate. Of course you know I am compelled by my father's royal mandate to speak of these matters only with those with a need to know. I will however make an exception for a Redflower. What do you know of these killings?" He said. Flint pulled a rolled message from his pocket and handed it over to Carcino.

"A message from your father The King. He too, it seems, makes exceptions for Redflowers. He petitioned us to assist you in your investigation. This is my territory after all, and being honest I would appreciate some assistance solving this riddle myself," he said. Carcino read the message and then handed it back to Flint. He looked back and gestured for his captains to approach.

"Very well son of Brewster. We will collaborate and bring these brigands to justice," he said as he remounted his horse and took up the reins. Flint pulled another message from his pocket. This one was still sealed with the sigil of Hall Lamb. He held it out to Carcino as his escort filed in behind him. Carcino leaned down and took the massage from Flint and examined it. He saw the yellow seal and the anvil pressed into it.

"What is this?" he said. Flint spun his toe in the air.

"I do not know. A rider hand delivered it me just an hour ago with the instructions that it was for your eyes only. You've been difficult to reach it appears," Flint said. Carcino looked at Flint for a few moments then back at the message in his hand. He broke the seal and read it. His expression remained unchanged but he let out a loud chuckle. He turned and looked at his captains.

"I suppose we drink wine tonight when we make camp. Celebration is in order. My brother has been betrothed," he said and looked back at the others down the road. He whistled to them and procession then resumed their movement. Carcino turned and looked at Flint.

"We will make camp near Glosten Hill at nightfall. Your rangers are welcome to dine with us," he said as he and his men continued on their way.

"It would be an honor," Flint shouted. He then turned and walked back into the trees.

A ranger was perched up in a tree just outside the Keep of Gromgoth, which was the lair of the infamous Witches of Horde. The ranger had crept up the tree to get a better a better angle to take a shot at a lookout posted on a stone wall not far from the keep. His party waited down below concealing themselves among the rocks that lay strewn around the area. Carefully and quietly the ranger nocked his arrow and drew back. His eye focused like an eagle across the span at the unsuspecting lookout. Dice fell from Sully's hand and bounced around until they came to rest. The roll was good. The table erupted into a 'Huzzah!' as the arrow met it's mark. Experience points went to Sully. He was doing well for a beginner and truly enjoying his time learning how to play the game. The others were very patient and Fate of Fortunes was being perhaps a bit more lenient than he would otherwise. This is not to say there hadn't been a few close shaves. The party barely survived the crossing of the Sparrow's Bridge. One bad roll would have spelled doom in the chasm below. The pizza was gone by this point having been eaten by the players or the others in the room who had gathered to watch them play. Quiz was here now with his crew getting prepped for their game at the space mini figurine filled table on the other side of the room. There were still plenty of Cheetos and Mountain Dew. No Mountain Dew for Salazar per Estrello's orders. He instead drank that dark green concoction with odd hints of lemon and ginger. He was also a bit salty that he had died at the hands of skeleton warriors when he rolled badly. His spell failed and he had to wait for a period of time before the party was in a place were he could be resurrected. He lost experience points as a result. The other's fortunes were far better. They had made it past the Sparrow's Bridge and through the army of skeletons to the very edge of the Keep of Gromgoth. Sully was eager to see what challenges they would run into next. Just then the door opened behind them. Standing in the doorway was Angelica. She was not in her security uniform. She was wearing a bright turquoise dress and had a brown leather backpack slung over her shoulder. She glared at Estrello.

"Hermano! Es hora de ir a la iglesia. Venaca por favor," she said. The group then all looked at Estrello. He picked up his phone and clicked it on to check the date.

"It's Sunday?" he said. Antonio gave him a puzzled look.

"Si es Domingo. Are you sure you're not the one with the head injury?" Antonio quipped and took a sip of his green concoction.

Estrello gave Antonio a narrow eyed look and then stood up from his chair. He looked around the table.

"My apologies. I must depart. It was a pleasure sharing this adventure with all of you. May the dice continue to show you favor," he said.

"Huzzah!" the group shouted in unison. Fate looked around.

"We got a spot open. Any takers?" He shouted. A hand went up. It was Ted Frost, a snarky looking copper top, who worked on the garden level, which provided a backup to the air component of the ship's life support system. His character was named Red Frost and a fighter like Nick's character. Fate looked over at him and waved him over to Nocivo's seat. He high-fived Nelson who was the party's Bard and then sat down to down to focus on his character sheet.

"No augmented stats. You jump in with newbie stats and gear. Only the strong survive!" he growled in his Fate voice. Nocivo threw Ted a thumb up and walked over to his sister. Angelica held out the backpack to her brother.

"You're not wearing scrubs and ranchero boots to church," she said. Estrello took the backpack and unzipped it. A blue buttoned down shirt was neatly folded inside along with a pair of slip on sneakers.

"Gracias," he said. Angelica frowned.

"I had to track you all the way from the infirmary. You're buying lunch," she said. The two of them walked down the hall and around the corner.

The rain had lightened into a slow drizzle and the wind had died down for the most part. Thunder still clashed in the distance. Lightning still lit up the forest around the small group of dwarves that huddled in a shallow cave in an outcropping of large rocks. They had built a fire with the dry wood and kindling they had smartly thought to pack with them before the rains came. They were able to scrounge more wood from the surrounding area and used their knives to scrape away enough of the wetness for it to catch. Raltec and Balocan had been in many of these situations before, but the two young ones, not so much. Pulcan looked exhausted as he tiredly ate a piece of dried meat. Dirt clung to his short dirty blonde beard. Manati looked worse. The older dwarves knew the signs of illness. Raltec crushed up herbs with a small stone mortar he kept in his pack. He hoped they would mitigate much of what could be afflicting Manati. He handed the mortar to the young one. Manati scooped the rendered mush out and began chewing it up. It was horrid tasting, but he chewed it and swallowed it down. He then lay back against his pack and held his hands out to the fire. Balocan could sense that something was troubling him. It was something other than the fever.

"What's on your mind lad?" he said. Manati looked over at the old dwarf and brushed aside the dark hair from his eyes. He seemed to be struggling with something. He looked over at Pulcan who nodded. He then looked back at Balocan.

"I saw something. Something in the storm," he said. Balocan leaned forward and rubbed his hands near the fire.

"One can see a lot of things in a storm. Even more in a bad one. Like just now," he said and looked over at Manati again. Manati scooped more of the herbs and chewed them down. He shuddered at the taste again.

"It weren't the storm sir. It was a person. Tall like a staff. Moved wrong for a staff," he said. Balocan looked over at Raltec who shrugged his shoulders. He looked back Manati.

"Just the storm lad. All it was," he said. Manati looked over at Pulcan.

"I saw it too sir. About a hundred paces behind us. Ducking behind the trees. Moving side to side. Fast. Like there weren't no wind. Like Manati said. Looked like a staff. Didn't move like one," Pulcan said. Balocan looked at him for a few moments then back at Raltec. Raltec looked at the two young ones. They both looked genuinely alarmed.

"When is the last time you saw it?" he said. The young ones looked at each other. Pulcan then looked at Raltec.

"Not long after we got hit with that big gust of wind. Didn't see it again after that." he said. Raltec frowned and then stood up. He picked up his hammer and walked out of the cave. The clouds kept the sky dark despite the sun already being up. Raltec could see around well enough. He climbed to the top of the rocky outcropping and crouched down. He scanned the area for a while. He saw nothing but forest and mist in all directions. He looked around for a while longer before being satisfied there was nothing to see. He then made his way back to the fire. In the distance a shadow disappeared behind a tree.

The morning cool was still very much in the air. The village of Riti was farther north down the river. Genesis had departed her father's house before dawn to make the journey up river to perform a reading for a man too infirmed to travel. The road was well travelled by goat herders and tradespeople travelling from town to town. This morning the route was busy. Horse pulled carts rocked and creaked as they rolled over the uneven rutted dirt path. Some of the faces she had seen before while walking this road. Many of them recognized her as well and nodded to her as she passed. Riti was smaller than her village but it was more important given it was near a crossroads to two northern roads. They called this area The King's Y because it had the shape of that letter and old King's mausoleum stood there. The name of the King however, had been lost to time. Genesis had grown hungry and stopped at the roadside to eat some of the bread she carried with her. She found a large rock and sat down to eat. She was passed by a number of people going either north or south.

After a time she had had her fill of bread and was preparing to continue on when she glanced north. Some two hundred paces away approached five hooded figures on horseback. They were dressed in much the same way as a man she had seen in her village earlier in the month. They stood out greatly from everyone else on this road. They carried no pennants and wore no sigils on their cloaks, yet their horsemanship was proficient in ways riders in this area were not. Their gate was far more orderly and they travelled with a deliberate purpose. Genesis was wary of them and pretended not to pay them much notice as they passed. She continued to watch them for a good while after they did. She again prepared to continue on her way until she noticed one of the riders separate from the group and head back in her direction. Genesis stood up and stared walking north again at a calm pace. A short while later the rider trotted up next to her and adjusted the horse's gate to match her speed. Genesis continued to walk forward not giving the rider any obvious attention. The rider responded by advancing ahead and stopping at the side of the road. Cloaked in a long brown robe with a large hood, the rider dismounted the horse and walked toward Genesis stopping about ten paces head of her and pulled back the hood. It was the face of a wanderer. A she-wolf stood before her with gold fur and almost burning emerald eyes that glowed with an air of nobility. She walked up to Genesis in a non-threatening way.

"If you beg my pardon. But might you be Mystic Genesis Payne?" the she-wolf said. Genesis gave the she-wolf a careful look over. If the she-wolf was armed she kept her weapons concealed. There was no way to tell whom she rode for given she wore just a plain brown cloak. Many wanderers served with ranger packs, but not all of them. It was poor judgment to throw around one's name, even along a road as safe as this one generally was. Even so there was something about this wanderer that stood out as trustworthy.

"I am. And who might you be?" She said. The she wolf smiled and held out her paw in greeting.

"I am Southstar Redflower. Corporal__ excuse me, sorry. Lieutenant of the Barley Lands Rangers. Newly promoted. Still getting used to my rank. I have travelled a long way to meet you," she said. Southstar looked trustworthy and the Redflower name was known even here, but Genesis was still guarded.

"What business do you have with me?" she said. Southstar could sense her reservation and tucked her paw back under her cloak.

"I do apologize for approaching you like this. I am here in regards to the Autumn Solstice?" she said. Genesis wondered why a southern ranger would want to talk to her about the Autumn Solstice.

"What is it you want to know about the Autumn Solstice?" she asked. Southstar looked up and down the road and then back at Genesis.

"I'd rather speak about this away from here," she said. Genesis sighed and looked at the she-wolf impatiently.

"I will be free later. I have business in the next town. When I am done I can talk all you want about either Solstice at length. My normal fee is ten coppers for a full reading. Is this acceptable?' she said. Southstar smiled.

"It is," she said. Genesis hadn't noticed Southstar's companions had ridden back to them as well. They remained a good thirty paces away. She glanced over her shoulder at them and then looked back to Southstar.

"Very well. I live at the end of the road of the town south of here. Meet me there when the shadows are an arms length to the east," Genesis said. Southstar looked at her companions and then back at Genesis.

"Agreed. We'll entertain ourselves somehow until then," she said as she walked back to her horse and mounted. Genesis watched them as the rangers departed south down the road. Southern rangers this far north was strange. It was yet another oddity building up to The Days.

Estrello and Angelica stood near the back of the church. They both sang 'How Great Thou Art' along with the other members of the congregation. They would normally be in one of the middle pews, but they had arrived later than usual. Something noticed by some of the older ladies that Estrello and Angelica called The Abuelitas. They were a group of gossipers who would no doubt have something to say later. No matter how many sermons Pastor Dale Sugar preached about the price of gossip, The Abuelitas still engaged in it. Particularly Mrs. Mendoza. She was the oldest and worst of them all. Only about half of them were here today. There was a Mission Trip to Guatemala some of them were on. When the Nocivos arrived there were of course looks thrown their way by Mrs. Mendoza and her clique. A group awfully invested in Angelica's personal life. They didn't concern themselves much with Estrello after finding out he was already married. Apart from asking every once and a while about his wife's scientific work abroad they left Estrello alone. It was a cover story, but one that was technically accurate. She had to be seen distancing herself from Estrello or else she would be targeted by those who burned him and his career down. Simply killing him was not enough. Corroding his entire existence and separating him from those he loved was part of the plan. Departing on an Antarctic scientific expedition made for sufficient optics while also not attracting the wrong kinds of attention. The outside observer assumed estrangement. Angelica had been similarly defamed. Her law enforcement career had been tarnished beyond repair with fabricated ties to drug dealers and human trafficking hung around her neck. It made her a wanted woman. Here on Gary's world she faced a different kind of scrutiny that was less of the criminal nature, but nonetheless annoying. At the end of the song Pastor Sugar stood at his podium and looked out at the congregation with a kind smile.

"Please rise and go forth my brothers and sisters and have a blessed day and a blessed week. Show everyone you meet the kindness and love we have all shared here today in the name of The Father, of The Son, and of The Holy Spirit. And the people said, amen," he said. The congregation echoed his petition for grace. The organist began playing again and Pastor Sugar walked down between the rows of pews to take a position at the doors to the narthex so he could bid everyone good day.

The deacons took their positions at the front pews and began ushering people from them. As they reached doors beyond the last pews they warmly shook hands with the Pastor. Estrello and Angelica watched as each row before theirs was ushered up and down. After several minutes it was their turn. They were the last in their row to exit their pew. Deacons George and Stanley gave them both warm smiles as they made their way to the narthex. When they got to Pastor Sugar he gave Estrello a big handshake.

"We were worried y'all might not make it. Mrs. Mendoza was asking about you right up until the service started," he said. Angelica smiled.

"It's good to know that we're missed. We're still pretty new here," she said. Pastor Sugar chuckled.

"Oh now. It doesn't matter if you're new or a longtime member. You're still family here," he said warmly and shook Angelica's hand as well. She smiled and walked into the narthex with her brother. It didn't take Mrs. Mendoza and the others long to notice her. She, Mrs. De La Hoya, Mrs. Duran and Mrs. Glendenning approached her with enormous smiles.

"Ay que linda! So good to see you! I was worried you wouldn't make it mami," she said and gave Angelica a hug. Mrs. Glendenning had a very large smile.

"Such a beautiful dress Angel. You look so lovely," she said and continued to before giving Angelica a hug as well. She did make it a point to dress well for church. She also saw Mrs. Taylor, another Abulita, out of the corner of her eye. It was then she knew the interrogation was about to commence.

About forty minutes after the service a Bobby Brown song played on the radio playing in the restaurant. It wasn't the version Estrello was accustomed to. This one had less of an early 90s sound and more of a Four Tops 1960s flavor to it.

Estrello took a sip of his coffee and set it down. He then picked up his East LA taco and dipped into the spicy green sauce he loved when he and his sister ate their post church meal at their favorite Las Palapas restaurant. She always had the chorizo and egg tacos. What had become routine every Sunday the questions about what Mrs. Mendoza and her crew threw at Angelica would come up. But Estrello wanted to finish his coffee. Though he would take the opportunity to ask for more as a waitress passed by.

"Mas café' por favor," he said. The waitress smiled and topped his off mug from the carafe she was carrying. Estrello enjoyed the aroma and set the mug down. Angelica knew something was coming by the smirk on her brother's face. Estrello was not one to try to hide his enjoyment for teasing his sister.

"So?" he said and smiled before taking another bite of his taco. Angelica rolled her eyes.

"Yes. They asked about Antonio. We take him to church with us one time. One. Time. And they think I'm dating him," she said with a sigh. Estrello laughed a little.

"Oh I've gathered that. What do you tell them?" he said and finished off his first taco. He picked up a second one and dipped it in delicious spicy green sauce. Angelica had become used to this torment.

"All that I can say is that he's been working hard. I didn't mention quite a bit. The less you say, the better," she said. Estrello finished chewing his food and laughed.

"Claro. Esto es cierto. All it took was one time and they're ready to marry you off to Tony," he said and snickered before taking a small sip of his coffee. Angelica rolled her eyes again and sighed.

"They know he has money. A lot of money. Or else they'd be trying to match me with one of the young guys at church. They evidently think I'm high maintenance," she said with a slight scowl. Estrello smiled.

"Well you do like the fancy peanut butter hermana. They mean well I guess," he said. Angelica scoffed.

"Anyway I'm not dating any of your weird friends. I don't care if they have money," she said. Estrello nearly spit out his coffee. He coughed a bit trying to catch his breath.

"Oh my goodness. Holy shit," he could barely say. Angelica just gave him a dirty look. Estrello held up a finger.

"Well, you're not wrong. Tony is an odd egg," he added once he regained his composure. As cringe inducing as this conversation was she was glad they were getting it over with now, and not have to visit it later in the week. Even so she still had a few gripes.

"They said they loved his TV commercial. They said he was very handsome and I should snatch him up quick before some other woman does. I don't think they know what he's really like," she said. Estrello nodded.

"I guess not. Though you may not know as much about him as you think you do," he said and took another bite of taco. Angelica turned and gave Estrello some side eye.

"Oh, what don't I know?" she said. Estrello finished chewing his food.

"Can't say I know a great deal more, but I think he's had a rough time. There's a lot about his divorce he doesn't talk about. He loves his Codona. His girl means the world to him. That's why he fights like I fight. But I think there is also something he feels he's missed. I think that's the family life that goes along with being a father. He's mentioned a few bad false starts after Jessica. I think he's jaded and he hides it. He's not like us. He's frequently dishonest about how he's feeling. It makes his motivations harder to follow. I think he's just a regular guy in this respect," he said and took another sip of coffee. Angelica almost felt like her brother was trying to sell the idea of Tony to her.

"Yes, well, I'm not the solution to his problem. I do hope that he does find someone that doesn't just break him more," she said. Sensing the reasoning behind some of the resistance in her voice Estrello clarified his intent.

"I do too. I don't know how comfortable I'd actually be with you dating someone I worked with. Seems like a bad idea. But Tony is going to have a hard time no matter what he does. What we do makes it hard.

I already have Laura and a way to get back to her. Tony won't, should he meet anyone when we're out. We don't go back to mission scenes after we're done. Too much risk of shear," he said. Angelica looked out the window.

"This is a big city. There are no ladies out there for a rich guy who drives an expensive car?" she mused. Estrello gave that one a bit of thought and looked out the window as well.

"I don't think he has a hookup in mind. That's all there seems to be in the culture right now. Blame social media if you will. This place is a weird mash-up of the 70s and 80s from our universe, but social media still has the same corrosive effect. Even if it's far less here," he said. Angelica smiled.

"So somebody on the crew then?" she said and laughed. Estrello grimaced.

"Hijole no. That's a whole other can of worms," he said while shaking his head. Angelica sighed and picked up the saltshaker next to her.

"He's going to figure something out if he wants it bad enough," she said. Estrello took a sip of coffee and set his mug down.

"Claro que si. All the best to him though," he said then finished off his taco.

Jack was still plenty caffeinated from his campaign earlier. His party triumphantly defeated the Skeleton Baron and his boney minions, even with the newbie Sully playing. Jack was still in the mood for winning. He peered out at security officer Chandler Moon from under the furry brim of his fuzzy hat. The sly competitor had paddle in one hand and a light white ball in the other. The pair of them glared at each other looking for weaknesses. Any crack or dent in the other's armor. Others looked on from their seats in Common Room 16. Behind them animatronic animals played instruments on a stage. Pauly, taking a break from the range, sat next to Ted who had a six-pack of beer riding on Moon. He always bet against Jack, no mater who he was playing, or what. This match was special though. It was the playoffs. The winner would go onto the next round to play Dougie who also sat and watched. This was Sunday Funday and there was always a ping-pong tournament going on. When one concluded, another one started always on a Sunday when both Angelica and Estrello would be at church. Members of security in particular took this time to gravitate to Common Room 16 to have a bit of fun. Until Chelsea Towers eventually showed up to harang people into taking safety modules they had neglected to.

Everyone understood it was her job, but when she showed up there were the inevitable groans and rolled eyes. Jack bounced the ball on the table and grinned at Moon. Moon grinned back. Jack dropped the ball again but this time struck it. It sailed over the net and landed on Moon's side. With a knock of his paddle, Moon returned it over to Jack. It bounced with good height so Jack slapped at it sending it cross-court only to be caught by Moon's reflexes. The ball sailed back over the net. Jack pivoted to his backhand and tapped it back. Moon seized on the chance and quickly batted it back. Jack swung, but just missed. Moon raised his hands in victory. He then pointed over at Dougie who shook his head and waved him away dismissively. Ted clapped and looked back at Nelson Cho sitting behind him.

"Pay up good sir," he said sarcastically. Nelson looked over at Jack and frowned.

"Damn it Jack. You said you had it in the bag," he said. Moon chuckled.

"In the game of ping pong, never bet against the man with one nipple," he said and laughed. Jack just raised his hands. Pauly looked back at Nelson with his bearded smirk.

"Far better is it to dare mighty things, to win glorious triumphs, even though checkered by failure, than to rank with those poor spirits who neither enjoy nor suffer much, because they live in that gray twilight that knows not victory nor defeat," he said still smirking. Dougie raised a brow.

"Teddy Roosevelt ain't playing Moon next. I am ha ha. Go get an ice cream sandwich and let Teddy rest in peace," he said. Ted snickered.

"I'm pretty well rested, but I appreciate your concern. I'm just going enjoy collecting my 12 beers and watching Bubblegum Crisis after my shift," Ted said and chuckled. Dougie groaned at the bad joke and stood up to stretch. Moon pointed at Dougie.

"Remember, if I win, you have to watch Tron Legacy with me. That was the wager," he said. Walked over and picked up a paddle and then pointed at Moon.

"And don't you forget I'm taking you to Chunky's. I'm going to watch you take at least one bite of that Ghost Chili burger if you lose. Best believe that," he said. Ted snickered.

"Isn't that a bit excessive. I mean aren't you a believer in the greatness of Garrett Hedlund?" he said with a smile. Dougie tapped on the table and then pointed at Ted.

"Okay I liked him in Eragon. Yes, I liked Eragon. I thought it was a pretty cool movie. I like shit with dragons," he said and then pointed over at Jack who was sitting down and pouting after his loss to Moon. Jack pulled out a coin and looked over at Moon.

"Okay call it," he said. Moon thought for a moment.

"Tails," he said. Jack nodded and then flipped the coin up onto the table. Both the competitors looked at it. It was heads. Dougie laughed.

"Prepare to eat fire my brother. Your ass is going to Chunky's," he said and laughed again. Moon tapped on the table.

"Oh we'll see. I hope you like Daft Punk," he said. Dougie grinned from ear to ear.

"Listen to him. Listen, to him. You about to spit fire my man," he said and served. Near one of the entrances to Common Room 16, Chelsea entered as the animatronic band began playing an Adele Dazeem song, carrying her clipboard. She also brought with her a cheerful demeanor some found unsettling, but others found quite pleasant. Ted glanced over his shoulder and caught sight of her. He tapped Jack on the shoulder.

Neither was up to date on their safety modules. Jack pointed to the arcade cabinets nearby. Both of them got up nonchalantly and headed over there. They ducked behind the Arkanoid machine and looked around the other side of it. Chelsea was walking toward another group of crew near the ice cream vending machine. Jack looked around for the east exit but saw a couple of crewmen pulling a pallet of bottled water through the exit door on a pallet jack and a wheel was caught on something. They tugged at it forcefully but had trouble pulling the pallet back. It just rocked back and forth. Jack looked back around the Arkanoid machine but didn't see Chelsea. Then he looked back at Ted to see her standing right behind him. She was smiling big and bright.

"Hey guys. Playing some Arkanoid? I love this game," she said. Jack and Ted smiled.

"Greatest game ever," Jack said and chuckled uncomfortably. Chelsea smiled even bigger.

"It sure is. Guess that's why you guys haven't watched a bunch of your training modules. Too busy playing Arkanoid. I get it. I do. But what neither of you will get is my high score. Boom!" she said and pointed to the leaderboard on the cabinet screen. There in glowing letters was 'CTR' next to a ridiculously high number. Ted grinned.

"What's the 'R' stand for?" he said. Chelsea smirked.

"It stands for 'Rules' because I rule. Neither of you chumps have what it takes to knock the queen off her throne. Now, if you'll follow me. The both of you owe me some modules," she said and gestured to Jack and Ted to follow her. Ward and Ian sat down next to Pauly and watched as Chelsea led away a dejected Jack and a grinning Ted.

"Looks like she hooked her a pair of fish," Ward said. Pauly nodded and took a sip of his drink.

"Guess they should have showed up to the training seminar," Ian said and laughed. Pauly smiled.

"Oh and I have both of them slated for firearms qualifications today. They're not going to avoid that either. As Teddy Roosevelt put it 'There has never yet been a man in our history who led a life of ease who's name is worth remembering.' He also said 'The first requisite of a good citizen in this republic of ours is that he shall be able and willing to pull his own weight.' They will at least have some fun doing that on the range. Training modules, not so much though" He said. Ward and Ian chuckled and began watching Dougie and Moon.

Tents dotted the area around Glosten Hill as Flint expected. He was followed by Raven, Tracker and Alpine. All were his brothers from later litters. Raven was the largest of them standing taller than Flint himself. He had jet-black fur with tufts of brown fur near his paws. Tracker was yellow in color like his twin sister Southstar. They looked like Brewster's great grandfather Sunrise Redflower. The third born pup in Southstar and Tracker's litter was Pepper. The youngest sibling was Alpine who had light fur. It was a pale gray much lighter than Flint's coat. He was smaller but gifted with a blade. He carried the pennant of The Barley Lands Leaf on high. Prince Carcino's soldiers rode out to greet the wanderers and the small group of men they brought with them.

The highest ranking of them was a Corporal named Ridel Ammai who transferred from a northern ranger pack from the north of the Borderlands. He was well versed in the cultures of The Midlands and became helpful whenever perspective was needed on northern affairs. The north was not of great concern this evening though. As afternoon faded the rangers escorted by Southgate soldiers made their way to the center of camp. They could hear sounds of celebration already. Flint could smell ale in the air. He knew the brew well. This ale came from a small town east of Glosten Hill. It was a particular variety only made from a certain type of barley and brewed at only one time of year. Prince Carcino had apparently sent men into town to purchase it. From the aroma in the air, they purchased quite a lot of it. Much of that aroma was coming from one tent in particular. It was far larger than the rest. The Southgate soldiers led the rangers to this one. The door flaps were wide open and dozens of soldiers and officers stood around facing inward.

Flint could hear a loud voice coming from within. Then he saw the Prince standing in the middle of the tent with a flagon of ale in hand. He appeared as though he was going to make a toast of some sort. Their arrival was timely it seemed. Carcino held up his flagon and looked around at the men in the tent.

"The Day Has Come! My brother is to be betrothed. To whom I do not know. Our King's message was not that specific. I could make speculations to whom my future sister-in-law may be, but I won't bother. I'll find out eventually. But whoever she is I make a toast to her as well as to my brother. A miracle is truly unfolding before us. Prince Attheon is about to put his arrow in a target not made of straw!" he shouted. The tone felt somewhat crude but the men around Flint laughed. He'd heard that southern humor was bit rough and brash. He hadn't heard much first hand until now. Prince Carcino continued.

"To my brother. Your Prince. Your future King. And his future Queen. To Attheon!" he yelled. The men cheered loudly and all began taking drinks from their flagons. Carcino spotted Flint and his rangers then. He beckoned them forth. The small group of rangers walked into the tent graciously. Prince Carcino announced them to his men.

"Men! I want you to welcome Flint Redflower. First born son of The High Chieftain, Brewster Redflower of Pack Redflower. And High Captain of The Barley Lands Pack." he said loudly. There were looks of awe coming from the men in and around the tent. Flint and his brothers knew this look. They saw it often when their father's name was mentioned. Wanderers did not formally have a system of royalty in their culture. But there was a hierarchy of esteem. High Chieftain was considered an equivalent title to that of a King by most outsiders despite it being more of a spiritual position usually passed down in the culture itself through a committee of elders and other pack leaders. Though pack Redflower had been the favored family to pass the title down for quite some time.

They inspired the kind of strength pack elders respected. Other races with hierarchal systems looked at the High Chieftain as something of a King regardless of how wolves felt about it. It's something wanderers had become accustomed to over the centuries despite their efforts to clarify. Hundreds of years ago Redflowers were not rangers. They were brewers and masters of their craft. Flint's father's name came from this bit of family history.

"You honor us Prince Carcino," Flint said. Carcino managed a smile, even if it was just a small one.

"Please Flint, call me Carcino. As I see it, we are both Princes. When your father passes you will take his place as High Chieftain. They are the Kings of your people. You and your brothers are as much Princes as I am in my eyes. You need a drink," he said. He'd clearly had more than a few flagons of ale before Flint and his brothers arrived. Carcino snapped his fingers to a few of his men who started filling up cups for Flint and his party. Flint took a flagon and held it up to his men.

"To Prince Attheon and The Hall Lamb. May the Strength of Southgate never falter," Flint toasted to his rangers. Carcino was moved to hear these words. Especially from the pup of a legend such as Brewster Redflower who was a warrior that even a Prince of Southgate could look up to. In many ways a King he looked up to more than his own father.

"Hear Hear!" Carcino said. Raven wasn't partial to ale but to took one and drank out of respect for Attheon of Southgate who was a man known for his prowess with a bow. A skill he had respect for. Tracker loved a good ale himself especially a nice dark one from the Barley Lands. Alpine could take or leave ale. He just wanted to talk to the southerners and hear all their stories. Carcino had heard that like himself Flint Redflower was a business-first type of man, and on most nights Carcino himself would dispense with the frivolity, but tonight was not most nights. He snapped his fingers and another flagon of ale was handed to him. He took that cup and handed it to Flint who had just finished off the last one.

"Grim tales have their time High Captain, and will. Tonight there is necessary merriment to be had. I'm sure you would agree," he said. Flint did agree, but only because he understood what something like a royal engagement meant to all of the lands south of The Midlands. He was also wary of what kind of news this was to the rest of Gatheria. The decline of Southgate had long been predicted since the death of its Prince Mercurian and the virtual absence of it's next in line in Prince Attheon.

Many regarded Carcino as Southgate's last best hope for survival in this changing world. Many supported him that did not support Attheon. Politically speaking, this would shake some things up. This made Flint nervous. It had been three generations since the last real war. The Barley Lands were fortunate this war was confined to the west beyond the lands controlled by Hall Redflower. He also saw what such a war did to the Hall Brian, which was the only Hall in the south with a might anywhere near that of Southgate. Still, their armies were significantly smaller. They could never have waged the kind of full-scale war a power like Southgate could unleash. There are many good reasons that Southgate was feared as much as The Empire itself. So much balanced on a thread. Flint did not know what role the ranger packs would have in any war. They were forbidden to take sides in any conflict. There would be dissenters. And where would the packs go while their territories burned? Where would the people go? How would the Midlanders treat refugees?

All these questions weighed on Flint's mind. He was sure he wasn't the only one. Carcino drank deeply from his flagon and cheered on one of his men who danced around with a burlap sack on his head. Flint was not a superstitious wolf, but he'd heard of The Tides. A dark paw rested on his shoulder. Flint turned to see the face of his wife Midnight Stardance-Redflower who had retired recently as a Lieutenant of the Grass Lands Ranger pack. Her belly was large with at least two of his pups. Flint embraced her warmly. He was surprised to see her here. But at the same time not.

"Wife, why do you venture out?" he said. Midnight laughed.

"Would I miss a party such as this? I think not husband. The house was dreary and I grew tired of listening to the midwives chatter on," she said. Flint laughed.

"Rascal of a woman. I should get you a chair," Flint jested. Midnight waved her paw around.

"You'll do no such thing Flint Redflower. I won't be here long. I just wanted to see some dance, hear some song, and tender my congratulations to Prince Carcino on his brother's pending engagement. Flint smiled and took her paw. They walked over to where Carcino was. He was watching two of his men dance in a circle with sacks on their heads. The two wolves caught his attention.

"May I introduce my wife Midnight," he said proudly. Carcino greeted her with a shallow bow as was customary for one royal to greet another.

"Princess Midnight. Your reputation precedes you," he said formally. Midnight smiled graciously. Even though her people didn't use that particular title she appreciated the gesture and the respect paid.

"Thank you Prince Carcino," she said. Carcino shook his head.

"No no. As I explained to your husband. Call me Carcino. He is as much a Prince as I," he said. Then he noticed Midnight's belly. A look of joy came over his stony face.

"Oh and look. Praise the Wind. You carry pups. Grandsons of Brewster! Sons of Flint! I raise my cup to a new generation of

Redflowers! May they call me Uncle Carcino," Carcino said and the men behind him clapped their hands loudly with gusto. Flint smiled at Midnight and placed his paw on her belly. He felt a kick then. His heart skipped a beat and his eyes glinted with love and pride.

The day was waning and a chill was beginning hover in the air. Genesis wrapped her shawl more tightly around herself as she walked down the road to her father's house. Her reading with the old man didn't take as long as she expected. He desired to know if his son's goats would be fertile in the coming spring. Her reading was favorable. It was good to see the joy in his eyes. It helped her forget her meeting later in the day for a time. But she had had plenty of time to dwell on it during the walk back to her village. As she neared her father's house she saw a few horses hitched to the fencing in front. The riders clearly knew which house she resided in. The wooden door creaked open as she entered. Her father's happy face greeted her. He was not alone though. Three others sat in the room with him. One face was of course that of Southstar Redflower. She looked up as Genesis walked over and sat by her father. Another wanderer with white fur sat beside Southstar that she was not acquainted with. The other visitor was a human man who was bald and rough looking. All wore the Leaf sigil and sat quietly as if they expected her to lead in with some sort of introductory proverb. She had no such wisdom to impart.

"Good evening father. Good evening rangers of the Barley Lands," she said. Her father hugged her around the shoulder.

"Good evening my child. How was your reading?" he said. She smiled.

"It was gladly pleasing. Old Handby will have a successful spring. He was most relieved. Last spring went poorly for him and his sons," she said. Her father poured her a cup of tea and handed it to her.

"Fresh mint from the garden that we've been enjoying while we waited," he said. Genesis took a sip. The herbs were greatly refreshing. She detected a bit of lemon. Southstar took a sip from her cup as well and set the cup back down.

"I'm sure you would like me to expand on what we spoke about earlier," she said. Genesis set her cup down and folded her hands in her lap.

"Yes. You mentioned wanting to know something about the Autumn Solstice. In these lands we call the arrival of autumn the festival of The Days. It's a week of feasts, games, and music. I'm quite fond of the joust, but father thinks it's too violent," she said. Her father chuckled.

"My child it is a dreadful sport. I have no taste for it at all. I don't know what appeal it has for you," he said. Genesis laughed.

"It's fun father," she said. Vincent Payne sighed and shook his head. Genesis looked back over at Southstar.

"Was there anything specific you wanted to know about The Days and the festivities that happen on individual days, or do you just have a general curiosity about them? I don't mean to sound rude, but you and your rangers did travel a great distance about something you could have asked anyone in these lands about," she said. Southstar looked over at her rangers and then back at Genesis.

"You're right. We could have asked anyone. And we did. Many people. Many with the same gifts as you and your father possess. Earlier in the month we came here and asked for a reading of The Days. We came away with more questions than answers. So we consulted more mystics. Much the same result. We heard from one of them that you were a talented reader as well. You father did not mention that when we were here last. I imagine he didn't trust us. At least not initially. We've come to a better understanding this time," she said. Genesis looked at her father.

"I wanted to protect you child. The ranger who came here before did not identify himself as such. I was afraid. But a daughter of Brewster Redflower arrived at my door. It was then I knew my fears were unfounded. Please forgive me. Both of you," he said. Genesis held her father's hand.

"There is nothing to forgive father," she said and looked back at Southstar.

"I concur most wholeheartedly. Any father would want his child to be safe," she said. The rangers that sat by her appeared to grow impatient. Such was the temperament of rangers, always on the move. Genesis picked up on their restlessness and set her father's box of runes down in front of her.

"I believe that was ten copper for a full reading," she said. Southstar cocked her head to the side.

"We really only have one question to ask, but we will pay in full," she said. Genesis was a bit taken off guard.

"You would be paying too much," she said insistently. Southstar just shook her head.

"Think nothing of it," she said. Genesis looked at her father and then back at Southstar. She took the runes from the box and held them out in her hand.

"Okay, very well. What is your question?" she asked. A serious look overtook Southstar's face.

"How do the humors fare in the winds upon the fourth day?" she said. Genesis without thinking threw the runes up and let them fall to the floor. She looked down at them. To her surprise all the runes faced down. Everyone in the room fell silent and looked at the runes. She recalled the readings her father had made for himself. She looked up at Southstar. Her face was grim as she looked over at her companions. Southstar looked over at Genesis.

"If you'll forgive me. We hoped for a different outcome. But it seems there is a great deal more we need to know," she said and took out a small bag of coins and set them down in front of Genesis and her father. Vincent picked the bag up. There felt like more than ten copper in it. He was speechless. Genesis wasn't.

"What brought you to ask about the fourth day? Why does it command the runes so?" she said insistent seriousness. Southstar looked down for a few moments. Then she looked back up at Genesis.

"What I tell you mustn't go farther than you two," she said. Genesis and her father looked at each other. Genesis nodded. Southstar looked over at the others. They seemed disagreeable but did not voice dissent.

"On the fifteenth of last month a man was found barely alive riding alone along the northern edge of our territory. He had been gravely injured. All he could say before he passed was The Runes. The Solstice. The Fourth Day. He died while repeating these things over and over. We never learned the man's name. All he had to identify him was a pendant with the symbol of the wind engraved on it. The same symbol carved on the stone in the center of town. The same one painted on this house," she said. The story shook Genesis.

"Oh how awful," she said and held her father's hand. He looked at Southstar.

"Truly a terrible thing. He was probably from these lands. Followers of the Winds are common here. I will say a prayer for him tonight," he said and smiled at Genesis.

"I wish we could tell you more, but I have never seen readings like this. You may try a Temple of the Winds or maybe even inquire about it at one of The Wood Lodges," he said. Southstar looked away for a moment.

"The Temple of the Winds we could try. A Wood Lodge I already have. I have a brother who studies at one. I sent a feather some time back. He hasn't responded. We haven't been very close in recent years. Such a thing is regrettable," she said. Genesis knew how she felt.

"These things can be hard. I hope he does respond. Family is the most important thing. I will pray for him that he finds his way," she said. Southstar appreciated the gesture. It was time to depart though. She smiled at her hosts.

"Thank you for your hospitality. We will retire to our inn for the night. May your festival be joyous," she said as she and her companions stood up. Vincent and Genesis did as well.

"Many blessings for you on your journeys. My prayers will go with all of you," Genesis said as they began to file out of the house. Vincent then turned to her and hugged her.

"May the winds be kind to them," he said.

Chapter Six: Some Minutes Ahead

It was hot day toady. Oktoberfest was set to begin on Saturday the 21st. It was the 17th now. Estrello Nocivo could reasonably expect JP and Martha to be in New Braunfels for the weekend. JP's father may have been from Finland, but his mother was Hungarian. JP had been talking about Wurstfest for months now, since the event had been moved up do to outside circumstances, changing his November plans. Some of the crew of the Bumppo would be going with him. Their plan was to rent a party bus. Conceivably they could get home safely even if the lot of them were shitfaced drunk. Not that there was much fear. JP would be along. On his list of snafus, drunkenness was not among them. Martha did not have a driver's license for Gary's World that he knew of. Ironic given that she could co-pilot a Pathfinder, a vehicle substantially more complex than a bus. Despite no need for her to be a designated driver, JP would not be allowing her any of the variety of fermented beverages available at the event. Estrello sat alone at wooden park bench near his favorite taco truck run by a colorful character named Roscoe Reynosa. Good for a laugh and made great tacos like Estrello's grandmother made in Mexico. The corn tortillas were freshly made just like hers. She called him her El Pequeño Rubio. He wasn't an actual blonde. Instead he had form of albinism that made his hair appear blonde while his eyes remained a very dark brown. If he did not have this condition his hair would be the same color as his sister's. The albinism came from his father's side of the family. He'd seen photos of his great grandfather and two of his sisters standing next to their brother who had black hair. If it weren't for some common facial resemblance one would assume they might not be related. Family lore seemed to indicate the albinism shows up about every 3rd generation or so. Estrello expected to see one of his grandchildren carry this trait.

He knew they would have the same sensitivity to the sun as he did, but the virtually odorless sunscreen Antonio Salazar developed for him mitigated that greatly. He would gift that to them so their time in the sun would be more comfortable than his was when he was growing up.

He hoped they'd enjoy a good squeeze of lime on their tacos as well. He picked up a wedge and gave it a good pinch. Delicious citrus dripped down. A low hum then emanated from his phone. He pulled it out and clicked it on. He'd received a text from Jack. JP's CityNet project was about to be activated. Through Salazar, key properties had been purchased all over the city and at each of these location devices were set up to conceal the massive energy surge that occurred every time the Bumppo was dashed. A fact everyone found out the hard way the last time the ship was launched. The city was visited by The US Nuclear Regulatory Commission, which investigated the city thoroughly for what caused the energy spike. Suspicion that radioactive material had been leaking somewhere in the city had begun raising alarms. The Bumppo had to be put in dark mode for several days, which meant minimal systems. It made for an uncomfortable weekend without heat once the vessel's internal temperature began to drop. CityNet was meant to prevent this from happening by blocking the Bumppo's dash wake the same way the ship itself concealed the dash wake of individuals or small craft. Estrello and JP talked about this extensively and both came to the conclusion that a second detection would bring the Civic Protectors in force to San Antonio. This was something both men wanted to avoid. Nocivo clicked on the app the Jack had installed on his phone. A map came up with green dots all over it. This meant, at least in theory, everything was running, as it should. He clicked off the app and called Jack's number. The phone rang for a few seconds. Then Jack picked up.

"Skipper! Is it all green on your end?" he said. Nocivo did not place a lot of faith in technology.

"The app indicates green. We will see if it holds up to testing. Is Evie ready to begin?" he said. He could hear Jack on the other end tapping on his tablet.

"Looks like we're good to go Skip," Jack said. Nocivo hated this part. He took his tablet out of his satchel and clicked it on. It took a minute to boot. As soon as it was up he clicked on app installed for the test. He picked his phone back up.

"Hit it," he said. Just then the graphic on his tablet came alive indicating the testing had started. The numbers looked good here at the onset, but Estrello was still wary.

"If it get's to 51% shut the test down Jack," he said.

"Understood," Jack replied. The test would last only a minute but it would soon become a very long minute. The percentage rose from 2% to 12% in just a few seconds. This was troubling. Then it jumped to 18% and then 27% at only twenty seconds in. This was not good at all and a few seconds later it jumped again to 39%, which was far faster than any of the simulations projected. Nocivo was ready to pull the plug. But ten more seconds went by. No change. Another five went by. The number dropped to 32%. It held steady there until the test was over. Nocivo could hear Jack high fiving people in the room with him.

"Hell Yeah! Stable at 32% baby!" Jack yelled. Nocivo wiped the sweat from his brow.

"Damn fine work Jack. Damn fine work," he said as he could hear cheering on the other end. He hung up and shut off his tablet. After taking a deep breath he finished off his last taco and collected his things. His motorcycle was parked nearby. Now he was going to take a relaxing ride.

Antonio stood at lane 3 waiting for his paper target to return. He hadn't shot at anything since getting back from Phoenix. He wanted to put himself thorough the paces. He wasn't pleased thus far. His head was foggy and he was having trouble focusing on his work. All of his scheduled research was suspended until he was confident he could hold a beaker without his hand shaking or losing track of what he was doing.

Behind him Quiz was collecting spent casings with a brass retriever. Pauly watched on and perhaps the only other person in the room disappointed with what the paper showed when it arrived. Antonio dropped his magazine and racked the slide of his Walther P99 a few times. Then he laid it down with the barrel pointed down range and pulled the target from the clips holding it. He examined his grouping and frowned when he saw how many minutes of arc separated it from the strays. A single stray would be normal. But not a few that deviated so far away from the main grouping. He held the paper up to show Pauly and Quiz. They both grimaced. Antonio sighed and pressed the button rendering his lane cold. Blue lights came on.

"Cringy as fuck," he groaned and took off his cans. Quiz shook his head. Pauly shrugged his shoulders.

"You're being too hard on yourself. You got shot in the head man. Shot in the head. Repeatedly. Nearly everyone that does, doesn't walk away from that. Most that do, aren't the same. Granted, none of them were wearing an advanced helmet made from materials cooked up by a master chemist, that are impressive even by 25th century standards. But you get my point," he said. Quiz patted Antonio on the shoulder reassuringly.

"Don't beat yourself up man. Sometimes you have to take the hard road back," he said. Pauly took his cans down from around his neck and laid them down on the table next to him.

"I've been sitting here watching you fight yourself for the last hour. It's sad to watch, because I know you're a guy who likes to have his shit together. When it's not, well, you fight yourself. Sad to see. As Emerson put it 'Life is a succession of lessons which must be lived to be understood' which means no short cuts. Challenges will come. When they do, don't make yourself just another enemy you have to defeat. Take each shot as it comes and build up slowly, because we can all see you're not zeroed in. And that's okay. Build back to it," Pauly said in his deep radio voice. Antonio folded his arms.

"Thanks man. You have a way with words bro. Good at putting things in perspective," he said. Quiz set his brass collector against the wall and sat down on a stool next to it.

"A good motivational turn of phrase is good at sanding down the rough edges. But they're just words to get you going. In other words 'Well done is better than well said.' It's still you that has to put lead down range. Ain't nobody else's hands holding the pistol. Just you. Work with you," he said. Antonio smirked and looked over at Pauly.

"He's been hanging around you too much Pauly. Now you got him quoting Ben Franklin," he said. Pauly shrugged his shoulders again.

"I could have him quoting The Legend of Bagger Vance but that would be a little too on the nose. Even for us," he said and picked his cans back up. He pointed back to the lane.

"Lock and load Tony. Hang up another paper," he said. Antonio smiled and turned back to the lane to pick up where he left off.

Traffic had picked up some but overall wasn't bad for this time of day. Nocivo sat on his Indian behind a loud diesel truck he was glad wasn't rolling coal. To his right was a basketball court with several teenagers hanging out on it. They weren't playing basketball though. Speakers had been set up. Sick beats emanated from them from Ludacris, but not how he was used to. This sounded more like late 80s KRS-One. He liked the old school spin on the 'Get Back' that just seemed to work. He was impressed. He was also impressed by the vibe of the kids break dancing to it. Antonio and JP showed him one time all about the movement from when they were growing up. They started breaking down cardboard boxes and he asked them why they were doing that. They explained to him that he needed to learn about something called 'Pop and Lock.' To which they subsequently engaged in what they described as a dance battle where they tried to one-up each other by throwing down dance moves with ever increasing complexity.

It became intensely competitive at one point. He was surprised neither of them injured themselves. The light turned green and Nocivo continued on his way. A few blocks later was a residential neighborhood littered with campaign signs. There were a lot for the Whig candidate. There were still many with signs for the candidate endorsed by the outgoing Federalist incumbent. President Sanders. On his world Sanders went on to coach college football after retiring from the NFL. On Gary's World his massive grin did it's work in the Oval Office. Nocivo wasn't a registered voter here, but if he were he had more than a few issues with economy and would vote thusly. He wasn't under any illusion that special interests wouldn't always be out there to mitigate any meaningful changes regardless of whoever took office. He did have the advantage of knowing which hands shook and what money lined which pocket. Knowledge most voters did not possess or look for themselves. They tended to vote straight ticket without much thought which was acceptable for those disinterested in meaningful improvement.

"Get out and vote!" rang a commercial playing through his ear buds. He rolled his eyes and pressed on. Nocivo's private practice lay at the far edge of this neighborhood, which he made a point to visit periodically even though he almost never saw patients there. The man in charge most of the time was Doctor Trent Martinez. A man who didn't know Nocivo was stopping by. He took a right and began travelling down the neighborhood street that ran its length. A few blocks in and he began seeing emergency vehicles. Something went down here recently. A police barricade had already been set up. Several SAPD officers stood around the perimeter keeping an eye on activity around the cordoned off area. He road past a news van that was getting set up to start covering the story that was unfolding here. Nocivo stopped just short of the barricade. A SAPD officer walked up to the police tape and held up his hands.

"Sorry sir. This is a crime scene. You'll have to go around," he said. Nocivo took off his helmet and got off the bike. He set the helmet down on his seat and looked up at the officer.

"I'm a doctor. I have a private practice at the end of this street," he said. The officer shook his head.

"Sorry sir. Still can't let you by. Some bad shit went down here. You'll have to go around," he said. Nocivo looked around. He caught traces of blood in the air of multiple different scents. He figured there were many injured or dead in the immediate vicinity. No gun shot residue. No explosives. Violence was likely committed with edged or pointed weapons. Blunt force trauma was also a possibility. He wouldn't know until he was where the crimes took place.

"From here it will take me an hour or more if I have to go around. I can provide medical assistance if y'all need it," he said. The officer looked over at one of the others and then looked back at Nocivo and shook his head.

"EMS is already on scene. We have it covered. Thanks for the offer though," he said. Nocivo continued to size up the scene from where he was standing. From the chatter around the scene he pieced together that there was a single assailant and multiple victims. Perp was in custody.

Detectives were already here asking questions. He could see one nearby who was an older bald black man with a gray mustache wearing a gray sport coat over turquoise undershirt. His coat did not match his slacks. He didn't appear to have been on duty when the incident was called in. He was talking to a pair of officers who looked liked they'd seen something horrible. Given the strength of the scent of blood Nocivo put the scene of the crime about five houses down from where he was standing on the north side of the street. The officer started to grow impatient.

"What's the name of your private practice?" he said with hints of doubt in his voice. Nocivo looked at him.

"Hidalgo Family Medical Clinic. I am Doctor Estrello Nocivo. I own the practice," he said. The older detective turned his head slightly when he heard the name hit his ear. He turned and looked over at Nocivo. Then held up a hand.

"Sit tight boys. I have more questions for you. I'll be right back," he said and then began walking in Nocivo's direction. He stopped on the other side of the police tape and looked Nocivo over and folded his arms.

"You say your name is Nocivo? Any relation to private detective Angelica Nocivo?" he said. Estrello nodded and then shook his head.

"I am her brother. She is not a private detective though. Only a contracted researcher," he said. The detective held out a hand across the tape. Nocivo looked at it and then shook it.

"She's one hell of a researcher then. I got PI's dropping her name all the time anymore. New whiz kid on the block. Her intel has helped put away some damn bad people. And that's just in the last six months. It's a pleasure to make your acquaintance Doctor. Detective Ross Staples. Pleased to meet you," he said. Nocivo smiled.

"Likewise Detective," he said. Detective Staples gestured to one of the officers to lift the tape.

"Maybe EMS could use a hand," he said. Nocivo glanced in the direction of where he reckoned the ambulances were parked though he could not directly see them past the fire truck parked in front of them. He turned and retrieved his medical kit from his saddlebag and walked under the tape. The officer who stopped him earlier narrowed his eyes.

Nocivo and Staples walked past the fire truck out upon the bulk of the crime scene. Estrello's eyes immediately began reading it and breaking it down in his mind. In seconds he had mountain of information about what went down. He had many questions. They walked up to an ambulance where and EMS was tending to the wounds of an injured man. Staples caught the look in Nocivo's eyes. There was an intensity there that caught him a bit off guard. Estrello glanced around at the other EMS workers and the people they were tending to. Then he began scanning the scene again almost robotically. Staples didn't know what to make of it.

"It got pretty bad here. Of course I can't get into the details just yet. Open investigation and whatnot. A lot of hurt people here. But it looks like you sussed that out. Maybe a bit more," he said and rubbed his chin. Nocivo looked over at him.

"I'll get to work and write up a report if you need one," he said. Staples looked at his eyes then he looked around the scene again.

"That wont be necessary. Your help patching these folks up will be good. I'm curious though. What do you make of all this? If you don't mind me asking?" he said. Nocivo looked around again and then back at Staples.

"Not much without being closer to site of the incident. Though the injuries I am seeing look like defensive wounds caused by an edged weapon of some sort. I assume these are neighbors that tried to intervene, with something. I noticed your forensics team does not appear to be investigating a shooting. Nobody is photographing spent casings. Firearms could still be a factor isolated to one or more key areas inside the residence. But I doubt it. SWAT isn't here. No active shooter or hostage situation. I would gather this was domestic situation that turned deadly. The number of wagons here would indicate multiple fatalities. Traces of vomit in the air would indicate this scene is very bad. Semi-relaxed scene would indicate the perpetrator is either dead or in custody. Still, there is an edginess around," he said. Staples was blown away at what he just heard, looked around, and then turned to Nocivo.

"You pieced all that together just standing there? It must run in the family," he said. Nocivo raised a brow.

"I don't follow?" he said. Staples smiled uneasily.

"Investigation. Seems like your family just has a knack for it. Not your first time dealing the fallout from a crime scene I take it. Never gets easier does it?" he said. Nocivo sighed.

"No, it doesn't," he said. He would not mention that he was better at creating these kinds of scenes than he was at investigating them but only slightly though. He wasn't thinking of himself much at the moment though. At the moment his ears were awash with despair.

All around him all he could hear were utterings of shock, disbelief, dismay, horror and grief. What went down here uprooted this neighborhood. A street he drove down often past all of these very people. A cameraman was out scouting all the angles he could. He hoped he could catch a glimpse of the attacker. His view was blocked off considerably. Officers would only let the crew get so close, so he had to make his way along the tape a good distance until he ran into a tree. He mumbled his frustration under his breath a craned his neck around it to see if he could see anything.

A smile reached across his face. He could see a squad car in the distance. There was someone sitting in the back of it. The unit was too far away to see clearly with the eye, so he rushed back to the news van to get his camera. After retrieving it he rushed back to the tree and began zooming in. His heart skipped a beat and his blood ran cold when the camera focused to reveal the man in the police unit staring right at him. Through him, felt more accurate. The cameraman panicked and pivoted away and sat against the tree not wanting to move. Nocivo had taken off his jacket and cleansed his hands before he started tending to the wounded. If Staples wasn't coordinating with his officers he was watching Nocivo work. The EMS first responders appreciated the extra set of hands. After finishing applying bandages to a middle aged woman for her trip to the hospital Nocivo snapped off his gloves and tossed them into a bio box before turning to Staples who was still observing him.

"You are a good doctor, but if you were to ever consider joining the police academy, or even your sister for that matter, I could put in the good word for y'all," he said. Nocivo smiled. The irony never failed to hit him every time someone suggested he take up law enforcement.

"I appreciate the offer, but I'm forty years old, and I think Angelica is comfortable doing what she is already. Maybe it's my fault. I bought her a really comfy office chair for her birthday the other day," he said. Staples chuckled and pulled out a business card and handed it to Nocivo.

"It's all good man. Wish her a happy belated birthday for me. If you change your mind, here's my card," he said. Nocivo smiled and took it from him. He glanced to the side as an ambulance transporting wounded away drove off. Behind it a distance away was the vehicle containing the suspect. The cameraman picked himself up off the ground and began moving along the police tape for a different angle. Hopefully he could get a shot of the suspect where he wasn't being directly looked at.

He felt himself shudder and a cold sweat began to hamper him. He found a space that wasn't available just a while ago. Some vehicles had departed which gave him a better vantage point. He started to pick up his camera again but his hands were shaking too much. The news crew sound man walked up behind him and laid a hand on his shoulder. The cameraman jumped some and looked back. The sound man was surprised to see his colleague so jarred.

"Hey man what's wrong bro?" he said. The cameraman took several deep breaths.

"Got a look at the perp. Something is really bad wrong with the guy. Like seriously bad wrong man. It ain't normal bad wrong man," he said. The sound man looked past him at the police unit in the distance. He could barely make anything out. He looked down at the camera in his colleague's hand and took it. The cameraman looked at him in horror.

"You don't want to do that man. Nah man, you don't want to do that," he said, but the sound man had already started zooming in. The man in the police unit wasn't looking in his direction. The cameraman was right. Something was very wrong with this man. Then suddenly the man snapped a gaze at the sound man. His head lurched unnaturally to face him. All the sound man could do was gasp as it felt like all the air had been sucked out of his lungs. Then a cold wet sweat began oozing out of his pores. He tried to pull away but he couldn't move. The man's cold stare seemed to reach out and drain away the warmth from his body. A smile as thin as a cutting razor slit it's way across the man's face. An ugly glee then filled his eyes as terror silently spilled out of the sound man.

Then suddenly the man stopped smiling and his head lurched to the side. His expression then changed drastically. The sound man ushered all his will to pan to the side, but whatever the man was looking at then was obstructed by an ambulance. Nocivo stood steely eyed. Unrelenting. Without averting his gaze he inquired from Staples.

"If I may ask, what was the modus?" he said with his gaze still fixed. Staples glanced over at what Nocivo was looking at and quickly turned back to him.

"It's a fresh scene. Shouldn't say. You don't look like a talker though," he said and rubbed his forehead. Nocivo didn't have to be looking at him to know he didn't want to look in the direction of the police unit.

"I don't care for talking to news people if that's what you mean," he said. Staples nodded uneasily.

"Yeah. I can't say much about the details you understand. But as far as motive goes. The guy claims a demon told him to do it. Then he said he was a demon," Staples said and wiped some sweat from his brow. Nocivo snickered.

"Oh, is that right? Funny thing about them. Demons aren't so bad once you understand what they are afraid of. Still, they can be dangerous. I have seen people do truly terrible things without making these claims though. People are more than capable of creating destruction without demonic motivation," he said as he remained still. Staples didn't know what to make of the look in Nocivo's eyes or what he just said. Intimidation didn't quite wrap up what he saw in a nice easy bow.

"Well, yeah. So that's what the suspect said. I can't go into anything else like I said. Papers will have the official SAPD statement later," he said uneasily. The sound man had been unable to move but watched as the man in the police unit had backed away until he right up against the far door of the vehicle.

He was still staring at something a distance away from him. The intensity of his gaze was still there, but all traces of glee had vanished and were replaced by something else. The sound man couldn't place it. It almost looked defensive. As if he were observing a threat. Nocivo took out a stick of Juicy Fruit chewing gum from his front pocket and unwrapped it. He put it in his mouth and grinned. He turned to Staples.

"I understand Detective. There's always a bigger lion. Anyway, a more interesting afternoon than I bargained for. But I'm glad I could help," he said and held out his hand. Staples shook it. The detective's grip was cold, clammy and weak. Staples looked into Nocivo's eyes. He was unstirred. Balanced. A strength and confidence seemed to emanate from him. A warmth began to build up in the detective replacing the cold as he shook Nocivo hand. Reassuring. Estrello smiled and nodded. Staples smiled in return.

"Thanks for the assist man," he said as Nocivo began walking over to the kit he left laying by the ambulance. Staples just stood and watched as he left the scene. Scarcely able to process what just happened. By the squad car a pair of officers reluctantly approached their unit. One looked up at the other uneasily. They stood on either side of the unit. Neither wanted to be the first to open their door. One of them reached down and cautiously pulled up on the handle. The loud clank startled them both. Then they both got in the car. Slowly. Then they looked back to see the suspect bunched up against the door with a fixed gaze. His blood stained clothes were now drenched in a cold sweat. The officer's looked at each other in puzzlement. Without looking at the officers, the man addressed them.

"It's too early. Far too early. But it has begun. Drive me away from here, At Once! We speak of this to no one. We speak of this no more! The time has come! What calamity has been wrought?" he grated in a wispy and raspy unnatural voice. Then he went quiet. Quiet, like the stillness of a cemetery. The officers looked at each other again. Then the driver put the keys in the ignition and started the vehicle.

Life at the Eastern Lodge went on just as it did day in and day out. Brothers tended to their duties or their studies as they did the day before with little variation. All except Pepper. He was about at his wits end. It had been many days and he and Grain had gone through half the rare collection searching for the mysterious glyph to no avail. In this time Garrett had begun to learn one of the dwarven mountain languages. It was an older dialect spoken little in recent times. Many of the books in the collection were written in it. Dwarves were well known to record everything meticulously and always had since their people began using a written language. Some texts still survived that where sixty thousand years old or more in dialects that were still understandable.

Any older and the language became more and more murky. Scholars were at odds to this day what some of the oldest surviving texts even said. Garrett supposed that was just a consequence of time. Pepper found the consequences of time equally frustrating in the small scale in the here and now. Every other day a brother would saunter through his door and ask about his progress. He was growing tired of telling them the same thing over and over. When they asked if he needed any assistance, he informed them that Grain was enough help. They would always leave with the same dejected look in their face. Pepper didn't care. They knew what he would say before they even bothered to come to this wing to bother him. He would find that glyph when he found it. Since nobody bothered to share with him why it was so important, he had little motivation to allow any of their oafishness anywhere near this vault. Grain was at least a smaller man who Pepper reasoned could do little damage. As long as he was reading, he was keeping quiet. He would ask the odd question though.

"Brother Pepper?" Garrett said. Pepper snapped out of stupor he was in and looked over at Grain.

"What is it Garrett?" he said. Garrett picked up a book and opened it.

"I have been reading about the history of dwarves from their earliest civilizations in The Midlands. I keep coming across references to a mountain called Asirnos. I've looked at all the maps we have of The Midlands. There are eleven named mountain peaks in The Midlands. None of which have ever been called Asirnos. At least not according to the resources we have here. I've asked the other brothers about it. None have ever heard the name," he said. Pepper gave him a good long stare.

"And I suppose this has been an itch in your mind," he said. Grain knew the tone well by now. Pepper was not the least bit interested in anything than what was right in front of him.

"Yes. Yes you could say that it is," he said. Pepper turned back to his book and turned a page.

"And could you say that this curiosity is helping or hindering you helping find the glyph?" Pepper grumbled. Grain gave this some thought.

"I would say it helps, at least in part. If I have a better context, I reason I'll be better able to spot when I'm on the right track," he said. Pepper looked back at him with a questioning expression. Then he turned back to his book.

"Very well. Carry on looking for your pretend mountain," Pepper said dismissively. Garrett sighed and continued to read the book he held. It was another in a stack of books that dealt with early dwarven cartography. The dwarves of old scoured the world for sources of gemstones as rich as the Midlands. The crown of King Tamaltu was said to hold the twelve Divine Stones. Those stones were said to represent the months of the year.

Grain was born in the spring in a month where the Green Sky Stone found only in The Sentinels around Southgate was represented. He had never seen an example of the stone but had heard it resembled the color of pine needles. Grain had thought to ask Pepper about what month he was born in, but decided against it. Pepper may not find the question to be productive.

Garrett instead focused on the books around him. When he turned a page he caught a glimpse of a symbol. It was not the one he was looking for. But something about it stood out to him. Some of the contours around the outer edge looked like the glyph they were searching for. I was not a match but Grain picked up a quill and made note of it in his journal. He set the book aside in a pile of books he'd found most interesting. A knock at the door caught his attention. Pepper was already up at the door as if he'd anticipated an arrival, or simply that his keen wolf ears heard their visitor's approach. When Pepper opened the door, Garrett heard a familiar voice.

"Please, come in," Pepper said and welcomed the visitor inside. It was Brother Alvin. He'd been by before a few days ago and was a far more welcome sight that some of the other Brothers who seemed to agitate

Pepper by their mere presence. Alvin turned to the brothers that had arrived with him.

"Please wait out here for me. I won't be long," he said and walked into Pepper's office. Pepper shook his hand and invited him to sit down.

"Such a comfort not to see the face of Dobey, Straw or Batten souring before my eyes," Pepper said. The comment got a chuckle out of the old Brother.

"Now you. Acting on behalf of The Delegation is enough to sour any man's face," Alvin said. Pepper had his doubts.

"You can imagine my joy then, to see The Delegation has not soured you Brother Alvin," he said jokingly. Garrett marveled at what a different wolf that Pepper was around Brother Alvin. Gone was the cynical and dismissive curtness. In its place was what passed for friendliness. There was a respect there. One that appeared baked in after a long period of time. It was a sight to behold as was the caring and almost fatherly look on Alvin's face around Pepper.

"Oh lad they have certainly tried. Believe me. It doesn't matter who sits on it, they all seem to have the same temperament. Dreary lot. But they still need compassion, which is an order, often a challenge to fulfill. But still we try," Alvin said and sat down. He looked over into the vault and invited Garrett over. The halfwyn got up from his stack of books and walked over to the other men. Pepper had heard Alvin's plea before. His position was still unchanged.

"Ha! I'll leave all the compassion to you Brother Alvin. I will continue to regard The Delegation as the malcontents they are and view the Brothers they send as the tepid buckets of water I know them to be," Pepper mused. The statement was not one Alvin hadn't heard before.

"Oh I see. Do you view me as a tepid bucket of water as well Brother Pepper?" Alvin said. Pepper snickered.

"Certainly not Brother Alvin. A cultured and measured man like yourself could never be a tepid bucket of water. I leave that characterization for others," he said. Alvin shook his head and looked over at Garrett who sat upon a small footstool.

"And how are you today my boy?" he said. Garrett didn't really have anything impressive to say about his day. He'd been sitting in the middle of the same dusty pile of books for the last few days. Apart from a few interesting finds, there wasn't anything revelatory to mention.

"The day treats me well Brother Alvin. Good to see you come around," he said. Alvin smiled and then rubbed his hands together. He looked over his shoulder at Pepper.

"Must you always keep that garishly large window open all the time? Don't you get cold up here?" Alvin said and folded his arms. Pepper chuckled.

"Fur coat Brother Alvin. It takes stronger weather to put a shiver in me," he said. Alvin gave him a look.

"What about young Brother Garrett here? He doesn't have a coat of fur" He said and pointed at the halfwyn. Garrett didn't want to seem lacking though.

"Oh I don't mind Brother Alvin. That's what a good hot tea is for," he said. Alvin smiled at him.

"I see. Well, I suppose I should ask about your research while I'm here. Shouldn't waste the walk up here making pleasantries. What would The Delegation think?" Alvin said. Pepper laughed.

"What would they think indeed? Banter? Gods, and tepid buckets forbid," Pepper mused and took his notebook from his pocket. He flipped through a few pages and handed it over to Alvin.

"As you can see Brother Alvin. Not much to report. It's certainly been interesting to discover all the magnificence and oddity this vault contains, but alas in terms of anything of interest to The Delegation, this vault has proven to be frightfully empty," he added. Alvin skimmed through the most recent pages. The old man's face looked forlorn. Pepper wished he had more to give Brother Alvin. The opinions of others didn't matter so much to him. Alvin's did. The old man closed the journal and handed it back to Pepper. He looked over at Garrett.

"And you lad. What have you uncovered during your time assisting Brother Pepper?" Alvin said. Garrett thought about this for a moment. Then he got up and walked over to where his notebook sat. He reached down and picked it up. As he did he recalled the book he'd just been reading and picked it up as well. He carried them both over to Brother Alvin and handed them over. Alvin opened the journal and thumbed through a few pages and nodded. He set it down and turned his attention to other book. The writing on the cover was faint so Alvin held it up closer to the lantern that hung from a load-bearing beam near the table.

"Chronicles of Thagnar the Stout. Oh it's an old ogres' almanac. Plenty of accounts of seasonal forecast that may have turned out more or less accurate. Obsessed about the weather those old ogres were. At least that's how all the old texts describe them," Alvin said as he opened the book and flipped through the pages. Garrett waited until the old Brother reached the page that had caught his eye. Alvin almost passed it by, but turned the page back and took a second look at the glyph stamped onto the page. He looked at it carefully. He seemed to notice the similarity in the outer contours as Garrett did. The old man looked up at the halfwyn. Pepper leaned in to get a closer look.

"Curious," he said and looked up at Garrett as well. Garrett felt a weight on his shoulders as both men looked at him with the expectation he had context to add.

"It is that I agree. The similarity there caught my eye, so I set that one aside to read later," he said. A look in Pepper's eyes he had not seen before appeared. Pepper smiled.

"Good work Brother Grain," he said. Alvin was pleased at the wolf's tone. It was something he was hoping to hear. Something he'd hoped to hear for many years in Pepper's voice for someone other than himself.

"Agreed. Good work lad. I eagerly await what you discover in these pages. I'd give it a read myself, but my eyes aren't what they used to be," Alvin said and closed the book. He handed it back to Garrett and pushed himself up out of the chair with a grunt. Pepper helped him up and patted the old Brother on the shoulder.

"Off so soon Brother Alvin? You just got here," Pepper said. Alvin shook the wolf's paw and smiled.

"Oh, I'll leave you boys to your studies. Don't need an old man doddering about getting in your way. Besides, I'm told rhubarb pie is to be served at the dining hall shortly. Mustn't miss that," he said and began walking to the door. Pepper followed to see him off.

"Always a pleasure Brother Alvin. I hope to see you by again soon. More so than others," Pepper said and glared at the other brothers standing outside on the colonnade. It put a fright in the pair and they gripped their sticks a little tighter. Alvin caught Pepper's display and looked up at the other brothers.

"Oh don't let the wolf spoil your stomachs. He's all bluster. Come along," Alvin said and gestured the Brothers to follow. Pepper watched as they walked away and then went back inside.

The ships to High Canyon Keep were still a half a day's ride out. The weather had been calm and the road was fair. Just a slight breeze enveloped the landscape. The small fleet was docked at a port on one the Southwest's largest lakes. The lake connected to a river that flowed northwest into the Canyon Lands where High Canyon Keep resided. The lake, river, and canyons were all controlled by Hall Brian. Near the center of the Canyon Lands one could find the cool valleys carpeted by vineyards that produced a particularly prized varietal outsiders called The Red Serpent. After being cut off from the coast, wine had become Hall Brian's main economic commodity. Interestingly enough a key reason even those who despised and envied Hall Brian, coveted their wine. Few would consider risking the destruction of Brian grapes, their production infrastructure, or silence their knowledge for the craft. Many land's economies were dependent on the buying and reselling of their wine.

Entire military campaigns had been funded by barrels of The Red Serpent. Many lords have offered their daughters to one of Lord Kastor Brian's sons, especially to his eldest Banathir. The wind blew around his light brown hair. He was a man in his early thirties who was well travelled by now. Much to his father's chagrin, along with fighting for the minor lords and barons of the Canyon Lands, the young Lord Banathir had reputed to have bedded many a tart and strumpet. The nickname Coin Thrower followed Banathir around. Old Lord Kastor expected one of these unfortunate souls to request audience with him one day with a bawling babe begging for his name.

Such a thing would not come to pass. No bastard child would be called Brian as long as he lived. Banathir had finally relented after 20 or so years of noble Ladies' names thrown at him. The old man was in a far better spirit as he sat in his carriage sipping some of his family's own special reserve. Banathir on the other hand was in far worse spirits as he rode along side his father's carriage. This arraignment sat poorly with him. He regarded his family's lands safety and security above all else. Starting a family of his own would greatly reduce his role in keeping that security. But an engagement to a young woman not much more than a child also put him in a foul spirit. It would be years before The King could present her formally. Years Banathir feared his father may not have. A father that had hoped that by now he'd run across a maiden in some Lord's Keep that would inspire him in the same way protecting the people of his lands did. This would not be. All he met were more deeply concerned with themselves and disinterested in anything outside their own small little worlds. He didn't expect much different from Princess Vanadia Lamb. But the number of days his father could know his grandchildren grew fewer with each passing year. His older sister Pallas had a colder heart than the statuary that filled the High Canyon Keep. She would bear him no grandchildren. His two younger brothers were more concerned with wine and fighting to take any offer of marriage seriously. His younger sister was even younger than Princess Vanadia. He hoped she didn't grow into the kind of vacuous vanity he'd seen so much of already. Sir Haldan Barlow rode up beside him. In his mid 50s now he'd served as a squire for Lord Kastor Brian's brother before being knighted. Now he served Banathir

"That is a dour face m'Lord if I say so. You look like a man on his way to marry a woman half his age," Sir Haldan mused. The joke made Banathir smile.

"I'll warn you Hal. That kind of remark may have you shoveling pig pens for the next month or so if he overheard you," Banathir said. Sir Haldan chuckled.

"But every good joke has some truth to it m'Lord. Didn't you know that?" He continued to muse. Banathir chuckled himself.

"You think I'm joking. You remember when we didn't know where Sir Mabren had gone? We all thought he gone off to deliver a message to Lord Tolliver all the way in the Barley Lands. Well, that was Sir Cafro.

Sir Mabren was in the pins shoveling for seven weeks. All because he said he thought my father walked too slowly. Sir Mabren still doesn't know how to whisper, but he's never commented on my father's walking speed again," Banathir said. Sir Haldan chuckled again.

"Well I suppose there's worse fates," Haldan said. Banathir looked over at him.

"Oh, do tell," he said. Haldan grinned.

"Going off to marry a fifteen year old girl," he said and then forced himself not laugh out loud. He loved a good cheerful barb, but shoveling pig shit was not particularly appealing. Banathir just smiled and shook his head.

"The man we should be praying for the strength of the Mountain for is that poor Prince Attheon," Banathir said. Sir Haldan put his hand to his heart.

"Oh if you please m'Lord don't you mean your future brother-in-law?" he said and smiled at Banathir.

"Indeed we shall be brothers-in-law. But unlike Attheon I am not marrying into a political hornets nest like Seastorm. The gods only know what sort of trouble is really brewing out east. This is a military marriage for him. Mine is merely economic," Banathir said. Haldan considered what his Lord just told him, but he disagreed.

"If you'll forgive me m'Lord, but war and money are never not in each other's company. I'm sure Prince Attheon will be wading into troubled waters first, but I would not so quickly assume those waters won't greet your shores thereafter. If Southgate is drawn into war, the south is drawn into war. The Canyon Lands are part of the south regardless if we think it is not. I'd hoped your years of fighting had granted you that insight," Haldan said less humorously. Banathir turned to his old friend.

"The Canyons are not in the south," He said. Haldan turned to him as well.

"Anything that is not The Midlands is the south m'Lord. Would you care to know The Emperor's opinion on that matter? What Southgate fights, sooner or later, we all fight. Hall Falco is going to end up fighting somebody. Any man who's swung a sword can see that. When their first arrow flies the candle is lit. When the light goes out, war is at your doorstep. Fighting for Southgate is the last thing any Canyoner would see himself doing. But some wars are just going to get fought. And when they do, well, best to fight for the winning side," he said. Banathir pondered this for a moment or two.

"What if I don't care if Southgate wins?" he said. Haldan could understand his attitude. He had no sense of obligation for Southgate either. But he did for his friend.

"I will tell you m'Lord. If Southgate falls, we'll likely have a new power in the south we cannot so easily ignore, and you will have a young wife who will fiercely loathe you and think you a coward. The Banathir of The Canyons I know would not let himself entertain such eventualities in his mind. The Banathir I know will fight back-to-back with that bothersome Southgater because he knows it's right. This is the Lord Banathir I know," Sir Haldan said and grinned. Banathir nodded and grinned as well.

"I see your point Hal. Good points as always. Who knows, I might get a blade forged from Sentinel Steel out of the arraignment. Only seventeen blades have ever been forged from their so-called Soul of the Sentinels ore. I may wield the eighteenth," he said. Haldan caught the sarcasm in his Lord's voice. He raised a brow.

"Oh, aye. But you'll have to put a ring on The Princess Vanadia's finger before The King puts a Sentinel Steel sword in your hand. You may be the holder of the eighteenth blade, if you're the holder of an eighteen year-old bride. These kinds of plans are best thought of in longer terms," he said. Banathir laughed.

"Too right. So almost three years until I have my hands on Sentinel Steel it is then?" he said and took a drink from his wineskin.

The afternoon was giving into evening as Estrello Nocivo pulled into Salazar's parking structure. From the moment he passed through the front gates to the moment his motorcycle passed through the concrete arch that led into the structure, an array of scanning and detection technology scrutinized every square nanometer of his person and the vehicle he rode. The "Parking" sign above the concrete arch itself was outfitted by cameras and ocular detectors. These were specialized cameras highly sensitive to the changes in UV and Infrared light levels caused by the movement of the human eye. These cameras recorded every time the structure was looked at by anyone. Other cameras were calibrated to detect a wide variety of camera lenses.

If the structure was being watched, the watchers had eyes on them as well. If the threshold exceeded 27% ocular activity, from either human or mechanical eyes, entry to the lower levels would not be granted. Even for Estrello Nocivo. Today the percentage was predictably low at only about 2.2%. Nothing showed up on facial recognition or heat profiling that would indicate a repetitive onlooker. Nor were there any suspicious hits in the auto VIN number database. Nocivo needed only speak his entry code and the enormous concrete doors opened for him.

The arena was closed to practice today. This is one of the reasons he chose this day to perform the CityNet test. The next day would be General Stratum's birthday, but not a lot going on today. Until that is, he received a text from Aloysius Clark who is the ship's Director of Foreign Technology Research. He wanted to speak with Estrello. His lab was located on the same level as Salazar's in one of the hardened areas of the ship. When he reached this area he waved to Antonio as he passed by the door of his lab. Antonio waved back and the then continued to munch on his bag of Andy Capp's Hot Fries while one of his machines completed whatever it was doing. Nocivo was largely unfamiliar with a majority of the equipment on this level or what purpose they served. Which made him curious why JP wasn't called in instead of him. Then he picked up the traces of Mane and Tail shampoo in the hallway air. JP had been here recently. From the strength of the scent he still may be. Estrello walked into the FTR lab after being scanned by the security team posted at the door. He passed numerous stations and greeted the handful of lab techs that seemed to work here around the clock. His destination was a holding area, which was a kind of vault for storing exotic technology that had undergone intense examination before being locked away here. The heavy composite doors whirred and clanked open for Nocivo. Inside he saw Director Clark garbed in his long white lab coat and shaded round-lensed glasses he never seemed to take off. It was explained at one time the glasses where tied into the network running through the lab, but he had forgotten the conversation. The Director had both his black gloved hands folded behind his back and was looking in Estrello's direction. There was a slight smirk on the Director's face augmented by his pronounced goatee and handlebar mustache.

"Good evening Skipper. Prompt as always," The Director said in his erudite manner. Nocivo approached The Director and noticed that JP was here as well sitting at a desk against the wall. He looked up at Nocivo as he drew near.

"Go ahead and tell him what you just told me Director," JP said and sat back in his chair. The Director pulled a remote device from his lab coat pocket and clicked a button. The heavy doors of a containment cabinet opened up in front of him.

Nocivo watched as the doors slid open and a glass shelf emerged from the interior and jutted out into the room. Sitting on the shelf was a clear container with what appeared to be cloudy water inside it with a label that read 08052435. Estrello leaned in to have a closer look at it. Then he stood back and looked over at the Director who seemed to have a disappointed expression.

"I was quite expecting a witty jab. Lofty expectation I suppose. JP generated a greater effort in this respect. Something to the effect of 'dirty dish water' collection. A description prescribed by our good Doctor Salazar, and repeated thusly," he said. Despite JP's rugged exterior his sarcasm was a notable behavioral trait.

"I would not presume to comment on something I didn't understand," Nocivo said. The Director was impressed. Humility wasn't something he was accustomed to.

"Yes quite. This receptacle sitting hence. A curiosity as it may be. It is not in fact dish water. It is the cloud of nanotechnology pulled from yourself and Doctor Salazar, as well as your equipment and the staging room itself, and is now contained safely here," he said. Nocivo grimaced. He recalled his experience inside The Director's Vantolotron machine.

"Something this dangerous is best kept under lock and key," he said. The Director smirked.

"This iteration of nanotechnology is not in itself substantially remarkable. In fact our good General Stratum regarded these nanites as

'Crude, Primitive, and Pedestrian' in design. Hardly a glowing review I should say," he said. Nocivo looked back at JP who nodded. He turned back to the director.

"I suppose not. I'm guessing there is a reason for this level of containment," he said. The director clicked his remote causing the shelf to retract into the cabinet, which shut and locked.

"Quite. Are you familiar with Interflux Causality?" Said the Director. Estrello shook his head. The Director put his remote back into his pocket and turned toward JP.

"In short Skip, it's a change made to what some refer to as the fabric of reality. An oversimplified term, but then again I name things Interflux Causality, so I'm not one to speak. The kind of change I'm talking about is one that occurs from outside a reality's own space-time," JP said. Nocivo was a little confused.

"You mean like reality contamination from misused dash technology?" he said. JP looked at the Director who wasn't quick to confirm. JP looked back at Nocivo.

"Yes and no. Yes in the sense the damage does come a dash device run amok casting its wake every which way, but whereas the damage done to Stratum's universe is the aftermath of very large contamination, the kind of damage we've been observing here with these nanites is evidence of smaller scale effect. A small change," JP said. Nocivo still seemed lost on the subject. The Director seemed to have something on his mind.

"It can be put this way Doctor Nocivo. For months myself and Commodore Persson have been trying to figure out how it was possible that a universe could be influenced without any dash contamination being detected. In essence we were trying to diagnose an infection, without evidence of an infection. Our earlier theory of universal collision wasn't holding the water the way we thought it did," The Director said. Estrello folded his arms.

"Could you explain this universal collision theory," Nocivo said. JP got up and tapped away at his tablet. A screen on the wall came to life with a graphic of what Estrello assumed were two universes represented by blobs. A third blob then appeared next to the others. An explosion animation then went off in that third universe sending it through one of the other universes. When the animation was over JP looked over at Nocivo.

"That about sums it. An incident causes one universe to move into another's locus. They don't physically touch of course, but there would be an effect on other levels. But the kinds of effects we've been observing are far too small to be the result of entire universes colliding," he said. Nocivo understood a bit more but his look of uncertainty spurred the Director on.

"Play animation two if you could please Commodore," he said. JP tapped away at his tablet and a second animation began playing. This time several universes were displayed. An eruption then occurred in one. Instead of the universe moving itself, tendrils began spidering out from it and hitting some of the other universes around it. JP stopped the animation and looked at Nocivo.

"It's still an incomplete theory but what it amounts to partly what we already knew. Dash device is activated and it affects universes around it. At this point we get lucky sometimes and get a hit on a major line from the epicenter. We go do our thing and follow it to the source. Bang, we've recovered another device. But we've been getting a lot of what we thought were just anomalous hits. Collateral damage from one universe colliding with another," he said. Nocivo rubbed his forehead.

"I would not claim to really understand any of this right this moment. But if I understand correctly, these aren't anomalous hits," he said. The Director and attempted to snap his fingers through his gloved fingers.

"Exactly Doctor. We were so focused on looking for the macro, we should have been looking at the micro," he said and pointed at JP who in turn zoomed in greatly into his animation.

"What we have here are micro hits. Micro contaminations with an infinitesimally small half-life. Once it hits, it decays almost instantly. Unlike the contaminations we've observed elsewhere, these don't get progressively bigger. They just die. Quickly. So quick nothing we have is calibrated to pick it up. We weren't even looking for it before. We just assumed we were dashing into dead ends. Picking up the pieces after the party had moved on and trying to learn what we could," JP said and switched off the screen. He looked at Nocivo what looked like he was on the verge of understanding.

"So you're saying these aren't necessarily dead ends?" he said. JP grinned widely.

"That's exactly what I'm saying. If we can calibrate our instruments to follow the scent, it is our hope wen can use micro contaminations to zero in on epicenters the same way we currently do with macro contaminations," JP said. Nocivo nodded.

"And what tangible evidence is there to support your theory that micro contaminations occur at all," he said. The Director whipped out his remote and reopened the cabinet containing the nanites. He pointed to them. And then he waved his hand over the entire wall of closed cabinets.

"A menagerie of novel artifacts all bearing a peculiar type of radiation we initially mistook as residue from dash travel. Except the decay of that radiation occurred in a different way than it would otherwise when comparatively conventional travel occurs. We overlooked it until we started comparing the artifacts to each other. A finger print if you will Doctor, began to emerge," said the Director. Nocivo looked back and forth at JP and the Director.

"What could a micro contamination do to any of these artifacts that would trigger Salazar and Martha's sight universes away, and make themselves such an important focal point?" he said. The Director didn't comment. JP kind of hung his head.

"We don't know Skip. Yet. But we're working on it. Lead is still fresh with the nanotech. We're dialing in there," JP said. Nocivo didn't like to feel like he was walking away empty handed, but he knew a lot more than he did before.

"Good work. Let me know when you two uncover anything else," he said and began to head out of the lab.

"Will do," JP yelled.

The gardens only had a few Brothers tending it this late in the season. Soon the air would grow much colder. Most Brothers preferred to work the soil in the spring and summer months. It was nearly autumn now. Only the seeds for late year plants were being sown right now. Few Brothers took interest in these. Garrett Grain was not among them. Though much was imported to The East Lodge, if a Brother wanted fresher produce they had to grow it themselves. Garrett was quite fond of sage, which he planted now. Farming was in his blood. There was an affinity with the soil. Even in the smallest scale here in the East Lodge covered garden, which was a serene place where many Brothers grew crops for themselves or others. Garrett was content to plant a substantial volume of sage because he knew other Brothers liked it as well, and he only harvested a small amount anyway. He was happy to put in the time and work though. It was one of the many small things that brought him joy. As he finished planting a seedling he felt like he was being watched. He turned to see Brother Alvin sitting a short distance away on one of the many stone benches that sat near the garden. He had a warm smile on his face. Garrett got up and brushed some of the dirt from his robe.

"Brother Alvin. So good to see you. What brings you all the way down to the gardens?" Garrett said as he walked over and sat on a bench near the old man. Alvin looked out at the garden and all the Brothers tending it.

"I just like to sit here sometimes and see how the garden is growing. And see how much care my Brothers put into their work here. One can tell much about them by how they tend their plots. You can tell if a Brother is in a good or a bad place. Those like yourself warm the soil with your good spirit and your seedlings feel that. They trust the ground more I feel when there is that warmth there. Others are under one burden or another. For most Brothers it's sadness brought upon the weight this place can put on one's shoulders. For many this is the first time away from their villages. The novelty of The East Lodge is not an immediate fit for many. There are some to which the fit never truly takes. Our Brother Pepper is one such man. An odd egg even before he got here. Odder still after coming here. Even after twenty years he's a lone wolf content to keep his distance from everyone. Save for myself. After all this time I couldn't say why the wolf has come to trust me more than so many others. He just does," Alvin said. Garrett agreed with how Alvin described Pepper.

He had seen much of that distancing in effect in his short time working with the wanderer.

"I have been around solitary types my whole life. Few though seem to engineer their solitude quite like Pepper does. It's made it a challenge to work with him. Just one of many. The first day I came to his door I thought he was going to eat me. I didn't want to go back after that first time. No matter how fascinating I found the rare texts vault to be. The Senior Brotherhood sent me back the next day though. If it were up to me I would have stayed in the library where I was before. I still don't know why I was sent back," Garrett said. Alvin smiled and laid his hands in his lap.

"That would be because I asked them to," Alvin said. This surprised Garrett.

"May I ask why Brother Alvin?" he said with a hint of distress in his voice. Alvin understood and had anticipated his reaction.

"I asked them to because I care very much for my dear friend Pepper. I care that he should have at least one Brother among the hundreds here that can take tea with him on equal footing and the mutual respect as I have built with him over many years. I want him to call someone else Brother, without it being merely a title we adopt when we take the robes to begin our study," Alvin said with hints of sadness in his voice.

"He has you though doesn't he Brother Alvin? He doesn't need me," Garrett replied. Alvin shook his head.

"I am an old man Brother Garrett. My health is good now. But only a fool would cast lots against time. Time always wins. I won't be here forever. A good harsh winter could put and end to me with these old bones. I need someone who can take my place when the time comes. Pepper may be adept at planning for solitude. I must, no We, must be adept at planning for the exact opposite. I hope you can understand," he said. Garrett couldn't help but be distressed with the direction this conversation was taking.

"I do understand, but at the same time why would you trust me over everyone else?" Garrett said. This was a fair question. Alvin paused a moment before answering.

"It became clear to me very early on after I observed Pepper opening up to me and no one else, his case would be unique. In the many years after that I have tried solve the puzzle that is Pepper Redflower. A daunting task. But one I never gave up on. Almost twenty years I have searched for someone with the qualities I felt would be most compatible with a stubborn solitary wolf. That solution came with you. Or so I hoped. To be perfectly honest I'd about given up at this point. Then I met an inquisitive young man that asked me if it was true that a farmer's horse started a great war. I then had the pleasure of saying yes, and handing that young man a book that told that story. Do you remember that day Garrett?" Alvin said. Garrett perked up then. He did indeed remember.

"Of course Brother Alvin. Just last summer. Right after the big storm that damaged the pier," he said with a smile. Alvin remembered that day fondly. Not so much having to deal with assessing the damage to the Lodge's pier, but something else.

"It was on that day I knew. I just knew. All it took was one book. Just one. A book that I had seen Brother Pepper take down from the shelf and read again, and again. There was something in him that engaged with the stories that book in particular contained. It struck me that he may connect with someone else who expressed curiosity with the same text. One might say that wasn't much to go on, but after twenty years it was really the only thread I saw to pull," Alvin said. Garrett began to see where Alvin's reasoning came from. He still didn't place the same faith in his friend's revelation.

"I do enjoy that book quite a bit. Especially how such a small thing could affect something so much bigger than itself," Garrett said. All Alvin could do is smile. Garrett waited for the old man to say something else. But all he did was sit there and smile.

"I can't guarantee that I can be the solution you need. But I will continue to help Brother Pepper with his task. I could not say what will become our collaborations from then on. But I can do that," Garrett said. Alvin turned to him.

"It is all I can ask of you. The rest must come from the two of you. I have heard it said that it is far easier to lose friends than it is to make them. Experience has taught me this is largely true. I will nonetheless hope," Alvin said. Garrett could feel the warmth returning to Alvin's voice.

"I hope that your hope is seen through. I suppose that all hinges on Brother Pepper," Garrett said. Alvin leaned on his walking stick and pushed himself up. He looked down at Garrett.

"Continue to work hard with him. Build that respect. Earn every bit of it. At the end of the day if he doesn't regard you how either of us would like, you still did all you could. I will retire for a spell to rest this old back. It looks like you still have another row to plant," Alvin said and pointed out to the garden. He then turned and began to walk away. Garrett sat there a few moments as he watched the old man make his way away from the garden.

Snow fell on the square in front the Temple of the High Mountain. Thick cloud cover had rolled in during the afternoon and now dropped its cargo onto the streets of Southgate. A man burst through front doors and ran out through the square. Priests of the Mountain watched as he did. Some even had to dodge him as he ran past. Remarks of condemnation promptly followed, but the running man did not stop to apologize. His gate and stride were determined. A path was before him and he put heels through snow as good as any steed in full gallop. At least that's what he thought of his effort. To onlookers he was wiry and clumsy young man sprinting through their placid evening.

He ran past the Southgate's Salvernuim and the salvers in the square before their institution. They were as equally offended by this audacious disturbance. The young man disregarded them in much the same way. He only cared about his destination. A small pub near the gatehouse leading out of the Brewer's Ward called The Burnt Barrel. He knew somebody he needed to find would be there. He made it there and nearly collapsed in front of it. The cold air stung his lungs and a great weight pressed down on his chest as if it were a foot pushing him down into the snow. But he kept going. Outside the pub men in armor stood about. None of them were the man he wanted to see. He walked into the pub, his chest heaved as he looked around at the men sitting around drinking their fill of ale. Some of them gave him a scornful look only to turn away dismissively. He spotted who he wanted to see near the back wall and approached his table. Freegale Lamb sat there enjoying as much ale as the barmen were willing to sell him. He would return home to his family in two days time. A journey he looked forward to.

He missed his children. The political atmosphere of Southgate encouraged him to drink too much. He finished off a flagon of ale when a skinny little Temple apprentice plopped down in front of him looking like he'd been chased down by a pack of wild dogs. The lad caught Freegale's eye as soon as he entered. A Temple robe was an uncommon sight here. The Templars preferred to drink with their own in the guts of the Temple of the Mountain. This lad was here. Freegale was just curious enough to inquire.

"What are you doing here lad?" he said and alerted a barkeep who promptly began walking over with more ale. The young man still did not have his breath. The barman handed Freegale a fresh flagon of ale. Freegale set it down and slid it over to the young man.

"This one's free. The rest will cost you a punch in the face. You walked in here with that vacant look you got there and then walked straight to me. I'm the one you want to see. Why?" he said. The young man had caught his breath and took the cup of ale and drank it a bit too quick. He coughed and set it down.

"Lord Freegale. I deeply apologize for disturbing you. I would not have come if it were not important," he said and then took another drink from the flagon. Freegale had already grown weary of the young man's company.

"I'll be the judge of that lad. Out with it before I start charging you for my time," he said. The young man reached into his cloak and produced a small rolled message and with a shaking hand gave it over to Freegale. He gave the boy a good long stare and read the note. He shook his head and held the message to the flame of a nearby candle. He placed the burning note in front of the young man and waited until it was completely consumed. He then got up from his chair.

"Well boy. Time respects no man, and there's other places for ale in this city. Run back to your Temple," he said and then tossed a nearby barman a few silver and copper coins.

A few other men stood as he did. The young man looked around. These men had the same rough look about them. It appeared that Freegale Lamb travelled with similar company. Company that followed Lord Lamb out of the establishment to their horses hitched outside. Freegale mounted his horse he'd named Noisy Beast. The others followed suit and the group was soon on their way. The young man watched as they departed on their way to the gatehouse. He then turned and began his walk back to the Temple.

The far end of Scanna was lively in contrast to the near side, which sat along the banks of the river. Inns and taverns inhabited this area. One such inn was the Flat End which this evening hosted Southstar and her rangers. They would be departing soon though. The group packed up their things in preparation for the journey south to The Barley Lands. A knock at the door interrupted them. One of the rangers walked over to the door and opened it. Standing outside was the innkeeper. A man named Barles.

"How can I help you old man?" the ranger said. Barles looked to his side. Genesis Payne stepped into view. The ranger looked at her.

"Oh," he said and opened the door further. Southstar turned and looked through the doorway spotting Genesis. This visit was surprising but she nonetheless beckoned her forth.

"Come to see us off Mystic Payne?" she said despite noticing Genesis dressed warmly with a pack over her shoulder and a walking staff in hand. It was easy to see the young woman's intent. Southstar had sensed some adventure in Genesis earlier, but this was far from her expectation. Regardless she treated the developing situation delicately. Genesis wasn't sure how her intentions would be received.

"I had something else in mind Lieutenant Redflower," she said. Southstar picked up her pack and threw it over her shoulder and picked up her sword.

"Off to another reading so soon?" she said hoping the answer would be yes despite everything about the look of Genesis this day said no. Genesis looked around at the other rangers and then back at Southstar.

"A reading yes. That would be one way of looking at it. But not the best way of saying it. I wish to join you on your way to The Barley Lands," she said. It was what Southstar expected her to say, but not what she particularly wanted to hear.

"Our journey will not be an easy one. What does your father have to say to this?" she said. Genesis looked down for a moment then back up at the group.

"He did have some disagreement. So close to The Days my absence would be hard on him. But I have put off my pilgrimage for several seasons now and__," she said but was cut off by Southstar.

"But you decide to join us as part of your pilgrimage? Why?" she said. Genesis leaned on her walking stick and gathered herself.

"It's true, you and your companions are little more than strangers. I trust rangers though. My own brother River serves in a pack in the far west near The Red Cliffs. My father and I talked greatly about your visit. Readings such as this are rare. We looked through all the texts we had in the house. We found only two instances where readings such as this were recorded. They both preceded war. One occurred before the War of the Forgotten and the other before the War of False Tribes," she said. The look in Southstar's eyes told Genesis much.

"You already knew this though," she added. Southstar sighed.

"We learned as much from the Temple of the Wind. They didn't have much literature about these wars. They only had references to them in regards to blank readings," she said. Genesis smiled.

"I would journey with you to The Barley Lands. But then I would make my way to The East Lodge." She said. Southstar tried to hide her distress upon hearing this. But it was difficult.

"The East Lodge will not receive you. You are a woman. Such a thing is forbidden without sponsored escort. The brothers will not allow a woman in alone. Even a mystic," she said. Genesis looked away for a moment. Then back at Southstar.

"I shall have to acquire one," she said. Southstar shook her head.

"You gamble Mystic Payne. And you may not rely on any ranger. We are cannot offer you sponsored escort. Out independent status forbids us from these types of affairs with the Lodges. It will be up to you to find a sponsor. Again, a gamble. Finding a man will not be easy. A trek to The East Lodge is a test few would take without more sliver than you are likely to possess. We can take you as far as Candleport. That is the northwesterly most edge of our territory. If you are truly fortunate a trading caravan may be willing to take you on as hired help. If not, Candleport is a good place to stay until you're able to journey back here. Are these terms acceptable?" she said. Genesis held out a hand. Southstar looked at it for a moment. Then she reluctantly shook it. Genesis nodded to the others and left the room. After handing in their door keys the group headed across the street to the small stable that belonged to the inn. Southstar mounted her horse and tipped the stable boy a few copper and walked it out onto the road. She looked around for Genesis. She would have assumed that the mystic would be out front waiting for them. Just then Genesis turned the corner riding a horse of her own which was a young light-coated steed with a dark mane and snout. She smiled as she neared. Southstar looked the horse over. The family did not own horse that she could observe from her time at their home.

"I would suppose this solves the issue of exactly how we'd transport you to Candleport. Where did this horse come from?" she said. Genesis patted the horse on the neck.

"I just became acquainted with this one. Part of your reading payment paid for him. I call him Trail Blazer," she said. Southstar pondered the scene for a moment and looked back at her group.

"Rangers! Ride!" she barked.

Canyon Lake was a modest port southeast from the Canyon Lands. The body of water itself and its adjoining river were deep enough for larger ships to traverse without much trouble if there were no drought conditions. The seasons had been favorably wet the last few years so sailing would not be an issue. Seven ships belonging to Hall Brian were docked here at the Canyon Lake port flying the red Fire Serpent. The people of Canyon Town eagerly awaited Lord Kastor Brian and his escort. The Lord's carriage came to a stop near the harbor. Around two-dozen of Kastor Brian's personal guard enveloped the area around it and Banathir. He and Sir Haldan dismounted and handed their reigns off Brian soldiers who would take them to their own ships. Sir Haldan promptly gave Banathir a half salute and headed off to the nearest tavern. The ride had made him thirsty. Banathir waited at his father's carriage. A guard set a wooden stool at the door of the conveyance and opened the door. The Lord of Hall Brian stepped out and waved to the townspeople who had gathered here. They applauded for him. He was most beloved here. He was a firm, but generous man. The Canyons were a wealthy region, and taxes were modest. Kastor saw to that. He greeted his son Banathir.

"Banathir my boy. Please walk with me to my ship," he said as he waved to the people around. Banathir placed a hand on his father's frail shoulder and walked with him amidst his personal guard.

"Our season has been productive this year. Our wineries have produced a significant yield. But not so significant boy, that the value decreases to an unacceptable point. Supply should never exceed demand son. One of many things you will need to understand when the time comes for these people to cheer for you. And the Princess Vanadia when her name is Brian and has bore you sons of your own. They will need to know this as well. So they may teach their sons. This is the way of things," Kastor said to Banathir as the walked. Banathir patted his father's shoulder.

"Yes father. This is the way of things," he said. Kastor sighed.

"This is why it disheartens me to hear such sullen words come from you. The sun is rising on our Hall my son. I can feel it. The people can feel it. I hope that some day you can feel it too," Kastor said. Banathir hung his head a bit. His father had heard his conversation with Sir Haldan.

"Forgive me father. I lack your experience," he said. Kastor chuckled.

"I would have hoped you could see boy, that even though you may lack my years, you do not lack my capability. You have talent my son. Not just with swinging a sword, but by being the man your family needs. A man I trust will fill my seat well when it is his time to govern these magnificent canyons. Better than any Atheon will fill the throne of Southgate. His sister is in better company here. She'll certainly keep warmer. Family has more value than any fancy Southgate steel or silver my boy. Legacy outweighs the world itself. Remember this well every time you look into your first born's eyes," Kastor said. Banathir patted his father on the shoulder again.

"I will endeavor to do so father," he said. His father stopped walking and looked into his son's eyes.

"I know you do not truly mean that son. Not yet. In time you will. As did I. As you will then for the rest of your years. I don't expect you to understand all that needs to be in a season. No true wine man expects the grape to give over its richness promptly. The vine must be cared for and the soil kept favorable for the grape to do so. Patience boy. Patience cultivates the strongest vines," he said and watched as his words took hold in his son's eyes. He rarely had the chance to talk to his father like this anymore.

"I will work toward that," he said. Kastor smiled and patted his son's hand. He resumed walking.

"I know you will son. That is the Brian in you. And remember you said the word 'work.' This word will become more and more important to you in the years to come. More real. No man who doesn't work hard deserves the respect of any man who looks him in the eyes boy. The higher the station. The more one must work to earn that. Marriage is much the same," he said. The pair said nothing for a few moments as they walked. Kastor grinned and turned to Banathir.

"Oh, and you can tell that scoundrel Haldan, he need not worry about shoveling shit. You needed to hear his words as much as you needed to hear mine. I am relieved his council is not all drinking, fighting and pursuing. That is all young men seem to care about anymore. A distraction should never replace a man's real life and purpose. Keep that in mind," Kastor said and laughed. Banathir laughed slightly as well.

"I will father," he said as the pair neared their ships.

Thunder rolled over the waves off the eastern coast. The seasons were changing and soon the summer heat would be replaced by cooler days and rougher seas. The Seastormers called it the Autumn Breeze. Soon the spice traders would start flooding the port as they did every year. This year they may not be as abundant. Lady Marea Falco stood at her balcony, which looked out at the city and harbor of Seastorm. Her olive cheeks still carried warmth in this cool overcast light. Her wavy brown hair wisped around in the modest breeze. There were fewer ships than usual flying the familiar colors of the spice trade. The recent surge of violence north likely meant only the boldest captains would dare sail here. Their wares would reap them more silver she expected. Few ships meant a higher price. It was unfortunate that so much of that silver would be headed out of port. But that was the cost. Marea's grandmother Terosa walked out to the balcony to sit with her granddaughter. She snapped her fingers at the servant girl in the room behind them.

"Olives and pickled onions girl. And some wine," she directed. The girl promptly darted out of the room to fetch the food and drink. Terosa watched to make sure she was gone.

"A little something to upset our appetites for supper grandmother?" Marea mused. Terosa huffed.

"Gods no. I just wanted that silly girl doing something other than standing around earning coppers eavesdropping on a grandmother talking to her grandchild about things best kept from the wrong ears," she said. Marea turned to Terosa.

"Now what deep secrets would that be?" she continued to muse. Terosa held out her hand and invited Marea to sit down with her.

"Firstly, I just wanted tell you how much I'm going to miss you when you're off in Southgate freezing your backside off and drinking that horrid southern ale. I'll be sending you barrels of proper drink for as long as I am able. I will visit when I can as much as I disapprove of those southern brutes and their primitive ways," she gruffed. Marea laughed.

"Grandmother please. Do you have to be so dramatic? I've met Prince Attheon if you remember," she said. Terosa wasn't impressed.

"Oh child you were five and he was already of thirteen years. Old enough to train with a sword. You're twenty and three now. Shall I do the arithmetic for you?" she huffed again.

"There you go again. I'm sure I've changed more than he has. I'm sure he hasn't turned into a southern brute. And besides I will be Queen one day. If I recall a year ago you were already convinced I was going to end up taking vows at the Temple of Tides or turn into a prickly bitter grouse like Pallas bloody Brian," she said and smiled at Terosa. Terosa squeezed her hand.

"I know child. I just worry. The worst that's ever been said about Attheon Lamb is that he spends too much time alone. Men like that are often hard to talk to. They can live in their own worlds they create in their own minds. They care too little for the real world around them. They need to be shown all that there is in this world that is magnificent. You have such a challenge ahead my child," she said.

"I'm sure I'm ready to handle whatever idiosyncrasies Prince Attheon Lamb can bring to bear," she said. Terosa sighed.

"Such bravado. I hope you're right," she said. Behind them the servant girl arrived with a tray of food and drink and set it on the table between the two women.

"Oh lovely my dear. I forgot to mention bread before. Mustn't have wine without bread. Be a dear and go fetch some and make sure it's sliced and toasted," she said. The servant girl curtsied and rushed off to fetch the bread. Marea looked over at Terosa with a sly grin.

"Really grandmother. You never have bread with wine," she said and picked up a plump olive and took a bite from it.

"I just wanted to send her away for a while longer. I can't stand her looming around leering all the time. She's the one who leers. I can't do with leers. Always leering," she sneered. Marea just laughed and ate olives.

Freegale dismounted his horse outside the Far Ward's Sheriff's station. He detested running errands for anyone but his presence was specifically requested. A deputy was posted near the door beside a fire. Freegale walked up to the deputy who looked up at him. Upon recognizing him he rose to his feet and stood to attention. Freegale looked the deputy with disdain.

"I'm not the King lad. I'm just his nephew. Sit back down or you'll hurt yourself," Freegale grumbled. The deputy relaxed some.

"Begging your pardon m'Lord," the deputy said. As was typical Freegale was very poor at hiding his annoyance.

"You have it. Now bloody relax. I'm here to see Sheriff Birch. Is he in?" Freegale said. The deputy nodded nervously. Freegale sighed and rolled his eyes. He looked back at the men who accompanied him.

"Keep the fire company boys. I won't be long," he said and walked up to the station door and rapped on it loudly. A few moments later a small window on the door swung open. A pair of eyes looked out at Freegale who stared right back.

"State your business," a voice said through the window. This was a hassle Freegale was not prepared to tolerate. His evening was already unraveling and he felt like reaching through the little window and grabbing whoever stood behind it. He kept his cool as well as he could.

"Would you like me to wake my uncle from his nap to ask him to what I should say my business is, or are you just going to open the fucking door so my arse doesn't freeze off?" Freegale growled. The eyes peering out widened and the little door slammed shut. Freegale rolled his eyes and sighed again. His men just stood by the fire shaking their heads. On the other side of the door Freegale could hear muffled yelling he could just barely make out.

"It's Freegale Bloody Lamb!" a muffled voice shouted. Moments later the sound of clanking locks being opened rattled the door and it swung open. Another much slighter deputy stood in the doorway with a panicked look on his face.

"Begging your pardon m'Lord. Just following procedure. Sheriff Birch is expecting you," the small deputy said. Freegale waved him out of his way and stomped through the door. Inside a half dozen deputies sat at a table eating bowls of salt pork stew and flatbread. They all had the same look on their faces as the one at the door. Freegale paid them no mind and headed back to Birch's office. He knocked on the door. A muffled voice made it through.

"Come in," Freegale could hear it say. He pushed the door open and saw a familiar face on the other side of a man he'd known for years standing by his fire.

"We have to stop meeting like this Bernard. I do this and we're even. Understood?" Freegale said as he walked up Sheriff Birch and shook his hand.

"Understood fully m'Lord. How have you been these last few years?" Bernard said. Freegale forced a smile.

"Well, I feel like I've been called away from a flagon of ale to help an old friend with a problem. Speaking of the problem, who does he usually have come and get him? I've always wondered that," he said. It was a fair question, but Bernard knew Freegale wasn't going to like his answer.

"We manage one way or another. But you're not here by my request, but rather, by his," Bernard said. This wasn't what Freegale was expecting to hear.

"I don't follow. He might as well have asked us to organize a parade with trumpets, jugglers, and dancing bears. Why the spectacle?" Freegale said. Sheriff Bernard picked up his ring of iron keys from his desk and hooked them to his belt.

"That would be a question for him I'd say. If you'll follow me," Bernard said and walked with Freegale out of his office and down a hall. They passed by stairs that led to the cells on the floor below. Freegale expected that's where Bernard would go, but they turned the corner instead and ended up at a door at the end of an adjacent hallway. Bernard unlocked the door and pushed it open. A tall lanky man was sitting on a small wooden stool looking cold and in quite a bit of distress. Bernard looked back at Freegale.

"I present to you his Eminence, The High Priest of the Mountain Errol Travis and current occupant of my linen closet," Bernard said. Freegale gave Travis a stern look. Travis managed a slight smile.

"How good of you to come for me Lord Lamb. I am deeply pleased to see you," he said. Freegale did not return the smile.

"That makes one of us. Why am I here Travis and why aren't you hiding in a barrel being wheeled back to the Mountain Temple by now?" he said. Travis didn't respond but looked over at the Sheriff instead. Bernard sighed and looked at Freegale.

"From what I understood through all the sobbing earlier the High Priest lost an alarming sum of money on a wager earlier in the night to someone with a particular reputation in the Far Ward," Bernard said. He didn't need to be told much else. Freegale already knew where the High Priest had been.

"One of those West Bend Street people. How much is he in the hole?" Freegale said. Bernard closed his eyes and tilted his head.

"Thirty and eight thousand C," Bernard said somberly. Freegale looked over at Travis in astonishment.

"By the Bloody Fucking Gods Man! How do you lose thirty eight thousand coppers? Does the Temple even have thirty-eight fucking thousand to bet? I don't suppose so, or you'd be over there handing it over to that West Bend Street trash instead of cowering in here. What the bloody fucking hell were you even betting on?" Freegale shouted. Travis sat there trembling.

"I'd rather not say m'Lord," Travis said through a breaking voice. Freegale scowled at him.

"If I'm to somehow find thirty eight fucking thousand tonight to get your holy arse out of a pinch, you'd better tell me how you got it in that pinch in the first place!" Freegale growled and leaned down at Travis to look him right in the eyes. Freegale's growing rage radiated out from him. Errol Travis could feel it and continued to tremble.

"Well, you see m'Lord. We were betting on two young strumpets fellating two gents to see which would curl his toes first. I bet on the dark haired one. The fair haired one won," Travis said. Freegale was speechless. He looked at Bernard. Apparently this was the first time he was hearing this too. The Sheriff's face mirrored his own. He looked back at Travis who was trying to smile slightly.

"Never bet against a tow head with a cock in her mouth. Now you have your arse in a vise. Congratulations are in order. Why should I not walk out of here right now and let The Council of the High Chaplainry elect a new representative to the ministry after they find your body floating in the Far Ward moat come dawn?" Freegale snapped. Travis nervously tried to collect himself.

"Th__ The__ The Temple's gratitude would not appear to be enough to sate in this situation," he said. Freegale was out of patience and could feel himself already sobering up.

"You're damn right Priest!" he yelled. Travis sat there a few moments trembling and looking down at the floor. He looked back up at Freegale. He was a truly defeated little man and would not make it through the night, and he knew it. He knew Freegale knew it as well.

"I'm your only hope then. You figure no trash from West Bend Street is going to try to slit your throat as long you're with The King's nephew. You figure you'll take advantage of my friendship with the Sheriff here. You figure I'll just find thirty eight thousand for you out of the goodness of my heart. I'm getting the picture you're a bad gambler Travis. Why should I help you then?" Freegale said. Travis gave him a long nervous stare. Then he looked over at Bernard.

"This needs to be between the two of us m'Lord," Travis said. Freegale had had enough of the evening. He looked over at The Sheriff.

"I'm feeling peckish Bernard. Could you fetch me some of that bread," he said. Bernard was not happy about being sent away in his own station. He relented though and frowned at Travis.

"Aye m'Lord. I'll go get that," he said and walked off down the hall. Freegale watched as he left and turned the corner. He then looked back at Travis.

"You've got something on your mind Priest. What is it?" Freegale said. Travis looked down at the ground. Several minutes later Freegale stormed out of the Sheriffs office in the poorest mood his men had ever seen him in. He walked over to his horse and mounted it. His men did the same. Freegale turned to one.

"Blaine. I'm going to need you to crack open one the petty caches we have and hand it over to that skulking gent up there on the wall," he said and glanced up at a figure a ways away watching the Sheriffs station.

"What's going on m'Lord?" Blaine said. Freegale shook his head.

"I'm having a bad day. That's all you need to know," Freegale said then snapped his reins.

Chief was tired. She'd been running from floor to floor, level to level, and section to section for the better part of seven hours straight fixing one problem after another or sending her people to do it if she couldn't get to it. She sat in in Common Room 16 at a table near the ping-pong area. Pauly and Phil were enjoying a bit of off time smacking the little ball back and forth while trading quips and a quotes. How two men could carry on such a deep philosophical conversation and play at the same time was beyond her. She was more focused on the burned out capacitor in front of her. An hour ago this room was uncomfortably warm. Complaints had started to come in while she was working on getting a pair of lift doors open a level up from here. She assigned that task to one of her team while she came down here to fix the cooling system for the series of rooms connected to this one. The other ones weren't in use. This one was. Up on a screen above her, a commercial ended and the grinning animated visage of the dapper host of Prime Time in San Tejas with Donny Page appeared along with the opening theme music of the show. It was a sports and superhero clip comedy show where athletes and heroes alike got roasted a few nights a week. The screen was connected to the internet via a computer that stitched together various live streams into a kind of television station. After throwing out a few quips and addressing some comments made by watchers on social media Donny waved his animated hand and an image of Proto Jay appeared on the screen. Donny laughed as he introduced the clip.

"Tonight on the Hot Seat is ace sidekick to The Night Eagle out in National City. Looks like some weapons grade cringe kicked him like a mule. Here he is all the way up in the Big Apple doing his best to keep it together in front of a reporter. He's a good little trooper. Oh boy does he really want to say something. Just look at him smolder," Donny said gleefully and started playing the clip. A reporter for a Fox affiliate had his mic up in Proto Jay's face. He stood his ground in his green uniform, amazing blonde hair, and seasoned resolve. The hero didn't look happy though.

"Again, there is no cause for alarm. The Night Eagle has already said so. As has Admiral Mercury, Jafus Powers, Kaepa Jaime and others. I can appreciate your concern. We take the safety of all Americans seriously. We came here to assist some friends of ours take down a dangerous bunch of characters who'd been up to bad business is all. Together we rained on their parade and returned stolen property to their rightful owners. The Ace of Clubs Gang are off the streets now. I think that's pretty swell. We're the Civic Protectors, and that's what we do," he said with a wink to the camera. Donny laughed and zoomed in on the wink for a replay.

"I don't know how these guys do this everyday. I'd be punching this mic waving guy in the face. Homies just looking out for the homies. That's all. Street life son. You feel me?" he said and then fast-forwarded to later in the video.

"Oh and that's not all Chat. Check out Full Scale with the photo bomb! Can we get some points up on the scoreboard Pedro!" he yelled at his animated sidekick who was a mustachioed gent in a white hoodie and Bermuda shorts. Just then a few points on an animated score keeper on screen chimed and numbers appeared under a photobomb header. The Donny pressed play. Full Scale walked into frame behind Proto Jay to give a pair of thumbs up. Donny chuckled and then began to preface the next clip.

"It's preseason again and the Spurs are back on the home court vs. the Timberwolves, but hold the phone Chat, that ain't the big story! Tanner McGovern just went and__," Chief smiled some as her attention gravitated back to the burned out capacitor on the table in front of her. Martha walked into the room and spotted Chief sitting around looking dour. She walked up and sat across from the ship's chief engineer who looked at a damaged device in front of her. The very sight of it vexed her. She looked at the object and then up at Chief.

"Bad thingamajig?" she said. Chief sighed and picked it up.

"You could say that. Overloaded capacitor. Don't know how it happened. No power surge recorded to explain it. Just went tits up," she said. Martha giggled. Chief raised and brow and set the device down.

"And what are you doing up so late Miss Martha? I thought you had an exam in the morning," she said. Martha smiled mischievously.

"Yeah, don't tell my dad I'm up. I did try to get to sleep but it's hard to get my head to calm down after The Sight. Tony told me walking around helps him," she said. Phil overhearing this chuckled. Both Chief and Martha looked over at him.

"That's not all he does, but I don't think you quite ready for that eh," he said. Martha didn't follow. She just shrugged her shoulders at him.

Phil smirked and served the ball to Pauly. Martha rolled her eyes and looked back at Chief.

"I don't know about any of that. I'm going down to The Cove to pick up a chamomile to go. Then back up to bed to try to sleep," she said. Nearby Pauly raised up his hands in victory and did a little dance. Phil grinned and shook his head. Gracious in defeat. Chief had an idea then.

"Hey kid. You want to work off some of that anxiety before you have your tea?" she said and pointed over to the ping-pong table. Martha looked over at it and the back at Chief with a smile.

"One game? You're on!" she said giddily. Chief got up and walked over to the table. She snatched up a paddle. Phil sat down after surrendering the table to Chief and Martha. Pauly sat by him feeling good about the free drink Phil owed him now. The stream up on the screen had a commercial pop up that wasn't skippable. A breaking news jingle filled the space and a reporters face emerged from a flowing graphic. Then an image popped that Phil recognized as soon as the reporter started talking. Pauly turned to Phil.

"Hey isn't that that guy you know? The cartoonist?" he said. Phil sighed and nodded.

"Yeah that's Cliff. Met him through Warhammer. He ran a stream about it before he got arrested. I watched it for a while before he invited me on. Really good guy. The charges against him are bullshit. Some people in Parliament are ass mad over some of his cartoons. It's just satire. They call it incitement. Like I said. Bullshit. He has a hearing pretty soon. I figured I'd fly up and hang with his people," he said. Pauly leaned back and looked at the image that popped up on the screen. It was one of Cliff's cartoons. Pauly laughed.

"Seriously? What a fucking joke. He got arrested for that? Fucking joke," he said. Phil shook his head.

"Yeah my guy. A lot of other cartoonists are rallying around him. Not just up there, but all over. My boy got done dirty. Good to see other people see it too," he said and stood up.

"Gotta get back to the bar. Whisky on the rocks?" he said. Pauly grinned.

"Read my mind. Let's jet," he said enthusiastically. The two men left the room as Martha giggled at a joke Chief told her and then served the ball. The two rallied for about a minute before Martha snuck a shot past Chief. She raised her hands.

"Whoo!" she yelled. Chief laughed and pointed at her.

"You're getting good kid. May have to stop holding back now," she said with a wink. Martha snickered.

"Oh? Oh? Oh is that so? Well bring it sister," she said slyly. Chief grinned and set down her paddle. Martha watched her with a bit of confusion. Chief then pulled out her phone and found something on it.

"Look at what I found. Actually getting your dad to let you go would be a small miracle, but__," she said and then trailed off. Martha set down her paddle and walked around the table to Chief to see what she was looking up. Chief found it and then showed Martha. Her eyes grew wide.

"No way! Backstreet's back! I missed the show in Cancún! They're coming to Texas! Oh my god! Oh my god!" she yelled. Chief laughed.

"March 30th 2025," she said. Martha gave Chief a hug and then began bouncing up and down.

"I could see Brian Littrell live! He's so gorgeous! Oh my god Chief. Do you know how amazing that is? They've all been dead for hundreds of years in my universe. I could see them alive, and not just old music videos. Oh my god Chief. Thank you for showing me this. I have no idea how to talk dad into letting me go. But thank you," she said and gave Chief another hug.

Dougie yawned widely and loudly and sat back in his chair. His shift had ended hours ago and he would otherwise be asleep, as would Nelson and many others in the room waiting on Angelica to arrive to conduct the Bumppo monthly security meeting. Chelsea sat near the far wall looking through her clipboard and grimacing at all the gaps in sign-offs. Chandler Moon sat behind her leaning against the wall asleep. The other fourteen people in the room looked exceedingly bored as the minutes dragged on. Finally after what felt like an hour Angelica walked into the room. The room stood as she did so. Chelsea turned around and poked Chandler, waking him. He groggily rose to his feet and leaned against the wall. Angelica set down her mug of tea and tablet and looked back and forth at the people in the room, which made up less than half the total number of security personnel.

"Please be seated," she said and everyone sat back down. Angelica reached down and picked her tablet up again and switched it on.

"I know it's late so I'll be brief. This hasn't been an easy month so far. For this place, that says a lot. I'll address the elephant in the room before we get into anything else. It's one the most poorly kept secrets on the ship at this point. On the fifth of this month my brother and Doctor Salazar dashed into mission numbered 72. On this mission a snafu occurred which instigated a fight between them. Many of the particulars insofar as how are still being investigated. I don't have those answers right now in other words. What I can say is that there is no lingering hostility between my brother and Doctor Salazar, and should be no cause for further concern," she said as she looked around the room at faces that displayed a varying range concern despite her reassurances. Angelica took a sip of tea and set her mug back down.

"I'll continue on by praising the response time to the colors alert. Unfortunately there still remains much to be desired from the detection structure, as it currently exists. It makes it necessary that security be at the top of their game, and in this instance, it was. My thanks. We don't work within conventional expectations. How good would your batting average be if all that was thrown at you were knuckleballs and curves? We do our best. Anyway I'm sure some of you have questions," she said and looked around again. There was silence and people looking around at each other for a few moments then Chelsea raised her hand. Angelica pointed to her.

"It's nearing the end of the month and I still have almost a quarter of the crew that haven't gotten up to date on their safety modules. I am so sorry. I am trying my hardest to get everyone caught up," she said and looked down at her clipboard. Angelica saw that there were still many names not checked off. She didn't show much disappointment.

"Don't be so hard on yourself Towers. It's hard to track down everyone on a ship this big. Circumstances being what they are at present, I am extending the deadline through the first week of October.

That should give you a little more time to work with. The Chemical Cleanup module is the only one scheduled for next month so you should be in good shape," she said. Chelsea smiled and relaxed her shoulders. Nelson raised his hand. Angelica pointed to him.

"Most of the security doors on level 27 only open halfway or not at all. I have put in three work orders this week. What is being done about it?" he said. Angelica nodded slowly.

"What can be done, is. I'm sorry to say that Chief and her team are already running around every which way fixing what they can. Automated platforms that are still operational are working around the clock as well," she said. Nelson wasn't very impressed but he kept his comments to himself. Chandler on the other hand was far more talkative.

"Okay great. It's starting to look like flying through a space war wasn't such a great idea. What was the reasoning behind that again? My teeth are still rattling," he said and sat back in his chair with arms folded. Angelica frowned and then sighed.

"I can't get into much of what went down. I hope you can understand. The dash to the intended destination was interrupted by shear. Not every trip is a clean one. It's a risk we run sometimes. That's why we don't dash the Bumppo unless we absolutely have to. Mission 71 called for it. Optimal exfil dash point was in a bad spot. That's the Cliff's Notes version," she said. Dougie's brow narrowed.

"Flying around the war wasn't an option?" he said sarcastically. Angelica took a deep breath. What she wanted to say was above the clearance of most of the people in the room. She considered what she was going to say next carefully.

"Not from my understanding. The optimal dash window was in a state of rapid decay, which made it necessary to fly through an active battle zone. A call needed to be made right then and there. I get by the looks on most of your faces that this is not the explanation you want to hear, so I'll give you the bottom line. Nobody is doing what we are doing. Nobody knows it needs to be done. If they did know they would still have to be dependent on the guys and the tech only they can use. This doesn't put us is a great position having to make things up as we go. But no precedent means we have to think on our feet more than any of us would seek to. It's the dirty part of adventure," she said. Some eyes appeared more convinced than others, but it would have to do for the time being. She was sure this would be brought up again and harbored no illusions that this would be last time the subject would come up which was the down side to blazing new territory.

The chambers of the Senior Brothers was infrequently busy this time of night, but activity kept the candles lit and a fire going on the hearth. Five longtime Brothers sat here discussing one matter or another. Much of the conversation pertained to the construction work going on all round the Lodge. Other talk involved food stores for the late fall and winter months. However the mood shifted when they saw Senior Brother Alvin enter the room. He gestured for his escort to wait outside the room while he made his way in and to his seat. The others halted their conversation as he approached. Alvin was not in the best of moods to be here at this late.

"I expect I will be relieved to hear that my journey here this late in the day has a substantial reason behind it," Alvin said as he sat down. Brother Lorry was quick to respond. His frizzy white hair, greatly receded, caught the firelight next to him

"We do thank you for joining us Brother Alvin. I must apologize for summoning you so late in the day. Myself and the others have been kept so busy with setbacks in the construction project we couldn't schedule at a better time. There are matters, which must be discussed now. The Delegation expects a feather. As much has been laid out in no uncertain terms," Lorry said. Alvin sighed.

"So be it then. I do appreciate you explaining it. It seems that The Delegation has become something of a bothersome and overbearing entity as of late. But even so what must be done, must be. What role in this particular discussion should I be assuming here on this night?" Alvin said. Brother Corbin spoke up.

"I'm sure you are aware of the many problems we're having with the ongoing construction project and how that will affect the harmony of this great Lodge come winter. While this is the most proximate issue it is by far not the most paramount issue to The Delegation," he said. He was a larger man who projected his voice better than most in the room. Nonetheless Lorry chose to interject.

"That would be rather the progress our Brother Pepper and his new, protégé I could say, Brother Garrett have made in their curious glyph assignment. Do you have anything to add to what we already have had difficulty gleaning from that stubborn wolf and his dusty vault of horrors?" Lorry asked almost snidely. Alvin took a moment to answer.

"I do understand your frustration Brother Lorry. I would ask you impart a bit more compassion to Brother Pepper. He was given an unusual task and not given much in the way of help from The Delegation, who have up until this very moment not tendered anything more than a scribble on paper and a demand to know what it is. Any of us would have the same challenge Pepper has had to contend with, and none of us need to be belittled for our trouble. Please remember that Brother Lorry," Alvin said with a hint of sternness in his voice. Brother Lorry softened his tone.

"My apologies Brother Alvin. The night asserts itself and the weight of all this is heavy. My words carry too much that I would not truly like to convey," he said. This seemed to satisfy Alvin who sat back in his chair. Brother Rolan took this opportunity to speak up. He was a shorter and slighter man with mostly grayed hair. He sat forward in his chair and cleared his throat.

"Even so however Brother, the question still remains. We will need to tell The Delegation something in our feather. I know nobody wants to hear the word 'audit' here. None more than myself. But they have been keenly insistent," he said. Alvin knew this pressure well. There had been audits before in the past when The Delegation felt ignored. This time felt particularly precarious.

"I understand completely Brother Rolan. What I can say from the last time I spoke to them was that they'd run across and image that bore some similarity to the one they have been charged with finding. Though they did not explicitly state as much, I got the impression this find had renewed their vigor. This is not a much, but it is at least more to offer than more of the same," Alvin said. Corbin's demeanor seemed to brighten upon hearing this.

"This is far better news than I expected. It seems that young Brother Garrett is proving to be a valuable asset. Though I don't care much for Grain, I don't recall Brother Pepper working well with anyone else in the past. He always struck me as a wolf set in his ways. An iron forged conviction so marvelously present in his father, but so misguided in him. It is my feeling that Brother Garrett should stay on to assist Brother Pepper for the foreseeable future. You can't be the only Brother in this Lodge the wolf won't turn his nose up to Alvin. Not now anyhow," Corbin said. Alvin was pleased to see he wasn't the only one to recognize Garrett's importance. As he looked around at the eyes of the men at the table he saw this was the general consensus.

"Well observed as always Brother Corbin. I will continue to do my part in guiding them. I have found that given the right support, even a stubborn wolf, or man for that matter, can find the right way," he said. Lorry had his reservations about Pepper, and always had since he first arrived as teenaged pup younger than Brother Garrett. If any other brother would deal with Pepper's rare collection they would be up there instead of him. Lorry would make sure of that. But those books were feared. Superstition was a powerful thing. Even among the so-called learned men of The East Lodge. Pepper was their only option. Other Brothers had threatened to leave The Lodge rather than deal with books they regarded as cursed.

"I concur with Brothers Corbin and Alvin. We will continue to encourage the collaboration of Brothers Pepper and Garrett. As I see it, we have no other prospects anyway, so we might as well play the pieces we do have. I regret I have to put it that way, but things are the way they are," Lorry said. Alvin did not like Lorry's attitude when it came to Pepper, but he did appreciate his frankness.

"I thank you for speaking plainly nonetheless Brother Lorry. And if there is no other need of my input I would like to take my leave and get some sleep. I would recommend the rest of you do the same. None of us are young enough to be burning this much midnight oil," Alvin mused as he got up from his chair. Brother Rolan did the same.

"I think what we've already discussed here will make a meaty enough message for feather would you all not agree?" he said. The other Brothers around the table nodded. Their desire for a warm bed far outweighed their desire to argue at this point. Corbin echoed his colleague's statements.

"I do believe you're right Brothers. I'll get everything down on paper and in the air before my tea gets cold. It's already been a very long night," he said and picked up his quill.

Chapter Seven: Cacophony

The FTR had a few visitors this Friday morning on the 20th of September. The break room was rather full. A coffee maker gurgled on a counter next to a table were several senior members of the Bumppo crew sat. Stratum sat in the hallway just outside the break room peering through the open doorway. He'd spent the last couple of days re-watching a video of his friend Geoffrey Hollis singing him happy birthday and some other songs he liked during his birthday party. The evening put him in a good mood he was still in. Not everyone shared his warm disposition. Around the table sat Nocivo, JP, Salazar, Jack, Chief, Hammer, and The Director. Terry watched through a tablet set up next to the coffee maker. They awaited a presentation generated by E.V.E., which was compiling. The conversation seemed to jump back and forth between the NBA upcoming season and recent Martin Lawrence stand up special the group had watched as a holographic progress bar floated above the table. Nocivo showed up wearing a San Antonio Spurs jersey. Antonio wore a Houston Rockets jersey. JP wore a Dallas Mavericks jersey. They glared at each other for a few moments when they first sat down. Their basketball conversations tended to become spirited. They kept the trash talking modest among their current company though. Enough headache fuel permeated the present situation. There had apparently been a few breakthroughs in the last few days regarding micro contaminations that JP and Director Clark made. Now this group was gathered to hear the findings. As the progress bar completed The Director took a sip of coffee from his large FTR Labs mug then stood up from his chair.

"My sincerest apologies to you all for convening in this venue. I hope you'll forgive the cramped quarters and bothersome noisy coffee maker. But ship wide diagnostics testing has limited the number of places in which give this presentation. Power demands being what they are. I feel somewhat sympathetic to everyone having to walk around with flashlights at present. I would formally request the default settings on emergency lighting be increased, but other matters need attending to," The Director said. Chief grimaced a bit.

"Testing will be done when it's done. Shakedown has to happen one way or another. I'll see about the lights," she said. Nocivo understood the pressure she had placed on herself to get The Bumppo up and flying again. He felt some considerable responsibility for it to be in the shape it was in. He still would have given the same order. But acknowledged the consequences had been immensely costly.

"You're doing what needs to be done Chief. As is everyone here. This is a team operation. We all have important work to do and roles to fill," Nocivo said. Director Clark gestured in agreement.

"Indeed Doctor. And perhaps what myself and The Commodore have discovered after quite the epiphany may help all of us understand what we are doing with greater clarity. Observe," The Director said and pulled out his remote device. Upon clicking it the holographic progress bar changed into two sets of flowing code. The Director turned to JP who stood up as well.

"Everyone I suppose you are wondering what it is you are looking at," he said. From the looks around the room this assessment was accurate. Chief was giving it a good hard look, as was Stratum. Chief pointed one of the lines of code. Her brain lit up like a Christmas parade as something deep within her revved up like a Formula 1 car. In almost an instant she recognized what she was looking at.

"This looks like an executable for high energy frequency amplitude oscillation," she said. For most in the meeting code was nothing more than a sequence of numbers. To Chief it was a language that told her a story. Stratum also recognized the code.

"That's the code extracted from the nanotech we got from Skip and Salazar," he said. JP pointed up at the floating image.

"Well yes and no Strat. The code on the left is the one we extracted from the nanotech we found inside Tony's helmet. The code on the right, well, it's the original code we took off of Barnes's laptop, which Tony retrieved from the scene and is thankfully now under lock and key at Site 55. They aren't the same code," JP said and brought up two differing portions of code. Chief looked at them closely.

"Brilliant," she said as she marveled at the drastic change in direction between the two iterations. JP expanded the graphic to show how many highlighted sections of code there were.

"That was just one of thousands a changes to the later code," he said. Nocivo got up to have a closer look himself, though he was very far outside his area. He looked over at JP and The Director.

"So Barnes uploaded a later version to the nanotech?" he asked. JP and The Director looked at each other for a moment and then back at Nocivo.

"Not exactly Doctor," The Director said. This was obviously confusing for Nocivo.

"Clarify then please," he said. Stratum poked his head through the door as something caught his eye. He looked over at Chief.

"No fucking way," he said. She read the expression in his yellow eyes. A sudden realization hit her and she shot an astonished look over at JP. His eyes confirmed what was going on in her mind.

"The later version wasn't coded by Barnes. We poured over that laptop and looked at everything he was doing from start to finish. Barnes was nowhere near being able to fathom the pieces he'd need to figure out just to make his nanotech actually do what he wanted it to do. He was years off. Decades maybe. Maybe never. He was a bright fellow. He just didn't have the mind it took to look in the right directions," The Director said. Antonio having brought Barnes down himself was a little off-put.

"So if Barnes didn't cook up this code. Who did?" he said and folded his arms in disgust. JP looked over at his friend and colleague. What he had to say may agitate Antonio even further but it needed to be said.

"It's not such a matter Who, but rather What, altered that code Tony," he said. Tony's expression was understandable. JP continued.

"To answer a question Skip asked earlier. As to what connection did micro contaminations have with nanotechnology we recovered from Mission 72, the answer is right here in this code." JP said. Nocivo still looked confused.

"In what manner?" He said. The Director cued up some new figures. Dates and times seemed to be among them. JP gestured to them.

"Four days and eleven hours before he launched his attack he uploaded a new version to the machine Tony dashed to Site 55 for containment. It in turn began building nano bots for Barnes updated with the new software. But the breakthrough for him actually occurred two months prior according to the video bad guy amateurs like him always insist on making of themselves. Video of him running tests on the nanotech to record their mass responses to a master control signal, and as you would guess. Failure after failure, until one day, after being forced to reboot his systems after a power outage, the nanotech started responding how he wanted them to. The code however that sat in his system was not the same code that was there before the reboot," JP said. Antonio rolled his eyes and looked away.

"He got too excited that he didn't fuck up again he neglected to look at the code to see why it was suddenly working, right? Fucking amateurs should stick to Angry Birds. Make the birdie fly, casual!" Antonio grumbled. JP wished Antonio was taking this better, but he understood.

"It looks that way Tony. He instead concluded a newer design in the nanotech's signal receiver he included in their newest build was responsible. Somewhat understandable. But you're right man. Amateur move." JP said. Antonio's expression didn't change much.

"So I did all that legwork after nabbing that hack Barnes__," Antonio began saying but just trailed off in further disgust. The Director picked up where JP had left.

"Undoubtedly, the prevailing question here is what caused the change to the code. What The Commodore and I propose is that the micro contaminations themselves altered the code. One of a trillion trillions of alterations they could have made universe wide sending countless events off in different directions they would have otherwise not gone in. It seems infinitely daunting in the face of that; this would be proverbial raised nail. But there it is," said The Director. Nocivo looked at the dates and times from their end as well as those pulled from Barnes's laptop.

"The dates do not line up to our timeline of events. How do you explain this discrepancy? Also why the nanotech specifically triggered The Sight in both Tony and Martha, and nothing else in this universe appears to have?" Nocivo said. The Director pointed to JP. He felt put a little on the spot, but answered nonetheless.

"What we had understood about contaminations themselves was wrong. We lack a complete enough picture of what was going on. Simply put. What we understand now is that contaminations occur in stages. At least two that we can observe at this time. Maybe more. When it comes to The Sight, we just don't know enough now why The Sight would trigger when it does. Even less why it focuses on what it does. We do have a somewhat clearer idea of why their sight seems to dial in on these events exclusively, and it has to do with Iso Harmonics," JP said. Antonio looked over at JP.

"Now what now?" he said. JP continued.

"The Iso Harmonic signature that produces the Iso Lock with the dash tech is also minutely present in the nanotech. It's not our Iso from that universe. Harmonics are too minute for it to be. But the similar harmonics would go far to explain why so many of the worlds we dash to are other versions of Earth, or are otherwise Earth-like. It's perhaps the place in most destinations more likely to carry our Iso signature or a number close to it. Proximity and adjacency, in theory," he said. Something bothered Antonio about that explanation.

"Okay so how does Martha pick up the same events as I do? She's not a dash tech compatible Iso. Her Iso Harmonic profile is different and should pick up on other things going on. Why the synch?" Antonio said. JP and The Director looked at each other again.

"We don't know. There is so much we don't know. We discover what we discover, when we discover it. We're toddlers playing with matches most of the time. Each of us in this room is driven by the same scientific, medical and engineering curiosities that get us asking questions about all the things we don't know," JP said. Nocivo chimed in.

"And taking a second look at everything we thought we understood," he said. The Director pointed at him.

"Precisely Doctor," he said and then shut down the hologram. JP rubbed his face and sighed through his grogginess. He looked over at Antonio who still looked fairly soured.

"Thanks for hard flashing the nano tech firmware back to Barnes' first build by the way. Not a loose thread that that universe could afford to have just laying around. It also opened up some source code for us. One more dot on the map to connect," he said and nodded at Antonio. Salazar threw him a thumb up as he perked up some.

"I'll take a win whenever I can get it. Besides, I got to try out a new formula I've been working on for a good while now. It far exceeded even my expectations," he said with a sly grin. Nocivo gave him a side-glance. JP narrowed his brow. Chief was a bit confused.

"I'm sorry? A source code? What source code?" she said as she raised her hand. JP looked up at her.

"It's not so much a source code. Only a nickname we have for snippets of information we get from 'Fixing' a contamination. It gives us clues to where a rogue dash machine might be. Fix fails 'bring on the blues' as Tony puts it. Leads get muddy and make it that much more critical to get it right the next time. We try hard not to fail in other words. Sorry to get you excited over the nomenclature," he said. Chief frowned. Then she held up a finger.

"Can't a predictive model be constructed based on the information you already have to plot points farther down the line?" she said. The Director took a sip of coffee and then shook his head.

"Alas no. Regrettably the 'source code' has proven to be confounding and random. Seemingly that is. Evie has attempted to build models, but sadly none have withstood rigor. Clues would not equate to a road map mildly put," he said. Nocivo pushed his chair back and stood.

"The best we can do right now is grind through the missions as they occur, and make the most of what we learn, when we learn it," he said. Chief grimaced. Many in the room shared her expression.

Hours later the hanger echoed with a discordant chatter of competing noise on a late Friday morning. The work on Pathfinder N-37B was steady but an absence of new replacement parts slowed down progress considerably. Amadou stood on the platform next to it wearing a headset directing the operator of a crane lowering a heavy section of the ship's roof back into place. His thick Senegalese accent could be heard throughout the hanger calling out directions and asking for the operator to go slower.

The crews in the hanger were happy to have him back. JP was a big help but Amadou was certainly a big part of helping the machinery of human collaboration operate well. JP was still here helping out, but he was now at N-37B's flight controls finishing up the calibrations that Martha had started the other day. He had come to the conclusion that the remaining erroneous 1.8% wasn't in the avionics, but rather an issue with another part of the craft. A conclusion he made sure to write down in his notes. Down on the floor the hanger on this level was itself being cleaned up.

Ernie and Ian were below the N-37B mopping a degreasing agent on the flooring, which had to happen frequently due to so many oily viscous fluids deposited on the floor by machinery leaking. Ernie began to laugh seemingly out of nowhere. Ian looked up and set his mop aside.

"What?" he said. Ernie grinned and leaned over.

"Hey Ian, what do you call fish of low intelligence?" he said and waited for Ian's response. Ian dropped his shoulders and looked at Ernie.

"What Ernie?" he said. Ernie was trembling. The laughter was difficult to contain. But he prevailed.

"Dumb Basses," he said and shook harder. Ian cracked and smile, and couldn't help but laugh a little. Ernie burst our laughing loudly.

"See, I got the laugh! There it is!" he said and continued to laugh.

"Son of a bitch Ernie. That was bad. The General is a bad influence on you man I swear," he said which made Ernie laugh harder.

Antonio had volunteered some of his time he would otherwise spend in the lab to pitch in. He drove a Unicarriers 30 Goliath series electric forklift moving crates around for Ward and Nick. He'd operated one for over five years in his father's company. Mauricio Salazar didn't like slackers or moochers. If Antonio wasn't in the lab, he was making himself useful elsewhere.

He didn't get a free pass because he was the boss's son. He put in a full day, one way or the other. A week after his eighteenth birthday he was in forklift training. One of the ways he spent his time was loading and unloading trailers. He took to singing while he was driving around. The people working in the warehouse always knew he was coming. Antonio moved forward and tilted his forks down to slide under a plastic pallet that had a stack of hydraulic fluid canisters secured onto it. Once under he tilted the forks back and raised them a few inches off the floor. He looked over at Ward and Nick. They were standing in the red light that indicated the safe distance away from the forklift. He gave them a look and they both stepped back out of the light. They got kind of a chuckle from that, but did appreciate Antonio's emphasis on safety.

"Okay where do you guys want it?" Salazar said. The guys chuckled again.

"Bay Ten, please" Ward said. Antonio threw them a thumb up. He honked the horn and put the forklift in reverse. A familiar repetitious beeping followed as he moved backwards. He threw the controls back in to forward and drove in the direction of bay ten. As soon as he accomplished this task he drove to the equipment parking area and stopped on one of the available spaces. As soon as he got down sensors detected his movement and tire locks automatically raised and clamped the forklift down into place. Antonio walked out of the hanger area and into the hall leading to lift to the upper levels. He took off his hardhat and the reflective safety shirt he was wearing and stepped into the lift. It took him to the floor where Common Room 16 resided. It's where he'd left his tablet before going down to the garage level. The room was fairly active with 'All Night Long' by The Mary Jane Girls playing on the room's audio system. He sat down on one of the easy chairs near where Jack, Chief and Pauly were sitting during their off time. Given the tone of the meeting earlier he understood the desire to kick back and enjoy themselves. Jack looked up from his laptop and gave Antonio a wave.

"Hey Tony," he said. Antonio didn't say anything but just smiled. Chief was a bit chattier.

"So how is the N-37B looking?" she said. Antonio just kind of shrugged his shoulders.

"She's coming along. I was just forklifting stuff around down there for the most part. They were putting the roof plating back on last I saw. Amadou was there so it got installed without much hassle. He's good at directing the crane. So that's a win," he said and stretched his arms. Chief opened up a tab on her tablet and looked at the current progress reports on the N-37B. There were things she was pleased to see but other things, not so much. She frowned slightly and closed the tab.

"If she gets off the ground before Thanksgiving it'll be a gosh darn miracle," she said. Antonio didn't disagree with her. So much of that operation was out of his wheelhouse so he deferred to people who knew what they were doing. But he was in a particular mood.

"Well, didn't ya know Chief? We are in the business of miracles," he said. Chief rolled her eyes and looked over at Antonio.

"We're in the business of working with pretty dangerous stuff Tony. And then high fiving when we don't die on a daily basis, because we work with some pretty dangerous stuff," she said while giving Antonio a judging side stare. Again Antonio did not disagree. Pauly chimed in though.

"Well I don't know Chief. Hemingway stressed it was more important how one lives as the ultimate metric, so in our case we're likely to die in a variety of interesting ways. I'd put emphasis of the word Interesting. A boring death is just that. If you think of all the ways we could die in our daily to-do's, if we were doing something else less cutting edge than we do, you begin to paint a fairly uninteresting picture," he said. Chief looked over at Pauly who was grinning.

"Well Pauly I'd rather not die don't cha know. Imma make sure things around me work right so my workspace doesn't yeet me the next time I think I gotta handle on things. When ya girl Chief double-checks her settings, she's watching her own ass. I got that drip. Tony can keep his miracles. I have a checklist. Respect the checklist," she said and flipped her tablet around and waved her hand around her checklist. Something she was very proud of. Jack decided to chime in then.

"Hey Tony you talk about miracles. What the weirdest thing you have ever seen doing this Iso thing?" he said. Antonio looked over at him. He thought about it for a bit and then turned to his backpack and pulled out his laptop. He woke it up and searched for a moment or two until he found what he was looking for. He opened a video file and then pressed play. He set the laptop on the table in front of him with the screen pointed at the others.

"So Jack there's a lot of crazy shit I have seen out there on dash. Shit that scared the absolute fuck out of me. Shit that was unbelievably awesome. And then you have things like this that are nothing short of miraculous. For lack of a better description," he said. The others leaned in to get a closer look at what was on Antonio's screen. Jack studied it for a few moments and looked up at Antonio.

"What are we looking at here?" he said. Antonio smiled and looked around at all of them.

"You are looking at footage we took during some of our earliest experimentation with dash probes. We decided to run what is called a double slit test. What you are looking at here are quantum particles passing through two slits in a setup we placed in a nearby universe. The camera recording this experiment is on a probe outside that universe observing what slit the particles passed through. On a larger scale ordinary matter will pass through these slits in a predictable pattern. They'll just simply go though in line with the slits. Waves will pass through these slits and create interference patterns on the other side as the waves interact with each other on the other side. Quantum particles do both. However when closely observed they will change their behavior. Almost as if they have an awareness of the observer and act differently as a result. Wild stuff. What do you notice here Jack?" Antonio said and then tapped the side the laptop screen. Jack looked closely.

"I don't know what I'm supposed to be seeing," he said. Just then a second view window opened up on the video. Jack looked at that for a few moments and then up at Antonio.

"I don't know what this is," he said. Antonio smiled.

"The smaller window there was footage taken ten minutes prior before the probe began observing. A third window is about to appear showing the wall sensor behind the double slit setup. As you can see, there is no change. Quantum particles are being observed without them being aware they are, and thus, do not behave any differently. Like I said. Wild stuff," he said. The group was just sat back. Chief was both fascinated and horrified at the same time.

"Isn't this impossible?" she said. Antonio could sense the trepidation in her voice. He had little to assuage her concern.

"Yes. If current understanding of physics is anything to go by this should be impossible," Antonio said then the view changed on the video. Now the footage showed the quantum particles alternating their spread pattern on the sensor. Jack looked up at Antonio with a puzzled look.

"What's happening there Tony? Now they're behaving differently," he said. Antonio nodded.

"Yes they are Jack. That footage is from an earlier test where we put an in-universe sensor right at the double slit setup. It behaved just at it did when other researchers tried this experiment. JP and Stratum have their theories. I asked one time and I all I got from it was string theory this and quantum entanglement that. I was drunk at the time and the Rockets were playing. You may have better luck retaining the conversation," he said. This didn't give Jack the answer he was looking for, but he just sat back in his chair and continued to watch the screen. Chief was tying herself in knots though.

"Okay Tony I have seen some dangerous shit. I maintain the Bumppo's weapon systems. I know what kind of shit we can bring if we want to. But this is on another level of dangerous. These probes can see anything and not even quantum particles know they're being watched. Holy shit Tony. That's scary as fuck. You could spy on anyone. Who should have that kind of power?" she said. Antonio understood every point she just made.

"Obviously we shouldn't. When people talk about the proverbial 'wrong hands,' that generally means us. A squad of squares didn't run across dash tech. We did. Insofar as abuses of power go, we've been fairly modest. When we weren't, it bit us in the ass. No way of knowing if the original creator of dash ever figured out how to reverse engineer his own work to create something like the probes. No way of knowing if he would find something like that useful," he said. Jack looked up Antonio with a very worried look.

"He could be watching us right now man," he said. Antonio and the others looked at Jack. Then they all looked at him. He turned the laptop around and stopped the video.

"Chances are remote. But never zero. He would likely be working with the same limitations we are. First off that test you saw burned off an immense amount of dash. It caught us flat-footed. Got a hit a day later. Couldn't run the probes very long. We dashed in with shit intel. Nearly got our assed shot off. Wasn't fun. A lot of running. Second problem he's going to have is dialing into a locus. Without that number he could be looking everywhere in existence but here," he said. It didn't seem to ease the group much. Pauly had something on his mind.

"Forgive me. I know the room is pretty freaked out right now, but theoretically a dash probe could see what's inside a black hole from outside the universe it's in right?" he said. Jack and Chief looked at him with narrowed eyes. Antonio pondered this while he shut his laptop.

"Theoretically yes. A few problems though Pauly. You'd have to have its locus. Having one number for one part of a universe doesn't mean you free reign over the whole universe unless you actually went there. As soon as probes are deployed they're burning through juice. We can only cover so much ground before we start running out of the mojo for ourselves. Es no bueno. It's also what's making tracking down The Dealer so hard. It's not like we can do some sleuthing wherever we please. Limited dash means we have very narrow windows. That we've been able to recover four devices thus far, is nothing short of a miracle," he said. Pauly just sat back and grinned.

"Okay all that aside what is the first weird thing you experienced?" he said. Antonio thought about this for a moment.

"You're probably asking for something mission related. But instead, I have this tale to tell. My family and I were driving up to visit my grandparents in Albuquerque, New Mexico back in 1983. December 23rd to be exact. My father didn't believe in spending money frivolously, so no air travel. Anyhow we stopped at some kind of Motel 6 type of place in Sweetwater, Texas. It had a pool. Anyhow that evening I was listening to radio through my tape player through my headphones. By this time I was having minor Sights and doctors really didn't have an idea of how to treat me, so I was taking these pills that made it hard to stay asleep. Music seemed to help so parents didn't mind me listening to music until I got tired. A song came on I'd heard once or twice before so I recorded it to a mix tape I was building. Wasn't paying attention to the

DJ before it started playing it so I never got the actual title or band that wrote it. Station went to commercial after it played. Whatever, went to sleep after that. Took the tape out and put it in my pajama shirt pocket. Dad liked to make mix tapes too. I didn't want this song to get recorded over. Lights out then. So I woke up later in the middle of the night. Of course everyone was sleeping like a rock. Even my little brother Marcelo. I was laying there just staring at the ceiling and the walls hating life when I saw something. The wallpapering began to change. It looked like a fractal or when steel wool burns. But the flat teal that was there when I went to sleep changed into a kind of jungle motif. That pattern was still there when I woke up. Asked everyone about it. They looked at me like I was an idiot or took too much medicine. Couldn't gather much from the experience, but what I did understand is the doctors didn't know shit about my condition. My parents made me stop taking those pills after that. Slept much better. Wouldn't be the last meds I'd get put on, but at least I wasn't taking that one anymore," Antonio said and then stuffed his laptop into his backpack. The group had a number of problems with what Antonio just said. None more than Chief, but she kept much of that to herself for the time being. She could see this coming up again in the future. She had one observation to note though.

"You saw a Mandela Effect happening in real time?" she said. Antonio looked up at her with a puzzled expression. Jack and Pauly looked at her with the same expression. She was a bit taken aback.

"You haven't heard of the Mandela Effect where you all are from?" she said. The others just looked at each other.

"What is a Mandela?" Pauly said. The others looked at Chief.

Activity was going on down the hall in the treatment ward of the infirmary. Not so much that Estrello felt compelled to snap on some gloves and pitch in. It didn't sound like many people were being treated so he knew his nurses had it covered. He was instead sitting alone in his office. Nobody would disturb him while he was shut in here. This was his place for relatively quiet reflection. With his keen hearing there were few truly quiet places for him to go. But his office was quiet enough. His aquariums containing all his pet sea horses cast the room in a topaz glow. A laptop sat on his desk in front of him. He opened it and booted it up. When the desktop appeared he searched for a file. It didn't have a name other than a date of October 13th, 2010. He opened it. Inside was a video file, which he clicked. Just then the sound of waves filled his ears. He saw himself standing on the Cole Park Pier in his hometown of Corpus Christi, Texas. His younger brother Diego was holding the camera. He remembered the day like it was yesterday. He chuckled a bit seeing how long his hair used to be. Then he saw her. His Laura. She had gorgeous dark hair but with frosted highlights. She wore her hair that way back then. Then he heard her voice. A beautiful British accent fluttered around like a melody. A Londoner. They had been dating for four years by then. People of their haplotype had spread all over the world over the course of tens of thousands of years. She came from one of the European families. Estrello's brother Diego introduced them on President's Day five years prior. They began dating a year later. On this day in October of 2010 his family had gotten together to celebrate an early Halloween and Dia De Los Muertos. Laura was studying at The University of London at the time for a degree in marine biology and had to fly back for mid-term exams.

Estrello took this opportunity to do something that scared the living daylights out of him. Dressed as Formula 1 driver, Estrello fell to one knee before Laura and took a small box out of his pocket. He'd spoken to her father while they were both in the UK a few months prior. He had his blessing and now he asked Laura a very important question. Dressed as 1960s hippie girl, and with tears in her eyes, she said yes. Estrello paused the video just after she said it. Tears rolled down his face. He stared at the frozen image for a time then rubbed his eyes clear from the tears that flowed through them. He reached over and pulled his laptop closed. As he did the glint from his wedding ring on his finger caught his eye. A picture of his wife and himself at a county fair three years after their wedding sat in his line of sight sitting on a shelf just past his desk. In the hurry to flee it was the only physical photograph he had of her. They were both smiling as both their faces poked out from a plywood cutout. She was a sunflower and he was an ear of corn. He smiled slightly and looked at it as tears continued to roll down. Then an alarm screamed all around him.

"Colores," he said out loud. He stood up and wiped the tears from his eyes with a towel and flipped his laptop back open. There was her face again. It gave him pause for a moment but then he minimized the video file and clicked on the app connected to E.V.E.

"Evie, Sit-Rep if you would," he said and waited for a response. A moment later E.V.E. appeared on his screen.

"I'm getting a hit at a locus farther down the line from the last one. Still waiting for final numbers. But the assigned tag is universe Charlie Oscar Sierra Foxtrot Papa.3857000009-Alpha Echo Romeo pattern group. GN designation," she said.

"Understood. Can you give me a location for Tony and Martha?" he said. E.V.E. brought up a schematic of the ship. Two yellow dots appeared in different areas.

"Tony is in Common Area 16 just above the garage level. Martha is in Classroom 5 in the Ship Library 3," E.V.E. said. Nocivo picked up and put on his medical coat.

"Send a med team to Martha's location. Tony is closer to me. I'll go myself," he said. E.V.E. gave him a thumb's up as he left the room.

In the infirmary ward nurses Tyson and Rhonda were the two on duty. Nocivo signaled to Rhonda to follow him. They rushed down three levels to Common Area 16. They found Antonio sitting with Pauly, Jack, Chief and now Seijin sitting at the far end of the room by the vending machines. They seemed to be engaged in some kind debate. Antonio noticed Nocivo and Rhonda approach and looked up. The rest took notice too. Chief turned to Estrello.

"Hey Skip, you've heard of Nelson Mandela right?" she said. This wasn't what Estrello was expecting the lead off question to be.

"Yes, he was a South African politician," he said. Chief turned and pointed at everyone.

"Skip knows who Nelson Mandela is. I'm not crazy. He was a real guy," she said mockingly. Nocivo didn't quite get what was going on.

"What about Nelson Mandela?" Nocivo said, hoping this bore some relevance to The Sight. Chief turned back to him.

"They've never heard of The Mandela Effect," she said. Nocivo just stared at her blankly for a moment.

"What is a Mandela Effect?" he said and looked at Antonio who shrugged his shoulders. Chief grimaced in dissatisfaction.

"Looks like mama has to do some explaining here," she said. Nocivo had other things on his mind.

"With due respect Chief, I think that can wait. I came here to see Tony, who just seems to be sitting here eating ice cream sandwiches," he said. Antonio was about to unwrap another one but set it down slowly, almost sarcastically.

"What can I do for you Skip?" he said. Nocivo studied him for a moment. Then he looked around the room and raised his hands. Antonio did the same in puzzled mimicry.

"I don't know what that gesture means man," he said. Nocivo pointed to his head. Then Antonio knew what he wanted to know then.

"Oh yeah the colors. The locus is a good distance away, which sucks. The Bends are gonna be rough when I get there. I was heading down to see Terry in a bit. Figured that's where you'd be going. You showed up here instead. Unusual but fine whatever," he said and unwrapped his ice cream sandwich. The others turned and looked at Antonio. This scene was making Estrello's head hurt. Pauly was particularly confused at what was unfolding.

"What? When?" he said. Antonio remembered Pauly had seen the state of him the last time around.

"A few minutes ago. Farther out The Sight is, the easier the hit. But not always. Been surprised before," he said. This seemed to somewhat satisfy Pauly. Antonio looked back a Nocivo.

"Medical precaution Tony. After last time I wrote up a new protocol. Why is everyone just sitting around? Didn't you hear the alarm?" he said. Everyone looked around at each other and then at Chief.

"Fuck me, the alarms don't work in this room either!" she groaned and whipped out her tablet and began tapping furiously. Nocivo just shook his head and looked over at Antonio who was eating his ice cream.

"Hijole Tony. Get down to the records room after you finish that. Pauly we may need your expertise in a while. Chief please fix the alarm in this room. And Jack, get with Hammer. I have a feeling we have a lot of shit to sort out this time around," he said before turning away and walking out. Jack looked at Antonio.

"So what about that song? Did you ever find out who it was by?" he said. Antonio took out his laptop and began searching for something.

"No as a matter of fact. I kept that mix tape around for years until the mp3 format was invented. I ported a lot of my old stuff. When it came labeling it I couldn't find a damn thing about it. Like it didn't exist. For years I played it for people and nobody had a clue what it was. Exhaustive internet searches and audio matching apps. Nothing. It may be called 'Like the Wind' or "Blind the Wind,' or some permutation therof. No clue. Told JP about it. He said it sounded like an artifact. Something displaced out of space and time, theoretically. I never considered that something like that could be possible until I started thie gig. But whatever. Messaged you a copy man. Enjoy," he said and stood up. Chief snapped her fingers and pointed at Antonio for a few moments as she grinned widely. Then she snickered as she looked back at her tablet.

"Skip's heard of Nelson Mandela," she said and snort laughed as she continued to tap away.

In Classroom 5, behind some display cases, which housed a myriad of antiquated technology that had been restored and powered, Martha sat watching a lecture on the philosophy of the mind. Not particularly exciting to her but there would be an exam later in the week and she wanted to do well. Certainly much better than she did on the pre-calculus exam earlier in the morning, which still stung. She was very unhappy about that. As far as this universe was concerned, she didn't exist until a year and half ago. Now she was in a Clonlara home learning program. Her father wanted her to have a diploma from somewhere. Anywhere. So now she sat at her desk taking notes as a professor spoke to a classroom of students. A knock at the door interrupted her. She paused the video and looked up as two members of the medical staff opened the door and entered the room. She was not happy about that.

"Okay look I had to stop my class once already for the alarm. Now you two show up. At this rate I'm never getting back to work on flight controls," she snapped. Her reaction was understandable. But the medical staff had a job to do.

"Sorry Martha. Skip's new medical rules. Have to check up on you and Doctor Salazar every time the colors alarm goes off," one of them said. Martha was annoyed but understood they needed to do what they were instructed to. If they didn't, they'd have to deal with both Nocivo, and her father. They could be scary.

"I'm okay. It was a distant Sight. Barely noticed it. The alarms were a bigger thing. Really I'm good," she said. They nodded cautiously. Just then Martha's phone began ringing. She held up a finger and the medical staff stepped back and closed the door. She answered the phone and heard a familiar voice.

"You okay sweetheart?" she heard her father say.

"I'm okay dad. The Sight wasn't bad this time. Medical people have already checked up on me," she said. JP was still concerned for her.

"Okay kiddo, but I'll be up there in a bit anyway. Heading down to the records room to see what's going on, but I'll swing by there first. Do you want me to bring anything?" he said. She was okay, but she did appreciate her father's concern.

"Okay dad. A peach tea would be great," she said.

The activity in and around The East Lodge had been fairly humdrum all day. Pepper was on his way to the dining hall to fetch himself a plate of steamed mussels for the afternoon. He liked to arrive early so he wouldn't have to wait in line behind the other brothers. Brothers who gave him acknowledging nods as he passed them on the colonnades, but those who tended to take their time serving themselves. Most of these same faces he saw every day as he made this walk. He wasn't particularly hungry but he knew mussels helped him think. It's not as if he'd made a considerable amount of progress this week or the last. Only three books in his entire collection had anything resembling the glyph he'd been assigned to find. One book Grain found. Two more Pepper found himself only yesterday. He knew a handful of brothers would visit him soon after he got back to ask about what he'd found like they did every day.

Every day they saw the same expression on his face as he gave them the same answer he always gave them. The others' opinions he didn't care about. But he didn't like disappointing Brother Alvin. Mussels would be good for that stress. But he just had no appetite. He stopped and stood there for a moment while he wrestled with his thoughts. He could get food now, or he could see what was left later when he did have an appetite. Pepper didn't like the idea of walking down here again, but he also wasn't going to force himself to eat. An upset stomach would not do. He turned around and made his way back. His break in routine stood out the brothers who watched him walking past in the other direction.

"Sour stomach?" one of the brothers said. His tone wasn't mocking. The tone was more curious than anything else. Pepper understood he had a reputation for being a creature of habit. He liked structure.

"Not peckish for whatever reason," he replied and continued walking on. Brother Grain was probably in the library as he always was cross-referencing everything he had in his notes. At least Pepper would have some peace and quiet for a while before he'd be inundated with a flood of questions from the small man. Not something he was looking forward to particularly. His path back up to his office was not as easy a walk as it had been going to the dining hall. Most of the brothers were walking the opposite direction.

Pepper had to stand aside and let groups of them pass as they headed where he had been going. He worried all the hot food would be eaten before he got back there himself. After a longer stroll than he would have liked he was finally on the walkway to his office. Something was amiss. A scent hung on the timber. One he did not recognize. As he continued to his office, alarm grew in his mind. It may be a new brother he hadn't met before. But he put this thought aside. New brothers generally avoided him and this wing. Also there wasn't a vague scent of lavender oil from the washing powders used to cleanse Lodge robing. There was an odd musk of dirt and grit here. As he drew nearer he could hear activity from his office. In a moment his mind focused in on the construction area. A worker! A thieving worker! Anger began boiling up in him and he quickened his pace up to his door. He furiously threw it open.

"Cur! How dare you insult our generosity!" he yelled as he stepped into the room. In the corner of his eye he spotted a wooden box sitting on his desk. Inside it were the three books he and Grain had run across, as well as all of his notes. His mind had only a split second to process this. Out of the corner of his other eye, A Shadow. A stunning crack, and he slammed back into a cabinet behind him. Snapping wood. Starry eyes. He crashed hard to the floor rattling baseboards. He tried to stand. A clapping of a box shut. The shadow took hold of it and swung it at Pepper. A hard thump to the chest and the wolf staggered back out of the room and onto the colonnade. His back wrenched around the railing hard knocking the air from his lungs. The shadow lunged out at him swinging the box again. Pepper couldn't move. A whoosh of air and then a bashing wham! He was on the ground. The world spun. He could taste wood splinters and blood in his mouth. In the eye he could open he saw the glint of steel.

"Stop!" he heard a voice cry. He looked up to see Brother Alvin and two others rushing towards them carrying sticks. They surrounded his attacker. It was at this moment he actually saw him. He was dressed head to toe in dark blue save for his eyes and his hands. A brother jabbed at the assailant who dodged the stick and plunged his blade into the young man's side.

Alvin grabbed his robe and tried to pull him away but the assailant pushed them back and sank his blade into Alvin's heart. He twisted and released. The third brother came swinging his stick wildly. The assailant dodged back and forth and slashed at the Brother's chest. He staggered back against the railing holding his wound. Pepper felt a hand on his shoulder. He looked up. Grain's horrified face greeted him. Garrett looked up to see his lodge brothers laying a few feet away in pooling blood. No thought. No calculation. Brother Grain ran over and picked up the fallen brother's stick and rushed the assailant striking him hard in the back as he struggled with the other brother. A loud scream, a hard elbow, and Grain was on the ground. Dazed he looked up. A blade pierced the brother's throat and he fell back clutching the spurting fount of crimson from his neck. Grain picked himself up as the assailant fixed his eyes on him. Steel slit the air down on Garrett.

He swung up defensively. A knocking thunk and the blade hit his stick. Grain staggered back from the force. The assailant came at him again with eyes glinting with glee. Garrett swung his stick to keep him at a distance. The attacker kept advancing. Garret heart raced and his hands vised the stick in his hands. The assailant slashed at him again. He jumped back to avoid it. He is foot came down on the body of Brother Alvin. He toppled backwards and crashed onto the timbers. His head rang off the floor. The assailant slapped the stick from his hands and grabbed him. With little effort Grain's mass rose from the ground and slapped against the wall behind him. He saw the glinting eyes again. The blade was raised. Grain's heart stopped, and then a bloody scream erupted from the attacker's covered mouth. Pepper's teeth clamped down on the assailant's shoulder. The wolf flexed and bit down harder forcing another bloody scream. The grip on Grain loosed and he fell back down onto his feet. The assailant arced his blade and stabbed down into Pepper's leg. The wolf released and howled. The assailant let the blade go and pushed Pepper back into the railing. He picked the box up again and set his feet for the blunt kill. Grain lunged at him knocking him off balance. The attacker snatched the halfwyn up and twisted him around forcing Grain into the railing. The assailant kicked at him with all his weight. The wood behind Garrett gave way and he plunged into the rushing river below.

"Nooo!" screamed Pepper. In a split moment his eyes opened like they never had. The pain disappeared. A snarl erupted from him and he was on the assailant with slashing claws and snapping jaws. The pair smashed through the railing and spiraled down biting and punching all the way down before stopping with a slap on the surface. Pepper shot right down to the riverbed and bashed against the rocks, and all went dark.

JP passed through all the checkpoints on the way to the records room. Even if he did own the ship he agreed with the security measures the group insisted on, and abided. Some new ones were added in the wake of the last mission. Everything about this operation was a work in progress. He had no illusions they had nearly enough figured out, and he was sure there would be plenty more hard lessons in the future. He wasn't sure how going on mission with Salazar would go now.

He was not overly thrilled knowing that Antonio had been studying him like that. He would be lying if he said that he wasn't observing El Gitano as well. But it was a shock to hear him confess like that. He'd come to appreciate Salazar coming clean since then. He could have tried to lie his way through the debriefing. But he didn't. Nothing he did was easy. It told him something very important. Salazar respected the people he worked with. The door to the records room slid open. And JP stepped in. Terry turned around in his chair and waved.

"Hey JP!" he said cheerfully. JP smiled and waved back. Terry never failed to make him smile. An Australian guy who took even the worst days in stride. Amadou was the same way, always upbeat and looking at the brighter side of things. Sitting down and talking with either of them just made a lot of the stress fall away. And speaking of stress, JP looked to his right to see Salazar sitting down stress eating licorice ropes.

"How the hell you burn off all those stress calories I will never know," he said. Antonio gave him a puzzled look.

"Oh I think I'll get my cardio in soon enough," he said sarcastically and continued eating ropes. JP shrugged it off and found a place to sit down to wait for the others. Up on the wall screen Terry was deep into a game of The Warriors. JP liked the movie, but had never played the game. JP looked back at Antonio who was still snacking. He looked fairly relaxed. Looks could be deceiving.

"How long have you been here? I came straight here after I checked up on Martha. Thought I would be the early bird," JP said. Antonio finished swallowing licorice.

"Not too long before you got here. Terry was playing Mega Man 6 just a little while ago. He complained he didn't like the slide mechanic because he'd just been playing the first two games of the series, so I told him to play Mega Man 9 and 10 because neither had the slide mechanic," he said. JP just looked at him for a few moments.

"And how do you know so much about Mega Man games?" JP asked. Antonio was about to take another bite of licorice but held off and gave JP a look.

"Interesting story. Kind of surprised it's never come up before. Well, if you'll remember I spent six years in an institution after my conviction dosed up to my eyeballs on some really powerful shit. I would know because I know what goes into making them. Anyhow, of the few personal items I was allowed I had a rechargeable gaming device that had Mega Man ROMs installed on it. I don't know where my brother got it, but it was made of clear plastic and had a crappy eight inch charging adaptor," he said. JP laughed and shook his head.

"Are you being serious right now Tony?" he said. Antonio expression didn't change.

"Well, yeah. Mega Man 3 was always my favorite. Shadow Man stage theme slaps," he said. JP still wasn't sure if he was being serious.

"Really," he said. Antonio didn't know what more JP wanted from him.

"Well yeah. Shadow Man stage theme slaps. I don't know what more I can say. Play it for yourself," he said. JP didn't have time to respond. The door to the Records Room opened behind him and he turned around. He saw the face of Nocivo. Behind him stood Pauly. JP looked way up to see Stratum had joined the group as well.

"Did you all come here together? I'll bet the security screening process was fun," he said. Nocivo and Pauly looked at each other and then up at Stratum. Pauly looked back at JP.

"No worse than before. Apart from Stratum getting frustrated that he kept having to shrink because the scanners were being finicky, nah it was fantastic. Thanks for asking," Pauly mused. Stratum couldn't physically roll his eyes but the group knew he was doing the nearest equivalent his body could manage.

"Oh yeah. Feels like my underwear is riding up my ass, and I don't wear clothes. Missing a fantasy hockey stream for this. Pre-season fever baby," he mumbled as he found a spot on the wall he could lean on. Nocivo and Pauly found some chairs to sit in and checked the status of the number crunching being performed by E.V.E. and the dash device. Nocivo looked up at the game Terry was engrossed in so much he didn't say hello.

"A game based on The Warriors film. Novel," he said. Pauly turned to him.

"Solid?" he said. Nocivo was going to answer but the progress bar floating in mid air changed into an image of E.V.E. who didn't look particularly happy.

"So guys, would you like the good news or the bad news first?" she said. Everyone looked around at each other, even Terry, who paused his game. Then they all looked at Estrello.

"Good news?" he said. E.V.E. smiled and brought up a graphic showing the approximate level of dash they had to work with. It was substantial.

"Sure thing Skip. As you can see even with a rough estimate of probe usage already factored in you'll have four days worth before pattern instability starts setting in, instead of four hours. Already scheduled your dash in the staging room for the 25th," she said. Nocivo looked away for a moment then back up at the graphic.

"What is the bad news then?" he said. E.V.E. frowned. A feed from the destination locus popped up. The groups could see a moving object. Then E.V.E. zoomed the camera in. Then they all saw what it was.

"As you can see Charlie Oscar Sierra Foxtrot Papa.3857000009-Alpha Echo Romeo has been identified as a 'Sword World,'" she said. The room collectively groaned as the grainy image of an armored rider rode by. Salazar threw his licorice ropes on the ground.

"Son of a fucking bitch! Now I have to program in another new pattern for valiant Generation Six. Exactly how I wanted to spend the next two days. I had better not be fucking related to any nobility this time around. I'm not going to spend the whole time with some asshole mean mugging me because he thinks I'm going to try to steal his castle because I look more like his own father than he did. Fuck That Noise!" Antonio growled. Stratum chuckled.

"I remember that. Funny shit man. Dude you were his cousin by blood. DNA lottery win man. You were the one who insisted we dashback to run the test remember. There was enough political upheaval. You could have challenged him for the throne of Spain and been King Antonio. That would have been legendary," Stratum said and burst out laughing. Antonio scowled.

"Stay in the land of leeches and leprosy? No thank you. I'll stick to my modern problems of micro plastics and smog," Antonio grumbled. Estrello couldn't help but laugh and comment.

"Rey Antonio el Pirmero. The Gypsy King," he mused. Salazar huffed and picked his licorice ropes back up. Stratum held out his hand. Vibrations from it emulated a song from The Gypsy Kings. Estrello sang the song for a bit but gestured for Stratum to stop. They both looked over at Antonio. He was seated again with a look of disgust on his face.

"Oh, don't stop on my account," he said and resumed eating licorice. Estrello and Stratum chuckled and Nocivo looked back at E.V.E. who had a smirk on her face.

"Okay enough of that. I got the sense that you had more bad news to tell us Evie," he said. He was correct.

"I do. Apart from obvious fact that Salazar is going to have bad bends this go around, this Sword World is not a version of Earth of any time period. That being said it bears a number of similarities to an Earth-like world based on what the dash probes have been able to ascertain thus far. Things like atmosphere, mass, gravity, range of ultraviolet to infrared light, and fresh water are all similar to Earth. It has roughly half the population of Gary's World coming in at just over 4.6 Billion spread over three major continents and a crap ton of smaller islands. The level of technology is roughly analogous to Earth of the 13th century, but reports of some more advanced technology are also coming in," she said. JP needed a bit of clarity about that last bit.

"More advanced technology. Such as?" he said. E.V.E. brought up and image.

"One example is something akin to a primitive attempt at a Franklin Stove that wasn't invented until 1742 here on Earth. It's the most recent example found thus far," she said. This both relieved and disappointed JP.

"Good, I was afraid I'd have to pack extra magazines for this one," JP joked. E.V.E. gave him a look.

"Equipping modern weaponry would not be advised for Mission ID Tag 73," she said. Pauly frowned. This was not what he came here expecting to learn.

"Well Fuck. That makes my job harder. Guess I'm going to have to get to work fabricating some old school shit now. Get a good look at their gear Evie?" Pauly said. E.V.E. smiled.

"Sure thing hon. I'll send you over the specs of their current state of the art once the dash probes finish their run," she said. This put Pauly at ease somewhat. He wasn't going to be completely useless this go around. Nocivo had a few things on his mind.

"Evie, you said there was a population of over 4.6 Billion. I'm going to assume there are some fairly substantial cultures," he said. Another graphic that seemed to be in a state of constant update came up then.

"Good assumption. I'm sorry to say that all of you will have to learn a considerable amount about much of them. And you only have a 96 hour window of time to do it," She said. Antonio looked the growing list over.

"Evie, have the probes been patched with the new update so they can search for things like carboxylic acid? It might save some time," He said. E.V.E. looked over at him with a smile.

"Of course hon. Probes are running all the latest patches," she said. Pauly was a little lost by that.

"What the hell is Car Boxy Lack Acid?" he said. This pronunciation struck Antonio as funny but he didn't laugh.

"It's a gas given off by paper as it ages. Hydrogen peroxide from parchment would be another example. The new patch has chemical detectors configured to sniff out the chemicals given off by numerous writing materials. It's so we can locate and read their books without having to get a library card," Antonio mused. Pauly was stunned. The video he'd seen earlier was scary enough a display of the power of the dash probes. This was terrifying as it was fascinating. As Pauly fell silent to ponder, Nocivo had more questions.

"Are there any cognates coincidences this time around or do we have to learn everything from scratch?" he said. Highlights appeared on large portions of the list of cultures.

"Occurrence of linguistic coincidence is highest in the southern portion of the largest landmass in both spoken and written forms. Occurrences decrease farther out from that point as populations skew more toward non-human," E.V.E. said. This statement got everyone's attention, none more than Nocivo and Stratum. Neither of them being Homo sapiens. They looked at each other and then back at the graphics.

"We're going to need the Cliffs Notes on them as well. Emphasis on customs. I want to know what isn't going to piss them off, apart from simply existing in their spaces," he said. Just then a separate window opened. JP studied this list for a few moments and looked over at Nocivo.

"I think we're going to need to bring Jeremy in. If I'm reading what I think I'm reading. We can't bullshit through this one. Nobody knows this kind of thing better than him," he said. Nocivo wasn't looking forward to paging Jeremy to come down to the records room. He hated coming down here.

"Agreed. We need Fate of Fortunes to get us up to speed. He's going rub a lot of this in our faces," he said. JP knew this all too well.

"Oh I have no doubt," he said and dialed Jeremy's number.

The Drowning Wench was the last great watering hole south of the Borderlands. Great was a relative term, given that the grog sold here was poor even by sailor's standards. But it was cheap and abundant. Two things sailors liked, especially those who've had a rough time at sea. Men like Captain Mortimer Slade.

His smug confidence was now replaced by broken despair. Most of his crew abandoned him after they made port. Just a handful of men now sat around him doing their best to drink memory away, and failing utterly which was a pathetic reality that put coppers in the barkeep's pocket. As long as they weren't rowdy, those salty gents could sit there and drink themselves to death for all he cared. A dead man's copper weighed as much a living man's. Mortimer didn't care at this point. His name was tarnished. His vessel, cursed. No man would accept his offer once they learned who he was. They knew he'd seen them. He was good for nothing but an arse on a stool in some backwater tavern surrounded by men of similar repute. Mortimer threw back the last of his grog and stared despondently at the bottom of his flagon. Footsteps in front of him made him look up. He saw a very dark skinned man wearing the armor and sigil of Hall Falco staring down at him. He was accompanied by several others wearing the same garb. A few of them with the same complexion. Despite his condition he inquired.

"Falco throwing silver at Western hirelings now? Eh? And what would Western hirelings carrying Falco silver want with a worthless dry-dock like me? Or am I sittin' on yer stool and you want my arse off it or you'll run me through? Go ahead Westerner. You'll be doing this port a favor. Barkeep might miss my copper. Fat vulture he is! Always perched on that bar waiting for me to slam me flagon. Ha!" Mortimer mumbled through the haze of grog. The young man turned and looked back at the plump barkeep who was watching him and his group. The young man smiled and looked back at Mortimer.

"We'll let the fat vulture rule his roost again once we have what we came here for," the young man said. Mortimer had heard confidence like that before. Confident words that spewed from his own lips.

"Oh and what would that be Westerner? You're so very far from home, you and your lot. Get tired of those western seas? Or Falco just pay better than your western lords?" Mortimer said and laughed drunkenly. The young man didn't seem too phased by the washed up sailor's scorn.

"We were hirelings yes. At one point. But we found serving Lord Falco to be a far more meaningful arrangement than the mere weight of coin," he said. This made Mortimer laugh.

"Balderdash! Save your sentiments hireling. The glint of silver is your true calling. Don't try to fool me. We both covet the same thing. You are no better. Wear all the fancy Falco steel you want. At your heart you are after just one thing. It makes a wonderful shimmering ring when you drop it on the table. Such a sweet sound ain't it? Oh don't feel ashamed lad. I know the lust for that luster," he said mockingly. The young man wasn't here for chat or banter.

"Was it your lust that took you out into the mists old man?" he said. The smile left Mortimer's face.

"Oh aye lad. Aye," he said as the spirit left his eyes. The young man pressed further.

"Tell me old man, was this where you saw The Shadow Fleet and it's Black Admiral? Rumor has it your eyes have seen what other men only tell tall tales about. Did his wake truly curse you and your boat, or have we been misled?" the young man said. Mortimer said nothing for a few moments. His head drooped down and he closed his eyes. He opened them again and looked up at Falco's men.

"It's true. All of it! They came out of the mists like they were birthed from it. Silent as the dead of night. Hundreds strong. If we had silver and gold we'd be dead men! Food for the crabs!" Mortimer yelled. Other patrons looked in his direction and sneered before turning back to their grog. The young man chuckled.

"Oh I see. Passed you over for bigger and fatter fish? I guess being a nothing nobody on a no-count tub can still be a useful thing. Not even The Black Admiral would waste his time on you," the young man said with a grin. Mortimer had had enough of his new company but he didn't have the strength to fight back.

"Oh aye lad. I'm only good for feeding fat vultures now. Worthless as they come. Be gone with you. Mustn't deprive him of my copper. You've heard my tale. Go report to your Sardis Falco," he said as the darkness began to take hold. The young man shook his head.

"You sell yourself short old man. It turns out you're not worthless after all. In fact you and your rabble are now in the service of our Lord Sardis Falco. Unless of course you have other things to do," the young man said and gestured to his men. They walked around the table and seized Mortimer's men. Those that resisted had steel drawn on them. Mortimer looked up at the young man bewildered.

"Who might I ask is escorting me to Lord Falco?" he said. The young man turned slightly and then looked back at the old captain.

"I am Sir Enifack Vekk, a pleasure to make your acquaintance," he said and turned as his men made their way around the table and took hold of Mortimer.

The air was wetter here this far south. Genesis had never ridden this far before. Candleport was still a few days ride away but the druid mystic and the rangers she rode with passed by many who were bound for a river ship east from the Candle Lakes which lay in the southern most point of The Borderlands. She had not encountered many Southerners apart from her present company. Growing up she'd heard stories of a brutish and savage people that clung on to the old ways. A people who had to be contained by dwarven magic lest the southern men march their armies and take The Borderlands for themselves. She'd always had her doubts. Many of her own methods of divination came from the southern cultures, and she did not believe brutes would be capable of building cities like Southgate. Even so she was nonetheless wary. Candleport would be thick with Southerners. The rangers would be a protective escort for a time, but they would depart, and she would be alone.

It would then be her decision to ride back north, or risk trusting a stranger to escort her east. These were just a few of the things weighing on her mind. Pilgrimages were supposed to be treacherous by design. A friendly road was no test of faith. This was an aspect Genesis didn't anticipate would scare her so. One of the rangers, a young wanderer with longer solid light gray fur rode up next to Genesis. He'd observed the way she tightly held her reins as if she was an anticipating an attack. In his time in The Borderlands he'd been asked many times about the brutes of the south, and if he was afraid of wearing The Leaf in a land of savages. This experience helped him to understand what may be going through the mystic woman's mind. If all she had ever heard growing up were stories like these her behavior now was understandable.

"My name is Hawk Quartermoon. I am a Junior Ranger as autumn looms but I may earn my Corporal's Leaf sometime before the spring," he said. Genesis turned to him. He had a very youthful look to him. His eyes looked less weary and road hardened as some of the other wanderers that rode with them.

"Pleased to meet you Ranger Quartermoon. I apologize. I have not taken much time to become very acquainted with everyone," she said. Hawk had observed her gazing at a number of things on their way here. He interpreted it as the mystic reading things like the clouds or the way the wind blew through the grasses on either side of the road. In her own way she was following tracks as he had grown up learning to do. Her approach was more metaphysical in nature though.

"No need to apologize Mystic Payne. You look like you have a lot on your mind. You must not travel very often," he said. Genesis had not wanted to stand out quite as much as she did.

"This is as far south as I have ever been. Already so much is new to me. Even the flowers that grow by the road are strange to me," she said. Hawk has already seen so much that was new to him by this point in his time as a ranger that encountering new things was not the novelty it had once been. It was more expected now.

"I'm not from a very big or important family. My story is not special. My family are river fishers like so many others. Before I left to join the Rangers I would ask my father if it were true that wolves rode horses. He would always tell me that yes, just like staffwyns, wolves did ride horses. I knew horses were scared of the low wolves. It seemed strange to me that a horse could ever trust a wolf. Even a high wolf. It wasn't until my training began an old kobold pulled me aside and shared with me a bit of his wisdom. He told me that if my heart and mind were true, trust could grow. He told me that from the very first time a horse sees you it is testing you. Trust can be there at the beginning, but it will test. It will know if you intend to harm it. Wolves and dragons do scare horses yes. Lessons from older times I should think. Less trust will be there in the beginning. Testing will be a greater challenge. But with time what is true will be proven so. What is false will also be so. A horse has a wisdom. Mine tests me even now. I will prove to be a worthy rider. Challenge is everywhere. This is life. This is how we greet the trees," he said.

Those close enough to hear his words echoed this motto. Genesis looked around at all who travelled with her. They all seemed to carry with them the same energy like wagon wheels turning in the same direction at the same speed. The young wolf rode ahead then. Genesis loosened her grip on her reins and relaxed her shoulders. Trail Blazer's steps became less stilted then. Genesis then realized that she was being tested as well. She understood Hawk's words better now. Genesis patted Trail Blazer on the neck gently.

"Good boy," She said softly. High up on a ridge a dark hooded figure stood in the shadows. The cloaked observer watched the group closely. As they moved farther down the road the figure turned and disappeared into the brush.

The bridge over the Blue River was dotted with rangers from The East Pines Pack. They were on the trail of bandits who had robbed a farming convoy in the night. Captain Snowbrace Quickwill would have told the farmers not to travel at night. Their haste was spurred on by a late harvest and a desire to get their crops to market. But now they would arrive penniless and missing part of their yield. Now they could only hope to sell the rest for a good price to make what they could. The robbery took place on this bridge. It still smelled of fear. Snowbrace took his time collecting the scents of all he suspected to be bandits in his memory. Their only hope of escaping him would be to already have put many miles between themselves and this very determined wolf. Other wanderers were on the bridge as well, all with the hope of putting bandits in chains or at the end of a rope. It depended on whose land they happened to be caught. With any hope the farmers' silver and copper could be recovered. The bandits would face justice regardless. One of Snowbrace's corporals, a man named Thorne, approached him. He'd been interviewing the victims of the robbery. Snowbrace was eager to hear more of the specifics.

"What do you have to report Corporal?" he said. Snowbrace didn't like long reports, but he did insist they be thorough. Corporal Thorne endeavored to do his best to find a medium.

"They were attacked in the early hours before dawn. Nine men with covered faces arrived from the south and met them halfway along this bridge. They had nowhere to run but backwards. But they couldn't outrun the bandits. After they took what they wanted they headed north together toward Runyard Pass on foot. They have a big lead on us but their scent is still fresh enough Lieutenant Vadom says. We should catch up to them in a day if the trail holds." He said. Snowbrace grinned.

"Promising. I like promising. Report to Vadom. We ride soon. I have what I need," He said. Thorne saluted his Captain.

"At once Captain," Thorne said and began walking away. The farmers and their carts sat on the northern bank of the river near the end of the bridge. They looked dejected and downtrodden. Snowbrace had seen this so many times. All these people wanted to do was sell their crops. Now they had to deal the possibility of going hungry.

A sound caught Snowbrace's ear then. The sound of hooves approaching at high speed filled the air. He looked in the direction it was coming from. A rider kicked up a cloud of dust behind him on the road that led to the bridge. His horse came to a stop when he met some of Snowbrace's rangers. One of them was Feyiyak. The rider took a message from under his cloak and handed it to the kobold. Feyiyak looked at the seal on the message and then he looked over to Snowbrace who watched from afar. The kobold walked over his Captain and handed him the message. Snowbrace took it and looked at the seal. It was from The East Lodge. He looked at Feyiyak. The look in his eyes told him the rider did not inform him what the message pertained to.

"All the rider told me is that it was feathered in only a short while ago," Feyiyak said. Snowbrace looked back at the scroll. He broke the seal and began reading. Feyiyak saw his Captain's eyes widen and horror flash in them. Then he saw wolf's arms begin to shake. The message fell from the wanderer's paws and drifted in the air down to the kobold's feet.

Snowbrace dropped to one knee and a deep and sorrowful growl began to rumble from within him. The wolf's shoulders started to shake, and then all at once the wolf lifted up his head and let out a loud agonizing howl. Ears of the other wanderers in the surrounding area picked up the cry. They responded in kind, letting out howls themselves. None of them knew what for. Feyiyak picked up the message and read it himself as Snowbrace buried his face in his paws. The kobold's heart sank as he finished the message.

"No. Please no. I am so sorry Captain. I am so very sorry," Feyiyak said. Snowbrace picked himself up and regained his composure. He looked over at his lieutenant.

"Bring me my horse and my spear. Proudwinter will have heard the howl. He and I have new prey to run down. I leave you, Vadom and Kitt in charge until we return. Find those fucking bandits and give them what's coming to them," Snowbrace said in an eerily calm tone. Feyiyak saluted his Captain.

"It will be done," he hissed. Snowbrace laid a hand on the kobold's shoulder.

"I am likely the first of my family to hear of this. Make sure a feather goes out to all my kin. The Pack Hunts!" Snowbrace snarled. Feyiyak looked on as his Captain stormed off. The kobold hung his head. He said a silent prayer in his head out of respect for the dead. Then he went to where he knew the other lieutenants would be. As he walked wanderers passed by him that responded to the howl. They saw the sad look in Feyiyak's eyes and they knew something was terribly wrong. Vadom met him a short distance from the bridge. Feyiyak looked up at his fellow ranger.

"Something's happened. You'll find out about it soon enough. But what you and Kitt need to know right now is that the Captain has put us in charge for the time being. There is something he must do. What we must do now is send a quick rider back to Falter's Marsh with enough silver and coppers to buy a slew of feathers. Who is our fastest scribe?" Feyiyak said. Vadom thought for a moment.

"Junior Ranger Teal can write up a storm," Vadom said. This wasn't a ranger Feyiyak knew well, but he knew the lad could write. Only some rangers had been taught to.

"I'll go and speak with him. You're needed with our Captain and the other wolves. Be prepared for the 43rd call of the Wind. I'm sure you know this prayer," Feyiyak said and walked off. Vadom watched him sadly depart, the wolf's mouth agape. He took a deep breath and turned toward the group gathering around Snowbrace.

The Autumn Festival was a day away and activity was high in the town of Bell Store. Tass and his father were in the town center helping other families prepare the area for the following evening's festivities. Vill normally did this task alone while the boys stayed home and helped their mother prepare for supper, but this year he needed help. His leg prevented him from doing much. His voice worked well enough. Tass provided the work that Vill could not. It was also educational his father felt. Years ago when his older boy was younger than Tass was now, Vill sent him with an older relative from another town to help prepare for the Autumn Festival. He had a summer fever then. His ailment was much worse now. Salvers gave him a long recovery at very best as an outlook on his future. His boys learning their roles in the community now when they were young would reap much in the future.

People remembered a helpful and responsible lad. He looked on in pride as the boy rolled empty barrels into place where others would later place wooden planks to make tables for festival patrons to sit and eat. As Tass was doing this Vill noticed something. A rather large presence in the town center he'd never quite seen before. Men who looked like hirelings to him stood around drinking from flagons and talking among themselves. Vill had heard of troubles across the rivers to the west, but he could not imagine the need for hired muscle here. He wondered how much it was taxing the village coffers to have them here, as well as holding the festival itself. He then looked to his boy. He'd wondered if Tass had noticed them. He feared the lad might be disturbed by their presence.

"Hurry now young man. Set those barrels. Shouldn't keep your mother waiting. Supper will be cold before we get back. Put your heels into it lad," he said. Tass responded by rolling the barrels a little faster. He had to correct more once he got them to where they needed to be, but he did as he was told. Vill looked up again and saw two farmers he knew from the other side of town. Gloss, a bald man with a strong brow and Tiller, a man with a long bushy beard. There appeared to an argument going on between them and their voices were growing loud enough to hear.

"The Tides Gloss! You've seen the signs clear as I can. The moon grows large. The Tides have arrived while we revel like simpletons!" Tiller snarled. Gloss just shook his head at him agitating him more.

"Deny it if you will. I won't be dancing around like a sickly sparrow while the gods are angry. The winds blow ill Gloss! Do you stand there and deny it?" Tiller continued to snarl. Gloss had had enough of Tiller and his naysaying.

"Listen to yourself man! Get a hold of yourself. Look around you. The village elders have listened to all of you chattering hens and bought swords to watch out for shadows and specters and whatever the hell else you people are afraid of," he said condescendingly. Tiller did not take this well. He waved his finger in Gloss's face.

"When the moon shines bright, the dark shadows grow. You know these words as well as I! That moon has come! I saw it! You saw it! You mocked me when I said it bodes ill! You mock me now!" Tiller yelled. This ruckus had caught the attention of some hirelings who stepped in between the men. Tiller scowled and stormed off. Gloss shook his head and walked away as well. This had caught Tass's attention. He looked back at his father. He saw fear in the boy's eyes.

"Hurry and finish up lad," he said. Again, the boy did as he was told. On the way home Vill could feel there was a great weight on the lad's shoulders. He didn't think it was healthy for a boy his age to be burdened by fears cast down to them by adults so poorly controlling their own. Vill knew the world could be viscous and cruel, and he knew he could not protect his boys forever. They would see for themselves sooner or later. But they would grow to have a love of life beforehand. He was determined they would not grow into bitter fearful men like Tiller, or even scoffers like Gloss. He looked down at his boy who lent him a shoulder to rest some of his weight on as they walked.

"Now listen to me good boy. I want you learn the right lesson from what you saw back there. Some men spend their lives fearing too much. They never let themselves truly live and love their lives or give that love to those who matter to them most. Some men spend their lives fearing too little. They walk around in a cloud of self-importance with no appreciation for what life gives them, or what it can take from them. They both are a danger to everyone around them. The challenge lad is to be the man in the middle. Fear just enough you don't put others in danger, but don't fear so much you don't live life with others. You catch my meaning boy?" Vill said. Tass looked up at his father and nodded.

"I do papa. But who were those men in the square?" Tass asked. Vill was reluctant to answer. He gave it some thought.

"Those were hirelings son. Men who fight for silver and not a sigil, Hall, a god, or even a people. When the silver runs out they ride to the next man who will pay them to fight. Their swords will guard the village for a night, maybe two, while the festival is going. And protect it they will. Fiercely. Their reputation is what get's them hired. After that they ride away and take their swords with them. That is their way," he said. The boy had more questions then.

"Why would the village elders want hirelings?" Tass said. This was an even harder question to answer.

"When enough fearful men appeal to authority. Authority will respond. It only cares about quelling a ruckus. It doesn't care so much about the concerns of the fearful men further than silencing their chatter. So they act. The stronger the chatter, the greater the response, the less regard for concerns boy. Fearful men never think about that. So they chatter louder paying no mind to anyone else," Vill said. Tass still had much weighing on his mind.

"But can't they see what will happen papa?" he said. Vill shook his head.

"Fear is a mist in the mind of a fearful man. The greater the fear, the less they can see. The less they care to. That's why it's important to challenge fear and question," Vill said. Tass was young though. His mind was not sated.

"Won't that upset them?" he said. Vill laughed.

"Like you wouldn't believe lad. For some that fear becomes as much a part of them as their own names. When you question their fears or ideas, you become part of their fears. Then expect no reason," he said. Tass looked down the road with his head down. Vill saw this and pat the boy on the shoulder.

"Some things a boy must come to understand. Time and the world have lessons to teach. Can't always choose which ones get taught. Just make sure when they're taught, they're taught right. Learn when you're being taught. Not always an easy thing. First you have to realize the lesson. Some day it will be you doing the teaching. And I hope you will teach your sons the right way when it comes time. Saying that, I'm going to be blunt. There will always be others more than eager to make you a part of their turmoil whether you asked to or not. When that time comes you need to be prepared to fight for every bit of life they try to take from you. It is not theirs to take. They cannot take your time without fair compensation. They cannot take your goods without fair compensation. They cannot take your freedom without fair law justly applied equally to all by those who rule. They will try to take as much as they can from you. Sometimes they will succeed. Takers kill inspiration, innovation, and a man's individual spirit. What is taken must always be fought to recover. Make no mistake about that boy. I know I may sound like an idealist blind to the world. But anyone who loves and respects life, will fight for every inch and hold themselves and others to account. While still respecting their lives as well. You are young still. But in time these challenges will meet you on the road. The question then becomes, will you meet them as a fearful man, a conceited man, or a man in the middle?" Vill said and tousled the boy's hair.

The sun was beginning to set in the southeastern forest. Manati's illness had slowed the group down considerably leaving them nearly two days behind where they wanted to be by now, but they were at least at the river now and had fresh water to drink and cook with. Their rain water had begun to sour. Manati lay against a rock near the banks. His fever had broken the night before. Raltec's herbs had worked well enough. He didn't want to slow the group down and offered to stay behind, but Raltec refused to leave a man. It was not his way. Others may have said their peace and let the forest take a man. It was a tough, perhaps even cold, but customary tendency for dwarves. Any dwarf left behind was often never found alive again. Raltec never agreed with the approach. Some saw him as a sentimentalist. He brushed it off. Balocan was of a similar philosophy. He was in the forest collecting as much dry wood as he could to keep the fire going.

Raltec stood at the river's edge with a line in the water waiting for a bite. He had little luck so far. Maybe the fish didn't like the crawlers he'd dug up for bait. Pulcan sat by the fire near Manati boiling water in a kettle to refill their water skins. An iron plate heated on the coals so he could use the last of their flour for more flat bread. He had become quite good at it in his time in these woods. Raltec wasn't enjoying his time here near as much. There had been no game apart from very small birds that fed on the crawling creatures that made up most of the wildlife in these woods. They weren't worth going after. It would take more strength than they would replace just to catch enough to make a full belly. All the stories of the desolation of this place were true. Fish did not even appear to want to swim in the waters that border it. He jammed the end of his fishing pole between some rocks at the bank and sat back. Perhaps the fish knew of his frustration and mocked him from beneath the surface. Ridiculous, but that was the image in his mind though. He would grin widely at their scaly mouths agape as they sizzled above his fire tonight. Swimming cretins. They could have their fun now.

But the skewers and fire would wait for them. Raltec almost chuckled. Was it the frustration? Was it the lack of tread root for many days now? Was it the water and flat bread every day for what seemed like months walking through these woods? He didn't know. He just felt fortunate to be out of them. He knew he'd be on his knees thanking the god of the Mountain for the first wild boar. He'd thank the god of the Mountain for the first boiled chicken if he were being honest with himself. Chicken with mashed yams sounded like ambrosia from the Mountains to Raltec at the moment. A meal from a dream served to him by large breasted dwarven women. His imaginative excursion came to a halt. Just up river he spied something odd. It was a large object floating on the surface. He stood back up and squinted. As the object grew closer it looked like some sort of animal. An animal draped rags. It looked to be entangled in some tree branches, which kept it afloat. Raltec turned to Pulcan.

"Pulcan! Assist Me!" Raltec yelled as he walked down into the gently flowing river. Pulcan stood up and watched as Raltec made his way to an approaching object. The young dwarf ran over to the water to get a closer look.

The water was shallow but it was up to Raltec's chest at it's deepest. He stretched out his hands to intercept the floating creature as it neared. Pulcan had already reached him by the time it did. Both dwarves caught hold of the branches it was tangled in and pulled. It took both of them to drag the mass of it all against the current. After some struggle they managed to drag it ashore. The two of them stood above it. Neither of them spoke for a few moments. But Pulcan broke that silence.

"Is this a ranger?" he said. Raltec shook his head.

"This is a wanderer. But not a ranger," Raltec said. Pulcan was relieved. Rangers were not the kind of people desirable to deal with even if you weren't the focus of their scrutiny.

"I say we push him back. The river took him. The Winds obviously claimed him. The god of the Mountain would be angry we sought to defy his brother the Wind," Raltec looked up at Pulcan. His eyes had a foolish innocence about them. He considered pushing the wolf back out for a briefly, but something caught his eye. A glint peeked out from underneath a fold by the wanderer's throat. He reached down took hold of it and pulled it out. He rolled the object around in his hand and looked at both sides of it. It took a second, but then the hair on the back of his neck stood up and his blood ran cold. He set it back down on the wolf's chest and looked back up at Pulcan.

"This wolf wears finery of dwarven make. Not just this. He wears the sigil of Pack Redflower. You see the four ruby petals with smaller river pearl inlays between them? That is the Red Flower. Only the pups of Brewster Redflower wear these. I know you know that name. I don't know how this Redflower pup got here, but we court death trifling with their Pack. Every ranger pack in Gatheria would be after our heads. We treat this pup with respect. As soon as Balocan gets back we're going to need to come up with a plan. And a good one. Help me get the body off this muddy bank," Raltec said and grabbed hold of the wanderer's garment.

Pulcan did the same. The two dwarves dug in their heels and pulled hard. Just then the wanderer let out a moan. Pulcan let go and ran back a few steps. Raltec though alarmed did not run. He laid a hand on the wanderer's chest. The wolf slowly opened his eyes and rolled his head over to look at Raltec.

"dwarf," he said weakly. Raltec waved Pulcan back over. The young dwarf did so cautiously. Raltec looked back down at the wolf.

"Easy now wolf. We're going to get you closer to our fire. Help us if you can. If not, we'll manage," Raltec said and then nodded to Pulcan to begin pulling again. The wolf did what he could but he was very weak. His time in the water had taken most of his vigor. The two dwarves set the wolf near the fire and stoked the flames. The wolf responded to the warmth. He'd begun shivering terribly after he'd regained more of his faculties. The fire felt good. He tried to move some but and sharp pain shot up his side. He weakly lifted a paw and laid it down on an area of his robe covering his upper leg. He did not have the strength to pull the fabric away. Raltec bent down and did so for him. He took hold of the cloth and pulled it away. What he saw shocked him. A knife was there protruding from the wolf's leg. The fabric around the area was stained crimson. Raltec looked the wolf in the eyes.

"You've been attacked wolf. The blade is here still. I'll see what I can do," Raltec said and then ripped the fabric way. As he did the wound around the blade bled. He bent down closer. To it to see how bad the wound was. There was no rot in the odor but there was something else though. He couldn't quite place it. But then it occurred to him. And he sat back to process what was going on in his mind. Then he looked over at Pulcan.

"Fetch my bag lad. I need my herbs," Raltec said. Pulcan ran over to where the dwarves' packs lay. Manati awoke from his nap as Pulcan picked up Raltec's bag.

"What's going on?" he said. Pulcan didn't have much of an answer.

"Trouble," he managed to say. This alarmed Manati and he sorely pulled himself up. Pulcan ran back to Raltec and handed him his bag. Raltec retrieved his supplies and set them down. He looked back at the wolf, who seemed to be gaining more wherewithal.

"I'm going to pull the blade and clean the wound. We can give you a branch to bite down on. There will be pain," he said. The wolf looked at him and weakly shook his head. Raltec nodded than then picked up a handful of herbs and crushed them in his mortar. He then wrapped the pulverized mash in a clean rag. He looked up at the wolf that appeared to acknowledge what was about to happen. Raltec set the rag of herbs under the wound and took hold of the knife's handle. He began to pull carefully. As he did he could feel the wolf's leg muscle tense up and cling to the steel. The wolf clacked his jaw shut as prickling ache like a burning hearth poker to his flesh bit down into him. He let out a twisting whine as the blade slid out. Raltec quickly pushed the herb rag onto the wound and tied it around the wolf's leg. The wolf let out a long breath of agony. He opened his eyes and looked at Raltec. He said nothing, but there was thanks in the wanderer's eyes. Raltec smiled and looked over at Pulcan. And threw him something from his pack.

"Boil that thread. I'm going to need to stitch this fellow up," He said. Pulcan walked back to the fire with the ball of thread. The wolf relaxed as the herbs began to dull the pain in his leg. Then the blackness covered his eyes as he passed out. Other eyes cast their gaze upon the scene. They watched from a distance away.

As night fell on the city of Castigo a line of fifty men carrying the pennants of Hall Falco arrived at the garrison there. Among them was a horse driven cart hauling a handful of very weary and sobering sailors. Large wooden doors opened allowing the Falco fighters through. They were led by their Captain, Enifack Vekk. He stopped his horse in the middle of the bailey and dismounted. His lieutenants did the same. The cart of sailors was intercepted by Falco men stationed there and driven off toward the garrison's holding cells. Vekk watched as the men were taken. He then looked to his top lieutenant. A man named Borate Hunter. Another westerner with a well groomed goatee.

"Make sure our guests are comfortable. Lord Falco's sheriff will be here in the morning to question all of them. Post a man with good ears outside. I want to know what they talk about amongst themselves. Borate saluted his captain and gestured to his brother Bomas to follow him. Vekk passed his reigns off and headed toward the garrison Marshall's office to meet with her. She sat at her desk reading through all the day's feathers as she did every night before retiring. Streaks of gray intertwined themselves among the dusty brown in her tight braids. This night like many others recently carried with it a tremendous volume of messages from up and down the coast. She looked up, as there was a knock on her door.

"Come in," she said. The door opened one of her lieutenants walked in followed by a dark skinned man wearing the armor of Hall Falco.

"Lady Marshall. This is Captain Enifack Vekk of your cousin's Northern Guard. He's brought some 'witnesses' with him," the lieutenant said. The Marshall set down the message she was holding.

"Vekk? That's a very western name to carry this far east. The stories about the Northern Guard are true it appears. Or should I call it the Western Guard?" The Marshall said. Vekk smirked.

"Call it what you like Lady Marshall. We fight just at hard for Lord Sardis Falco as the Southern Guard or the Lord's Navy. Some of us just happen to have western names, and western faces," Vekk said. The Marshall face remained steeled for a moment then she smiled.

"Please sit Captain." The Marshall said. Vekk pulled up a chair and sat down.

"Much obliged Lady Marshall," he said. The Marshall was indifferent to westerners. They were far friendlier with the Empire than her liking, but it wasn't a sin that could be applied to all from the west. Hirelings on the other hand she held an immense suspicion of. She didn't trust a man only loyal to money and the ones who could give him the most of it. This Vekk was young, less than forty, but old enough to have spilled much blood for silver and gold. More gold she reckoned. But this Vekk, looked to be a natural fit in Falco armor. She wasn't sure why.

"Oh please Captain Vekk. Men under my command call me Lady Marshall. You may call me Hellen. Or Lady Hellen if you prefer formalities," Hellen said. Vekk didn't care this way or that. He was content to finalize the handover of his cargo and step back into an observer's role when Lord Falco's sheriff arrived.

"As you wish Lady Hellen. I'm here to hand off some witnesses to your care until a Seastorm sheriff can arrive to question them," he said. Hellen picked up a message from her desk and looked at it.

"I received a feather from my cousin, the young Lord Denato, this morning informing me of your arrival. He did not go in specifics. You might say I have more than a few curiosities. For instance, what are these men actually 'witnesses' of?" she said. Vekk was silent a moment. His eyes shifted to the direction the garrison lieutenant that was standing behind him. Hellen looked up to her man and gestured for him to leave the room. The lieutenant gave Vekk a scowl and then walked out, closing the door behind him. Vekk looked back at Hellen.

"The men in your cells were witnesses to The Black Admiral and his Shadow Fleet. He and his crew are some of the very few men who have seen The Shadows and still draw breath. Your cousin, Lord Falco, is very interested in what they have to say. You could say they're very valuable," he said. This didn't impress Lady Hellen very much.

"I would think their value would be assessed by the sheriff, and not the Northern Guard. With all due respect of course Captain. I have seen many so-called witnesses come through here begging for my family's asylum and clemency for their piracy. I have no reason to feel differently about the characters brought here. As I said, the sheriff will determine their value. Until then they're mouths to feed until they're worth the silver being spent on their behalf. Would you say that's a fair assessment Captain?" Hellen said. Vekk trusted his own instincts. He knew what he saw when he spoke to Mortimer himself. But he couldn't expect anyone else to be able to see the same who hadn't looked the man in the eyes.

"Fairly put Lady Hellen. I'll have my own men stand guard so none of yours need be distracted from their duties," He said. Hellen could see that Vekk was trying to make things easier even if he didn't fully realize how disruptive his presence here was. He was a hireling being called a captain after all. Hellen didn't expect he understood how to run a garrison, or what it took to keep one running well. He was an arm with a sword.

"I'll expect you and your men to depart back north as soon as the sheriff arrives. Plenty of activity up there to keep a man like you busy," she said. Vekk picked up a hint of hostility in her voice, but this did not concern him. He had his orders, and would follow them through.

"I expect I will be leaving as soon as the sheriff makes his assessments. Not before," he said. Hellen did not expect this kind of resistance.

"I see. On whose authority may I ask?" she said. Vekk had heard this tone many times here in the east. People saw a western face. Heard a western name. Saw Imperial gold. The spite in their voices spat venom on that gold and the throne that mined it. He would not be throwing that venom back.

"On the authority of your Aunt. The City Minister of Seastorm, The Tradelands, and the White Cliffs. Lady Terosa Falco," Vekk said and pulled a wrinkled folded message from a pouch on his belt and handed it over to Hellen who gave him a skeptical glare. She took the note and looked it over. The look of skepticism was replaced by one of disappointment. She looked up at Vekk and handed the message back to him.

"That is my aunt's hand, and that is most certainly her signature. She names you personally. I can't fathom quite why, but she has her reasons. Maybe enough of the Emperor's gold dust has rubbed off of you by now. Maybe it hasn't. You wear my family's sigil and seem to carry some esteem with some of us with a much louder voice than mine. You remind me of my son. Lauded by the family. Captain of his own ship before he knew what his limits were. Glory was his gold. He lives with our goddess now. The goddess, or one of her brothers, will have you soon enough. You just don't know it yet. Young men like you think you have things sussed out. Fame and fortune is the currency of fools. Spend wisely Captain Vekk," she said. If the woman could hiss like a kobold, Vekk imagined she would try. He could nonetheless sense his welcome had become overstayed. He stood up out of his chair and managed a smile.

"I suppose I should take my leave. It was a pleasure to make your acquaintance Lady Hellen," he said. Vekk had tried his best to leave a good impression, but one could not draw water from a stone. Hellen did not find anything specifically offensive about the Captain, but young men like him had always attracted trouble in her experience and she could not have that here in her garrison. The sooner he was gone the better.

"Likewise Captain. A very good evening to you," she said coldly. Vekk could feel that barb, surely as if it were made of steel. But he had felt them many times before as he left a room rife with mistrust. The shadow the Empire cast was broad, and followed him wherever he went. He called it the Midlands Pall. He walked back to his men who had made camp outside the gates of the garrison for the night. The bailey was far too small to accommodate the Northern Guardsmen and guest quarters were too few. Vekk preferred to camp with his men rather than sleep on a straw mattress with a flagon of ale looking down on those tents his men were forced to sleep under. He could not respect himself, nor would he expect any from the men under his command if they saw him pampering himself. He was a captain, not some lord, duke, or baron. Borate stood near where Vekk's men had set up his tent. The look on his face gave away what he anticipated Vekk would have to say about his meeting with Marshall Falco. Vekk would not stray too far.

"I can't say I would have had much cause to see that going differently," Vekk said. Borate nodded.

"Went well did it?" he said. Vekk shook his head and pulled off his gloves.

"Midland Pall. I might as well have been covered in the Emperor's gold and carrying his pennant still. Aye, the woman heard what I had to say, but she had much to say herself. Nothing we haven't heard before. Sheriff will be here in the morning. Once he's done we go north," he said. Borate was not much of a talker. Unlike Bomas who couldn't be shut up once he got going. The Hunter brothers were great grandsons of a southerner who journeyed to the westernmost point of Gatheria, which was the city of Aganton. Old tales tell this was the last place a cyclops was seen in Gatheria before their tribe crossed the western sea to their ancestral home of Hastonia. His name was Hastosh The Culler. An entire continent came to be named after him. A stone said to have been cleft in half by his great sword sat at the heart of Aganton. A last reminder of an ancient battle that saw the cyclops army finally driven out of Gatheria which was said to have kicked off a decade of celebration.

It was a rock that Borate and Bomas played upon as children. Their father would take them to see it often on the way to market. It was the last place they saw their father before both of them struck out on their own. They met Vekk shortly after. Enifack remembered that day. Two rough around the edges teenagers looking for a fight. Vekk wasn't much older and he knew where the fighting and the gold was. The attitudes of all three men had changed since those days. They'd seen their share of fights in the north. They made their share of gold from the Emperor or one of his Warlord allies. The trio sailed with a company of loyal Imperial Soldiers and hirelings off the northeastern coast on their way to sack Shalnishan, which sat on disputed land. Years of political turmoil had erupted in violence when Shalnishan declared itself a free city. Vekk's ship was one of hundreds sailing east when a typhoon cut the fleet in half. The vessel was battered and barely stayed afloat. Many aboard were killed by the storm.

They lost all bearings and drifted far off course. Living off what stores of food were not spoiled by the sea the survivors and the crippled vessel floated adrift for weeks until another storm forced them back to land. They ran aground far south near a Borderlands city that was coincidently hosting Lord Sardis Falco at that time. He met with the survivors himself and heard their stories. He had them fed and clothed. He gave their dead proper burials. Vekk, Borate, Bomas and all the other hirelings from the north and west saw in Falco a different man than the ones that had paid them to fight in the Midlands. He was a man that inspired them. A man they wanted to follow. Not for gold or silver, but for an honorable Hall and it's Lord. Sardis Falco brought them to the keep for his Northern Guard and gave them uniforms. In time Vekk had risen through the ranks to become that keep's captain. The other hirelings earned respect from their new southern brothers. The Midlands Pall cast no shadow there.

The summer sun began to rise high over Chicago. The day's forecast called for high winds and partly cloudy skies. Highs in the mid-90s Fahrenheit with a moderate UV index. Humidity was also high. Proximity to Lake Michigan regularly dumped considerable moisture on the city if the winds were right. The office was mixture of laser printers, phone conversations, gurgling coffee makers, ringing phones, and the click clacking of heels on tiles down the hallways that ran this way and that. Chief sat at her desk trying to figure out how colleagues in another area had so badly misunderstood how to use a program she wrote just the month prior. On her desk to her right sat a steaming mug of coffee with 'NHL's Little Ball of Hate' on it that she bought from a Happee Stax because she thought it was hilarious. To her left sat a solar powered Hula dancing figurine with a bit of electrical tape covering the solar collector. The dancing proved to be distracting. Distractions would not do with deadlines and expectations looming. The hum from the fluorescent light was distracting enough. It was thankfully drowned out for the most part by her desk fan keeping the heat at bay.

Barbara had been by earlier for a 45-minute chat that could have easily been avoided with a 5-minute email. Barbara was her direct supervisor so Chief couldn't just ask her to come by later when she wasn't as busy. That cost her 45 minutes of productivity and now she had to work faster just to make up lost ground. An hour later she was still playing catch-up. Her mug was empty though. It was time to swing by the break room for a refill. The elevator beeped as she passed it. Behind her a handful of her colleagues exited out into the hallway, which she reckoned, they were just getting back from their lunch break. She wasn't able to take hers because she wanted to get this assignment done before she left and wouldn't have to worry about it over the weekend. A fresh pot of coffee would help her to do that. When she got to the break room nobody was in it. Odd on most days, but it was a Friday. It wasn't odd on either a Monday or a Friday. Today it was very Friday. Break room shouldn't be packed. She looked around for creamer in the fridge. Nothing. She searched the cabinets above the coffee makers.

None could be found. Today certainly had a theme. No creamer. Not even the powder. Not only did people fail to understand a program she knew worked but was nonetheless told to re-check line by line, but also nobody thought to get more creamer. She sighed and just poured in more honey. There was at least there was plenty of that. Her walk back to her office was oddly quiet. Nobody seemed to be around in the halls. Friday or not, this was out of place. Regardless, she dismissed it and kept walking. When she arrived she sat down at her desk and lay her mug back down. For a moment all was humdrum. She drank her coffee for the next while in an unsettling silence, hearing not even so much as the sounds of others typing in the next office over. Then her phone began humming. Normally she would disregard it in favor of getting things done. But for whatever reason she picked it up and clicked it on. Twystar was abuzz with posts from all her online friends. There was something big going on. Everyone was posting videos of something called Blaire 2008. Just then Chief could hear commotion out in the hall. She looked up to see several of the people who worked on this floor rushing past her door. She stood up and walked to her door to see what was going on. Two people rushed by her she as peeked out into the hall. They ran in the same direction everyone else seemed to be heading which was the balcony at the other end of the building. She turned and picked her phone up and stuffed it in her pocket before heading out to see what everyone was sprinting off to. She was moving at a much slower pace than everyone but she arrived soon enough. On the balcony there were a dozen or more people from this floor here looking out at something. Tall people worked on this floor, taller than her at any rate. She walked out and worked her way through the crowd to see out. They were all pointing to something in the sky. Up above she could see a bright object moving past the clouds at an incredible rate of speed. Like the others she watched for a good while. They weren't alone. On the balconies above and below them workers from the other floors were out watching the object as well. Looking around at the surrounding buildings this was the thing everyone was paying attention to. Every window, balcony and rooftop had people watching. After about five or so minutes the object disappeared past the horizon. Once it was gone nobody said anything for a few moments. Then conversations started up. A woman from her floor began talking to her, but she couldn't understand what she was saying. In fact she couldn't understand anyone. A very bad feeling crept up in her mind. A bright flash filled the sky. Everyone lurched back and covered their faces. Then they looked back at the horizon. A purple tinge began to creep up replacing the blue. Chief and the crowd around her looked at the transition in astonishment as the light that fell upon them began to change. Below them sirens began to blare. Tires squealed and thumps of impact from the traffic below echoed off the buildings. The rest was a blur. Running. Screaming. Phone alerts. A lock. She couldn't get through. Fighting. Swinging. Bashing. Crying. Shaking.

"Shit!" she yelled as she bolted up. Chief looked around her. She was in her quarters on the Bumppo again in bed. The dream had struck again. A shiver ran down her back. The cold sweat again. Tears ran down her face. The panicked faces of her co-workers still very fresh in her mind. She wiped her face and got up. There was no sense in trying to get back to sleep. She would not be able to. Many times over the last year and change she had tried, but failed. A walk around the ship would help. The hallways were always empty this time of night. Graveyard shift people were probably at their stations. Kitchen would be open at The Cove. At least she could get some hot food not from a vending machine. When she got there she sat at her usual table and ordered hash browns and scrambled eggs like she always did when a bad dream woke her up in the middle of the night.

Not many people were around right then. Most of the late-nighters would have already come and gone by now. The stragglers were all that still hung around. She noticed that Antonio was sitting alone at the bar. Phil was off to the side wiping down glasses while he watched the television mounted to the wall behind the bar. She'd seen Antonio here many times in the last year when she couldn't sleep. She just figured he was a night owl and just liked being up all hours of the night. After paying her check. She walked over and sat next to him. Phil noticed her out of the corner of his eye. He walked over with a big grin.

"What'll ya have eh?" he said. Chief thought about it a moment. She didn't come here for a drink, but since she was already sitting here.

"Bloody Mary. Easy on the ice," she said. The recipe appeared in Phil's mind instantly and he turned to set about making it. Chief then looked over to Antonio. He didn't even seem to acknowledge either of them. He just sat there. An empty glass of what she though once contained Jim Beam sat in front of him. Rise, by Herb Alpert played softly in the background as Antonio sat there. Chief sat there as well not saying anything. Phil set her drink in front of her. They both glanced at Antonio and then at each other. Phil shrugged his shoulders and then went back to what he was doing. Chief took a sip of her drink. It was very good. Hit the right notes, and its bite was just peppery enough. Antonio picked up his head a bit.

"Bad dreams again?" he said. Chief was a little dumbstruck. She didn't recall ever mentioning this to anyone before.

"Good guess," she said. Antonio's peculiar set of abilities was still a hand of cards he kept close to his vest. She wondered if he had telepathic abilities as well. He looked over slightly.

"I can't read minds. I just see you here a lot at bad hours. Figured it could be bad dreams. Left you alone. Wasn't my business," he said. This was a relief. She had hurled a substantial amount of criticism at him in her mind the last several months. She'd worried sometimes if he could hear what she was thinking. He could be lying to her now.

"I see you're up again as well. Running experiments?" she said. She expected a nod. He shook his head instead and threw two fingers at Phil. Tabs stopped what he was doing and walked over with a bottle and poured him another glass. Antonio lifted it up and looked over at Chief.

"Salud," he said. She raised her glass as well and they both took a sip.

"Having bad dreams too?" she said. Antonio didn't give an immediate response. He picked his glass up, and then set it back down again.

"Always, after The Sight. Usually never good. Tonight it was bad. Slept maybe three hours," he said. Phil overheard this.

"Yeah my guy got here right before you did. Like twenty minutes eh," he said and looked back up at the TV. He was watching something called The Ghost Host that featured a character named Justin Apparition. Animated sketch comedy Chief had watched a few times since arriving on Gary's World and she enjoyed it. She took a sip and set her drink down. She knew it probably wasn't the best question to ask but she was nonetheless curious.

"Was it the high school speech in your underwear dream?" She said. Antonio shook his head.

"No, that dream would actually be nice. How about you?" he said. Chief wasn't actually prepared to answer that question. The guys knew a good amount about her already. But still, this was not an easy question. Even so Antonio and Phil were guys she felt she could trust.

"My dream was about Chief One's last day. I don't know how much of it actually happened the way I remember it, or dream it. My memory is a reconstruction of what could be pulled from Chief One. Fragmented would be putting it lightly. She was lucky though. They got to her early. The rest is a mashup of second and third hand information from other people, social media, recordings, photos, and other things. I couldn't put a number on how much of me is directly her. How much is concrete verbatim, or how much is abstract, I don't know. Much of who I am now could very well be who I once imagined myself being at one point or another. I don't know enough about how memory actually works to tell you. I do know my memory set is more complete than either Chief Two or Chief Three. The Rescuers technology and understanding of human memory had advanced considerably by my time," she said. It all just came rolling out. Chief didn't talk about herself much. It felt good for some reason, which was an interesting discovery. She was still learning about who she was. Shades of personality seemingly came from nowhere. Jokes she didn't know she knew would pop up in her mind and just made her start laughing. She often wondered if this is what it was like for Chief Two. Would bits of Chief One slowly emerge over the course of forty years in her mind and personality?

"Chief Two was cool to hang out with. You would have liked her. We never met Chief Three. Only heard stories about her and her new family in the New Earth colony," he said. Chief winced in her mind. This hit more than a few emotional nerves for reasons she understood, and many she didn't.

"Chief Two helped build New Earth for Chief Three so she could take her place when she was gone and go where she couldn't. First generation clones, had flaws. Many. Two could never leave the Moon outpost like many others," she said. She had many memories in common with Two during her time as Administrator, a name that Two called herself.

"She told us that part. Talked with her and her rescuers quite a bit while we waited for the juice to build up. Dashed to the wrong universe. We made a lot of mistakes then. Early days. Two loved N-37B as much as you seem to, even if she could never fly around in it. And our stories about our adventures. I expect that's why The Rescuers snuck your sarcophagus into our cargo hold. So Four could live the life Two could not," He said. There it was again. The emotion.

"And Three could live the life Two could not, just as Two was able to live while One was already gone," she said, stammering some. She took a big gulp of her drink. Phil looked to be preparing a second one for her like he knew what she was thinking. Antonio may not be the only one at this bar who could read minds. Or it may be that both of them were good at reading people. Phil was a good bartender. Not just for making drinks and cracking jokes. But establishing a good rapport with his patrons. The good ones just knew when a customer needed a refill. Antonio was mostly done with his. She suspected he'd be signaling Phil soon for more bourbon.

"So if it wasn't high school underwear than what was it?" she said. Antonio didn't say anything for a few moments. Then he sighed and finished off his bourbon and another two fingers went up. Phil walked over with Chief's second Bloody Mary and a bottle of Jim Beam. Once Antonio's glass was filled he spoke.

"You've seen the replay. Pretty much that. Only sometimes I don't pull the trigger. Then I wake up knowing that was bullshit. I damn well know I pulled that trigger. I see the muzzle flash in dreams that don't lie to me. I've killed over sixty men Chief. This was the only one I regret. None of those other douchebags wake me up at night. They were trying to kill me as much as I was trying to kill them. I won. This guy was just walking home one night," he said and took a sip of bourbon. Phil had had conversations about bad dreams with Antonio many times before. But he hadn't known about this one, or even the incident itself until recently.

"It seems like to me eh. There's some common ground here. Chief, you couldn't control a rock the size of Paris exploding over your Earth. You couldn't control how things shook out for Two. You also didn't put yourself on the Pathfinder. But from what I've seen, you made the absolute best of what you can in a different universe living a different life. That's some pretty spectacular shit. And Tony you couldn't control what your mind does on a long dash. But from what I understand, you've taken responsibility for that. You've made sure as best you can that that doesn't happen again. I know saying all this doesn't fix things. But maybe it'll help you both going forward. I don't know. I just work here," he said. Antonio raised his glass and took another sip. Phil was right. Chief could feel the booze start to kick in. But the conversation was more of help to her in her mind.

"Thanks Tabs," she said. Phil smiled and nodded.

"Don't mention it kid. It's what I'm here for," Phil said and then resumed watching TV. Chief and Antonio didn't say much more before she finished her second drink. Her nerves had settled down enough by then and returned to her quarters. Antonio stayed where he was. His night wasn't over. Phil was there to look after him though.

Pauly was working late tonight. Reconstructing older weapons tech came with more than a few challenges. From what the probes had been able to ascertain so far there were more than a dozen varieties of tree that both matched species on Gary's World, but were also suitable for fashioning bows. He'd settled on a variety of hickory after testing several others for durability, strength, and flexibility. Both Nocivo and JP would be carrying bows. Each had his preference. Estrello would go with a short bow. A long bow was most practical for a man of JP's height. After looking at all the bows the probes documented, hybrid style designs of the most common bows were formulated and fed into the machine Pauly had craft for them. It was a machine originally designed to craft furniture, but adapted to create these older type weapons. The wood grain was optimized down to a cellular level.

A fact became apparent after the last Sword World the team ended up in. Bows they happened upon while they were there proved unsatisfactory. Going in better prepared became a priority. Nick and Quiz wheeled carts filled with arrows tipped with heads hand forged by Salazar. The range had suspended regular operations while the particulars of Mission 73 could be attended to. Foam targets had been set up where paper targets would normally go. Pauly had spent a few hours thoroughly sweeping the area to remove as much unburned powder as he could. Not that it mattered if he did, but he hated tracking it around. Nick and Quiz set the carts next to the wall just inside by lane 8. Nearby Pauly had laid out several variations of each design for Nocivo and JP to test out. Quiz had been itching at ask since he and Nick had picked up their carts from Jack's storeroom.

"Hey Pauly, you think they made enough arrows? There's no way in hell they're going to be able to carry all of these." He said. Pauly knew he was being sarcastic.

"Well obviously they don't intend to take them all. But they do need to get a feel for whatever they're going to ultimately settle on. Of course no matter how well designed any one of these are Skip would argue that shooting at a static target is no substitute for real battle. The tool is only part of the equation, or as Socrates once put it 'The way to gain a good reputation is to endeavor to be what you desire to appear,'" Pauly said. Quiz looked a little confused.

"Who the hell is Socrates?" he said. Pauly looked up at him and blinked a few times like he was genuinely disappointed Quiz was unfamiliar with the name. Nick chimed in.

"He was a Greek philospher," he said with a chuckle. Quiz looked at him and then a Pauly.

"See, this is what I mean when I say that these 21st century people are really smart. People look at us from the future and think we're all geniuses because we have all this great advanced technology. No, we're dumb as shit, but our toys are really cool. People don't get that. They think I'm going to hold up my hand and say something profound. Well, no. I'm going to say something stupid and try to sound smart," Quiz said.

Nick laughed. Pauly could understand where Quiz was coming from. All the Bumppo crew not from the 25th century did assume a great deal about him and others from the future.

"I think that's one of the great illusions about time most would not consider. I would even go so far as to point out the arrogance of people of what we'd regard as the present Quiz. The case could be made this attitude has always existed for those of the respective 'present times' when discussing people from the past. I talk to Skip and Tony all the time and I am floored every time I do because even I am guilty of this. These guys blow me away at just how much more of everything they know than I do. In our time I would be regarded as well read, but when I get into a deep philosophical conversation with Skipper, I realize I'm breaking even," he said. Nick had a point to make though.

"Oh yeah, but he is a doctor," he said. Pauly did acknowledge that, but also wanted to make a point.

"But he's not the only one from the past I've interacted with obviously. I always get a kick from talking with you for instance. I know I will always come away with something that will absolutely blow my mind. Skip took me and Tony to his favorite taco truck guy, I don't remember what his name was, but I must have stayed and chatted with the guy for three hours or more. Very well rounded guy. Makes a great taco. My point being, too may people take for granted that people will be smarter in the future. We just aren't," Pauly said. Quiz had something to add to that.

"Well yeah of course. If you assume that people will just figure everything out in time organically you're doomed to failure if you don't put the burden on yourself to know more to teach to younger people. They won't have anything to pass on to the generation after them. The responsibility rests on those living in the here and now," Quiz said. Nick laughed.

"Yeah man, but nobody wants to look it at that way," he said. Quiz nodded and pointed at himself.

"Exactly! That's why people in the 25th century are dumber that dirt. Nobody wants to take that responsibility. They're the end result of people from the 22nd, 23rd and 24th centuries that just thought things would work themselves out in the future. Well, no. No they don't. It doesn't work that way, and it never has. Cashless society? What's the worst that could happen? I could go on for days about that. We finally sobered up from that stupid shit," he said. Nick laughed again.

"Yeah man, modern science wants to dismiss any possibility that advanced civilizations have existed on this planet before. They can't come to terms with the idea that we, humans, can get dumber over time. We certainly can. Our capacity to do stupid things is at least as great as our capacity for brilliance. Even if we're talking about the same person. I can say there is no easy way of passing things down because we're too good at fucking that up. Everyone has their own idea of how to do it. Everyone is wrong. Some people are more wrong than others, but all of us are wrong. You get enough people that are wrong about too much, even if the wrong they are about disagrees with each other, civilization declines, and will collapse. Even the most advanced ones. All because we lack the objectivity we need to look each other in the eye with the kind of honesty we need to actually solve problems just because they need to. No agendas," Nick said. Quiz smiled and looked at Pauly as he pointed at Nick.

"This is why I like talking to people from the past. I never have conversations like this back home. Thank you sir," Quiz said. Nick chuckled.

"Hey no problem man. Sorry to hear you don't get those really good conversations in the 25th. At least Pauly got out in pretty good shape," he said. Pauly really appreciated that.

"Aww thanks man," he said. Quiz agreed highly.

"Yeah JP really knew what he was doing putting this crew together. I shit you not man, he found the only interesting people from the 25th century and brought them here. Everybody else? Talking blocks of wood. You might find the technology interesting. The people, not so much. You're better off in the here and now," Quiz said. Nick was a little disappointed.

"I guess the future is spoiled for me now," He mused. Pauly shook his head.

"Nah man. The future did that to itself on it's own. You want to know how I got on this crew?" He said. Nick had wanted to know this for a while now.

"Let's hear it," he said. Pauly sat down on a shop stool near him.

"I met JP about seven years ago. He was part of this group of ship captains called the 360. There weren't 360 of them. They just met at this hole in the wall place called The Loten next to where I was working at the time. They only hung around for about two hours before they got tired of talking or ordering food. I used to hang out with a group of people who called themselves The Minions. We were all a bunch of knuckleheads that worked around The Loten. That's how I met Quiz, Chandler, Ted, Terry, and a bunch of other people. Yes Terry too. I know crazy right?" he said. Quiz laughed. Nick was surprised. Terry never went anywhere. Just wasn't his way.

"Wow, Terry out in public. That's wild man," he said. It was true though. Pauly continued.

"The Loten was owned by this guy named Frank. Always wore these retro Coco Pops t-shirts. The place had a stage where people could perform on open mic nights. Or they could sit up on stage with Frank and two friends of his when they would sit around telling stories. Tori and Scribbles. I don't know what his name actually was. People just called him that. Anyhow my friends would go to this place and hear Frank and the others sit around and tell stories. These crazy ship captains would show up and watch too. When Frank and them finished their set these guys would start talking among themselves. A lot of people would crowd around them to hear all their stories too. Every now and again one would join Frank and the gang up on stage. Our friends would do the same. A lot of fun times," he said. So far this was turning out to be an interesting story. Nick had something of a similar story to tell, but he'd wait for another time.

"That's awesome man. Great bunch of people just getting together and telling stories. Love it," he said. Pauly and Quiz looked at each other for a moment. Pauly sighed and collected his thoughts.

"Well it wasn't all great. There was a handful of those ship captains that started stirring up trouble for everyone else. Some started picking fights with us. Difference of opinion is one thing, but it got ridiculous. Some of them went to picking fights with other people who worked the shipping lanes people called The Tubes. But that's a whole other story. To make a long story short too much bad blood in the 360. They stopped showing up altogether. A few years later Frank closed The Loten down. The Minions started hanging out by a zoo down the street at an outdoor barbeque place owned by Reggie. Really nice lady. One day JP and Martha show up. She'd wanted to see the giraffes. Something of an endangered species in the 25th," he said. Nick wasn't happy to hear that. He loved giraffes as a kid. He'd collected wax figurines he gotten from the San Antonio Zoo's Mold-A-Rama machines.

"Aww man. Y'all killed off the giraffes too?" he moaned. The 25th century was beginning to sound grim but Pauly needed to tell the story.

"Oh yeah a space port experienced catastrophic orbital decay that couldn't be fixed in time so it crash landed in Africa and wiped a bunch of them out. Happened about forty years ago. Sad story. Anyhow so JP recognized us and we all got to talking. We wanted to know what he'd been up to since all the 360 drama went down. He told us he'd been doing some travelling. Yeah, he said travelling. None of us really knew what he meant. He told us he met this really awesome alien guy, and later two really intense dudes. Skip and the guys. JP was pretty vague about a lot of things. Really cagey when we'd ask about specifics. It was a cool conversation just the same. About a week later he shows back up telling us he was putting together a new crew for a ship he'd just got his hands on. Offered us a job," he said. Nick was really invested in the story now.

"Just like that?" he said. Pauly and Quiz just nodded. Quiz continued.

"Just like that. We asked why he wanted us on his crew. He told us that we were some of the good ones. Some of us were surprised he didn't even ask for a resume. He told us that hanging out with us at The Loten and hearing our stories was all the resume he needed. Dude, we were floored. Floored! Getting a job on a ship is The Amazing job that everyone wants. It's the single most difficult job to get. Planet jobs. Space port jobs. These are easy. Anybody can get those. But a job on a ship. A cruise ship? Holy shit man. A dream come true. This was a prime gig. Nobody even cared to ask where we'd be flying. This was a VCS 64 Rho man! Big as fuck! Great crew quarters. Better than working for some crappy movie streaming service. Those people were assholes," he said. Nick and Pauly laughed. Pauly picked up one the test carvings of JP's longbow. He looped a string onto one end and grunted as he tried to affix the other end. He seemed to be having a lot of trouble. Even putting his weight on it was going nowhere. Nick gave him a hand. The two of them put all their weight into it and managed to string it. Pauly was breathing a little heavy. He was astonished JP had given him these specs.

"Holy shit what does the man eat to want a bow like that?" he said. Pauly then tried to draw the string back. He couldn't. Nick was surprised as well. Pauly handed him the bow for him to try. Nick pulled hard but could not draw it back very far.

"You gotta be kidding me. That's amazing. I know he's a big guy, but wow!" he said. Quiz couldn't believe it was that hard and took the bow up and tried to draw. He almost threw his shoulder out. He was stunned how many pounds JP's bow had.

"Guy has to be on steroids like seriously man!" Quiz said as he handed the bow back to Pauly.

"I'm not a small guy, but JP is a battleship of a man. It's like Immigrant Song was written just for him. I'm supremely envious of the guy. As Tacitus put it 'When men are full of envy they disparage everything, whether it be good or bad.' That being said, he looks like he bench presses Buick LeSabres. I merely drive one," Pauly joked. The guys laughed. Nick was curious what Pauly was doing before The Bumppo.

"So how does a guy who hangs out next to a zoo get a gig as a range master and man-at-arms on ship like this?" he said. Pauly sat back down. It was a good question.

"I was working weekends at a gun range that was part of a gun store while I was working on my dissertation. Guy I was working for was a hard man to work for. Shadowed the gunsmith that worked there. Learned all kinds of stuff. As for that dissertation. It took me three years to write that damn thing. Professors hated all my drafts. Kept making changes until they liked it. Philistines. Kept working at the range until the old man ran the business into the ground. Hard thing to do in the 25th century. Firearms market is strong. Plenty of off-worlders. Can't be too careful. Especially if your old boss owed some gangsters a lot of money and they thought you knew where he was, and subsequently start showing up at your apartment threating to do very bad things to you unless you talked. That was not a fun experience. They kept coming back and hassling me until I met JP. Subject came up. Goons didn't come around bothering me anymore. He told me the matter was 'taken care of' and there had been a 'misunderstanding' and 'everything was copacetic now' and for me not to worry about it anymore. I didn't ask him to clarify," Pauly said. Nick was even more curious now.

"So JP had a sit down with these guys?" Nick said. Pauly didn't have a good answer.

"When it comes to JP, there's questions you ask. And those you don't. Do we work for some kind of Space Capo? There's a good chance. I wouldn't bring it up though. Look up the word Omerta and then you'll know what I mean. Guy follows the code," Pauly said. Nick just laughed. Pauly was being serious. JP had a lot of layers.

"Trust me if you asked Skip, Tony and Strat about JP they wouldn't tell you anything. They follow the code too. There's a lot these guys will tell you about themselves and each other. We're their people. Not outsiders. And there's a lot they won't. Because the four of them are their own inner circle. There's things they keep just between them," Pauly added. Nick was a little concerned about a few things.

"How do I know where the line is drawn?" he asked. Pauly thought about this for a moment.

"I couldn't tell you much more, but I know to never ask why Skip doesn't take contracts anymore. Never ask JP about how he makes his real money. Never ask Tony about his conviction. And I am being very serious, never ask Strat about the wars. Angel won't talk about her brother either. Don't bother there," Pauly said. Nick nodded. He was curious about some of that. But now he knew not go looking for those answers.

"There's just some shit I don't need to know," Nick said and laughed. Pauly smiled.

"See, there ya go. That's the spirit," he said.

The night was chilly and the wind largely still. The calm flow of the river nearby blended with the night to create a blanket of placidity that enveloped the dwarven campsite. Raltec had the watch for the time being. He'd taken over for Balocan who had first watch and was now sound asleep. When Raltec could no longer stay awake he would roust Pulcan and he would watch until first light. It had been the same routine for many nights now.

This night was different. This night Raltec watched over this strange wanderer, a Redflower, which was a very unexpected complication, but one that had to be addressed. Redflowers were not a pack to cross, in particular its patriarch, and he had to wonder who had the temerity or the folly to attack one. Even one who appeared to be as humble as this wolf. That person courted a very slow painful death if the tales of Brewster Redflower were to be believed. He was called The Red Wolf for more reasons than one. The only thing Raltec had of the attacker was the strange small single bladed knife with bronze scales on the handle. He heard a sound then. The wolf appeared to be waking. A cloud of mist billowed from the wanderer's snout as he deeply sighed.

"Dwarf," he moaned. The aching throb of pain hit the wolf all at once as he came to. He picked his head up enough to look over at Raltec. The dwarf was glad to see the wolf wasn't dead.

"Wanderer, alive still I see. Good," he said. The wolf could hear the apprehensiveness in the dwarf's voice. Even through the pain, he could understand.

"Thank you for pulling me ashore and tending my wounds. Your fire is much appreciated. I'm sure you have many questions," the wolf said weakly. Raltec sat forward and stoked the fire some and lay back again.

"You could say I do Redflower. The first being, how did one of Brewster's pups end up in a river in these woods? Also what sort of fiend or fool put a knife in one? Anyone demented enough to cross your pack is likely to be a concern for me and my crew wouldn't you say?" he said. If the wolf could nod, he would have.

"I agree. I can tell you my name is Pepper Redflower. I'd gather you saw the sigil around my neck. No point in trying to deny it then. My family and I are not so close anymore, but I am a pup of Brewster Redflower. I would not imagine my attacker knew of my lineage. Or perhaps he was too demented to care. If he survived the river as I did, we will see how much a fiend, or fool he happens to be. My father has a long memory," Pepper said. This answered some of what Raltec was curious about, but not all.

"I wonder Pepper, of the pack Redflower, what this man's quarrel with you was. It seems you both had more than a mere disagreement," he said. Pepper was awake, but his mind was not altogether clear. He knew that dwarves liked to get straight to the point. Not a people known for mincing words. Finesse would not be advisable, or even really possible at the moment.

"I did not know my attacker. I'm not even entirely certain what he was after. All that I know is what he took, and what he did to myself and my brothers who tried to stop him," Pepper said. This seemed to elicit some alarm from the dwarf.

"Brothers?" he said. Pepper could feel the trepidation building in the dwarf.

"My brothers of The East Lodge. I am a Brother there. I am head supervisor of rare texts. The man who attacked me was trying to steal some of those rare texts. The men he killed were not my flesh and blood. But they were still my brothers," he said. Sadness overtook the pain in his voice. Raltec calmed some but this raised even more questions in his mind.

"You are a Brother of The East Lodge? Strangely enough myself and my crew were on our way to meet with the Brothers. What did this man take and why? Was he working alone? I'm sorry, you should be resting but there are some things I need to know. If I'm going to have to fight, I'd like to know as much as I can. I'm sure you'd agree," Raltec said firmly, but fairly. Pepper could only tell him what he knew.

"I could speculate about a number of things. As to why, I could not say. He had some books related to some recent research I was involved in. Believe me, I would like to know more myself. I don't know if he was working alone. That he knew to go after what he did, would suggest he was working for someone else. It wasn't the kind of material someone would go after unless they were put up to it," he said wearily. Raltec didn't want to press any further.

Pepper lay his head back down and exhaled deeply. Raltec resumed his watch. He knew more now than he did. But this was little comfort. If the murderous thief or his patrons didn't like loose ends, how thorough would they be to make sure no further complications would arise? Were they the sort would have thought that through? For them to send someone to The East Lodge for something that specific, little could be ruled out.

The morning sun was rising. A heavy jeweling of dew clung to the grass around Carcino Lamb's feet. It was the first day of autumn. Something like this would otherwise be a cause for good tidings and well wishes. This year it would not. The smell of smoke in the shifting winds before the dawn signaled Carcino and his men that something was wrong. They mobilized as quickly as they could and rode hard towards the rising sun. Now Carcino stood where he was, and saw what he did. A windmill spinning in the wind just stiff enough to move it. Then there was the sound of wood whining against wood as the blades spun, and the sound of metal scraping against board. And the thump of human flesh hitting the ground and dragging through the grit and gravel. A man lay dead a few yards away lacking an arm. Carcino figured he'd been chained to the blades sometime in the last day or so. It didn't matter the constant wind in the night kept those blades moving. He wasn't sure if it was the trauma or the exposure to the cold of the night that killed him. But he was surely dead. The mill had probably been throwing him over dead for hours until it twisted the arm free. Carcino's Captain, Sir Prose Vallamy stood behind him. He waited until his Prince gave him the go-ahead. Carcino looked back at him.

"Make sure this man, and all the dead here are given proper burials. Especially the children. They will be given the same respect as if they were born within the walls of Southgate. Is this understood Sir Vallamy?" he said. Vallamy could see the emotion behind his Prince's eyes. It's one thing to hear stories and read accounts. It's another to see it all first hand. And here he was. A Prince of Southgate bearing witness to the horror.

"Aye my Prince. And before that end how would you like the men to proceed?" Vallamy asked. Carcino looked back at the dead man. He walked a few steps and knelt down beside his mangled body. He answered without looking up.

"I want men who can write and draw going along. I want all the men going in to walk as a cat does. I want everything observed. I want everything documented. These killers are well practiced. No ordinary bandits. These knew what they were doing. They're smarter. Cleaner. But more brutal than any bandit gang I have yet seen. I want you to remember this Vallamy. Dark times breed dark men. Dark hearts fuel dark deeds to birth these dark times. They didn't just want silver and gold. They wanted to earn it the way men with dark thoughts do," Carcino said. Vallamy looked upon a man who wanted to fight so badly the very ground he walked on seemed to offer its back to stand on for that fight.

"Aye my Prince. I will take those words to my grave," Vallamy said. Carcino gestured to a few of his lieutenants to follow him as he proceeded into the obliterated village of Guppie's Gulch. As Carcino walked slowly forward he took note of the impressions in the ground. He noted their depth and shape. Most were deep and distorted.

The distance between them was long like the one who made them was running for their life, or to take one. Those prints didn't interest him as much as others. Even fresher prints but shallower. Better defined. They were closer together as if the one who made them walked about casually. Would they be out of place in a scene like this? Not to Carcino. These were the marks left by guilty men. He took note of them. The size of the heel, the point of the toe, the spacing of the tacks, and every other detail were important to him. Carcino heard one of his men gasp behind him. He looked up. More bodies lay nearby. The cold of the night had kept the rot at bay but he could smell the blood well enough. A woman lay face down in a pool of water she may have been drowned in. In one leg an arrow with the fletching snapped away was placed just above the back of the knee.

"You men tend to her," he said as he pointed at the drowned woman. He proceeded ahead followed by some of the others. They walk a ways past a farmhouse. Long smeared handprints stained its door as if the occupants had been pulled out through them. He looked at the ground to see drag marks everywhere. Drag marks that seemed to go in one direction toward the center of town. Dew on the grass scoured by violence told him they were made well before they arrived here. Had it happened after, the droplets would not glisten as they did. This told him the killings could not have happened later than few hours before the dawn. His brother Attheon taught him this when he was a child. Attheon could track a deer over miles through a rainstorm and taught his brother well.

"Hold your breakfast whatever we see here lads. I don't want your vomit covering an important track. And stop dragging your feet," he said. His men were quick to respond.

"Aye my Prince," they all said and started picking up their feet. As the group walked they saw more blood, smeared print and drag marks on the ground, but no bodies. Farmhouses sat open and quiet. The sound of the occasional whining door hinge moved by the wind broke the silence. And then they turned the corner. Two of the men stopped dead in their tracks and looked on in horror. Carcino kept walking forward with eyes to the ground trying to process everything he was seeing with every step that felt heavier than the last. He turned and looked back at the stunned men.

"I said stop dragging your feet lads," he said sternly. His tone snapped them out their stupors.

"Aye my Prince," they both said meekly. Carcino turned to continue on until he too stopped and stood silently. A Temple of the Wind sat in the middle of town. Around it were fifty, maybe a hundred, bodies tied like a chain around it. The town had been dragged here. Their bodies tied together like a chain of death that resembled a frilled garland with all the arrows buried into flesh. Some stood pinned to the building while others lay against it. As Carcino stood there more of his men carrying paper and quills looked on with mouths open and eyes sullen. Carcino took a deep breath and pulled one of them aside.

"You've gotten your orders, yes? Follow them to the letter. I want all of those arrows collected as intact as you can. Document, Everything," He said strongly. His man nodded. Sir Vallamy walked up then. His face was ashen.

"Orders have been given my Prince. A priest of The Wind in the next village has a rider going to him. I don't think he'll ever be forgetting the last rites he performs today," Vallamy said. There was the same shock in the faces of all his men here. Death in battle was known to most. Dead civilians were another matter.

"Have a feather flown to Flint Redflower, and one to Snowbrace Quickwill for good measure. I want information on bandit movements in this area. In case I'm wrong, and bandits have elevated their rancor, I don't want to be caught flat-footed. The rangers need to be contacted. I don't care if all they have to offer right now is rumor or gut instinct. We will fill in those blanks," he said. Vallamy saw the raw insistence in Carcino's eyes.

"At once my Prince," he said and turned back to have the messages written up. Carcino turned and looked back at the grisly scene. Something stood out to him. He walked forward toward the temple stopping just short of it. He knelt down and looked at one of the bodies. It was a little girl. In her hair were the kind of bows his sister wore on her birthday when she was a small child. As all small girls tied into their hair the night before their birthday in the south. He reached over and closed her still open eyes.

"Rest child," he said, and then fell silent.

The winds were low this morning on the Eastern Sea. The Storm Eagle and its Captain Lord Denato Falco of Seastorm sailed forth as fast as the weak winds would carry her. Behind sailed 20 ships of the Falco fleet. It was as big an escort as young Lord Falco could get away with and still maintain some stealth while sailing on patrol.

There hadn't been a proper encounter in months. Much of the scoundrel pirate presence desired neither to fight nor flee from the Falco fleet. They instead sailed in flying flags of truce scared out of their wits by what their accounts described as phantoms sailing under the flag of The Black Admiral and his Shadow Fleet, an unstoppable dark armada by every account.

Denato had heard the stories and seen men with hardened hearts built up thick over years of killing, raping and looting, break down in front of him describing ships blown by the winds of death itself chasing down seasoned cutthroats who knew the sea better than their own kin. Ships with infamous monikers captained by known names now lined the bottom of the sea. But these doomed vessels were not alone. Along side them were trading ships and fishing boats. Humble men making an honest living shared their watery grave with fiends. It was a difficult thing to fathom. But silver and gold appeared to be all the same in the eyes of the Shadow Fleet. A sailor who smelled too richly of it was gambling with his ship, his crew, and his own life. Scarcity bred opportunity. Opportunity tempted the weak and foolish, which spilled so much proverbial blood in the water to attract The Black Admiral. A Shadow Fleet that sailed with impunity and seemed to make port in the darkness of night itself. No harbor saw them drop anchor. Islands with suitably deep waters lay desolate. It was a mystery how such an immense fleet could just vanish on the horizon without a trace. Even a man like Denato Falco had more than his share of apprehension. He brought only the keenest eyes to keep watch for the swarm of black sails in the distance. Thus far after many months of patrols in waters of reported sightings, nothing was detected. This first day of autumn was appearing to be as fruitless as the last day of summer. Denato stood at the helm with his hands on the wheel feeling the sea speak to him through his fingertips. It didn't tell him much. His first mate Geosep Genodi sat on a barrel nearby cutting into a big green lime.

"Gods man, chasing off scurvy already?" Denato said. Geosep kept cutting until he split the lime in half. He held out a half to his Captain.

"Oh I take scurvy quite seriously m'Lord and so should you," he said. Denato smiled and took the half.

"If you insist. A good sour bite ought to take my mind off the fact the sea is guarding her secrets far too well. I knew I should have prayed harder to the goddess as a child. Now I'm paying for it by chasing after shadows and coming up emptier than a Midlander's promise," Denato said. Geosep chuckled.

"Oh I wouldn't call it a complete waste. We have plenty of limes m'Lord," he said. Denato sighed.

"Oh aye Geosep. We'll die of boredom long before scurvy kills us. If The Black Admiral rises up from the blackness he'll have to pry the fruit from our cold dead hands!" Denato mused. Geosep sensed the young Lord was being more scornful than sarcastic. From his tone it sounded like all of it was self-directed. Denato Falco liked getting results. He wanted at least some trail to follow, but the sea offered nothing but dead leads and a clear horizon. The young Lord frowned as he bit into his lime. Geosep stood up from his barrel and leaned against the railing.

"Should I have the boys take inventory again? Break up some of this monotony?" he said. Denato knew idle hands bred gambling, and the last thing he needed was a distracted crew on a hunt for The Black Admiral. It didn't matter if there was no silver, gold or even copper on board. Denato was not a superstitious man, but he still could not explain how the Shadow Fleet knew which ships were carrying riches and which weren't. The best explanation is that The Black Admiral had a formidable network of spies in his employ. Agents of the Shadow Fleet could be lurking in every port and none would be the wiser. This is why Denato only trusted men he knew himself. He kept to the people he knew and avoided the city. It kept him away from family but his singular focus had been The Shadow Fleet and it's commander for the better part of two years.

"Might as well. These men will get to playing tiles if they have nothing to do. We don't need to be breaking up fights and it make it even easier for The Shadows to evade us," he said. Geosep didn't need much prompting. He trotted down the steps

"Alright listen up! The Captain wants a count of every rope, nail and barrel of piss on this boat and he wants it now! Unless you want to get shipped high in transit, I suggest you get it done before that sun is overhead!!" Geosep barked. Denato almost laughed. It did certainly get the men moving. They darted fore and aft to start getting a count. Noon was fast approaching.

Some of the men ran to the forecastle to count the ropes coiled and stored there. One would count while another would mark notches on a stick.

"Four coils! And three coils! And five coils!" one yelled to the other. He notched just as he was told.

"Aye!" he yelled back and was set to run back with the stick but something caught his eye. He looked around for a lookout. He saw one just over his shoulder. He'd seen it too. The lookout turned to him.

"Get the Captain!" the lookout yelled. The stick marker ran back to the foremast.

"Ship on the horizon!" he screamed. Others looked up as he did. They began shouting back toward the helm. Geosep turned to Denato as the words met his ears. Denato's eyes flared up.

"Look alive men! Hoist the alert! Quickly now!" Denato shouted. Two men sprung into action. They pulled a red flag from its box and strung it high in haste. The red was seen. The word spread. Archers mobilized and swords passed around. The Falco fleet was ready for a fight. Geosep took the helm as Denato rushed to the bow next to his lookout. Flagmen waited for their Captain's order to fly yellow for a fight. Or green to stand down. Denato's eyes were fixed on the horizon like a soaring raptor on a fish swimming too shallow. His eyes shifted this way and that as the sighted object drew nearer. No other objects were appearing on either side. Whatever ship this was, it was alone. As least as far as he could tell.

"All I see is a lone vessel. Do you concur?" Denato said to his lookout.

"Aye Captain. Nothing trails it yet. Odd looking vessel m'Lord." The lookout said. Denato agreed. At this distance the ship appeared strange looking.

"It's massive. Not like any ship I've ever seen," Denato said. The lookout agreed. He strained his eyes to catch a first glimpse of her colors. Meanwhile flag men on the other ships kept a close eye on the other flags. As soon as they saw yellow, the archers who stood around them would know it was a fight. Denato's lookout saw something then that gave him pause for a moment.

"It's not one vessel m'Lord," he said. Denato looked up at his lookout.

"Are you sure? Another vessel trails behind it?" he said and looked back at the object. The lookout's head was beginning to hurt from the strain but he persisted. Then clarity washed over him.

"No Captain, it's two vessels lashed to each other by the rigging. Like they struck together in a storm and caught up in a snag," he said. Denato was silent for a moment.

"Adrift? Crippled perhaps? What colors do they fly?" he said. The lookout had been trying to catch a glimpse of them. The wind shifted then and enough of the sail flapped into view. The lookout's eyes widened.

"She flies blue Captain! Three orange crabs! All in a row! Exiled colors!" the lookout yelled. Denato's blood ran cold. He and the lookout stared at each other, each fueling each others growing sense of dread.

"Ilonnis Honestead. These are Honestead ships. Three crabs." Denato seemed to say to himself as his men watched him to get their next orders. He was dumbfounded. The theory that The Black Admiral sailed for the Exiled kingdoms seemed to be cast in doubt now if this was by his hand.

"What is your order m'Lord?" an archer near Denato said. The young Lord turned to him.

"They could have been damaged in a storm yes? But they still cling to each other. Why has nobody freed up the rigging? Crew is dead likely. Killed by the storm? All of them? Unlikley. If crew is dead, how? Who is responsible?" he said to the archer. The archer didn't have much to offer.

"I could not say Captain. Shadows maybe. Just two ships though. Common pirates more likely," he said. Denato nodded.

"Perhaps. We'll need to intercept and investigate to know for sure. Lookout, what else do you see?" he said. The lookout scanned the horizon. There was nothing else. He looked down at the young Lord and shook his head. Denato paused for a moment of thought then turned to his archer.

"Fly green," He said and headed back to the helm. The archer wasted no time.

"Fly Green!" he shouted back. A chain of others followed suit. Flagmen grabbed up green and hoisted it by the red. The message filtered back to the other ships. Archers eased and swords sheathed. Denato walked up to his first mate.

"Intercept course Geosep," He said. His first mate did as his Captain asked.

The subtle sound of Brazilian jazz filled the room waking Antonio from his slumber. He would not call it waking though. More accurately it was a failure to continue to be asleep. Awake would be strong language to describe his state. He sat up and let the brackish throb roll over him. Standing was possible, if not necessarily desired position at the moment. Nonetheless he stood and staggered across the room to turn off the alarm, sweet silence too over then. A thirst took hold then. He looked over at his mini fridge and staggered over to it and opened it. A container of green drink sat there.

He was then reminded of the pain in his head wasn't just the consequence of hanging out with his friend Jim Beam, but six well placed shots to the back of his head. Then he was reminded that he'd be looking forward to a day in the records room with the guys and E.V.E. planning out the next op. 73 it was now. Antonio frowned and picked up the green drink and flipped the top open. He took a swig and staggered over with a grimace to his computer desk where a bottle of painkillers sat. He took a few and lay back in his chair. He pushed his computer mouse, which woke up his computer. The monitor lit up the dim room and hurt Antonio's eyes. He took up the mouse and opened up a folder on his desktop. He looked for a video file and opened it. The image of his daughter at 11 years old materialized. She held a bat while she listened to his instructions. He remembered this day. It was weeks before her little league softball season was to begin and she wanted to work in some extra batting practice. She wanted video so she could watch herself. Codi was always keen to spot where she needed work. The little slugger was truly her father's daughter. Antonio's younger bother Marcelo held the camera. Whereas Antonio's words were mechanical and concise, Marcelo was just trying to be encouraging to his niece. Practice for when his first child could hold a bat. His wife had been carrying him then and was nearly due. This was good practice for Marcelo. The encouragement took. Codena did well that season. Second on the team in runs batted in. Antonio smiled as he heard his brother's laugh as Antonio stood on the pitchers mound. Then came the throw. A good pitch that sailed over the middle of home plate, and then bat cracked. A good hit that flew just above Antonio's mitt. Codena turned around and high fived her uncle. The camera panned over to Antonio who clapped. That was a good day. Antonio stopped the video. He needed the extra motivation. His walk down to the records room was a slow and sluggish slog. He didn't feel particularly enthusiastic about clarifying the locus, but the image of him clapping for his daughter overruled that. The checkpoint guards could tell he had a rough night. They kept things light, even Moon, who held back his usual biting sarcasm. Antonio knew to stay where he was when the red light came on. It just was what it was. When he reached the records room he was the last to arrive. Jeremy was here too. He didn't look like he was in a great mood. He was in good company. He noticed Antonio walk in.

"There he is. Now we can start," he said. Antonio would have expected Jeremy would have already been well through his presentation by now.

"Y'all didn't have to wait up for me. I'm a walking hangover, brick, thing. I'll just lament over here in a corner until y'all need me to locus. Ignore me. You have the floor Jeremy," Antonio said as he staggered off to a chair. Jeremy rolled his eyes.

"Thank you Tony. I was hoping to have your blessing before my diatribe," Jeremy said sarcastically. Nocivo was less entertained with Antonio's state.

"I did tell you to lay off the booze didn't I Tony? But what do I know? I'm just a doctor," he said with a shade of darker sarcasm. He then turned to Jeremy who looked like he had a lot to say.

"First off I want to thank you all for inviting me down here. I can't tell you how much of a joy it was to go through all of your security checkpoints. I know my life is now fuller having been through that experience. But don't take my word for it. Have a look at Tony Sparklefinger to see a man who is truly sharing a morning I will cherish for the rest of my days," he said. Nocivo did understand Jeremy's dissatisfaction.

"On the bright side you would have never known you had a zinc deficiency," he said half musing. Jeremy recognized he was being messed with.

"Gee Skip, I don't think I could possibly gone on without knowing I have a zinc deficiency. My life can truly start changing for the better now," he said. The guys in the room started grinning. Especially JP.

"Hey man we all have to start somewhere. It's all about making to the commitment to living a better life through zinc," JP said. Jeremy added to it.

"Uh huh, and I am truly blessed that mad men and their technological horrors have given me the chance to understand the true power of zinc," he said followed with a chuckle. Though Nocivo did appreciate a bit of humor, he did want to move things along.

"Not if you don't get your zinc levels up. Just like we need to get our intel levels up. What can you tell us about what we're walking into?" he said. Jeremy threw a goofy grin around and then sat back in his chair.

"I can tell you that you boys are seven shades of fucked if you go in like you did last time. I really wished you'd talked to me before you guys went ahead with that one. That was some cringy shit and I am less cool now for hanging out with all of you," Jeremy said. JP seemed to have his disagreements with Jeremy assessments.

"Well, we thought we had a handle on things. We had not one, but two, Spanish speakers, and a sense of adventure. But at the same time yeah, they did look at us like we were mall ninjas," he said. Jeremy snapped his fingers.

"Mall Ninjas! Exactly the words I wanted to use. Thank you JP. I want to help you all now not to show up on this Sword World looking like Mall Ninjas in their back yard swinging around a Klingon bat'leth screaming 'Qapla' until someone's grandma has you put on a government watch list," he said. JP snickered.

"It's a little late for that with this crowd man," he mused. Jeremy rolled his eyes.

"My goal is to help you blend in a much as possible. I'll point out I didn't say as much as 'Probable.' I've known you guys long enough to know some shit just ain't in the cards. But I'll help as much as I can," he said. Nocivo brought up a map of the landmasses of the Sword World.

"What can you tell us about the cultures we'll be running across? In particular the ones in the approximate locus hits Evie has been able to pinpoint," he said. Jeremy picked up a tablet sitting in front of him and tapped away.

"There appears to be five major cultural epicenters on the continent you're gunning for. Y'all don't have to pay mind to the north or west. They're both too far away to matter, but I've made some notes if you insist on going there. I don't recommend it. You'll be dealing with enough of a shit show in the places that actually matter for this mission," he said. JP leaned forward and looked closely at the areas Jeremy highlighted.

"Thank you for the clarification. You saved us from agonizingly long boat trips," JP said. Jeremy took a bow in his chair.

"I aim to please. The three you have to worry about are some dipshits in a place they call The Midlands. Has an Emperor and some warlords and just generally comes off as a bad place to go. But y'all need to know about it so I covered it thoroughly in my notes. To the east you have a bunch of large islands the locals call The Exiled Kingdoms. Pretty much a bunch of Kings got fed up with being told what to do so they packed up their shit and sailed to these islands. We all know how that goes. Don't go there expecting The Virgin Islands though. They're not big on outsiders. Then you have a place called Southgate. This place is fucking huge even by today's standards. About twenty-two miles across if you only count the walled in portion. It has a population around 2.2 million if you include the city outside the city walls and all the villages inside the same mountain range. It's run by a king named Herald the Second. Most of the locus points are going to fall in lands controlled by the Kingdom of Southgate or one the lordships it's connected to. These are the primary people you don't want to piss off," Jeremy said. Antonio had kept quiet up until now.

"How would you suggest we accomplish that?" he grunted from the other side of the room. Jeremy snapped his fingers again.

"How about not doing all that Mall Ninja shit and take it from there. Seriously though you have a once nomadic culture that goes back almost ten thousand years. That's when they discovered how not to die where they are now. If this place were Earth, it would be roughly halfway between Argentina and Antarctica. Hoodie weather if you plan to go there. If you don't want to freeze your balls off you might try dashing in to one of the locus points farther north. If not, that's y'alls call. What this place has in 'Fuck You' weather, it more than makes up for with an amazing river system. If you don't like where you land, take a boat to somewhere better," he said. Antonio frowned and woke up his tablet.

"I'm going to need to make a lot of modifications to the team kit coach. Looks like I'll be debuting some new formulations early this year. New merch for the stadium shop. Really up the sales next quarter and fire up the fans," he said. Jeremy had a puzzled look on his face.

"I don't know what any of that garbage means. Just put in some time to make them look like y'all belong there. Of course all that will go out the window as soon as you open your mouths, start blowing shit up, or villagers ask about the fifteen foot tall metal alien with big yellow glowing eyes," he said. Stratum raised his hands.

"They don't have to glow. I just like the way that looks. It's my trademark. People like the glowing eyes. I read it on the internet. Glowing eyes brand well. Looks good on camera after we bust crooks," he said. Jeremy shot a side-glance up at him. Looking back on their track record the crew usually took two approaches, subtle or loud. The way JP was seeing it; this would not be a subtle op.

"We're not going to Rainbow Six for 73. But we're not going to Ratchet and Clank it either. There's ways of going about this where we don't cause an absolute clusterfuck. Even if that's more our forte. We'll need a good rundown of local customs, faux pas, and lingo. It helps that much of the language is cognate. Written and spoken. It may not be

Earth but it has a Gleasonian Framework," JP said. Jeremy stared at him a moment.

"A what?" he said still confused. JP was used to the others knowing what that was. He'd certainly talked up Gleason enough for them to, much to their chagrin.

"The Gleasonian Framework. It was a theory posed by James Orville Gleason in 2252 in his research that later formed the basis of 25th century multiversal theory. Simply put, he theorized a common developmental framework that could exist even for non-parallel worlds. Such as Earth and this Sword World. Two different worlds from two different universes but have a common framework that gives rise to biological, cultural, linguistic, and technological coincidence. Think of it like two ancient Earth cultures separated by continents, but developing some of the same technologies and facets of culture. And even similar language structure. My Iso theory contains elements of Gleason's work," JP said. Jeremy appreciated an informative tangent as much as the next guy, but they needed to cover more ground.

"Okay moving on then. Religiously speaking this Sword World has a lot of different regional faiths. The most mainstream one appears to be like the Holy Trinity, but instead of a Father, Son, and Holy Spirit, theirs takes the form of two brothers and a sister that represent The Mountain, The Wind, and The Sea. The key difference one is usually emphasized more over the other depending on where you are. All this will be in my notes as well as copies of their holy texts," he said. Nocivo wasn't paying particular attention. His focus was on the map as he plotted routes from areas of lower percentage to those of higher. JP had felt he'd said enough for now. Stratum was enjoying Jeremy's presentation and didn't really want to interrupt. Antonio on the other hand felt compelled to interject.

"So Crom, Poseidon, and central air conditioning?" he said sarcastically. Jeremy sighed and shook his head.

"I don't think you're going to make too many friends if you go in there comparing one of the key pillars of their faith to a Frigidaire. But while we're on the subject of the metaphysical, and this it something I'm sure you and JP will love to discuss, which is, the 'M' word," Jeremy said with a grin. JP looked over at him. Annoyance washed over Antonio's face.

"No. No no no. No!" he groused. Jeremy laughed.

"Oh yes. Give me more of your unexplained advanced para-cryptidy whatsits science rant Tony. Or better yet, let's not. This place has magic. Now whether you want to dismiss it as a clever card tricks or not is up to you. If you see weird shit happening around you, have a plan. That's all I'm saying. Don't just stand around while a witch turns your taint into a Ikea coffee table," Jeremy said and laughed again.

"I'll take a hex-head set with me. I'll be fine," he said. Jeremy's mood became more serious then.

"Look man, all I'm saying is don't get caught flat footed because you think everything you're seeing is smoke and mirrors. If people are using magic, they probably want to kill you. Get the hell out Dodge," he said. Nocivo liked this advice. The Isos had had a number close shaves in the past because they underestimated something they didn't understand.

"Sound advice Jeremy," he said. Jeremy nodded at Estrello. He wasn't confident that either JP or Antonio were taking things seriously enough so he took a different approach and looked over at them.

"Okay if you guys aren't going to take magic seriously you may want to read my notes on some of the 'High Fantasy Type' species you are going to encounter," he said. This caught Antonio's attention.

"You mean like manticores? I've always wanted to see a manticore," Antonio said. Jeremy grimaced at him.

"No, you don't. What the hell is wrong with you?" Jeremy said. Antonio understood his tone.

"I saw one in a book once. Thought they looked cool," he said. Jeremy gazed at Antonio and then rubbed his forehead out of frustration.

"It'll fucking kill you. Like so many of the other things on that planet. It's a 13th century era microcosm where creatures from folklore are walking around waiting for some idiot from another universe to walk up and say 'Hey look it's a manticore! How Cool! I'm gonna go pet it!'" he said. Jeremy had some exasperation in voice but he didn't answer Antonio's question.

"So they do have manticores?" he said. Jeremy stared at Antonio for a moment aghast. Then he snapped out of it.

"No, they don't. They do have giant cyclopses, dragons, wolfmen, and dwarves!" He snapped. Antonio didn't want to piss Jeremy off. Especially since he took the trouble to come down to the records room. But he needed some clarification.

"Dwarves? Like Danny Woodburn, Warwick Davis, Peter Dinklage kinda dwarves?" he said. Jeremy wasn't sure if he was being messed with here, but he'd answer the question.

"Like Golden Axe that'll fucking cut you in half for being stupid kind of dwarves. I'm serious Tony. Next campaign I'm gonna let the dire rats kill you and eat you. I don't care what you roll. Sparklefinger. How the fuck did you win a Nobel Prize?" he said. Antonio was a bit taken aback. He didn't want to incur Fate of Fortune's wrath any further. He was known to hold a grudge through multiple campaigns. Nocivo seeing what kind of grave his hung-over colleague was digging himself, stepped in.

"I'm sure we'll get a clearer picture over the next few days before we dash. I do thank you for your research and for coming down here," he said. Jeremy seemed to settle down some.

"Probes are going to end their run tonight. Whatever else they find I'll let y'all know. Evie has been updating the stuff I have to go through every hour. I'll go get to work. Each species has their own cultures and belief systems with some religious overlap. I just don't want you guys going in like mall ninjas and valley girls and start a war," he said. Jeremy was a man that Nocivo had come to respect.

He'd been hired mistakenly to run a comic book shop on the Bumppo. The space that would have been the shop had been converted into a magazine to store detonator components. He nonetheless stayed on when JP found out Jeremy was a Medieval History expert. Given what the Isos did, someone like that would prove useful. And Jeremy had. He was one of the best accidental hires JP had on staff.

"Great work man. If we do run into a manticore, I'll be the first to tell Tony, not to pet the damn manticore," JP said. Jeremy laughed. Antonio rolled his eyes.

"Well what about the wolfmen then? Are they the dudes who wolf out by the light of a full moon or are they just like that all the time?" he said. A halfway sensible question from Antonio and Jeremy supposed that's the best he was going to get from him right then.

"They're like that all the time. They're bipedal wolves that have paws with a thumb-like appendage that arches back when they're in a gallop stance. That's if they have to chase anything down. Which they usually don't. They have their own martial art. The way of The Spear and Bow. Not a flashy name, but there is an order with the same name that trains young wolves to join what they call Ranger Packs. Some kind of roving police force started way back in the day by these wolfmen and now they recruit from any race. Apparently this place has a big bandit problem. They're not the Adam and the Ants jolly kind from what I can see," he said. Sword Worlds were turning out to be get-hands-dirty kinds of worlds. Antonio didn't have much of a problem with that.

"I promise not to pet the bandits," he mused. Jeremy just shook his head.

"Thank you Tony. I'm sure they'd appreciate that," Jeremy said and stood up from his chair.

"Okay I'm gonna run off here. I've sent a copy of my notes to all of you. I'm going to go see what else I can dig up. Probes are sending in a crap ton of info. Gonna take a while to work through that. Terry has been a big help. Nobody can blaze through a mountain of texts like he can," he added. Terry chuckled and resumed playing. Bandits worried Nocivo. Antagonists like this would necessitate a certain style of combat and approach and in many ways a more difficult one. Slaughter was easy, far too easy for a man with his skills.

"Bueno. There's a lot of ground to cover in the next few days. We'll go over as much as we can. Every bit helps," he said and gave Jeremy a fist bump as he made his way out of the room. Just then Estrello got a text. He took out his phone and clicked on the text. He sighed.

"Iglesia," he said. Antonio snickered.

"Este vato. Decirle a las abuelas se dice hola," he said and laughed. Nocivo gave him a side-glance.

"Ven a la iglesia alguna vez y diles tú mismo. Until then work on the locus," he said. Antonio frowned and then sat back to focus.

The Storm Eagle and two other ships called The Starfish and The Turtle surrounded the two crippled Honestead ships. Lookouts on all three ships scanned the deck thoroughly for any signs of life. None could be seen. Geosep looked at his Captain. Young Lord Denato's expression and manner were guarded, for a very good reason. Ignoring these ships would be seen as provocative if word ever reached the Exiled Kingdoms that a Falco fleet sailed past and did nothing. Denato also understood that setting foot on a Honestead deck could be misconstrued as an act of aggression. Especially if King Ilonnis believed Falco ships caused this. This act could trigger open warfare between Hall Falco and Hall Honestead.

Something that Denato wanted to avoid if at all possible. But he was after The Black Admiral. Some chances needed to be taken. Denato turned to Geosep.

"Lower a tub. Assemble ten of our best swords. We're boarding," he said. Geosep knew what kind of fire they could be lighting, but he would obey his Captain.

"At once m'Lord." he said and gestured to the flagmen. They ran to their boxes and took out flags on sticks and took positions at the bow and stern to deliver the Captain's orders to The Starfish and The Turtle. A dozen or more men set about lowering a yawl down into the water. They worked quickly. Soon it was down and Denato was on board with his escort. Oar man set to paddling over to the crippled vessels. As they drew near Denato got a closer look at the deep scarring on the hull. It looked as if another ship had been dragged across it. The storm damage theory was gaining merit. The ships were eerily silent as they made their approach. The wooden vessels loomed high overhead like two giant floating corpses tied together in the calm sea. Hooks were thrown up and ladder men ascended. A rope ladder unraveled when they reached the deck. Denato made his way up. As he arrived at the top he saw the expressions of the men that were already aboard. Their faces were ashen and daunted as if they had awoken from a terrible dream. When he climbed over the railing he saw what they did. Like a grisly macabre menagerie, the deck was strewn with the corpses of the crew. Many of them looked nearly mummified with half their flesh eaten way. They had been dead for quite some time now. Weeks. Perhaps months, as the smell would be far greater if the scene were fresher.

"Looks like the sea birds already had their fill," one of the swordsmen, a man named Farrio said. Denato couldn't disagree. The birds had been here. The deck was covered in their excrement, likely leavings from the digested dead men of Hall Honestead.

"Storms did not kill these men. Ribs and limbs are cleanly cleft. Wind doesn't do that. I need to see Captain's quarters," he said and gestured to some of the swordsmen to follow him. Denato pushed open the Captain's door. What remained of him lay on the floor with three others. They appeared to have been cut down with axes. Bones were shattered as much as they were cut.

Denato said a silent prayer for him to the goddess and then looked around. The cabin was in disarray. The Captain's desk was covered in message rolls. He picked one up and looked at it. He soon realized it was one of many copies. He looked up and around the room.

"The Captain of this boat knew his ship was doomed. He was writing feathers. All the cages are empty. He must have had time to send at least some of them. The window is open. The Black Admiral may have taken what birds were left if all did not fly," he said. His men looked around at the cages as he laid out the scene for them. Denato brushed away some debris and found the Captain's Log. He opened it and began reading. One of the swordsmen not adept at reading saw the look making it's way across Denato's face.

"What does it say m'Lord?" he said. Denato looked up for a moment.

"It says these two ships were part of an armada seventy strong delivering silver, wine and weapons to one of the smaller Honestead controlled islands," Denato said. The swordsman's eyes widened. For a moment he did the math in his head.

"What happened to the other sixty-eight ships m'Lord?" he said. Denato didn't have a good answer.

"I would say a fair number of them are at the bottom of the sea. Any that didn't get away from The Shadows. Nobody really escapes The Black Admiral once he has the scent. Or so I've been told. A storm nearly sank these two. I expect that's the fate of many of them. It may have even been a tactic of The Shadows in the first place. Drive their prey into a storm. If they couldn't have their riches, they'd offer them to the goddess instead. But I only speculate. These ships didn't escape the sword before the weather had a go. The feathers tell of the attack itself. The Dark Fleet. And the location of the attack. Coordinates look to be four hundred miles from here. No doubt these ships were blown quite a distance south by the storm," Denato said. The swordsman looked down.

"Poor bastards," he said. Denato closed the log and placed it back on the table.

"Aye. Weather probably had them off course to begin with. Then they ran into The Shadows," he said. Just then one of his other men stepped into the cabin.

"Cargo hold is filled with more dead Captain. They took every copper. Didn't even bother with anything else. Was it Shadows m'Lord?" he said. Denato looked down at the log and the rolls of feathers lying on the table. He looked back up at the swordsman.

"I can't say no. If any message got back to Honestead, they know it too. This means we're in a less precarious position. We'll send a feather there ourselves. Get some men to attend to the bodies. We'll give them a proper sea burial according to Honestead traditions. Or at least our best understanding of them," he said. He looked back down at the log, and then picked it up again. Sadness flashed over his eyes and then tucked the log under his arm.

With Jeremy and Terry both doing research, E.V.E. churning through data, and Antonio designing field kit for the team, JP didn't have a lot to do and wouldn't until E.V.E. finished her work. It gave him an opportunity to spend some time with Martha. It had been their plan for weeks to go to Wurstfest for their Oktoberfest celebration. It was a bit too short notice to rent a party bus, but fortunately the Bumppo had a 2023 Mercedes-Benz Sprinter that could accommodate everyone who had expressed interest in going. It was heavily modified for heists, but it should get them all there and back in one piece. JP wasn't expecting to escape small weapons fire. The vehicle did its job perhaps too well. Cameras installed all around it picked up every highway patrol unit that came within a few miles of their location on their way up to the festival grounds north of San Antonio in New Braunfels, next to the Comal river. If JP had bothered to load the magazines, gun turrets would have sprouted out of panels and locked on to them. No ammunition. No lock on. The van's sensors still got angry when threats were around. JP didn't pay attention to them. Instead had fun joking around with everyone.

When they got there they were greeted by a live accordion music and the fantastic aroma of cooked meats and other culinary delights. It didn't take long for Martha to gravitate toward the bratwurst and pork chop on a stick, which JP graciously shelled out for. JP really stood out in the crowd. He was not a particularly small man. He towered over Martha and stood at least a head taller than nearly everyone around him save for some young men wearing Roadrunners apparel JP figured to be basketball players. JP and Martha would not be outdone in the style department either. The pair wore matching Mario and Luigi themed t-shirts. The group walked around taking pictures and buying food until they reached one of the bigger event halls. The two sat near the stage while the other enjoyed large mugs of beer while they watched the band play. Martha took this opportunity to pitch an idea to her father. She wouldn't lead off with it though.

"You and the guys are going pretty far out this time. One of the longest away I've picked up before. Hard to understand what all that really means," she said. JP looked down at her. There was worry in her eyes. Something he didn't want to see while they were here for a fun time. But he wasn't upset.

"What we do can be scary sometimes, but I have a good squad with me. Even Tony. He is actually highly effective in the field, if a bit unorthodox. Highly unorthodox. Confusing at times. Difficult to understand most of the time. But effective. Plus I have a great crew making sure we know all we need to before we have boots down. Same as always. Even when the locus is far away. I'll be back before you know it," he said and smiled before he took a drink from his mug. Martha took a sip from her soda and watched the band for a bit and then looked up at her dad.

"This band is really good. I wonder if they tour or they only just play this festival here. Is it true Wurstfest is in November in our universe?" she said. JP laughed.

"Yes it is. It would be in November here too, but the city has some new construction planned for then. So they moved it up. As for the band, I'm sure they have gigs all over the place during the year. You don't sound as good as they do if you only play one festival a year. Why, you want me to book them for your birthday?" he said and nudged her. Martha smiled.

"We'll I had in mind some live music, but it won't happen until after my birthday," she said with a smidge of sheepishness. JP picked up on that. He grinned and took a sip of his beer and looked back down at Martha.

"Backstreet Boys will be in town next year. I know," he said. Martha looked up at him in surprise. He just kept smiling.

"Chief thinks she just found out that tidbit on her own. She had a little help," JP said and winked. Martha didn't know how to respond.

"Dad I__," she said before trailing off. JP chuckled some.

"You do know who owns skybox seats at the Alamodome don't you? Let's say he and I had a chat a few days ago and worked out an arrangement. Thank him the next time you see him," he said. Martha set her drink down and hugged her father. He hugged her back and then they both continued to watch the show. Martha started looking around then. JP took notice.

"What's up sweetheart?" he said. Martha looked back at him.

"I wonder where the Gross Opa is. I wanted to get a picture with him and a button," she said. JP looked around.

"I'm sure we'll run across him sooner or later. I'll help you look for him. But first, how about a potato pancake?" he said. Martha's brow raised and she raised a palm. JP high fived it and looked in the direction he remembered them being sold.

"I'll take that as a yes," he said. Martha chuckled.

Chapter Eight: The Days Begin

The riverbank was livelier this afternoon. Pulcan and Manati were having better luck today than Raltec had earlier. Where they lacked in some areas, fishing seemed to be their strong suit. Raltec sat by the fire cooking the fish they caught trying not to let on to his disappointment. Pepper sat up against a rock. His leg was as stiff as a board but at least the wound was sealed and the herbs dulled the pain. Balocan was out foraging for what few things dwarves could stomach. This forest didn't provide much in this respect. Pepper had woken up from a very unpleasant dream. It was far brighter than his current reality. He was thankful to be alive regardless. His current company would not have been his first choice, but he was nonetheless grateful to the dwarves for pulling him out of the river. He had been watching Pulcan and Manati while they fished, but he then turned his attention to Raltec.

"You must forgive me, I didn't have the strength to familiarize myself in the night. I am aware that dwarves are not overly keen on sharing with outsiders. I haven't met many dwarves. I would like to know whom I can thank for saving me," he said. Raltec looked up from his cooking. The wolf was right. Dwarves were not very open people. Trust was hard to forge. Even often amongst themselves. But Pepper didn't strike him as being much of a threat.

"You are not wrong Redflower. Fate has bonded us for a time. You need our help not to die out here in this forest. We mustn't find ourselves catching the ire of your father. We both profit. But this does not mean we can't chat. I am Raltec Irontusk of the Western Sentinels. I don't come from a very well known family. Nobody is particularly afraid of my father. You and I differ in this respect. I am educated as my kind goes. I don't wear a robe of the Brotherhood of The East Lodge, but I'm clever enough some might say. No dwarf my age has ever been in charge of a survey team as I have. Some dwarves spend decades just trying to get a job on one of the teams. Helps to know someone of esteem. Most don't have that. I didn't.

Here I am though, before a single gray has sprouted, heading my own team, and sitting by a river in the middle of nowhere trying not to let a wanderer with a famous name die. Far more excitement than I expected to encounter before my team set out last month. The Mountain laughs at us sometimes when we think we have everything reckoned. Most times we truly deserve it. Not sure how I'd call this journey though. What thoughts would you have wolf?" Raltec said. Pepper looked down. He had a lot to say on the matter. The Wind and The Sea were not great communicators in his experience. He preferred to instead rationalize things the way he thought was the most correct given what he knew at the time.

"You could say I didn't fit in very well when it came to my family. I take after the brewmasters of old. Contemplative. Less, adventurous. Redflowers used to brew ale a very long time ago to sell to fisher mongers in exchange for part of their catch and money to donate to the ranger packs in the Barley Lands. They were studious wolves. Studying how to brew better and better ales. Why they stopped fishing for themselves is a mystery lost to time or muddled with conflicting family lore. I do know at one point a Redflower took up a bow and a spear to wear The Leaf, and walked away from the ferment. And Redflowers have been rangers ever since. I joined the Brotherhood as soon as I was of age. My nose has been stuck in one book or another ever since. I don't get away from the Lodge very much. I prefer not to run into maniacs with knives. I must say I am impressed with your dressing. It feels far less painful than I would have expected it to be," Pepper said. Raltec did admittedly feel some pride in impressing a Redflower, even if it was this one.

"Standard field stitching, and the herbs take care of the rest. It helped your wound was not greatly infected to begin with," he said. Pepper looked down at his neatly bandaged leg.

"I suppose it was the cold of the water. That river looks filthy though," Pepper said. Raltec looked at the river and then back at Pepper.

"I suspect it was all that lavender oil you have all over that robe. Good for rubbing on swollen limbs. Don't know how it works for wolves or open wounds. Wolves are different than dwarves obviously. However it works, you smell like a bloody garden. Has anyone ever told you that?"

Raltec said trying very hard not to sound overly critical which was a hard thing to do for a dwarf. Pepper took no offense though.

"Oh yes that. Many of the Brothers don't bathe very often. So they use lavender oil infused powders for washing their garments. Lavender is planted all around the Lodge. Keeps away scorpions. I use that much lavender not so much for them, but for everyone else. So I don't have to smell them as much. Not as effective as I would like. I'm a wolf after all. By comparison you and your crew take much better care of yourselves than many of the Brothers," he said. It was an odd compliment, but Raltec took it.

"You should have smelled us before we found this river. I expect it scared the fish away for a good spell. That, or your lavender. Maybe fish just don't like wolves," he said and chuckled. Pepper tried to laugh but it was effort enough just to talk.

The dwarves had been very fortunate reaching this river. Strawberries were quite plentiful here. Other berries could be found around but dwarves wouldn't eat them unless they absolutely had to. Balocan went for the easier of them all for the dwarf stomach. His sack was getting heavy now. He'd picked more than usual given there was an extra mouth to feed now. It was bad enough with a sick Manati. Now they had an injured wanderer. The outlook on their journey was becoming bleaker by the day. They wouldn't starve, this much was going in their favor. Strawberries were nothing compared to a nice juicy boar. The thought of boar or even some tasty fowl would be a delight right about then. His mind wandered to sitting by the fire and feasting on the fish the others were catching. His mind almost wandered too far. But then he noticed that he felt like he was being watched. It wasn't a strong feeling, but a feeling still. He continued to pick berries as he grew nearer to the bank. He was a long ways from camp.

The lack of anything in this forest had made him complacent in recent days. He'd grown accustomed to seeing and expecting nothing. Whoever it was would still have a fight on their hands. If they made a move Balocan was prepared to shatter skulls. That is if he couldn't shake his watcher. He was no amateur. He wanted to know what he was dealing with though. He kept an eye out for a useful distraction. The watcher had him at something of a disadvantage. It would take something almost spontaneous. But his usual methods would not be easy to manage with eyes already on him and watching his every move. He'd have to be clever. He continued to pick berries along the river for some time. He still felt the eyes from afar. Whoever it was exercised caution. This was both good and bad. Good in terms of actual threat. If the watcher was more scared of him, Balocan had the advantage should violence be the outcome, but bad in terms of finding an effective distraction. But then Balocan saw his opening. Just above him in the trees he spotted birds resting in branches. A good number of them sat in a nearby tree with a stout trunk. As he knelt down to pick berries he palmed a stone. He then worked his way to the tree. His eye caught a glimpse of a strawberry bush just beyond it and walked toward it. As he passed behind the tree he dropped his sack against it and threw the stone up startling the birds above. The branches erupted with flapping wings. Balocan's quickly scanned back at the forest. He saw his watcher looking up at the panic above. He took up his bag and then began foraging casually again back in the direction of camp.

Pepper picked the bones out of his fish and tossed them into the fire. This meal was satisfying. It had been a very long time since he had fish cooked over a campfire. He had grown accustomed to the fish the Lodge kitchens produced. Sufficiently substantial, but nothing like a well-cooked fish over an open fire. There was a smokiness to it that only a fire in the wild could capture.

He didn't realize how much he'd missed it. Being away from family it was easy to put things like this out of his mind. A fascinating book or assignment kept the mind on other things. But being out here in the wild, old memories were harder to gloss over. This Raltec reminded him of his father who was as much a part of the forest as the river and the trees. It was something that Pepper could never live up to. Raltec noticed that Pepper was watching him cook. An odd thing, but given this wolf was outside the norm to begin with, he didn't give it much thought.

"I can't claim to be a Lodge chef, but how is the fish?" he said. He expected some indifference but Pepper had something else to offer.

"Lodge chefs don't know how to use the smoke properly. They want it cooked quickly, not flavorfully in many cases. This is better than I've had in a while," Pepper said. Raltec was a bit surprised. He'd dealt with many higher born in the past. This Pepper was by far the least acrid and insufferable. His father was practically a King.

"My thanks. I cook for myself and my men. I want it to be good because they work hard and I want to offer something more than just a mass to fill their belly. They deserve as much. I'd like to be brewing them some tread root right now, but we ran out a good while ago. Didn't run across any on our journey here. Do you know if it grows around these parts?" Raltec said. Pepper didn't take tread root very often, but many of the Brothers did.

"A variety does grow near the Lodge. I prefer tea, but you will find it growing north of here," he said. Raltec seemed to perk up some.

"That'll do. Tread root is good for keeping a dwarf walking even in bad weather. Plenty of it on this trip. Walking that is," he said. Pepper knew what he was talking about.

"Bad time of year to be in these woods I'm afraid. Storms like to run up and down the coast the end of every summer. Things won't quiet down until the middle of next month at the earliest. Until then I don't recommend you travel back the way you came. Keep going north and farther inland. You'll reach roads controlled by Hall Falco soon enough. Sardis Falco has ties to Southgate if I'm not mistaken. Southgate is an ally of the Dwarven Kingdoms if I remember right," Pepper said. Raltec had not considered travelling into Falco lands, but given their circumstances there were worse places to venture.

"This is correct Redflower. I had hoped to keep a lower profile, but one can only do so much with the path set before him. Falco lands may be a favorable refuge. Even if only to use their roads to make haste," he said. Pepper had been curious about why these dwarves were here to begin with. He'd originally suspected they were just another survey party to ignore as they went about their commission for whatever interest directed them to operate. He assumed some minor lord had summoned their services through whatever channels these dwarves made available to those willing to pay to know what resources may be in their lands. But now he wasn't so sure. Nobody claimed dominion over these woods. It was ill-suited land for anything other than dying a slow death.

"If you don't mind my asking, what brought you to this forsaken wood?" he said. Raltec was very reluctant to share his finding with anyone but the elders of The East Lodge. He'd just met this wanderer. Even though this wolf was a Redflower he had his reservations. He reached back for his pack and pulled out a logbook regardless.

"Earlier in the month my team and I were at a site many miles from here. No survey team had been through there in a very long time. Only existing logs were scribed onto crumbling fired clay if that tells you anything. Unpopular location would be putting it lightly. The King wanted updated maps for these lands for whatever reason. I can only assume for the purpose of looking for new mining prospects. But whatever the aim, for many years teams have been sent out to measure little travelled lands starting well south of The Sentinels. This plot came up in the plan and my dwarves were sent out. We didn't find much at first. But then my team stumbled on something more than an eroded hillside or traces of copper. We'd have rather had that. We found instead, this," Raltec said and got up to hand the journal to Pepper. The wolf opened it and began looking through the pages. Raltec could see the concern in the wanderer's eyes as he read and examined the pictograms.

"We have larger rubbings. Those are some of the smaller carvings," he said. Pepper looked up at him.

"I have never seen this particular figure before. But it is most similar to carvings going back more than fifteen thousand years. Few examples still exist to this day. Anything else would be from drawings that have been copied and recopied many times over. What is this you say here about the site being unsettled?" Pepper said. Raltec looked away.

"It's a dwarf expression. It means cursed. I could not say why a stone floor would have that kind of effect, but it did. Not just for me, but for every dwarf that saw it. We are not people so easily shaken. When I tell you it had a pall. It had a pall. And a bad one. I know my own Antiquities Bureau. They are a startled ox upon a bed of flowers. They would not know how to treat something like that. It was my hope The East Lodge would have a better attitude," he said. Pepper understood. He could not speak to the dwarf's fear of the site, but if this were as old as he suspected, the right care would need to be taken.

"The East Lodge takes these matters very seriously. No doubt your Antiquities Bureau will take exception to The East Lodge stepping in. Your King will side with The Brothers in this matter. They must be notified as soon as possible. Following the river north would be the fastest way back in my mind. At least until we meet a road," Pepper said. Raltec concurred. He didn't like the visibility travelling by road would bring. But they had already been delayed considerably. The others would be near a dwarven settlement by now. Soon after the Antiquities Bureau would receive a standard account like everyone else did. If they found anything amiss, more questions would be asked.

"Good, it's settled then. I would very much like to speak with your Brothers about this site. It's all I have been thinking about for quite some time now. It will be good to know more. If you'd been there, you'd know why," Raltec said. Pepper seemed to be troubled with something.

"You will find what the Brothers have to say to be useful, but the one you really need to speak to no longer resides at The East Lodge," he said. This was not something Raltec wanted to hear.

"Come again?" He mumbled. Pepper could hear the disturbance in the dwarf's voice. He tried his best to put things delicately.

"The man you want to talk to is former Senior Brother Gospar Deonalli. He was the Lodge's foremost expert on ancient carvings and he lives in Seastorm. He retired there five years ago," he said. Raltec tried to take this news as best he could, but he was growing weary of complications.

"Bloody fucking hell! Now we need to go even farther north!" he growled. Even though Pepper knew Raltec's agitation wasn't directed at him, he still felt compelled to tread lightly.

"My apologies. I wish I had better news, but this is the fact as it stands," he said. Raltec wanted to pick up and rock and throw it very hard at the nearest tree. His eye even found one just right for the job. But then he spotted Balocan approaching. His colleague had a peculiar expression on his face. The older dwarf said nothing until he was close to the fire. He expression didn't change as he drew near.

"A son of Latalec approaches," he said and gestured over his shoulder. Raltec leaned to the side and looked past Balocan. He didn't see Balocan's watcher at first but then he did. He looked up at Balocan and sighed. Balocan shrugged his shoulders and sat down. Raltec looked back at the watcher and beckoned. In the distance up river a shape moved around in the bushes. Pepper had become curious about the scene and weakly peered around from behind his rock. His wolf eyes immediately caught movement. Slowly a small figure emerged from cover. Pepper's eyes widened. Brother Grain stumbled his way forward. His face and hands were bruised but he didn't appear too worse for the wear. Raltec grew impatient and beckoned again. Pepper looked back at Raltec.

"I know this halfwyn. He's harmless. Please don't hurt him. I thought him dead," Pepper said with a hint of joy in his voice. Balocan snickered.

"Of course I know he's harmless. He can't stalk worth a damn," he said. Raltec smiled and beckoned a third time. Grain approached cautiously and addressed the dwarves as loudly as he could speak.

His words were not that of the common Gatherian tongue. Grain belted out a series of greetings in an old dwarven dialect he learned from reading dwarvish texts. Raltec and Balocan looked at each other in bewilderment. Pulcan and Manati had taken notice of the scene by now and they looked over at Raltec and Balocan with much the same expression. Raltec looked at Pepper. The wolf was just a befuddled as everyone else. Raltec then looked back at Garrett.

"Come sit by the fire cousin! You're among friends here!" Raltec shouted. Balocan looked over his shoulder.

"And speak plainly boy! You sound like my bloody great grandfather! When he was drunk!" he barked. Raltec fought back a laugh. Garrett made his way to the fire cautiously looking back at the dwarves staring back at him. As he rounded the rock a he found a familiar bedraggled wolf. Joy filled his eyes and he ran up and hugged the wanderer. Pepper was not a hugger, but hugged his Brother back.

"Take care Brother Garrett, the river wasn't kind. So good to see you still among us. I saw you fall as well. Feared the worst," Pepper said as he weakly patted Garrett on the back. Brother Grain was in tears. He sat down next to the wolf.

"I saw you and that bastard fiend fall. I clung to a branch. I saw you fall and the river take you. Then the current took me. I was swept I don't know how long. I don't know how far. I managed to get to the bank when the current slowed. If I could make it so could you. I followed the river. I had to find you. Oh dear gods Brother Alvin. Oh dear gods. They're dead. That bastard murdered our Brothers! He could be out there still!" Garrett lamented as he sobbed. Raltec stood and knelt by Garrett. He laid a hand on his shoulder.

"If the bastard still draws breath, he'll have to battle us to get to you little cousin. Now have a seat closer to the fire. You looked chilled to the bone," he said. Garrett didn't realize how much he was shivering. He sat on a rock close to the flames and rubbed his stiff hands together. The warmth felt so good. Raltec sat back down and looked over at Brother Garrett.

"Where did you learn our words cousin? You pronunciation was shit, but you said them more or less correctly otherwise," Raltec said with a smile. Garrett had never met a dwarf before and didn't know anyone who had. He had been unsure how to greet one if he ever met one.

"The Lodge has copies of old dwarven texts. I learned enough dwarvish so I could understand them as best I could. It was important that I do so. I begin formal training in a few years, and I just wanted to know more about the texts," he said. Raltec nodded as he stoked the fire to give it more life.

"An older dialect. But it's viable. The Voyager would be proud one of his descendants practiced the older tongues. I doubt many halfwyns do anymore. Easier to do business speaking simplified dwarvish or as the staffwyns do I would imagine. We even do outside our cities and villages," he said. Garrett tried to smile as he wiped the tears from his eyes.

"I did my best. Dwarvish participles have odd rules to them. I wasn't sure if what I was saying was in present tense either," Grain said. Raltec smirked slightly.

"Aye they do cousin. And sadly you spoke in the future. Not the present. Common mistake to make for those who didn't grow up speaking dwarvish. Understood you well enough. We'll help you get a better handle on it," He said. Grain could smile now. He looked over to Pepper.

"That filth killed our Brothers. But he did not get away with his prize. I found it floating in an eddy a mile or two down from where I pulled myself ashore. It's over there behind the bush," Garrett said. Pepper managed a weak grin. Raltec looked over at Manati and pointed at the bushes Garrett had been hiding behind. Manati got up and walked over to them. He pushed the branches aside. Lying beneath them was a wooden box. On its lid was the sigil of The East Lodge. He picked it up and carried it over to Raltec. He took it from Manati and opened the box. The box contained three books, two journals and some rolled up scrolls. Raltec was pleased with their condition.

"Still dry, even after a spell in the river. Very well made box," he said. Garrett and Pepper were also pleased to see their books were undamaged.

"That's a Lodge document chest. Made for long journeys through rain or snow. Sealed to keep the weather out. I'd brought one up from the library in case we'd need to send our journals to the Lodge Delegation. The maniac thief must have thought it was a convenient box to put his ill-gotten spoils in," Grain said. Raltec was only half listening to Garrett. His attention was more on the books inside the box. He lifted one out. He opened it and thumbed through it. Then he gave Garrett and Pepper a very serious look.

"You boys know what this is?" he said. Garrett and Pepper looked at each other and then at Raltec.

"That's the Chronicles of Thagnar the Stout. He was an ogre, and that is an almanac of weather forecasts for growing seasons," Garrett said. Balocan seemed agitated at the mentioning of the name.

"Why is that name familiar? I know I have heard it somewhere before," he said. Raltec looked up at him.

"The Epic of Apaggosh. The Great Droughts. The drying of The Sea of Vabai. The old stories from before The Troubles. You don't remember the tales of Thagnar and The Ogres' Ring?" Raltec said. Balocan didn't seem to know what he was talking about.

"Do I remember some ridiculous old children's tales some old crone tried to tell me so I wouldn't make a nuisance of myself? Not so much.

But do be so kind as to tell me what an 'Ogres' Ring' is," Balocan quipped. Raltec flipped a few pages back and held it up for everyone to see.

"Ogres, though said to be masters of the very old world magics and in tune with the soil in ways even the old races could scarcely understand at the time, we're shit with a quill and paper. That's why they enlisted dwarves to scribe for them. They were called the order of the Moonlight Scribes. Their hands wrote the original copies of this book for Thagnar and his circle of prophets. You can see the border art there along the edges of these pages that has been copied again and again for thousands of years. All dwarven," Raltec said. Balocan rubbed his chin.

"So this stout fellow and his magic friends were this Ogre Circle?" he said. Raltec understood the tales told to children were only interesting to old grandmothers teaching them to their daughters to in turn tell their children. Unlike most dwarves Raltec still visited his grandmother from time to time. Just like when he was small she would tell him the old tales. While others his age would have forgotten them, these tales were still fresh in his mind.

"No old friend. The Ogres' Ring was not a group ogres, so much as what those ogres are said to have created to end The Great Droughts and refill the fresh water Sea of Vabai. That is the Ogres' Ring. An object of powerful old world magic. An object of great power lost during the Troubles. To most who have ever heard of Thagnar he's just an old farmer complaining about the weather. To others he's one of the co-creators of one of the most powerful magical objects this world has ever known. Still fewer know he was said to have discovered The Tides," he said. Balocan held back laughter. His friend and colleague was being very sincere, but what he was saying the old dwarf had trouble taking seriously.

"I'm sure you have a great time with your Gran and listening to all the old tales. But the world has truly gone mad if someone was willing to kill men over a book dictated by a long dead ogre. One who is rumored to have created a fantastic magic circle thing to bring back a sea that doesn't even exist. If it did, half The Midlands would be under water. Old grandmother's tales told to children to keep them from breaking things," Balocan said. Raltec closed the book and placed it back into the box.

"I did not say I believed the old tales. I just knew who Thagnar the Stout was. My question for our cousin here and his wanderer friend is why would you be interested in dead ogres and who would kill men to get a copy of a book one could get anywhere? Chronicles of Thagnar aren't exactly rare," Raltec said. Pepper pulled himself up some and looked past the fire at the dwarf.

"As for the larger motivation of the thief and killer, I could not say. We were charged with finding a glyph by our Lodge Delegation. They ask, we do. Could there be a connection? I cannot say. What I can though is say that copy of The Chronicles of Thagnar is the last one in existence outside Dwarvendom copied by dwarven hands. To my knowledge anyway. All others I have inquired about have been copies made by staffwyns who would have no appreciation for the subtleties of dwarven embellishments," Pepper said. Raltec pondered his words for a moment and then picked the book back up.

He examined the construction of the book and then flipped it open and looked over the pages within. He'd never personally read anything by Thagnar so he had no basis for comparison. He asked himself if the staffwyns would neglect to recreate dwarven elements they regarded as unimportant.

"The last real dwarvish copy with dwarven design outside our Kingdoms you say? If so it would be far easier to try to take one from a place like The East Lodge than it would be to try to filch one from a dwarven library in my mind. It brings up a lot of questions wouldn't you say? Who would be interested in your research apart from your Lodges? Who would know you'd run across that book? Who would know why it differed form other copies? Who would care that it did?" Raltec said. Pepper shook his head. Grain had nothing to say either. Neither of them were sheriff magistrates. They weren't trained to ask these sorts of questions, to say nothing of answering them. Raltec worked with men that were, and did. Such was common practice in his profession. Men Balocan worked with as well.

"I'm sure a lot of this matter will be cleared up once we get to The East Lodge," Balocan said. Raltec shook his head and looked over at his friend.

"We aren't going to The East Lodge old friend," Raltec said. A look of puzzlement took over Balocan's face.

"What's that?" he said. Raltec glanced over at Pepper, and then looked back at Balocan.

"I've been informed that the man we need to talk to about our hillside problem isn't at The East Lodge. We'll be going to Seastorm instead," He said. Balocan's puzzlement quickly turned to irritation.

"To dine with the Falco's I see," he remarked. His reaction was understandable. On the list of places a dwarf would ever want to go, Seastorm would rank one of the lowest. Raltec himself wasn't enthusiastic about making that journey either. But that was where he was determined to go now.

"I'd rather eat my own boot. But we're going to the city anyhow," he said. Balocan was not happy to hear about this. He looked over at Pepper and Garrett.

"What about this lot? Are we taking them to Seastorm with us? What about The East Lodge and their ships? I'd like to know how much our strategy is changing here," He said. He was right to feel the way he did. These kinds of departures were not the dwarven way of doing things. Raltec rolled a few thoughts around in his head, and then looked to Pepper.

"As I see it we're about out of simple options. Men were killed at The East Lodge. Killed over a book we have. Should we say it's a simple matter of a killer thief after a valuable rare book, craving the sliver someone would pay for it? I'm sure the Brothers have a lot of rare books worth a lot of silver to the right buyer. Am I right Brother Pepper?" he said. The dwarf was on the right line of thought. Pepper couldn't help but acknowledge that.

"Yes. We have many valuable rare books. The reason we rarely have thefts, is that only an absolute fool or madman would risk crossing the Stone Lodges. They deal with troublemakers, harshly. I have no doubt a force has already been sent to investigate," he said. Raltec placed the almanac back into its box and closed the lid.

"I suppose that's one good development. I do mean no offense by suggesting at least one of your number may not be the humble man of learning he makes himself out to be. If that is the case he may have a plan already in motion to protect himself. As far as he knows his plan to get those books out of The East Lodge to a buyer has failed and his conspirator presumably dead. If you show up with those books in hand who knows what he might do next. If they are valuable enough to him who's to say he won't try again sometime in the future? Who's to say he won't seek revenge against the both of you? And who is to say he's not already having other Lodge property stolen to line his pockets as we speak? The way I see it the both of you should stay as far away from The East Lodge as you can. Seastorm in a good place to disappear," he said. Pepper and Garrett looked at each other. Raltec made a lot of sense.

He was quite the critical thinker. It was becoming clearer why he'd been trusted to take on the job he had. Balocan had a lot of trouble with this plan though.

"So we take these lads with us. That'll slow us down even more. They know this Brother of theirs in Seastorm. This is good, I'll grant that. But we still needed The East Lodge to help us. How can we get that if we don't bother going there?" he said. Raltec sighed and thought that over for a moment. Then he looked over at Pepper.

"Who do you trust at The East Lodge wolf? I mean who do you absolutely trust? A man you'd trust to hold a knife to your throat?" he said sternly. Pepper's list was very small. He didn't care for many. The ones he did like he wasn't particularly warm toward either. Only one name stood out him. A name Garrett would not like to hear.

"I'm afraid I can only say Brother Corbin Hearth. I'm sorry Garrett." He said and looked down. Garrett was shocked Pepper would choose him.

"Corbin Hearth? Are you serious Pepper? The man who gave me chamber pot duty for two years because I corrected his spelling. A man I know for a fact you don't talk to!" Garrett yelled. Pepper was surprised by his reaction. He'd never seen him raise his voice before. But he understood why.

"If Alvin still lived, his name would be the one I would have spoken. It is true. I do not speak to Corbin. I don't find him pleasant to be around. This does not mean that I do not trust him. I have known him a very long time. However petty his actions have been in the past, he is an honest man who will put the interests of The Lodge, our Bothers, and the pursuit of discovery in the highest regard. Again Brother Garrett, I am sorry. He is the only choice," Pepper said. There was a lot of conflict in Garrett's eyes. Raltec saw it too. Dwarven Gumption his father called it. The face a dwarf made when challenged with a hard choice that did not favor him.

"Brother Corbin you say? How would you propose to contact this Corbin? A scoundrel may be among you. How would you say we get a message to him only his eyes will see?" Raltec said. Pepper sat there for a little while as he ran through the possibilities in his head.

"A straightforward feather could become widely known quickly. Anything formal or official would stand out. We could try sending a false rankings page. Corbin is an enthusiast for the joust. He'd be keen to receive the latest news from the tourneys. Nobody would care monitor one of those if it were flown into the lodge. Sporting is not a common interest among the Brothers. Frivolous un-academic malarkey enjoyed by the simple minded, tends to be the attitude. Acquiring a seal from a sporting firm will not be easy. We'd have to travel far out of our way to one of their offices. I'm afraid I wouldn't know how to steal one once we got there," Pepper said. Raltec smirked.

"I don't think we'll have to go to that much trouble. As luck would have it, you're among dwarves. It won't have to be perfect. But we can craft something convincing enough. The young one here needs to learn some of the old craft after all," he said and looked at Garrett.

The afternoon loomed over the keep of Bucklers Bend. Along the road south leading up to it a lone rider ragged from his journey approached. He rode almost day and night for weeks now. His ninth horse was weary and on the brink of collapse. Its predecessors had been traded or sold for each other, and now for him. His rider carried an important message for the Lord of Bucklers Bend. A message deemed too important for a bird. Pennantmen of Hall Marsh halted the rider short of the gatehouse of the keep. The rider took an object from his pocket and showed it to them. It was a small snail carved from alabaster. Lord Addar Marsh's men knew to be looking for it and let the rider pass into the keep. He proceeded forth to the stables where he left his horse with the ferrier and stable master to be looked after. He was then led to the Lord's gallery. Addar Marsh sat upon his Lord's throne attending to the business of his lands. A Marsh man held the rider to the back of the room.

"Lord Marsh will meet with you once his other business has concluded," the man said. The rider looked ahead to see an old man standing before Lord Marsh. The old man had a forlorn expression.

"Please Lord Marsh! Bandits raided my granary in the night and took more than half of my stores. I won't last the winter on what they left me. Others tell me the same tale. Our village has always been loyal to Hall Marsh and it's Lord. We may be able to buy what we need from the Borderlands, but we need more protection. Begging your absolute pardon m'Lord but this Midland Curse must be met with force!" the old man said. Addar Marsh took a deep breath and held the hand of his wife, the Lady Nasera who was born a Midlander of olive skin and piercing blue eyes. She addressed the man.

"No offense is taken good sir. I was born a Midlander to a noble southern Midland family. Part of me will always be a Midlander. My home is here though. In the south. With my Lord and my children. I do acknowledge the problems that originate from the land of my birth. I too have grievance with those I know to be responsible," Lady Marsh said. The old man nodded in agreeance. Addar looked to his love and smiled. He looked back at the old man.

"I put family over politics. And so too do you see does the Lady Marsh. The people of my lands are important to me as well. Additional men will be sent to patrol the forests around your village. I have already sent a feather to Lord Tolliver of The Barley Lands to offer my support during these troubling times. It is my hope to procure shipments in exchange. I assure you good sir, all that can be done, is being done," Addar said. The old man seemed sufficiently satisfied with the answer took a bow, and then took his leave. In the back of the room Marsh's man turned to the rider.

"Wait here,' he said and then approached Lord Marsh. He spoke quietly to Addar who looked up and then at the rider. Addar responded quietly to his man and then sat back and smiled at his wife. Marsh's man walked back to the rider and whispered.

"Follow me," he said. And then gestured the rider to come with him. They walked around to a staircase that led up to the don jon of the keep. There the rider was told to sit and wait for Lord Marsh. And wait he did. It seemed like he sat there long enough for the shadows to change shape. His body ached greatly from his journey. Somehow this wait felt longer. He'd waited so long to deliver his message and now he was required to wait even longer. He'd feel insulted if he didn't know something about how the mechanism of the keep worked to maintain the lands. Just as he was about to succumb to his fatigue he heard footsteps outside the door. One of Marsh's men opened it and Lord Addar Marsh stepped through and entered the room. He sat behind his desk and looked the rider over.

"Well, it appears you've ridden a long way to get here. What do you have to tell me?" he said. The rider looked over his shoulder at Marsh's guard. Then he looked back at Addar.

"If you'll forgive me m'Lord, you instructed me to deliver a message to you, and only you," he said. Lord Marsh sighed and looked up at his man. He waved him away. Marsh's man did what he was told. Lord Marsh looked back the rider and folded his hands on his desk. The rider pulled out a rolled message and slid it over to Addar. The Lord of Buckler's Bend read and frowned deeply. He held the message to a flame and laid the burning paper upon a bronze plate.

"It seems the troubles have increased, to put it lightly. I cannot thank you enough for arriving as quickly as you have. I can't imagine how hard a ride that was for you. You risked life and limb to get here. Hall Marsh has many enemies of late and sours my family's character unabashedly. This Hall repays its gratitude. This Hall never forgets," he said. The rider nodded his head.

"I was there m'Lord. I was there when Haddock was spitting fire at you and your Hall. If it weren't for The King, The Swift Fish would be in Bucklers Bend looking to hang every last Marsh," the rider said. Addar sighed. He'd heard of Lord Haddock's dislike of him. Ever since he married a Midlander a suspicious eye had been cast his way from Hall Haddock. Now he had proof of Haddock's disdain.

"Were you able to witness anything else?" Addar said. From the look in the rider's eyes a lot more was coming.

"I did Lord Marsh. I saw Haddock have a good long conversation with Lord Ivy after The King took his leave. I should say he's no friend of Hall Marsh either," the rider said. Addar was not surprised to hear that name. Ivys were plotters and schemers. Every drop of Ivy blood was political and had been for generations.

"I sense you have much more to tell me," Addar said. The rider shifted uncomfortably in his chair. Pains were starting to creep in. But he needed to tell all he needed to.

"Prince Attheon is on his way to Seastorm with almost seven hundred men. My source told me Lord Sardis Falco has accepted The King's proposal to join Hall Lamb and Falco with a union of Attheon and Lady Marea. An official courtship is soon to begin. A Royal marriage could follow very soon after," the rider said. This surprised Addar greatly.

"The predictors were very wrong. Lady Pallas continues to be a maiden. This is shocking. I imagine many wagers have been lost. Attheon will not wed Lady Pallas Brian. There will be no union of Halls Lamb and Brian after all," Addar said. The rider shifted again in his seat. He didn't know it, but what he had to say next would not be received well.

"I'm afraid m'Lord that is not the case. My source also tells me that hand of Princess Vanadia has been offered to young Lord Banathir. A union of Lamb and Brian will occur. A different Lamb and a different Brian," the rider said. The embers of anger stoked in Addar Marsh.

"Lady Vanadia? She's barely out of the cradle! To be wed to Banathir? It seems old agreements no longer hold value." Addar uttered coldly. Many years ago when Banathir was small Lord Marsh and Lord Brian entered into a gentlemen's pact to join their Halls in the future after the birth of Marsh's oldest daughter Callia. It was Addar's hope to increase the security and prosperity of his lands by having his daughter marry into a far more powerful family.

"I'm sorry m'Lord. There's more," the rider said. Addar gave the rider a stern look. He feared to say anything more. Some time later Addar emerged from his study and made his way back down to the keep's bailey.

From there he made his way to the aviary. The bird master looked up as his Lord approached. Addar handed him a message.

"This is to be flown out immediately to Cedar Point," he barked. The bird master took the message. It was stamped with the seal of the Marsh shield.

"At once m'Lord." he said and set about selecting a bird for the trip.

Prince Carcino Lamb sat in his tent sipping a soothing mint tea. The image of the dead girl was still very fresh in his mind. He'd sent a feather to Flint Redflower asking for his assistance in tracking down any bandits that could be responsible for the carnage he saw at Guppies Gulch. He had heard no response back.

No rider. No feather. Nothing. Seemed odd to him. The wolf gave him the impression of a very duty driven individual. He did not seem like an individual that wouldn't even respond with a 'No.' His ponderance was interrupted. One of his riders stopped in front of his tent and dismounted. He looked up to see a young Southgate soldier standing just outside. Carcino stood up and walked out to him.

"What news soldier?" Carcino said. The lanky young man barely eighteen with ill-fitting armor bowed to Carcino.

"My Prince. I bring word from the village of Fine Gray. They know of a new bandit camp they suspect just west of here," the lad said. Carcino was simultaneously pleased and unhappy to hear this. New bandit camps meant there was new movement of their activity in the area. On the other hand they at least knew where this camp was. Bandits tended to break camp quickly and disappear. Time was of the essence.

"I see. It looks like an afternoon hunt men!" Carcino shouted to his soldiers. He gestured to his squire Willem.

"Bring my blade and my horse. If our presence hasn't scared off our prey then justice will have a full belly before sunset. I intend to feed it fat! What say you Southgate?" Carcino yelled. His men responded by rapping their shields loudly.

"Mount up Southgate! We Ride!" he yelled. Willem handed up his sword as he passed by. The Golden Anvil twice the bandits projected number thundered out of camp. The men of Southgate rode to within a mile of where the young soldier heard the bandits may be. They dismounted and continued on foot taking cover in the forest. Lookouts on either flank ahead of the main force made their way to the bend of a small river where the bandits may have their camp. Carcino and the bulk of his men held back behind some rocks and waited for his scouts to report back. Much time passed as they sat largely silent. Then one appeared.

"Report," Carcino said just above a whisper. The scout responded in kind.

"Thirty men camped about a half mile from here near the river. Decently armed. Not rangers. Not Stone Lodge. No sigils. Broken chests and barrels in a pile outside the camp. Our best route with the best cover lays three hundred yards ahead just to the north. They have lookouts, but not very good ones. Shouldn't be too much trouble to shoot down my Prince," The scout said. Carcino looked around at his captains.

"We move at dusk. Clear sky and sun will give away our approach with the first glint of steel. I want plenty to question. Kill only those you can't disarm. Half of you will follow me to the right along cover. The other half of you will flank from the left. When you hear the fight, hit them from behind and cut off their escape. Is this understood?" he said.

"Aye my Prince," they all said one after the other. Carcino nodded.

"Spread the word," he said. His captains then fanned out to align all the men to the Prince's wishes. More time passed and the sun began to set. The warmth of the sun gave way to a chill that took hold quickly. Carcino waited there behind the rocks watching the wind move through the leaves of the trees up above. As the sun lowered the wind began to shift toward them. He knew then. It was time to strike. He got up and signaled to his captains. They turned and began signaling down the line. The seventy men of Southgate moved in, led by its Prince. Quickly they crept forward. Well trained. Well disciplined. Singularly focused. Predatory footfalls. Hands at hilts, and eyes steeled, distance vanished between Southgate and the bandit camp. The path was as the scout had described. Good cover to conceal their approach. Bandit lookouts lazily sat atop rocks near the end of the path. Arrows nocked. Strings pulled. Order given. Lookouts felled. Carcino and Southgate shifted quickly past their bodies to the outskirts of the camp. The Prince drew his sword Dread Thunder. Finely forged Sentinel Steel. He charged. His men followed. Southgaters shot forth like coiled springs snapping. Steel glinted as it sung out from leather sheaths into the chilly dusk air. Bandits looked up to see a wall of gold crashing down upon them.

They barely had time to draw before the wave of Southgate smashed into them. Screams shattered the air and metal clashed. Bandits hit the ground under the Anvil's fury. Some tried to run but more Southgate met them down river. A few tried to fight. They were cut down. The others threw down their weapons and fell to their knees. They screamed for mercy as they were seized. The battle was over quickly. Eighteen bandits remained breathing. Beaten severely. But breathing. Carcino wiped blood from his sword as he surveyed the scene. The fight was all too brief. No real test. Even for his relatively small contingent. His men had already begun to round up all the bandits who surrendered and those too beaten to continue fighting. He looked back to a few of his men.

"Collect the dead and bring them over here," he said. They went about this without any hesitation. Carcino turned back to the defeated bandits being lined up, the whole lot of them bleeding, broken, and pathetic. He walked up the line of them studying each down to the slightest eye twitch. Some dared look at him. Most did not. He stopped at the end of the line and turned around.

"Do help them up," he said. The Southgate soldiers then began picking the bandits up on their feet. Some of them winced and groaned in pain. Carcino's expression did not change. He began walking down the line again looking the bandits over yet again.

"I'm sure all of you know why we paid the lot of you a visit this evening. My manners are quite poor in these types of, social situations. Is this how I should view tonight's affair? I'm afraid I never did learn how to make friends. I am Prince Carcino of Southgate," he said. Many eyes widened and jaws dropped, that had not been dislocated. Carcino continued.

"But in case you hadn't pieced together why a Prince of Southgate would like to meet you lot, please allow me to educate you. You see I've just had the displeasure of having eighty innocent farmers from the village of Guppies Gulch buried in shallow graves. You might say something like that would make me want to travel to new places, and meet new people. Perhaps kill a few who thought law was a matter of, negotiation," Carcino said as his men carried the dead bandits and set them down nearby.

Carcino glanced over at them for a moment and then turned back the live ones and continued to walk down the line.

"I wanted to meet others with my same lust for travel and enthusiasm for meeting new people. People such as yourselves. The question I had to ask myself though, was I going to get along with the new people I met, or would I have difficulty finding common interests?" he said. One of the bandits in a great amount of pain had grown tired of Carcino's mockery.

"Fuck your interest Southgate shit!" he yelled through the pain. Carcino paid no attention to him. Instead he studied all the dead that been placed nearby. He turned around to the loud bandit and walked over to him and looked him up and down. Carcino smiled.

"I really like your boots. Have you had them long?" he said. The bandit looked puzzled.

"What the fuck do you care?" he grunted. Carcino stopped smiling.

"If I cared enough to ask, I care enough to hear you answer. Do you follow that reasoning? Or would you like me to ask again in a manner that doesn't involve talking?" he said. The bandit wanted to keep fighting, but he'd taken too severe a beating.

"Stole em' bout six months ago. Fit my feet," the bandit said. Carcino smiled again.

"I'm glad they fit. You all seem to have stolen pairs of boots that appear to fit you nicely. This makes all of you thieves. Theft is very bad. I don't care for thieves. But you're not murderers. At least not of the people of Guppies Gulch," Carcino said. Some of the bandits understood at least some of what Carcino was trying to say. Most didn't and just looked at him blankly. Carcino continued.

"Captain, who's land do we currently stand upon?" Carcino said and turned to one of his captains. His captain answered promptly.

"This is one of Lord Tolliver's lands my Prince," he said. Carcino nodded.

"You are correct. This is indeed Lord Tolliver's land. Captain can you tell me what penalty does Lord Tolliver's law give for murder?" Carcino said. The captain answered just as promptly.

"The penalty is hanging," the captain said. Carcino turned back to the bandits.

"Did you all hear that? Lord Tolliver's law demands hanging for murder. This is his land. This is his law. The rule of law shall be upheld! But none of you are murderers, that I know of, or can much less prove. Captain, I have another question," Carcino said and turned back to his captain. The captain was very attentive.

"Yes my Prince," he said and awaited Carcino's question. Carcino clapped his hands together.

"Captain, what does Lord Tolliver's law say the penalty for theft should be?" Carcino said. The captain with a stone face looked back and forth at all the bandits. Then he answered.

"Lord Tolliver's law demands a hand for thievery," the captain said. Carcino nodded and turned around to the bandits again.

"The law of this land demands a hand. I don't really care which one. I'm sure all of you would have a preference. Since I neglected to write ahead to let you know I'd be stopping by, I'll let you make that choice," he said. The sounds of blades being drawn filled the clearing. Southgate men began pulling bandits down to their knees as one of them picked up a heavy log and threw it down on the ground near the moaning and pleading bandits. Carcino snapped his fingers.

"Bring me the gobby one," he said and gestured. A pair of Southgate men picked the mouthy bandit up and brought him over to Prince Carcino. He looked the bandit dead in the eyes.

"While the others whimpered and cried you had the courage to speak. I say courage, but I really mean foolishness given that we could split you in half and let the wolves devour you. But you did show a kind of courage, and I have some respect for that. I'm afraid my respect for the law does not allow me to grant clemency to all your bandit friends. Consequently they don't get to keep their hands. That is the law. They'll need someone to sew them up with two good hands. Hands like yours. You get to keep your spare, for now.

We'll keep you and your friends company while you work. Then we'll bring you to Lord Tolliver. Whether you walk free or make your home in a dungeon is entirely up to him. I'll put in a good word for you. You could end up staying whole," Carcino said. Just then more Southgate men showed up with coils of rope. Carcino almost laughed.

"And to think. We could have used that rope for a hanging. I suppose binding you lot up is still a good use for them. I'm sorry, I didn't catch your name," Carcino said. The bandit winced in pain, but answered.

"Kade. Kade Marsters," the bandit said weakly. Carcino smiled.

"Pleased to meet you Kade Marsters. Looks like you have a long bloody night ahead of you," Carcino said gave the signal to his men to proceed with carrying out the sentence. Kade watched Prince Carcino of Southgate walk off into the darkness to the sounds of blades hitting wood and men screaming. Carcino's blood-splattered cloak swayed back and forth as he faded into the blackness.

The river city of Hopps Harbor was alive with the spirit of autumn. The Opal Cranes prepared for their performance inside their tent. It was the first night of The Days. The river peoples were strong followers of The Wind. Such observances were a key cultural facet that anyone with an enterprising spirit could take advantage of.

River towns and cities were where anyone who could juggle a ball or stand on their head was bound to earn a copper or two. Autumn and spring solstices were the Buskers Delight. A thousand years ago the Opals arose from the dark corners of the festival seasons. Groups of con artists, thieves and assassins gravitated to each other to form a single cohesive structure built of regional branches. The Cranes found Minly Kestral as an outcast from a ranger pack. Her antics had caught the ire of its captain one too many times. Her Leaf was taken away and her name crossed out. Now she sat in the Cranes' tent fixing her hair. Her shorter brown hair was harder to style so she wrapped what she could into a bun, placed a bonze basket over it, and held it in place with two short bronze pins.

Tonight was the first night of The Days. This was the night to make a great entrance. Good word of mouth was passed from town to town along the river system. A good performance was key to attracting viewers even though this wasn't how The Opal Cranes made their real money. A good façade was beneficial to conceal the very real passage of information, and execution of contracts and schemes. Agents of the Opal Cranes were hard at work miles from here completing such a contract. They were overdue to return. The group was growing concerned, none more than Fadis Frodare.

He paced about drinking his anise spirits and mumbling to himself. He wore his multi colored tunic with its bronze accents that jingled like little bells as he moved. His long waxed up-curled goatee jutted out in front of his face adding to the consternation of his demeanor. Preston, a tall portly man, called Porj by the group, watched Fadis as he walked back and forth. He served as kind of bodyguard for Fadis, despite the fact

Frodare was a dangerous man himself. Porj took his job very seriously and looked after his boss. The sounds of hooves outside the tent caught Fadis' attention. He ceased his pacing and walked to the front to the tent and looked out. The Crane agents had arrived. He walked out to greet them. Porj got up from his chair and followed Fadis out. The pair was gone for several minutes. Then Fadis stormed back into the tent followed by Porj and the agents. Fadis clapped his hands loudly making everyone in the tent look up at him.

"Listen up you lot!" he yelled. The tent suddenly went very quiet. Fadis took off his puffy hat, rubbed his forehead, and then looked around at everyone.

"It is my duty to inform all of you that the stamp on our former associate Wilter Gallow may have gotten larger. And if that is so, many of you in this tent will be on horseback following tonight's performance. If there is information to be got. We get it first! Do I make myself clear?" Fadis growled. Minly was deeply curious. The stakes on stamps tended to remain static.

"What has he done now? How large are we talking about Fadis?" she said almost flippantly. Fadis scowled and looked at her.

"You remember Backroad Tolly? That large," he said. Minly fell silent. Fadis continued.

"There was an act of theft and murder at The East Lodge recently. Yes, that East Lodge. One could not say for sure, but this botch-up has the smell of Wilter Gallow all over it. The kind of scent our people would recognize. But not just us. Other branches as well," he said. Another Opal Crane, a man named Nalor Crenshaw, spoke up.

"Who is going to miss a librarian?" he said. Fadis walked up to him with a deep glare.

"You seem ignorant about Lodges lad. Let me educate you. Lodges look after their own. That means Stone Lodges now have their people on the road to root out whoever done it. If that's Gallow, and they find him, we don't cash in. Follow me so far? Good. Now it's gets a lot worse. A lot worse," Fadis groaned, and he buried his face in his hands. Minly could scarcely see how much worse it could get than provoking the ire of The Stone Lodges.

"Honestly Fadis how much worse?" she said while almost laughing. Fadis looked over at her. His expression was almost disturbing. Something was clearly very wrong.

"Would you like to know who Gallow managed to kill? Would you? I'll tell you Kestral. Crenshaw is right. Who would care about some librarian? The Stone Lodges yes perhaps, but who else really you reckon? What if his name was Redflower? Have your attention yet girl? Do you know who Brewster Redflower is? Of course you do. You wore a Leaf. Anybody that has, knows," Fadis snarled. Minly looked away. She had been trained by a Quickwill who was a brother-in-law of Brewster Redflower.

"Dear gods," she muttered. Fadis threw up his hands.

"Dear gods indeed! So not only do we have other Opals and the Stone Lodges after Gallow. Now he has the Redflowers and all their kin and allies after him now. Wilter has become the most wanted man in all Gatheria. Would anyone care to guess what that means?" he said and looked around the room to mostly blank expressions. Minly broke the silence.

"Whoever brings Gallow in or points the highest bidder in the right direction makes the Cranes filthy fucking rich?" she said. Fadis turned to her with a big satisfied grin.

"Absolutely dear girl. And that is why ladies and gentlemen, Kestral gets the opening act tonight. This stamp belongs to The Cranes! The Coin! The Glory! The Prestige! Have a great performance everyone. Then get me a fucking lead. Am I clear?" Fadis said as he shifted into showman persona.

"To The Stage!" he shouted as he waved his arm theatrically. The group looked around at each other. Everyone had the same look in their eyes. The Gallow situation was quickly growing even out of their control. They all got up and made their way out of the tent. Not a one spoke to the other. Each one felt the growing dread. None more so that Minly Kestral. Any path attached to Brewster Redflower was a precarious one to travel. The end of that road may not only be bad for Gallow, but others as well.

The crowd was sparse this Sunday night at the HEB Plus supermarket. Antonio reasoned it had to do with the Spurs preseason game going on downtown vs. the Utah Jazz. He followed the Rockets so he didn't care so much. He'd been courtside a few times in the last season when Houston was in town. They didn't play San Antonio until November so the NBA was far from his mind at that moment. He was more concerned about replenishing his supply of mango Venom energy drinks. Deuce was philosophically opposed to energy drinks so never kept them in stock in the restaurant. The Skipper and JP controlled what went into the vending machines all around the ship and energy drinks were a no. If Antonio wanted them he had to take a trip down to HEB or Target and get them himself. They were cheapest there. On the Bumppo he wasn't Antonio Salazar of Salazar Chemical who could snap his fingers and an ice cold drink was just handed to him. On the Bumppo he was just 'Get it your Damn Self' Tony.

Dulcet jazzy aura from Jamiroquai filled the store, which made the wait in line not as bad. Ahead of him in the '15 Items or Less' checkout was an old lady buying a 12-pack of lime flavored sparkling water. She seemed to be having trouble with the credit card reader. The cashier was helping her through the process. This gave Antonio a chance to glare at the life-sized cardboard cutout of Patriot Man standing next to the checkout line. He had his usual saccharine grin plastered across his face and a thumb up. The Liberty Bell patches on his shoulders were printed with garish bronze foil that made them glisten in the fluorescent light. The cashier caught Antonio giving the cardboard hero ugly looks. As soon as the old woman got sorted out she rolled all of Antonio's Venoms to the laser scanner.

"He was here in San Antonio. Can you believe it? I didn't get to see him speak at the Alamodome. I had to be here that day," she said and gazed longing at the cardboard cutout. Antonio internally rolled his eyes.

"Interesting fellow," he said as she began ringing up. His tone was dismissive enough to get a reaction.

"I wonder what he's like," she said. Antonio looked back at the cutout. He turned back with a grin.

"That display is fairly accurate recreation. He's not too deep a guy. Somewhat pushy. Insistent would be a kinder way of putting it," he said. The cashier was both offended and amused at the same time.

"You know Patriot Man? How?" she said. Antonio never liked where these conversations led but he was already in it. At this point in the day he was too tired not to walk straight into that wall.

"I'm in the super science game. Hard not to cross paths with super people. They just kind of show up at your lab unannounced, without even a box of donuts, asking questions about one thing or the other. Insistently. Usually something weird a bad guy had or was using. Then they just disappear the second you turn your back. It's kind of rude," he said. It took a moment for her to process, and then a giddy look splashed across her face.

"Oh my god, you're that guy from the commercial!" she chirped. Antonio wanted to be far elsewhere right then.

"Yeah that's me," he said. The cashier smiled widely.

"I don't think so, but my dad says you look like a drug dealer," she said. Antonio's eyes narrowed.

"A lot of people do apparently. And they're not technically wrong. We sell bulk compounds to pharmaceutical companies to manufacture drugs. Over the counter things. Not the hard stuff," he said. The cashier giggled.

"If I got a science job do you think I could meet superheroes too?" she said almost gleefully. Antonio forced back as much sarcasm as he could.

"It couldn't hurt. You could always try supervillany," he said in the most mildly sarcastic tone as he could manage. She laughed.

"Oh like The Neon Skeleton? I could meet Patriot Man then. Or better yet I could commit some crimes in National City. Do you think

I could get Night Eagle to sign my Street Talon? It's the 2015 limited edition back when it used to be blue and didn't have the rocket engine upgrade he installed after he put The Surmiser away for the first time," She said gleefully and pushed her glasses back up. Antonio tried even harder to hold back.

"He'd probably just throw his Eagle's Claw at you and then hand you over the NCPD to be honest," he muttered. That didn't chase away her exuberance.

"Oh my god that would be so exciting. I could meet Proto Jay! He is so hot! Green is my favorite color! My friend has a replica of the Jayte Board he used early on in his career. It's super sexy with green LEDs even though the real one doesn't light up," she said. Antonio began to wish The Neon Skeleton would attack so he could exit this conversation. Nobody was in line behind him so the cashier was taking her time.

"I wonder what The Four Men are like. Got some love for the local boys too. Do you think General Stratum really is a space alien?" she said as Antonio slid his card through the reader. He sighed on the inside. Loudly.

"Yes," he said understatedly with a raised brow. The cashier almost jumped.

"Me Too! Or he just wears super high tech armor like Full Scale. Awesome either way!" she said as she handed Antonio his receipt. He just smiled and pushed his cart ahead wishing he hadn't opened his mouth in the first place. As he approached the exit he was greeted by large decals of Patriot Man stuck to the glass sliding doors. He was once again treated to Patriot Man's enthusiastic grin and thumbs up.

He muttered obscenities under his breath as he pushed the cart over to his car. He even muttered obscenities as he put his drinks in the trunk of his car. He arrived at the parking structure about 20 minutes later with the conversation still very fresh in his mind. He was thinking about it as he popped open his trunk and then began stuffing cans of energy drink into a backpack. Then he heard a familiar voice.

"Smuggling in more of the naughty drinks huh Pablo Escobar?" he heard Stratum jest behind him. Antonio turned around to see his giant friend.

"I used to be an infamous high technology thief. Feared! Respected! People beefed up their security just to keep my ass out. Mine! Shelling out mad cash for state of the art. State of the art. I pushed the envelope man. Now I'm reduced to sneaking highly caffeinated beverages behind my friends' backs into a space ship from the future. I used to be legit bro. Bona fide. The shit! You can go ahead and say it," Antonio groaned. Stratum chuckled. He wouldn't normally go for such an easy setup but Antonio did offer it up.

"Oh how the mighty have fallen?" he mused. Antonio turned back and finished stuffing his backpack.

"There it is," he muttered. Stratum laughed.

"Is that possession with intent to distribute there El Gitano? You're moving up the criminal ladder now. Watch out for this guy!" Stratum quipped. Antonio gave him a side-glance.

"Sadly no. It's all for me. If I'm going to burn gas, I get to drink it all. Everyone else can take care of themselves," he said and closed his trunk.

"Oh before I forget, I had the pleasure of meeting another one of our fans," Antonio added. Stratum was intrigued.

"Oh boy, I love hearing about our fandom," he said. Antonio looked up at his friend.

"This girl who rang my stuff up thinks you're a space alien," he said. Stratum truly enjoyed hearing this.

"Whatever gave her that idea?" He said and chuckled. Antonio shrugged his shoulders.

"Might be the 15 foot tall thing. Might be the metal thing. Maybe it's your accent?" he said. Stratum scratched his head making an awful metal on metal sound.

"What accent? I sound like I'm from Ohio. Or at least that's what they say on the internet," he said. Antonio shrugged his shoulders again.

"Maybe it's because you like Frisbee golf. That's a dead giveaway for space alien," he said. Stratum laughed again.

"Yeah, maybe so." He said as the pair walked to the other end of the garage level. Chief had been sitting around the Annex Lounge for the better part of three hours now reading Only For Me by Anissa Walker. The Annex Lounge was set up in a building adjoining the parking complex that served as a waiting area for Bumppo crew that had arrived when outsiders parked in the complex. It happened every once in a while when more opportunistic San Antonians would lift up the boom barrier so they could park there, or when an outsider followed behind a crew member thinking they were driving into a public parking structure. The former was the case right now with Chief. Her red 2024 Jeep Wrangler High Tide was sitting on the second level next to a dummy car placed there for the effect of normalcy. An outsider's car was siting about fifty feet away. Some college girls going to a club down the street Chief imagined. She had been waiting for an all clear alert for a good while now, even though there was the option to pass through a series of detection gates to enter the main complex. She disliked those scanners more than most. They always picked up that she was a clone, and she didn't need constant reminders of it. Chief pulled out her tablet and began running diagnostics on the alert system, which wasn't physically located in the building itself, but rather on the Bumppo.

If nothing were wrong with it, she'd have words with Salazar. He co-owned the towing company that the Bumppo crew called to haul away outsiders' cars. After a few minutes she scowled. The alert system had somehow set itself on standby. Chief took out her phone and dialed up JP. After a few rings he answered.

"Hey Chief, what can I do for you?" he said as he drank ginger ale from a Wurstfest mug he bought earlier in the day. Chief rolled her eyes and sent him a screenshot of the malfunction.

"I have been sitting up here in the Annex for the last couple of hours. Waiting for an alert to let me know that some drunk bitch's car has been towed. No alert. So I was about to call up Tony to give him shit about it when I thought to pull up the status of the alert system itself, and wouldn't ya know. System put itself on standby. I can't re-initiate from my end. And I can't access the camera feeds either. Lucky me. And the doors locked behind me so I can't go out and look for myself," she said. The frustration was fairly obvious. JP set down his tablet and mug then rolled in his chair to another station in the records room where he could access the surveillance system.

"What level were you on?" he said as he looked through the camera feeds. Chief had to think a second.

"I parked on two next to a maroon Saturn dummy. Party girls stopped on the other end of level. They were driving a bitchy little white Dodge Neon," she said. JP quickly found the feed. He expanded the frame and looked it over.

"Sorry Chief. No Dodge Neon. Motion detectors have towing guys hauling it off an hour ago. And then I have Tony driving slowly by your Jeep. He's just shrugging his shoulders and driving to the entrance," he said. There was a silence for a few moments.

"Son of a! Son of a Bitch!" he heard Chief yell on the other end. JP pulled up a command menu on the surveillance screen.

"Overriding lock and sending a notification to the entry guards about the malfunction. Sorry Chief. Why didn't you call earlier?" he said. Chief felt a little dumb now, but she did have a good reason.

"I don't like to bother you guys when you're in the records room. That's On-Mission kind of stuff," she said. JP did appreciate the consideration for the most part.

"Thanks kid, but I can't have our chief engineer stuck up in the annex. Call one of us up even if we're doing mission stuff," he said. Chief, though tired and wanted to be in a better mood after getting home from a movie, didn't want to take out her frustrations on JP. Or even Tony for that matter. She heard the door unlock and looked up.

"Okay, I'll remember that. Thanks for getting me out of here. Sorry, I wasn't going to go through your nightmare tunnel. I hate those gates so much," she said. JP laughed a little.

"I'll let you in on a little secret. It's a pain in the ass on purpose. If it was a breeze, nobody would have a problem with it, and feel comfortable going anywhere they wanted whenever they wanted. Sorry kiddo. Just how it is," he said. He heard an exasperated sigh on the other end.

"Understood. On my way down to have a look at the Parking Complex systems. It would be stupid to think that's the only thing not working right tonight," Chief said and hung up. JP put his phone back in his pocket and spun around. Terry wasn't gaming as he usually did. He and Jeremy were looking over aerial photos of some of the Sword World cities and keeps the group had surmised to be more important to study. Jeremy sat there with a look of utter fascination on his face.

"You look impressed," JP said as he wheeled himself over to where the others were. Jeremy glanced over at him.

"Are you kidding me? I'm losing my damn mind looking at these things. We have 13th century level technology for the most part. But their 13th century architecture kicks the absolute shit out of ours. It's not even close. We were nowhere near to building on this scale until the 17th century. And the Sheer Fucking Number of these structures is staggering. Earth had maybe and handful of cities near the size of this Imperial Capital city of Frest back in 1600. Nothing like it in 1200. Now you look at a city like Southgate on the southeastern-ish end and it's on a whole other level of ridiculous. It's almost the same size as the city we're in now in 2024. Both in population and scale. If you run into anyone wearing this gold anvil, don't piss them off," Jeremy said. JP leaned in and looked over at one of the cities.

"Roger that. What about this coastal city? What can you tell me about it?" he said. Jeremy highlighted the aerial photos of it and enlarged their frames.

"That is a city called Seastorm. It has a major regional lord, kind of like an eastern warden named Sardis Falco. The city itself is just over a quarter of the size of Southgate, and it's one of the larger ones on the continent. Navy town. Its port is one of the smaller ones on this landmass, but they utilize an island chain that runs along it to harbor a decently sized fleet. Not people you want to piss off either. We have some color hits there. More of them north of there." Jeremy said. JP looked over his shoulder and reached out into the air. A few moments later a frown made it's way across his face.

"We have a lot of turbulence. Not many good dash drop zones anywhere near right where we want to be," he said. He looked at an image of eastern Gatheria and pointed to a spot. Jeremy looked at where he was pointing and pulled up a map of the area.

"Right there Jeremy. East of that big river. Guess we don't have a name for it yet. But right there is where we need to put boots down. We're pushing it with 37% turbulence. Gonna be a rough dash for all of us. Not just Tony. A lot of quieter places to put down, but they're all too far from where we need to be. Get me everything you can about that area. We'll need to make a good case to Skip in the morning," he said. Jeremy gave JP a fist bump.

"Hey no problem man. Terry and I have this," Jeremy said. Terry chuckled and continued what he was doing. Nocivo lay in bed staring at the ceiling. He'd normally be nodding off to sleep but his mind was too active right now. He had the same feeling as if he had a song stuck in his head that kept playing in a loop and wouldn't stop no matter what he did, except there was no song.

His mind just wouldn't shut down. Like a silent circus cast in darkness, ever present, but unseen and unheard. He threw over the covers and sat up. He would take a shot at burning off some of whatever this was. He found himself on one of the Bumppo's basketball courts on one of the Recreation Levels. Ball in hand he stood at the free throw line. He dribbled a few times and then took aim. Then came the shot. The ball arced through the air. Net snapped as the ball passed through the hoop. He walked over and snatched it out of air as it bounced and returned to the free throw line. He took another shot. The net snapped as the ball passed through again. Again he walked over and snatched the ball as it bounced. Again, he returned to the free throw line. This is something he could do all night. Sometimes he would never miss. Tonight didn't feel like that kind of night. He felt eyes on him then and looked to his left. Angelica was standing at the edge of the court. He grinned.

"¿Has venido aquí a jugar al caballo?" he said. From her expression she didn't appear in a gaming mood.

"No. You'd win that one. Gonna do this all night?" she said. Estrello dribbled the ball a few times. Then he shot, then a snap of the net.

"Thought about it. Figured I'd keep going until I got bored. No puedo dormir. Es algo que acer," he said as he walked over to retrieve the ball. Angelica watched as her brother returned to the free throw line.

"Didn't feel like sitting around with the others planning things out?" she said. Estrello dribbled a few times and then just held the ball as he looked ahead at the rim.

"That's the good thing about having those guys around. I don't have to plan everything myself anymore," he said and shot the ball. Net snapped and the ball fell to the ground. Estrello walked over to get it. Angelica walked out onto the court.

"You trust them to come up with a good plan?" she said. Estrello rolled the ball in his hands.

"I trust them to come up what they think is a good plan. But that is not the same thing is it? I'm going to find problems with what they come up with. The advantage is that it makes it easier to work out the mistakes when you see other people come up with them before you do. Sometimes you need to hear it from someone else to know it's a bad plan," he said. Angelica watched Estrello take another shot. The net snapped and he went to get the ball.

"Yet I get the feeling you aren't feeling very good about this mission. Neither do I," she said as Estrello walked back to the line. He dribbled a few times and held onto the ball.

"I haven't felt good about most of these missions," he said and dribbled the ball a few times and then held onto the ball. Angelica expected him to shoot. But he didn't he just stood there holding the ball.

"What about this mission has you up in your ugly sweat pants throwing around a ball?" she said. Estrello looked down at his sweatpants.

"I like these pants. But you're not wrong. I'm not feeling this one. It's a Sword World. So no modern weapons. I'm not so sore about that. I don't need guns to kill a lot of people," he said. Angelica knew what her brother used to do, but hearing him say it like that made her more uncomfortable than she would like.

"You're worried you may have to kill a lot of people this time around?" She said. Estrello took another shot. This time it bounced off the rim and over to the wall.

"Es un miedo razonable, ¿no crees?" he said as he walked over and picked up the ball. Angelica watched as he returned to the line.

"I've seen all the movies. I've seen the shows. Battles happen. Taking lives isn't something you do anymore if you can help it. I understand. But you have to defend yourself. And you have to defend the others," she said. Estrello dribbled the ball a few times and the held onto it.

"Entiendo eso. But how much defending myself and others do I do before blood rains from the sky and I'm just an animal swinging a blade around. I'm not much of a healer then now am I? How much red is there to see? How long before all that's seen is green? Or silver, as I understand it to be there. I took no vows before the Lord to leave my past behind. But it feels like a betrayal nonetheless," he said. He didn't take another shot. Angelica watched him roll the ball in his hands.

"Do you remember the sermon this morning. Pastor Sugar was talking about The Book of Ezra? Chapter 8. Ezra was given the task of transporting riches over a great distance. He's refused all the protection offered to him and his people. Instead citing faith as the shield that would protect them. This put him in the difficult position to consider taking up the offer after he'd first refused it. He opted to instead fast for the three days before his journey. In that time of prayer and sacrifice he must have thought about a lot of things. But he did come up with a game plan that worked. He was rewarded with safety on his journey. His faith was rewarded," she said. Estrello dribbled the ball a few times and held onto it again.

"What will I fast?" he said. Angelica shook her head.

"I don't know Hermano. That's between you and God. You have a few days to figure it out." She said and the turned to walk away. Estrello watched her disappear through the doors. He dribbled the ball a few times and then shot. The net snapped cleanly. He picked the ball back up and looked at it in his hands. Then he glanced through the window of the check-in equipment room at all the other basketballs sitting in a row. One by one his eyes passed over them. In the back of his mind he could hear the singing of blades and screaming of men. The bloodied heads of dead men took their place. His grip on the ball tightened and he breathed deeply. Then his grip loosened, and he began to dribble again.

In the poorly lit area Antonio could see the faint reddish glow around Stratum as he contracted down to a smaller size to fit through the door of the garage's mid level office. At the back of which were the lifts up and down. Safety Officer Chelsea stood around with her clipboard as Amadou, Ernie and Ian sat at computers wearing headphones. They all seemed to be taking the Fire Safety module. They all appeared to be falling asleep. Antonio had a part in producing it. He wasn't told to make it exciting. Chelsea looked up from her clipboard and adjusted her glasses and brushed away her auburn hair, which had gotten trapped behind the lenses. She smiled warmly when she saw Antonio and Stratum.

"Good evening guys!" she said energetically. Antonio smiled slightly. Stratum may have been smiling but nobody would be able to see his aura. Chelsea flipped her clipboard over to show a list of names. Dozens of names had already had their boxes checked. She had been very hard at work getting everyone on the crew up to date on their modules. Behind her Ian grumbled.

"PASS. Pull out pin. Aim nozzle low. Squeeze handles. Sweep fire. I got it already. Dammit!" he said. Amadou grinned.

"Se sentir fatigué? Attends juste le test à la fin," he said and chuckled. Ernie began laughing. He didn't understand French, but Amadou's delivery was funny nonetheless. Chelsea rolled her eyes.

"Anyway, I need someone to sign off on page three. I got all the people on it. Just need a signature to make it official," she said and held out the clipboard and a pen. Antonio reluctantly took it and flipped to page three. Indeed all the names seemed to be checked off. He clicked the pen and initialed in the blank at the bottom. He handed the clipboard and pen back to Chelsea.

"The ship has an internal fire suppression system. I still don't see why I needed to help produce a module we don't really need," he said. Chelsea raised a brow.

"Ship systems can fail. They don't often. But they can. It's always good to know how to fight a fire in case it does," she said and smiled slightly. Antonio smiled in return.

"Good point. Good work Chelsea. Keep us up to date on the crew's progress," he said and began walking toward the lift. Chelsea watched him as he did.

"I will Doctor Salazar," she said. Stratum glanced at her as she did, and then looked over at Antonio as he was boarding the lift. Stratum pointed up.

"I take the stairs. This lift doesn't like me," he said as the doors began to slide closed. He looked back at Chelsea and nodded to her as he headed to the stairwell. He looked back briefly again to see her still looking at the lift even after the doors had closed. His trip up the stairwell was not long and arduous. In fact he negotiated it rather gracefully. A cushion of air helped lift him up as he used the railing to quietly climb up the stairs rather quickly.

When Antonio arrived at his floor he saw Stratum already there tapping at a light on the ceiling that was flickering. The giant looked down at Antonio. Salazar had become somewhat adept at reading his large friend in the time they'd worked together. He seemed disappointed by something. Antonio didn't inquire. He had work to get done on equipment designs.

Stratum could get chatty if prompted. He instead opted to leave him to his flickering light. He sat down in a chair in the fabrication room across the hall from his lab. He yawned and took out one of his energy drinks and cracked it open. He booted up the computer controlling one of the machines behind him. He also activated a holographic imaging program. Upon opening up a file several concepts of a new Generation Six helmets appeared. Some were more ornate and complex than others. He took his tablet out his bag, which automatically unlocked itself from civilian to ship mode allowing him access to features that would not automatically be available outside the Bumppo. He uploaded some new ideas, which updated the list of features hovering next to his concepts. He tapped on the comms and waited for an answer.

"What can I do for you hon?" a voice said. Antonio took a sip of his drink and scrolled through the concepts.

"Hey Evie, can I get you to mock up concept 11, 3, 8, and 1 in poly. I want to get a fitting in before I commit to a look. Hard to choose. Also how did JP's gear turn out?" he said. A holographic image of E.V.E. appeared then and testing chart of The Commodore's armor and accouterments appeared.

"Everything is five by five Tony. Fabricator didn't have any trouble with the new alloy formulations. Ukko has been brought up from storage and is with his kit that's been produced so far. We're looking good and ahead of schedule for a change. Pauly has his bow pretty much nailed down. He's had to figure out how to create a natural string strong enough to handle the pounds on JP's rig. But he thinks he's got it figured out," she said as lasers began running across a container of medium to cure out a form. Antonio raised a brow.

"What's an Ukko?" he said. There was a pause, and then an answer.

"It's the name of JP's sword. This it the third time I've said it. You keep forgetting," E.V.E. said. Antonio's attention was already elsewhere as a shape began to rise out of the medium. E.V.E. stared at him for a few moments, and then continued.

"So I suppose JP will hate not getting a jet pack this time around," she said. Antonio looked up at her a bit confused.

"I'm sorry what?" he said. E.V.E. rolled her eyes.

"Great attention span hon. I said JP will hate not having a jet pack this time around," she said frustratingly. Antonio sat back and gave the statement some thought.

"Well a jet pack might seem a bit out of place don't you think? I could see if Chief could build him some metal wings, but The Red Osprey already has that gimmick going," he said. E.V.E. started at him for a few moments more as she slowly shook her head.

"I wasn't being serious Tony," she said. Antonio looked up at her.

"I was being tired. Sorry Evie, post Sight is killing my circadian rhythm. Deuce may disapprove, but I'm drinking this Venom. And Skip gives me shit if I drink too much coffee now, because of that thing," he said. E.V.E. held up a finger and nodded.

"Oh yeah, I remember the thing. Never do that again," she said. Antonio rubbed his eyes and then took another sip of his drink.

"So yeah, almost at autopilot threshold here. But yeah no jet pack for JP," he said and laughed tiredly. Down on the range Pauly entered in his calculations into the rig Director Clark helped set up for testing prototypes for JP's bow. As Quiz looked on from his stool by the wall, The Director stood behind the bullet resistant barrier set up a few lanes down from the test. He was far more skeptical of Pauly's craftsmanship and the structural integrity of his own rig. He had an idea how powerful the bow could be. He was deeply dismayed the other two people here weren't nearly as concerned. Quiz snickered as he watched Pauly.

"And why is all this necessary again?" he said and ate a corn chip from the bag he got from the machine in the range lobby. Pauly looked back at him.

"Well since it takes two guys to draw the string back on this damn thing I thought a mechanism to allow for consistent draws we can measure, would be a good idea. I don't know if JP is descended from Vikings, or Sasquatch. But holy fuck," he said. Quiz laughed. The Director chuckled uneasily and moved farther back from the bullet resistant glass. Pauly finished entering in his calculations and placed an arrow on the string. He looked back at the other guys and held up a thumb.

"Alright gentlemen. Range is hot. As Freidrich Schiller wrote in William Tell 'Together, the weak are powerful,' hence the rig and the minds that constructed it," he said. The Director raised his hand.

"He also wrote 'The bow that's stretched too much, breaks,' I would remind you," he said. Pauly looked back at him and narrowed his eyes.

"But as Terence put it 'Fortune favors the bold' I would remind you," he said. The Director raised and brow and folded his arms. Quiz looked at Pauly quizzically.

"The only thing Terrence says is 'Thanks for bringing me chicken strips mate' even if I only heated them up in the microwave," he said. Pauly and The Director looked at him for a few moments.

"Terence the playwright, not the Australian in the Records Room," Pauly said and sighed. He wanted to say something more but opted to just press the button on the mechanism instead. The rig came to life and began slowly pulling the string back. The metal rig creaked and whined under the strain as it inched back.

Quiz picked up a bullet resistant vest that was lying next to him and held it in front of himself. Pauly retreated away a few steps, as the sound grew louder. He kept an eye on the pounds it was taking to draw and slowly his jaw began to drop. For the others it was the same. At JP's maximum anatomical draw point the arrow released and the string snapped back like a whip. All three men nearly jumped out of the their skins. The arrow split the air like a crack of thunder and thunked the target down range with a solid percussive thud. All three men looked back and forth at each other in awe. Pauly broke the silence.

"Tank shells didn't scare the shit out of me like this damn thing just did! Holy fuck! Tony is going to have to beef up JP's wrist guard like he wouldn't believe!" he said and wiped the sweat from his brow.

The wooden doors of the wall around the keep that headquartered the Northern Guard of Seastorm creaked open. Vekk, followed by the Hunter brothers rode out. Behind them rode Ronel Vastow from the southwest. People called him Cricket. Others were Ruter Aatbii formerly of the Imperial Capital of Frest. And in the back of the group was Cregg Shaw from The Borderlands. All of them were former hirelings recruited by Sardis Falco for his Northern Guard. All of them had fought together for years.

Now they rode out together yet again. A rider from Lord Falco arrived at dawn. Vekk left the highest-ranking man remaining at the keep in charge. He and his men were needed in Seastorm. It would be a few days journey by ship. Their next stop would be the small docks of the village just south of the Northern Guard keep. They rode for many miles until the sun was high in the sky. As they rounded the bluff Vekk slowed down to a trot. Before him were twenty of more Falco ships. Between them floated two vessels flying sails with a sigil he was unfamiliar with. He turned to his first lieutenant Borate.

"Ever seen that sigil Borate?" he said. Borate studied it for a moment.

"Three orange crabs in a line? Never seen that one at any Falco docks. Could be from the far south. I don't remember that one from The Midlands or The Borderlands," he said. Vekk had an uneasy feeling then. Borate was good at knowing sigils. If he didn't know one, that was not good news.

"Do you think it could be from the Exiled Islands?" he said. It had occurred to Borate but he didn't want to say it.

"Those ships look like they were captured. If that's so we could be looking an act of war. I don't like the looks of this Captain," he said. The Exiled Kingdom ships looked as though they had been sailed in by a skeleton crew. Though the ships were good distance off all of them aboard wore Falco colors. Uneasiness in Vekk grew.

"What would possess ships from the Exiled Kingdoms to sail this far south?" he said. Nobody had an answer. They just looked on with dread in their stomachs as they approached the village. When they arrived other Falco men greeted them. One of them waved Vekk over as they made their way into town.

"You must be Captain Enifack Vekk. Commander of the Northern Guard. I have heard much about you. I am Geonni Noritti. Captain of The Turtle. The young Lord Denato asked for you personally. I'm to escort you and your men to his ship," he said. Vekk wasn't shy about pointing out factors adding up that did not put him at ease.

"What kind of mess are we walking into here Captain?" Vekk said and dismounted. Noritti seemed reluctant to say much.

"A rather big one aye. This is all I can tell you. Lord Denato will be able to tell you more," he said and began leading the group down to the docks. Lord Denato's first mate greeted them by the gangplank that led up to the Lord's ship.

"Geosep Genodi. First Mate of The Storm Eagle. It's a pleasure to meet you Captain Vekk. You'll forgive me; I don't meet many westerners even in my line of work. I hope I said your name right," he said. Vekk had become accustomed to these types of introductions while here in the east and didn't think much of it.

"My family name is straight forward enough. It's my given name most people have trouble with. Most people just call me Vekk," he said.

Geosep was surprised by the authority and strength in Vekk's manner. Not a trait he'd come to associate with hirelings. His men carried much the same manner about them.

"Very well Captain Vekk. Follow me if you will," He said and began walking up the gangplank. Lord Denato stood at the helm of The Storm Eagle and watched Vekk as he approached and walked up the steps to him.

"Permission to come aboard Lord Denato," Vekk said and bowed his head slightly in the traditional greeting of ones' Hall Lord, even if he was still just the heir to his father's lands. Denato nodded.

"Permission granted Captain Vekk. You and your men will be shown to your bunks shortly." He said. The ride had not been long. He wasn't very road weary but he did appreciate the hospitality.

"My thanks m'Lord. If you'll forgive me but I have a number of curiosities regarding our presence here and the situation I see around us," Vekk said. Word would reach up and down the coast before the week is up that two Exiled ships were here at a Falco controlled port. He could only imagine the fallout that was to come from it. He needed as many assets working to his advantage as he could muster.

"You came highly recommended by my father. You are known as a man who can get things done. He's often spoke of you. You must have made quite an impression to be named commander of The Northern Guard. A position not easily earned. As for other matters, please follow me," he said. Denato turned and headed down to his stateroom. Vekk and the Hunters followed. The men entered the room below the helm and the door was shut. Denato walked to his desk and picked up the Captain's log from the doomed Honestead ship. He handed it to Vekk.

"These ships are from the Exiled Kingdom ruled by Ilonnis Honestead. Not a name familiar to many here on the coast. The Exiled Kings and Queens keep to their islands and don't bother with much this far south for any reason. You can imagine our surprise when we found this pair of vessels adrift 50 miles from here. They were part of a fleet of seventy ships that were attacked some time ago. Their assailant is someone you are familiar with I've come to understand," Denato said as

Vekk flipped though pages of the log. He came to the last page and read the last passage. He looked up Denato.

"The Black Admiral," he said solemnly. Denato walked to his window and looked out upon the Honestead ships.

"The very same. From what we were able to gather from the grisly scene The Shadow Fleet left for us the captain who kept that log may have been able to get word to his King. If so it takes blame away from Hall Falco for any mischief. If we are fortunate King Honestead will press no claim for conflict. If he does I would expect King Herald will be hearing grievances against my family's Hall. Let's hope for the best. But very much so, prepare for the worst. I need my father's best men beside me. He is still travelling back to Seastorm from Southgate. Hall Falco must prepare. Word of this will spread, and quickly. And when it does I fear war could follow. But maybe that is what The Black Admiral has always wanted. If the rumors are true, he's not been content to merely prey on the sea any longer. His shadows now darken the land as well," Denato said with uneasiness in his voice. Vekk had learned a great deal about The Shadows. This was the first he was hearing of attacks on land.

"I'm sorry m'Lord. I'm afraid I'm not familiar with these rumors," he said. Denato turned to him.

"My father journeyed to Southgate to speak with King Herald. It seems killings have been occurring in the area called The Barley Lands. Killings similar in nature to The Black Admiral and his Shadow Fleet. It was my father's feeling, and mine as well, the killings were connected. It was also our feeling that The Black Admiral may be connected to The Exiled Kingdoms. The slaughter we discovered would seem to suggest otherwise. It appears the Exiled Islands are as much under threat of The Black Admiral's blood lust for riches and war as we are. It could mean a potential alliance, or terrible conflict. Time will tell. We will meet with my father when he arrives in Seastorm to discuss this matter with him," Denato said. If what Vekk had learned thus far about The Black Admiral he could be a far greater threat than anyone had allowed themselves to entertain.

"Whatever The Shadow Fleet has planned, they've been making moves for a very long time. I would very much like to know exactly who, or What, The Black Admiral actually is," Vekk said. Denato nodded and turned back to the window.

"As would I Captain Vekk. As would I," he said and watched the wind blow around the sails of the Honestead ship.

As the sun began to dip below the horizon the fires of Candleport began to win the battle of light. The Candle Lake's waters were calm as the group rounded the shore. The body of water marked the halfway point of The Borderlands. It sat on high land and spilled into a river that flowed southeast toward The Bands. Here Genesis Payne would find a boat travelling east large enough to transport her and her horse. She hoped she would find a sponsor to escort her. Her current escort was due to depart west in three days time. She would be left alone to fend for herself on the long perilous journey east, or submit to failure and return north back to Scanna. Genesis was hopeful this trip was not a foolish excursion. The autumn festival was very much alive here in Candleport. Street performers stationed themselves at every corner. Genesis and her ranger escort passed by groups of jugglers on their way to the inn on the other side of town. Genesis had seen jugglers before, but none as proficient as these.

"They're so talented." She said to Hawk who was riding beside her. He looked around and smiled.

"Opal Sparrows. Carnival troupe that travels around these lands. Just one of many groups of entertainers that operate all over Gatheria. A long storied history that attracts many would-be Opals to their ranks. True professionals. Only a very few are ever selected. Take this in. An Opal show on the scale we'll see tonight is a thing seldom seen outside of autumn and spring. Apart from private bookings. Unless you're a Noble or a King, don't put that on your list of dreams," he said and flipped a coin to one of the Opals and nodded in appreciation for the show.

The Opal responded in kind. As they passed the Opal kept an eye on the group as they headed down the road. Once they were out of sight the Opal turned and exchanged a silent glance with the juggler standing next to her, and then they both walked off. Genesis and the rangers arrived at the inn and booked their rooms. They all gathered in the tavern below for a meal of mutton and root vegetables.

Outside musicians played and people cheered. The meal was under seasoned but filling enough. Genesis didn't care for mead but the inn had nothing else to drink. Outside the inn a pair of eyes under a dark hood watched the establishment from an alley cloaked in shadow. They watched as a group of jovial performers entered the building. One of them announced their arrival by ringing a small bronze bell, the trademark of The Opals. The groups looked up from their meals to see around a dozen costumed characters enter and start taking up their positions. The holder of the bell stepped forward and addressed the inn's patrons.

"Pleasant eve to you all! I am pleased to present to you The Opal Players! Tonight we bring you the story of The Elements! A tale as old as time. A story written by the gods themselves. Won't all of you join us on this journey of Wonder and Mystery? Watch as the pages of time are turned back!" the bell man hollered. A man in a gray tunic stepped forth as the bell man fell behind. The man in gray looked back and forth at patrons and then stomped his feet loudly on the wooden floorboards.

"I am the Mountain! Mighty is the strength in my hand that is rooted in the very bedrock of this world. Behold the great peak which soars above the clouds!" the man in gray bellowed and stepped to the side. A man in green stepped forth and looked around at the patrons. He put a hand to his ear.

"Hark and listen well. I am The Wind that speaks in the sky. I carry the clouds in my arms and bring the rains to bring all the green things forth from by brother's soil. Witness as I feed the rivers and streams for the creatures that swim," said the man in green. He too stepped to the side. A woman in blue stepped forward and looked around. She took a ribbon of blue fabric and ran it through her fingers.

"I am the blue. I am the waves that crash. I am the vast ocean. I am The Seas both warm and cold. I am both clear as crystal and black as night. I carry men, or claim them. No matter what direction you may journey, I will always be there at the end," she said as she looked around at all of the faces in the crowd. The bell rang. A look of disdain reached across her face. The man in gray also grimaced, with the man in green followed suit soon thereafter. The bell rang again and a man in yellow stood forth as the other three stepped away and stared him down. The man in yellow smiled and laughed.

"Forgive me brothers and sister. It was not my intention to intrude. But intrude I shall. I am The Fire. I am there as the lightning strikes. I am there when the torch is lit. I am there when the blood boils. I am the flame that brings warmth to the heart, or the destroyer of all that heart holds dear," the man in yellow said and looked around at his siblings. The man in gray stepped forward and stomped his foot.

"What is a candle to a mountain brother?" he said and stepped back and folded his arms. The man in yellow nodded and turned to him.

"I am the heat that men harness to forge steel from your flesh brother. I melt the rock, which creates new land from the sea. You are not apart from me," the man in yellow said and stepped back. The man in green stepped forth and scowled at the man in yellow.

"You boast. What are you to the wind that blows on high?" the man in green said and stepped back. The man in yellow nodded and turned to him.

"You soar high my brother and you do bring the rain. But do you also bring the light that makes all the green whose thirst you quench bloom? You are not apart from me brother," the man in yellow said. The man in green stepped back. The woman in blue stepped forward and hissed.

"You carry on as if your flame is anything to the waves that suffocate the fire," the woman in blue said and flicked her ribbon at the man in yellow. He turned to her.

"Oh sister. Your dominion may cover this world. Your waters may be clear as the finest crystal. Your depths may be dark as the blackest night. But I am the light that reveals all this beauty for eyes to see and the shadow that hides from it. You sister, are not apart from me," said the man in yellow. The woman in blue frowned and stepped back. The man in yellow looked at them all and then out at the crowd.

"I am what gives them meaning. But they too give me meaning. Without the earth to warm I have no meaning. Without the green that grows upon it what would there be to bloom? Without the sea how would warm hearts witness all that this wonderful world can show them? They are not apart from me. And I am not apart from them. Together we are this world. We are life. We all become death. It is the path all must take. But we take it together," the man in yellow said as the others walked up and stood next him. In unison they all took a bow. A round of applause lit up the room. The inn keep stepped forward and handed the performers flagon of mead and congratulated them. Genesis turned to Southstar and the others.

"I've always loved this story," she said. Hawk turned to her.

"There is a third brother?" he said. Hawk wasn't from The Borderlands. Few outsiders even knew who the third brother was.

"The Third Brother is not very well known away from The Borderlands. No temples still exist. The Fire was once worshipped the world over in very ancient times. After The Troubles fewer and fewer temples were built and The Fire fell out of favor. At least that's what the old texts say. Those who still give prayers to The Fire only do so as part of old family traditions. He lives on there and in plays like these," she said. This made Hawk even more curious.

"Those who pray to The Fire, what do they pray for?" he asked. A fair question, and others at the table seemed interested in what Genesis had to say.

"Sadly I know very little about that faith. I know very little about those who pray to The Fire either. I have never met one to ask. Much of what I know comes from the Book of The Seasons. I would guess the performers read the same book. Much of the phrasing comes from it," she said. Southstar had overheard the conversation. She had heard the title of this book before many years ago when she was very young.

"What is The Book of the Seasons?" she asked. All the others looked at Genesis keenly.

"The Book of the Seasons is a book written with children in mind to teach them about The Elements and their seasons. Fire is the Element of Summer. Mountain is the Element of Autumn. Sea is the Element of Winter. And Wind is the Element of Spring. Their influence over the world is said to be strongest during these times of the year. Right now the machinations of The Mountain would be said to be at work the most," she said. She was met with many blank expressions. Southstar stood up and looked at her flagon.

"I will return with more mead to hear more about these seasons," she said and walked over to the inn keep. Genesis was a little taken aback by her abruptness.

"Was it something I said?" she said. One of the other rangers shook his head.

"Nah, she just likes her head settled before she sits down to listen to a story. Busy as a beehive up there. Talks to herself sometimes. One gets used to it after a while," he said. One of the other rangers jabbed him in the ribs.

"Hey, I meant no offense. All of us got our wrinkles," he said. Southstar returned and sat down with a full flagon of mead. Genesis talked about The Seasons well into the night. She grew tired after so much talking. There were only a handful of people left in the tavern by then. Some rangers. Some performers. Some patrons. And one inn keep. Genesis retired to her very small room on the second floor at the end of the hall. It wasn't much more than a closet with a padded platform along the wall. Meager accommodations, but the mattress was comfortable enough. She thought of her father as she lay there. She thought of how much he must be missing her right then and worrying about her safety. She also thought about what she'd have to do while here in Candleport. She was so far away from anything. She fell asleep on that thought.

Chapter Nine: Forty-Eight Hours

A loud knock woke Genesis up suddenly. The light startled her. She didn't even realize she'd been asleep. A second knock jarred her up right and standing. She picked up her shawl and wrapped it around her before unlatching the door. She opened it to see the face of the old inn keep. He had a worried expression on his face. Something clearly was wrong.

"Begging your pardon miss. I do apologize for waking you so but I regret I have some rather complicated news," he said. Genesis was still barely awake at this point.

"Quite alright sir. I needed to be up anyway. What news do you bring?" she said. The inn keep looked down for a moment. It's clear what he had to say was not going be easy to express.

"Well you see miss, the matter is, your ranger friends, well you see, they've departed in the night," the inn keep said. Genesis had to give herself a moment to process this.

"What do you mean they've departed sir?" she said. The inn keep was having a terrible time delivering this news.

"Their commander said a personal matter of some sort had come up. She was talking to one of the performers last night you see. It was after you'd retired for the night. After what they talked about she got frightfully upset about something and brought her people aside. They talked a good while before she came up to me. You've been paid for room and board here for the next few days if you'd like to stay. Any friend of the rangers is a friend here," he said trying to smile. Genesis was stunned. How could they have just left her here?

"They've all gone? Did she say why she had to leave?" she said trying very hard to mask her panic. The inn keep could see how distressed she was and tried his best not to agitate her more than she already was.

"Yes miss they've all gone. I am so very sorry. All the commander said is that it was a personal issue. I'll tell you what; while you stay all meals are on the house. Again miss I am so very sorry," he said. Genesis smiled as best she could.

"I do thank you for your hospitality and generosity. I need a while to ready myself," she said. The inn keep felt very badly for her. He'd known she'd travelled a good long way.

"Understood miss. Whenever you're ready I'll make sure you have a good hot meal," he said. Genesis managed a smile and then closed the door. She sat back down on her mattress and buried her head in her hands. She didn't have the first idea of what to do. She was in a strange city surrounded by strangers. Her escort had left in the middle of the night. And the only person she knew even slightly was the inn keep. She did not imagine he could be persuaded to escort her to The East Lodge. She took hold of her clay pendant and held it tightly. She was on the verge of prayer when she opened her eyes and looked at the pendant. It occurred to her then, Candleport's Temple of the Wind. Downstairs the inn keep was drying off flagons when Genesis approached him.

"Where can I find the Temple of the Wind?" she said. The question caught the inn keep off guard. Then he saw her pendant. He realized then what Genesis was. It took him a moment to collect himself.

"You head down this road. Take a right at the anise bread baker and follow that road to its end. There you will find the Temple. Many prayers to the wind for you Mystic," he said. Genesis smiled and concealed her pendant under her cloak.

"You are very kind. May the day treat you well," she said and walked out of the inn. The road was busy. Evidence of the night's revelry had all but vanished. It was replaced with merchants lining the street selling their wares to passers by.

She had very little money at this point. She just smiled when petitioned and kept walking. As she did she couldn't help but feel like she was being watched. She subtly looked over her shoulder at the street behind her. She saw no one looking her way. She kept on for a while longer. She suddenly felt very self-conscious. As if the entire street had begun to watch her. She quickened her pace. The aroma of anise began to fill the air so she knew she was close to the bakery. The sound of breaking glass startled her and made her turn around. She looked down the street to see two men in an argument. They pushed and shoved each other while hurling insults at each other. A pair of town magistrate stepped in and separated the two. A hand gripped her arm and she was pulled back with force. Another hand covered her mouth. She tried to scream and break free but she could not. She was spun around and pressed against an alleyway wall. She saw her assailant then. He wore a dark cloak and hood that darkened his face.

"Do not scream again! Why are you here?" the cloaked man said in a deep grating voice. It was vaguely familiar though, but Genesis could not place it. The man slowly lifted his hand away from her mouth.

"I'm a mystic. I'm on a pilgrimage," she said. The man was silent for a moment.

"On a pilgrimage where? Here?" he said. Genesis shook her head.

"No, not here," she said. The man seemed to be growing impatient.

"I asked you where! If you don't tell, there will be trouble!" he snarled. Genesis tried to focus her eyes through the shadow to see who this man was, but could not. His voice was familiar.

"Who are you sir?" she said. The man fell silent again for a few moments. Then he lifted his hood. Genesis' eye widened.

"Brother!" she said loudly. The man held a finger up to his lips.

"Keep your voice down Genni. It isn't safe," he said. Genesis was having trouble believing this was real. She had not seen her brother in many years. His hair was short now and he was no longer a teenager.

"I might ask what you're doing here River," she said and frowned at her brother. River shook his head and sighed.

"I was shadowing the Redflower. And then I saw you riding with them. You are in danger," he said. This was all too much for Genesis. First she was abandoned by the rangers, and now her own brother accosts her in the street. She pushed River back and pointed a finger at him.

"Why are you following Redflower, and what danger am I in?" she snapped. River gathered himself and put his hands on his hips. He took a deep breath. A very somber look washed across his eyes.

"Some time ago the Ranger Pack of the Red Clay heard of an attack on a caravan near our borders. They were Priests of the Wind. Fifty or more were slain. There was evidence of torture. We never uncovered who the attackers were. We did pick up a trail of a survivor that somehow escaped the attack. His trail led us to the borders of the Rangers of

The Barley Lands. A priest died in their custody. Barley Lands means Redflowers. Barley Lands and Red Clay haven't been close in the last century or so. My commander feathered the High Chieftain himself telling him all we knew. I was sent along with two hirelings Red Clay trusts," he said and looked to his right. Two older men emerged from the shadows. One with faint traces of red in his hair and beard stepped forward.

"A pleasure to make your acquaintance Mystic Payne. I am Sir Pannos Rayley. I was once the commander of the Lord's guard for Hall Haddock. I ply my trade elsewhere now. Red Clays are good people to work for," he said. The other man stepped forward. His beard had black highlights in the gray. His head was neatly shaven.

"I am Sir Colvin Wheeler. I was once part of his Majesty's Royal Guard in Southgate. But I became long in years and was replaced by a younger man. It's how these things go I'm afraid. I still earn my way in this world fighting along side this gent here. Sometimes he can still keep up with me," Colvin quipped. Pannos would not be outdone.

"I have to slow down just so you can keep up with me," he shot back. Colvin grimaced and shook his head. Genesis wasn't interested in banter though.

"A pleasure Sirs," she said and then gave her brother a hard stare.

"What caravan? Why were you sent? Wouldn't Southstar's father send reinforcements from the Barley Lands?" she said. River looked over at the hireling knights. Then he looked back at Genesis.

"As to The High Chieftain's aims, I could not say. I suspect he has his reasons. It's my feeling there is something far greater at work here than priests killed for their offerings of silver and gold. I say this because there is indeed a shadow lurking about. Who they are, we do not know. They're difficult to track. We've had to keep our distance and observe them from afar. We've done so since you left Scanna. Redflower departed with a few of her rangers east early this morning. The bulk of her shadows departed in pursuit. None followed her two rangers that went west. Some stayed here. The only reason is that they must think you know something of interest to them. We saw a small group of men headed to the Temple of the Wind. I suspect they are waiting for you to arrive there. Which you will," River said. Genesis looked at him. She was deeply distressed.

"What are you thinking asking me to go where you know killers are? They could be waiting there to murder me!" she said loudly. This was not a reasonable thing to ask of his sister, but River had his reasons.

"You must go and pray. Speak at length to no one. Do what you need to do and come back to the inn. We will watch over you," he said. Genesis glared at him for a few moments. She then closed her eyes and exhaled loudly. She opened her eyes again.

"Very well. Father will hear of this," she said and pointed at River again. He held up his hands.

"I have no doubt. Go now. We will see you again later," River said. Genesis crossed her arms and glared at river.

"Do you honestly think after all this time you have any right to show up and start ordering me around like you have the authority? Do you really think you're in any place to act with this impunity?" she growled as she waved her finger in River's face. River was a little beside himself.

"Genni, please just do this. None of this is ideal for anyone," he said. Genesis wanted to throw something very hard at River but did not want to create more of a scene.

"We will be speaking about this later," she said angrily. Genesis scowled and walked out of the alley and continued on her way to The Temple. Sir Pannos walked up and slapped River on the shoulder.

"Should be a fun chat lad. Tell us how it goes," he said and headed off with Sir Colvin down the alley toward The Temple of the Wind. Much farther east the procession of Southgate men filed through the main road through Creendea. Another night of autumn revelry was being prepared. The warm colors of the season were everywhere. Onlookers applauded Atheon as he passed by on his horse. If he was being honest with himself he was very unsure about how he'd be received. He'd recalled his father was greeted with what was best described as ambivalence when he last visited Falco lands. Atheon expected much the same this time. Instead the people were very warm and appeared genuinely excited that he was here. Attention was still a very foreign thing to him. People looked down from the white arched stone walkways on either side of the road and pointed as they smiled. He looked over at Antimony. He didn't even seem to be paying attention to the crowd. Instead he appeared to be focusing his attention on the baked goods merchants they passed.

"Unhappy with camp rations brother?" Attheon quipped. Antimony looked over at his brother.

"Camp mutton and flat bread are fine enough, but have nothing on a fresh baked loaf. An army marches with its stomach as much as it's feet brother. I hear they have something in the Falco land called a shoe loaf. Given that it is the size and shape of a shoe. It goes wonderfully with oil I am told. I am quite keen to try it," he said. Attheon chuckled.

"I should think you'd want to fill up a cart with them to take back to Southgate," he mused. Antimony looked at him seriously.

"Do we have a spare cart?" he said. Attheon laughed. Antimony cracked a slight smile.

"I'm being serious brother. The aroma from the bakers' wares here is enchanting," he added. Attheon laughed again. The Southgate line proceeded to the other end of the city and started gathering around the Mayor's keep. Mayor Marto Runeo Stood outside with his advisers on either side of him. He appeared very pleased to see the Princes of Southgate in the city of Creendea. Attheon dismounted. Antimony and a handful of Southgate captains followed suit.

"Greetings and warmest of welcomes to Creendea Princes Attheon and Antimony. It is such a pleasure to have you visit our city. You will want for nothing. Food and drink for your men. You've arrived at a particularly exciting time. The Autumn festivities are in full swing to celebrate The Days," Mayor Runeo said gleefully.

"Pleased are we as well to be here in Creendea. It's been many years since I was here last. I recall the hospitality was quite exceptional. I'm sure my men will enjoy the evening's festivities, and I assure you they will be on their best behavior. We do have to depart on the morrow, regardless of how their heads feel," Attheon said giving emphasis to that last part at a volume many of his men could hear. Mayor Runeo extended a hand and beckoned the Princes to follow him.

"Please follow me my Princes. You've traveled a great distance to be here. We have wine and olives in the keep. As much as you would like," said Runeo. Attheon looked back at his brother and then back at Runeo.

"Would you happen to have any of that shoe bread and oil? The Prince Antimony had been interested in sampling that," he said. Runeo turned to one of his advisors and patted him on the shoulder. The advisor headed off in the direction of the city. Antimony smiled. Runeo clasped his hands together and began leading the Princes to the keep. The keep itself was fairly modest being just a front hall with an adjoining kitchen and bedroom. Attheon and Antimony sat at The Mayor's table graciously. Runeo could barely contain his excitement that they were there. Attheon was not really one to engage in much banter. He had a number of questions rolling around in his mind on his journey here. After one of Runeo's servants had filled his cup, Attheon took a sip and nodded his head.

"Northeastern wine lives up to its reputation," he said. Antimony took a sip as well. He favored ale and mead over wine, but this was quite good.

"My compliments to the vineyard. The climate does the grapes justice," he said and picked up a handful of olives. Attheon turned to Runeo.

"Mayor Runeo, if I may ask, I've had the opportunity to observe the many comings and goings of travellers up and down The Bands. It has come to my attention that a great many travellers have been following my battalion for some distance. Merchants I should suspect. What can you tell me of the spirit of these lands?" he said. Some of the cheer faded from Runeo's face, but he kept a brave expression.

"We are strong people my Prince. Being so close to Seastorm offers safety. Even so nearby villages still have their problems with bandits as you may imagine. Our sheriffs do what they can to deal out justice as much as they can. Recent troubles, that I can only address in rumor my Prince, from the coast as well I hear from The Barley Lands out west, have given the people of Creendea an uneasiness we're, unaccustomed to. Your presence here has certainly lifted much of the weight off the people's shoulders. Revelers have flocked here like they haven't since my grandfather was small. He's said so much himself," Runeo said. Attheon was distressed to hear that that. He'd started to realize just how grave a situation was brewing here in the lands along the coast, as well as west in the Barley Lands.

"I can assure you Mayor Runeo that Southgate is well aware of the troubles out west. My own brother, Prince Carcino is leading an investigation personally into the violence there. I am to understand he's coordinating with the rangers of that region as well. I'm sure that Lord Falco is also going to great lengths to get to the root of this Shadow Pirate I have been hearing so much about," he said. The mention of this character cast unease in The Mayor's eyes.

"Oh yes. That name has been a common topic on the lips of many in the last two years almost. The Black Admiral they call him. More of a myth than a man. A fiend and brigand said to command a thousand ships or more if you believe the stories. They say he rises from the waves like a specter and commands the night to follow him wherever he goes. Even when the sun is high. I don't really give into the fantasy. I just know that he's a nuisance and a threat to our way of life. Please forgive me my Princes. It is not for one of my station to utter such malaise. But I do believe this Black Admiral is intent on starting war," Runeo said and withdrew back into his chair. This was nothing that Attheon wasn't thinking himself.

"There is nothing to forgive Mayor. You love your people as I do mine. I suppose it's not a very well kept secret at this point that my marriage to Lady Marea Falco will mean your people will be mine as well. The people of Southgate will be hers in turn. Southgate looks after it's own. If this Black Admiral is foolish enough to make war with Seastorm, he will face Sentinel steel," Attheon said. Antimony was quite impressed with his brother of late. He had had some doubts how readily he would fit into the role of King. He was seeing the beginnings of what could be a King he would look forward to serving. He poured himself some more wine and raised his goblet.

"To the union of Hall Lamb and Hall Falco," he said. Attheon and the Runeo raised their goblets as well.

"Hear Hear," Runeo said and the men took a drink. Attheon raised his goblet.

"To the best worst kept secret to ever grace the southlands," he said and took a drink. The others did as well. Attheon looked over his shoulder for a moment and then looked back. He had a serious look on his face.

"Only a few rivers separate The Olive Lands from the eastern edge of the Barley Lands. Once I make my official proposal I will lead my men there to make a few inquiries myself. I can't let my brother do all of this alone. Southgate looks after it's own," he said. Antimony raised his goblet and took a drink. The door opened behind them and Runeo's advisor entered carrying a basket and a bottle of oil. He set them down on the table in front of Antimony who opened it and breathed in deeply. The look on his face was one of pure bliss.

"Oh what a truly sublime aroma. I hope they brought a basket for you too brother," Antimony mused. Attheon chuckled.

"An entertainer now I see," Attheon said and laughed as Antimony took out one of the loaves and passed it over to his brother. Attheon broke it in half and took a bite. The center was soft while it had a tougher and crisper crust on the outside. It was surprisingly flavorful on its own. He looked over at the Runeo who was smiling. Antimony followed suit and sat back enjoying the very flavorful bread. Attheon smiled.

"This bread is superb. If I had known these lands had this I would have courted the Lady Marea years ago," he said. Antimony laughed.

"And you would not think I'd speak in jest if I were to propose we hire one of these bakers to ply his trade in Southgate," he said. The younger Prince was certainly eager and unabashed to facilitate his access to his culinary tastes. Attheon smirked at Antimony.

"If we did that brother, we'd need to tell the armorer to let out your chest plate," Attheon said. Antimony looked at his brother as if he did not expect this level of wit coming from him. Then he burst out laughing. Runeo took out a glazed clay saucer and poured out a considerable amount of oil into it. He gestured to the greenish-golden pool.

"The bread alone is quite delicious. Please try it with oil," he said and dipped some of his bread in the oil and took a bite. The Princes did the same. The look on their faces told Runeo all he needed to know. He looked up at his advisor and snapped his fingers.

"More oil!" he said. The advisor promptly ran back out the door.

The citizens of Swifts Isles could feel the tension in the air as the Haddock ships pulled into port. The indigo color of Haddock sails stretched down one of the four rivers that ran by the island called Rushing Horse, which connected, to one of the lakes south of the Barley Lands. Lord Parnell Haddock's ship made dock. His imposing frame thundered down the gangplank catching the attention of everyone standing ashore. His advisors and several members of his guard followed him hastily. The fire in the man's face had not cooled considerably since his time in Southgate.

The Swifts Islanders darted out of the road to avoid the procession and catching the ire of their land's Lord. The Swiftriver Keep was equally on edge, except Miles Haddock who was the eldest son of Parnell Haddock. He stood in the keep's bailey flanked by his two sisters Hanela and Denia. It had been almost two months since their father departed to Southgate. Miles disliked when his father travelled. Distance seemed to directly contribute to the severity of his mood when he returned. His mother, the Lady Forah Haddock, chose to stay in her study. She'd tired of welcoming Lord Haddock in his post travel demeanor. She was wise to abstain from today's welcome. Miles looked back at his cousin Tyler who stood some distance away. The look of worry in his eyes mirrored his own. It seemed to darken his normally warm and vibrant golden hair and beard. The heavy wooden doors of the keep groaned open revealing the malcontented visage of Lord Parnell Haddock. Miles managed a smile even though he knew for the next good while or so he'd have to hear all about Lord Addar Marsh, just as he did in the day prior to his father's departure to Southgate. Parnell Haddock's mood was largely unchanged from when he did. He nonetheless greeted his children warmly.

"I hope the road was favorable to you father," Miles said. Parnell exhaled deeply and shook his head.

"There is nothing like long days and short nights to make a man dwell and drive him to the edge of madness. The next time King Herald Lamb feathers a request for my presence in Southgate, tell him I'm dead," Lord Haddock said. Miles was unsure if his father meant it in jest. His father tended to swing back and forth from hyperbole to deprecation and back. It was often difficult to know exactly where on the pendulum's swing the man was. Miles merely smirked subtly. Parnell embraced his girls with both arms and looked at them both. Hanela was within a year of her eighteenth birthday. Already interest in her hand had been floated Parnell's way from Halls both large and small. Few of them presented viable offers in his eyes. He hoped the field would be more fruitful with prospects by the time his younger daughter Denia was of age. Lord Ivy had already pitched his daughter as mate for his son Miles more than once in the last few years. He'd met the girl himself, and if honest, wasn't largely impressed.

"How have the Ladies of this Hall found their days these past months? I hope you've kept your mother preoccupied. She gets to her gossiping something fierce without check," Parnell said. Hanela held her father's hand and smiled.

"Denia and I have kept her from perusing the markets with a head full of whispers with many games of cards. Though I must admit it has become more and more difficult to let her win without giving ourselves away," she said. Her father's expression softened and he chuckled.

"Oh child, do you think your mother so easily duped. She's a clever one who knows precisely what you two are doing. Though I should say she does appreciate the attention you give her. I think that is most important to her. Go to her now and have the servants start preparing a meal. I hunger after my journey," Parnell said and gave his girls another big hug. As they departed he turned to Tyler who trailed a few paces behind.

"You, come here boy. You look dour as the clouds cover the sun. How fares my brother?" Lord Haddock said. Tyler though garbed in plate and leather walked up sheepishly to his uncle.

"Still with a sour stomach I'm afraid. He's gotten better since he feathered you," he said. Lord Haddock frowned and shook his head.

"Purcian never could pass up street food. Misguided by his nose to no good. I hope his week in an outhouse has been vivid enough a lesson. Good to hear he's doing better. Go now and make sure my men get my things back to the keep dry. If they drop anything in the river this time, there'll be a flogging," he said. Tyler bowed to his uncle.

"It will be done uncle," he said and walked off in the direction of the river. Lord Haddock then turned to Miles with a serious look.

"You and I need to talk lad," he said. Miles could hear the alarm in his father's voice, and it wasn't just from his travel stresses. Lord Haddock proceeded to make his way to his private study. He stood next to a narrow window in the room when he got there. He collected his thoughts for a few moments before turning to his son.

"What I say does not leave this room, do you understand me boy?" Parnell said. Miles was startled at his father's abruptness, but he was accommodating.

"You have my word father," he said. Lord Haddock turned to the window again for a few moments, and then looked back at Miles.

"They're fools. All of them. Especially that Sardis Falco. They play games with all of our lands. They think themselves wise and dismiss my concerns as if they were mere flights of fancy. They do not see the Midland threat as we do. King Herald sits comfortably in his palace behind his mountains without a care in the world. Falco looks out on his beaches like the sea isn't full of death looking for throats to cut. I went to their meeting and the number of clever men in The Old Hall was distressingly small," Parnell said as he left the window and sat in one of the large wooden chairs by his desk. Miles sat down in one of the others.

"Surely there were at least a few ears receptive to your case father," he said. Parnell rubbed his chin and looked up at his son.

"Very few. Lord Ivy was the only one of real influence that paid me any mind. This is not a small thing. Ivy is a formidable ally. And he and I do agree on more than one very important matter. The first being, we cannot trust or ignore a man like Addar Marsh whose connection to northern fiends is well known. Fiends who make sport of the south, because our King Herald and Hall Lamb pay no fealty to their Emperor. They gladly turn their backs on brigands bred in their lands robbing and murdering our people. May the gods grasp their throats when they take wine! Midland trash," Parnell growled. The name of Addar Marsh was bound to come up sooner or later. Miles was glad it had come up earlier rather than later.

"The King didn't even consider sending an inquiry to audit Lord Marsh? To ascertain what riches could be attributed to unsavory dealings with the north?" he said. Parnell was impressed at how much his son had grown.

"Sadly no my boy. Sadly no," he said. Miles understood just how much his father questioned the leadership on the throne of Southgate. His father had for years complained about the lack of action the throne took to the increasing banditry problems flooding the southlands.

"At least we have the support of Hall Ivy. On what other matters did Lord Ivy concur?" Miles said. Parnell sat back in his chair and then sighed.

"You should know my son. King Herald has abandoned reason and has favored his feral child Attheon to take the throne after him," Parnell said. This was surprising to Miles. This was not the Lamb he'd envisioned taking the throne after King Herald.

"If you'll forgive me father, I was not entirely convinced there was even such a man as Prince Attheon Lamb," he said. This had grown all too common in recent years. There was nothing unusual about young Lord Haddock's skepticism.

"Oh Attheon Lamb is quite real lad. Saw him myself. A wildness in that boy's eyes. Not becoming of a future King. Old Herald is a fool putting a crown on his head. It's a matter Lord Ivy and myself had words about. It's time our Hall started putting its support behind the younger Prince Carcino. A Prince of Hall Lamb better born to sit the throne. Still a mere shadow of Prince Mercurian, but many leagues better than the wild man King Herald intends," Parnell said. Carcino was a name Miles knew well and had come to respect in recent years.

"Prince Carcino is in the West Barley Lands the last I heard," Miles said. Parnell was proud to know his son was so well informed.

"Yes lad. And whatever aid Hall Haddock can lend, it will be lent. Attheon will falter. Sooner or later that feral boy will falter and his father will see. Attheon will never sit on the throne of Southgate. I don't care what pomp our King has invested himself in with this marriage to that Falco girl. A hollow and desperate gesture. Telling as well. If Herald had any true confidence in the boy, he'd send him on his way to court Lady Pallas Brian. But instead we get an obvious display of weakness that makes it very clear The King fears the death on Falco's doorstep. He'll throw his wild son into the bed of Lady Falco to secure the Falco fleet. A good move perhaps, if he'd negotiated with Sardis Falco to wed Carcino to Marea instead. He named that boy after one of Falco's ancestors for gods' sake. It should have been his move. But like every other decision from the throne, it is mired in folly. Why should this have been any different?" Parnell said. What his father was saying troubled Miles deeply. Not just the treasonous flavor his father's words were taking, but the truth behind them.

"Our King is trusting an unproven son over one who has proven himself many times over. This is a truly a dark time in the south father," he said. Parnell nodded and sighed deeply.

"That it is boy. Hall Haddock will not sit idly by and let the shadowy killers in the west prey upon our people. We will not allow the shadowy killers in the east come to our lands and prey on our people. And will certainly not allow the shadowy killers from the north and their fiendish conspirator continue to plunder! Prince Carcino will have our full support. I will begin preparations on the morrow. The future begins now lad. A storm is brewing. I can feel it. The Swift Fish is no stranger to the storm," he said and laid his hands in his lap.

"Addar Marsh will have eyes pointed south. He'll expect a move from Swiftriver and he's going to be prepared," Miles said. The boy was right. Lord Haddock could find no flaw in his reasoning.

"If we too are prepared. It won't matter," the elder Haddock said. Miles didn't know what his father meant by that. He suspected he'd be finding out soon enough.

The Records Room was an utter mess. If not for the garbage disposal system, it would look a lot worse. That was little comfort to Terry who barely had room for his gaming station. All other surfaces were taken up by open books, charts, notebooks and people trying to make heads and tails out of one Sword World thing or another. He chose to ignore everyone for the time being and concentrate on Pac Man. He'd already put in his time on research. Much of it was being looked over by JP, Antonio and Stratum. Nocivo stood off by himself looking through the list of medicinal plant life Terry worked hard to compile for him. He'd put together few lists of plants and spices local to this Sword World he knew would be most effective and easiest to find. Even with the many worlds they'd visited, the ones without comparable levels of technology were the most challenging. Matching a world's level of technology always was. Particularly for a group accustomed to working with higher tech, and none more than Salazar. But he would find a way around the moratorium on advanced equipment. He had the mind of a thief. There was no such thing as impossible. There was only a list of possible outcomes with decreasing likelihood of occurring instead. Nocivo by contrast had a better respect of the concept of impossible and chose his battles more carefully. Even so he expected Salazar was having Jack and Hammer help him create some kind of workaround. Firearms were an absolute no-go. Modern explosives were also out. With Antonio a normal walk in the park for some would render a sizable list in his mind with what he could use to make a bomb. JP didn't bother with anything so complicated as explosives even though he was no slouch in this area either. His methods were more old fashioned and hands on. Stratum was more a wild card. He strangely enough seemed to have the least amount of apprehension about the journey. He just sat in the corner offering feedback as if he were lounging in a coffee shop socializing. The behemoth had a particular manner about him that took some getting used to. He had the most reason to worry about this mission than anyone in the room. It's not as if he could blend in. Nocivo had thought about asking him to stay. But ultimately it would be better to have him than end up needing him. The rest they would figure out. Nocivo stretched and yawned.

  He thought back to what his sister had said earlier about fasting. He still didn't know what he could do to fast, but he needed to get out for a while before he and the team headed to the Staging Room. He took out his phone and texted Jack with instructions, a text that had Jack looking at Estrello like he was crazy as they met on the garage level.

"Are you serious Skip? Now?" he said. Nocivo didn't think it was that outrageous a request.

"Why not? Couldn't you use some fresh air and sunshine?" he said. Jack's face contorted even more.

"No. No I couldn't. I need to finish building things so you and the team don't die horrible deaths, badly, with bad death," he said. His objection was noted but Nocivo had other ideas.

"Noted. Meet me with the trailer in one hour fifteen at the coordinates I texted you," he said. Jack let out an exasperated groan. His expression didn't change much when he met Estrello at the location he provided later. Jack got out of the cab and held up his hand. There were fresh red marks. Nocivo looked at them and chuckled. He walked over to the cooler strapped to the back of his motorcycle and pulled out some ice. He wrapped it in a scarf he pulled out of his pocket and handed it to Jack. He took it and placed it on the reddened area.

"That damn horse better not have rabies. And I would not be shocked if it did," he said. Estrello was more focused on Blueskin to pay attention to the remark. He hadn't had him out for a good ride in a good while. He affixed Blueskin's trail saddle. This would be a good evening. Jack grumbled to himself and pulled his mountain bike from the bed of his truck. He snapped on a helmet and followed Estrello and Blueskin as they made their way up the trail. Texas hill country was rugged territory with limestone outcroppings on either side of path. The fringes of which resembled Swiss cheese.

This was a well-travelled trail so much of the brush along the trail had been cleared away by years of foot traffic. Estrello wasn't here to blaze any new trails. He was just here to ride and enjoy the evening. They rode for an hour or two not saying much. Just enjoying the air and scenery. Jack would complain every so often when their journey took them uphill. Nocivo would hang back and wait for him to catch up. The day had been warm but as evening encroached a cooler wind blew over the road. They were nearly to where Estrello wanted to be. He didn't think Jack would last very much longer. They still had the trip back. Jack seemed to find a higher gear though. Soon they were at their destination. Nocivo turned Blueskin to the side and he looked out at the horizon. Jack looked over in the same direction. Before him the setting sun washed the landscape in rich warm hues of red, orange and yellow. Nocivo did prefer beaches. That was a matter of nature. This view was still amazing to him and hit him very profoundly. The trio sat there for a while watching the colors on he horizon shift. Jack's stomach began to grumble then and he looked up at Nocivo.

"Hey man this is nice and all, but I'm getting hungry and we should get going if we want to make it back before it's too dark," he said. Estrello was getting a little hungry himself.

"Bueno. Let's go," he said and turned Blueskin around. Jack had been thinking of how to ask about why they were out riding for a good while now. He was a bit reluctant to ask a direct question. Even so he felt it was the right time.

"So what was this all about?" he said and looked back at Estrello. Nocivo recalled his conversation with his sister and the sermon of that Sunday.

"Ezra chapter eight. I suppose you could say I wanted to gain some perspective before I left for another mission. You also might say that I've had more than a few reservations about it," he said. Jack was not a spiritual guy. He didn't know Ezra from Ezekiel.

"Not a part The Bible I'm familiar with I'm afraid. What does Ezra have to do with your reservations?" Jack said. Estrello wasn't in a frame of mind to witness, but he would share his thoughts on the matter.

"Ezra eight is in short a lesson in faith and fasting. I wasn't sure what I could fast in order gain that perspective. I have enjoyed this ride and this sunset but I am no closer to gaining perspective than I was before I left. I don't have an answer. I have neither figured it out myself, nor do I feel The Lord has clued me in to whatever I need to know. The answer is still in the future it would appear. The same future where I will have to decide how much blood I am going to allow to spill. Principles are more of a challenge to live by when there are fewer restraints on everyone around you. I have the feeling Jack that I am about to be tested, as I have never been before. I am not at ease about that," he said. There was much that Jack glossed over in terms of the team and the missions they went on. It was easy for him to divorce himself from the realization that each of them were real people with real fears. He saw them as men on a much higher level than he. It was a self-imposed illusion, because they were in fact not so far removed from him.

"I'm sorry man. I don't know how to save the lives of the people who will try to kill you or the other guys. I just know what I can do help you not die yourself. That's all I can do. I wish there was a way that nobody had to die, but I know that's not how real life works. I've been part of this crew long enough to know that," he said. Estrello appreciated his frankness.

"Like most times before I set out into the unknown, I'll just have to see what I can do and hope for the best," Nocivo said. Jack tightened the Velcro straps on his gloves and looked ahead at the trail.

"That's what everyone does. Ones that bother to think about what they're doing before they do it anyway. Others just run into the night without much of a plan. At least you know you're going to a violent place and not assuming everyone will play nice. Or that everyone can or should. You can only control what you do. What other people decide to do, the consequences are squarely on them," he said and then began pedaling forward. Nocivo followed behind. This trip did bear some fruit. It was fruit already sitting in the bowl in front of him. There was just more of it now.

Chelsea sat near a pool table in Common Room 16. She'd spent the better part of three days reviewing safety procedures for anything she'd care to add or subtract. She understood full well each change would have to endure multiple levels of scrutiny before being considered for implementation or retiring. She'd have to talk to a number of different people in order to get approval for one thing or another. One such person walked into the room carrying a cue and stopped at a table nearby. It was Antonio Salazar. It had become a common occurrence to see him clear his head with a solo match or five before setting his sights on the staging room to dash out. He set a container filled with a thick greenish liquid on a table beside the pool cue rack. Antonio then pushed in a switch to release the clacking balls and picked up the triangle and set it down on the felt. Chelsea then watched as Antonio began setting the balls down in the triangle. This is when she noticed that he'd noticed her watching. He turned and took another cue from the rack and held it out to her.

"You break Towers," he said as he held the stick out. Chelsea sat there like a tangled cable unsure how to respond.

"I__. I don't want to interrupt your thing," she said. This didn't seem to matter to Antonio who still held the stick out. Chelsea set her tablet down in the chair next to her and stood. She took hold of the pool cue and held it with uncertainty. Antonio picked up a chalk cube and set it down near her, and then proceeded to finish racking the balls. Chelsea picked up the cube and watched as Antonio centered the triangle perfectly and lifted the apparatus away from the neat cluster of balls.

He turned and looked at her before rolling the white cue ball toward Chelsea who looked very much lost. Antonio walked to the other side of the table and stood there waiting for Chelsea to do something. She looked down at the blue chalk cube and the hemispherical divot on one side. Antonio watched curiously but felt compelled to comment after a few moments.

"You are familiar with general idea behind the game?" he said. His choice of words may have been poor but his tone was not sarcastic or scornful. Chelsea snapped out of her stupor and chalked the tip of her cue and smiled sheepishly.

"I am. I haven't played this in a while. I wasn't very good at it," she said. Antonio smiled and shrugged his shoulders.

"I don't play to compete. I just play. If you want to play to win, that's your call," he said. A simple, but at the same time complex answer. Chelsea picked up the cue ball and walked over to the other end of the table and set it down. She looked up at Antonio still looking unsure about the situation. He continued to look on patiently. Slowly she positioned herself and took aim. Chelsea pulled the cue back and then snapped it forward. The cue ball zipped up and connected solidly with the cluster with a loud clack. Balls on either side of the mass careened this way and that into the banks. The maroon seven ball found a pocket and rolled down into the channel under the felt. Antonio grinned.

"Guess you're solids. Good start Towers," he said. Chelsea smiled meekly. She looked for her next shot. Green six ball was near a pocket. The cue could have been better positioned. The purple four ball was another shot but she would need to bank it. Chelsea opted for the former and took aim. The cue zipped up to the six ball and struck it badly. It bounced off a bank and away from the pocket. On the far side of the Room Stratum sat and watched the pair. He looked back and forth at each of them. There was an aura of concern and melancholy about him. Antonio picked up the chalk cube and prepped before taking a position in line with the fifteen ball. He took aim and sunk it in the corner pocket. He looked up at Chelsea instead of evaluating his next shot.

"Looks like you have a lot on your mind. Penny for your thoughts?" he said. Chelsea looked up from the table unsure how to respond. She took a moment to come up with something to say.

"I don't really have a lot going on. Just some updates to the modules I have in mind. Not much else," she said. Antonio smiled slightly. He took a few moments before taking aim at the thirteen ball and sunk it without much trouble.

"Doesn't seem like a small thing," he said and looked around for his next shot. Chelsea leaned on her pool cue as she rolled his words around in her head. It struck her as peculiar, comparatively speaking. She looked up at him again. His dark eyes had a depth to them. He had a younger face than his years, but his eyes betrayed the miles he'd travelled. Chelsea fumbled around for a response.

"Yeah. Well__yeah. I'm not about to travel to another universe. I'm just going to do some video editing," she said. Antonio smiled and then sank the twelve ball in the pocket right in front of her. He picked up the cube again and chalked up his cue as he walked around to the other side of the table. Chelsea took a few steps back so Antonio could make his next shot. He looked at the table and then back at Chelsea.

"Apples and oranges. Orange is not a lesser fruit in the bowl. Security and safety aren't a small thing here. True what Isos do is dangerous with all that spectacle and scope, but that's not the only way to look at things," he said. Chelsea didn't quite understand what he was getting at. She was nonetheless appreciative.

"Thanks? Thanks," she said. Antonio spotted his next shot. Instead of taking it he pointed up. Chelsea looked up at the ceiling and then backs down with some confusion.

"Okay?" she said and tilted her head to the side. Antonio took aim and struck the fourteen ball. It was poorly positioned and just went rolling off to the far end of the table. Antonio looked back up at Chelsea.

"A fact, regard it as fun or not, is that this ship is docked beneath the city of San Antonio. Why would this be significant?" he said with a slight smile. Chelsea didn't have an answer to that. The question had crept up in her mind a few times before. Of all the places on Earth why was San Antonio chosen over anywhere else? Antonio continued.

"A number of reasons. Conversations for another time. A fact, regard it as fun or not, is that outside of Langley, Quantico, and Washington DC, the city of San Antonio has the largest concentration of military, intelligence and law enforcement entities in the country. And it goes deep. Deep. So deep I don't even think the capes quite understand what sort of city this is. But we do. Why do you think the movie Cloak and Dagger was set here? I'm sure the filmmakers could say one thing. But we know why. So I would say any measure keeping our ducks in a row with what sits above us, it one worth valuing. Your shot," he said and backed away from the table. Chelsea looked up, and then back down at Antonio.

"I wouldn't have thought__," she said before trailing off. She seemed to sink into thought as she stood there. Antonio's eyes were very dark. A ringtone interrupted the scene. Antonio looked down at his pocket and took out his phone. There was a message from JP. Antonio read it and then looked back up at Chelsea.

"Gotta run. Guess the table is yours. Good game Towers," he said and put up his cue. Chelsea tried to say something as he turned away, but the words caught up in her throat. Stratum still watching from afar stood, shook his head, and then turned toward the door.

Genesis arrived back at her room after spending time in prayer. She unlocked the door and pushed the door open. Her brother sat in the chair by her mattress. She was startled for a moment. But only just. She closed the door and sat down. There was aggression behind her eyes as she did. River didn't want an argument, but didn't reason his chances were very good. Genesis didn't hide her hostility very well.

"I put in my time for prayer. I'm not dead, so I'm thankful for that. At least one prayer answered by the Wind. We'll see if he answers any others today," she said and leaned back against the wall. River had his hirelings stationed inside and outside the inn. It gave him enough peace of mind to be here. If he expected any cooperation, this was a conversation that needed to happen.

"We followed you to the Temple and stood watch. Your tails were there just as we predicted. When you left they followed you back for a time. Then they met with some others we'd also had an eye on. They spoke about something. We didn't get close enough to overhear them. They seemed very concerned about a message they'd received. They departed east from what we could tell. We aren't sure there aren't more of them in the city watching you. We just know those look to be gone," he said. Genesis took a deep breath. It was some relief. But there was a fire in her heart.

"Why were you sent here? Out of all their numbers. The Red Clays send you. Why?" she said. This was what River was expecting.

"The leadership of the Red Clays sent me because of father. They knew he is a mystic and that he prayed to the Wind. If this slaughter was a matter of mystics, they needed someone with a background knowledge of them leading the inquiry," he said. Genesis chuckled.

"A background? I seem to recall you rejecting your background," she snapped. What she said was fair. River could not dispute.

"I did. But I was the best they had. So now I'm here. You never did explain much why you were if I'm not mistaken," he said. Genesis was not prepared to slide past this one. She'd had a lot to say to River.

"Why did you leave? Why did you reject the way? Why did you reject us?" she said angrily. He knew his answer would not be received very well, but it was what he had to say.

"I wish I could say it was something profound like receiving a message in the Wind that told me I had a great destiny in the west. But the fact of it is, I wasn't contented with a quiet life. I didn't have the patience father needed me to have to learn the ways. With mother gone I didn't want to have to discuss my grief. I was very young and there were a great many things I needed to learn. The Red Clays were more than eager to teach. They didn't care how ready I was to learn. I learned what they needed to train. I'm sorry I wasn't there for you. I needed to learn how to be the brother you needed, elsewhere. Nothing I can say will repair the injury. Let me have a chance that I don't deserve to earn what I can from the here and now," he said. Genesis was still very angry. She wanted to scream at River and unload every bitter thought in her heart at him, but she remembered her prayers. Her fire calmed some.

"If it is your goal to earn, you will earn. If you fall short, you have yourself to blame. I will not judge true effort harshly, as The Wind commands. If you are sincere, I hope you succeed. Do not fool yourself that this will be easy to complete. You will stand before father. When you do, may your report be better than the one you just gave to me. May the Wind guide you and help you," she said. River heard his father through her words. They stung, badly.

"I am prepared to do what my words cannot," he said. Despite the anger in her heart Genesis did not hate River. It was not hate she harbored. She had set out on the road herself when she could be with their father. In that he did not bear the guilt alone. Though he had no greater cause than himself when he left, she could not dispute he'd gained one now.

"You asked me in the alley what I was doing here in Candleport with these rangers. I have taken a pilgrimage. But only so I can follow signs sent to us by the runes. Uncovering what they mean will take me to The East Lodge. The survivor of the attack you were sent to investigate had few dying words. The Runes, The Solstice and The Fourth Day. Southstar Redflower told this to me. As a mystic the runes are a very relevant thing. We use them to conduct a portion of our readings. The solstice has just occurred. We are now in the third day. Tomorrow will the fourth day. Tomorrow I fear something terrible may happen. In regards to what, I cannot say. What I can say is that I am not alone in my readings. Others who have inquired about the fourth day have all read the same," she said. River leaned forward. He had a very skeptical look on his.

"How can this be sister?" he said. Genesis reached down into her bag, which sat on the floor. She took out a small leather bag and tossed it over to River. He opened it and poured out its contents into his hand. It was his sister's runes. He looked up at her with puzzlement.

"Ask about the fourth day brother. You have the gift. No matter how far you have run from it. The runes will listen to you. Ask with your heart," she said. Her eyes were earnest, but he only saw madness in her words.

"You cannot ask this of me. I turned my back on The Wind. On the way. On the family!" he snapped and tried to hand the runes back. Genesis held up her hand.

"The Wind knows the truth. Your sister knows the truth. The runes know the truth. They know your heart. Ask of them. Not of yourself," she said. River could not tell if it was pity he was hearing in her voice or something else. He closed his eyes and shook his head.

"You expect too much of me. I'm not worthy to hold runes, much less ask of them, or of myself. I am a ranger. I know my place in this world Genni," he said. Genesis nodded and then folded her arms disapprovingly.

"You sound certain brother. Prove it then. Ask of them about the fourth day. If the reading is nonsense then by all means pick up your bow and merely be the ranger you claim to be. Let the runes speak for themselves," she said. River looked at the runes in his hand. Their weight and their design was the first thing that entered his mind. As they sat in his hand his question formed in his mind. He asked his heart as his father had taught him so many years ago. Then he looked up at Genesis.

"Very well. Do the humors bode well for The Fourth Day?" he said and then tossed the runes up in the air. He watched them as they fell and tumbled down through the air to the mattress. They bounced around when they struck the surface. River's eyes jolted wide open and he stood bolt upright. He stared at the runes for several moments and then he glanced over at Genesis.

"It's a trick!" He yelped and picked up one of the runes and rolled it around in his hand, checking for an imbalance. Genesis sat back and snickered.

"It's no trick brother. The runes fell from your own hand and now lay blank. Do you believe me now that we have good cause for alarm?" she said. River placed the rune in his hand back in the bag and handed it back to Genesis.

"I don't know what we have cause for. I know I have more questions than answers. This will not do. Answers are at The East Lodge you say?" he said. Genesis collected her runes and put them back in their bag. She looked up at her brother. He looked alarmed enough to her.

"I would not be travelling there if I believed otherwise. I won't be able to address The Brothers without an impartial escort. Rangers cannot serve as sponsors regarding Lodges I am to understand. This is a problem," she said. The Lodges had their own ways. Only Glass Lodges allowed women without escort. Rangers had declared a state of autonomy in this respect. No direct interaction with the Lodge system without an outside arbiter in other words. It was a schism from olden times. River would not trespass. Even for his sister.

"You are correct. I cannot sponsor you. I do however travel with two esteemed knights of the realm. Working for silver as hirelings or nay, they are still esteemed. Their titles still carry weight. Choose one or both to escort you. I will refrain as you make your inquires. I will Greet with the Trees with the Barley Lands while you do," he said. Genesis placed her runes back in her satchel and stood up.

"The path is plotted then. Prayer has left me famished. We can discuss booking a river ship over boiled chicken," she said. River bent down and picked the bag of runes up out of his sister's pack and handed them to her.

"You'll want to have these on hand Genni. We will need The Wind's wisdom again soon I fear," he said. Genesis smiled and slid the bag into her pocket.

Music filled night in Creendea after the sun dipped below the horizon. Attheon sat aside from many of his men in a café near the center of the city. Sitting with him were his brother Antimony and

Mayor Runeo. Before them musicians played joyous and energetically spirited music as fire twirlers dazzled the crowd with their agility and skill. Attheon had abstained from wine for his evening meal. Opting instead to take tea. His head would be clear for the morning ride. Antimony decided to have some wine but had kept his consumption modest. He found he enjoyed music more if he could still stand unaided.

Attheon had not seen a show like this in quite some time. It wasn't like a peaceful night under the stars, but it was entertaining. His men seemed to be having a good time. After such a long journey east they deserved some fun to offset all the miles they'd put between themselves and Southgate. Some miles still needed to be travelled before their arrival in Seastorm. He was no closer to knowing how he would make the impression he needed to with Lady Marea. Their union was already a given, but he was not a man familiar with taking what he did not earn or feel worthy of. If it were not his father's wish, he would not accept.

Not without first facing challenge and winning favor. He was still very unsure what he would be taking away from his time in Seastorm before he journeyed to The Sentinel Landing. The ancestral site where royal marriages took place that stood at the foot of eastern edge of The Sentinels. His father was no doubt making preparations to travel there as Attheon sat there and sipped tea. To the side of the performers someone weaving through the crowd caught his eye. A young man dressed in a long brown robe made his way toward Attheon' table. A pair of Southgate men stood up and blocked his path as he approached. Mayor Runeo took notice of the man and recognized him.

"Do not be alarmed my Princes. This is Salver Carline," he said. Attheon looked the man over and then gestured to his men to let the salver pass.

"What business do you have with us salver?" Attheon said. Salver Carline laid a message down on the table in front of him. Attheon picked it up and looked at it.

"It has a Redflower seal on it," he said. Antimony leaned over to take a closer look at it. Attheon looked up at Carline.

"When did this arrive?" he said. The salver looked to be somewhat out of breath. He must have run here.

"It. It just arrived by feather my Prince," he stammered. Attheon looked back the message in his hand. He broke the seal and began reading it. What he saw disturbed him greatly. The message dropped from his hand and he stared off into space. This alarmed Antimony.

"What is it brother?" he said. Attheon refocused to Antimony.

"There's been a murder. A Redflower has been killed at The East Lodge," he said. Antimony's jaw dropped. Runeo gasped. Neither Lamb spoke for a moment. Antimony pushed his wine away.

"Madness! Utter Madness! Who would be such a fool as to beg wrath from the Redflowers?" Antimony said and slammed the table with his fist. Attheon was thinking just the same.

"Evidently someone ignorant of the consequences. The message comes from a Snowbrace Quickwill. Cousin of the wolf who was slain. A pup of Carbor I would reckon. He is requesting us to meet him on the morrow on an island called Cotter's Hill," he said. Runeo knew of this place.

"Cotter's Hill is an island between rivers near our border with the East Barley Lands. A quarter day's ride to Cotter's Bridge on a swift horse," he said. Attheon read the message again and then set it back down. He then looked over at his brother.

"We're gong to need some fresh horses for seven Mayor Runeo. Five of our fastest riders will join us. We will meet with this ranger. Now," Attheon said. Antimony did not like this plan.

"Brother, what about your courtship? What about Seastorm? What do we even know of this Quickwill ranger?" he said. Attheon stood up and picked up his sword.

"Surely you jest brother. Not even a Prince of Southgate has any business ignoring a petition from Redflower kin. Lady Marea and the city of Seastorm aren't going anywhere. We depart at once," he said authoritatively. Despite his misgivings Antimony nodded in agreement and stood up as well. Attheon turned to Mayor Runeo.

"Mayor if you would, feather Seastorm and notify them of the possibility of our delay and express our sincerest apologies for them," he said and stuffed the message into his pocket. Runeo downed his entire cup of wine and stood.

"It will be done at once my Prince," he said. Attheon smiled and departed the café with Antimony following behind him. Runeo looked to his advisors.

"Put a quill in the hand of our most eloquent scribe. I don't care if you have to roust him from bed. I want horses collected and brought to the keep post haste. Go quickly now. Not a moment to lose!" he yelled. His advisors jumped into action despite having plenty of wine. Attheon already had a list forming in his head of men he knew could negotiate unfamiliar terrain quickly. They would be the swords by his side. He had never met a Redflower in person before, but the name was long familiar to him. He was less familiar with the Quickwills or any other kin to Brewster Redflower. He understood his brother's reluctance. There was much he didn't trust about this as well. He did trust himself and his abilities enough, that if this were some sort of treachery, he'd have the ability to escape it. He didn't want to be wrong about this though. If he caught a single whiff of something he didn't like he'd make a swift exit from the scene. He understood the rivers in the area to be shallower and on the slower side. Crossing could be an option if the riverbed was firm enough. The soil on either side could tell him much. Strong sturdy trees would be a good sign of a rocky bottom versus silt. As many avenues of retreat would need to be scouted before crossing onto Cotter's Hill.

Bell Store was a quiet place again after the festival. Evening commotion was now fairly modest as smaller observances about town carried on. Tass had come home from such an event. It was simple gathering of farmers telling stories as men had ale and the children ate slices of spiced pumpkin. The hirelings had gone home after patrolling an otherwise subdued festival night. Tass doubted the town leadership felt like they got their money's worth. Not even an argument broke out. It was a jovial affair to be sure with music and dancing well into the night. He had fun throwing horseshoes with some of the other children. Many of whom he had met for the first time. Social events were few and far between. The rest of the calendar was taken up by work and left little time to meet anyone. The evening's fun had left him both energized and tired at the same time. It was usually one or the other. He began to fall asleep when he thought he heard the sound of someone running by his window. He listened for a while but he didn't hear it again.

He figured it was his dreams teasing him before he could properly nod off. He dwelled on his disappointment in his dreams. So much so he failed to notice that he had fallen asleep. He was in a field. Not his family's field. But one he knew nearby. It was wide open and looked freshly tilled. His feet sank deeply into the soil so he sidestepped into a furrow. He followed along it for some distance before he reached a round wooden table in the middle of the field. Sitting upon it was a single bright orange pumpkin. As Tass got closer to the table the pumpkin atop it began to frost over. The closer he moved, the more frost formed. When he was within several paces the air around him began to grow colder and colder. The layer of frost on the pumpkin grew very thick. When Tass was close enough to the table to touch it the pumpkin cracked and then fragmented. The shattered pieces then caught alight and began burning. Thick plumes of smoke started billowing out and down the sides of the table. A sharp crack woke Tass up. He heard a scream. His door burst open. His father, with horror in his eyes and a hatchet in his hand looked down at him in terror.

"Run Boy!" he yelled and looked over at the window. He then dashed back out of the room and slammed the door shut. Tass heard shouting. He jumped up and went the door.

"Papa!" he screamed. The door thundered and the wall shook as something smashed up against it. Tass grabbed at the latch and pulled with all his strength as a loud cry rang out from behind it. It wouldn't budge. Wood splintered and a jolt of hot pain ripped down the boy's arm. Tass pulled away from the door to see a blade punctured through it. It started to twist as the injury around it oozed dark red blood. Tass groaned in agony as he noticed his arm bled as well. He didn't remember running then. Just flashes. He only reckoned reaching the window, falling, and hitting the dirt as if it were a stone slab. Couldn't breathe. Feet kicking. Running to the barn. Finding Bess. Throwing on her bridle. Climbing onto her back. Galloping. All around him was fire. All around him was screaming. All around him were people running. People lay around like they were asleep. But their eyes were open. Tass pointed Bess east past his family's field and away from town. Everything was a blur. The world slowed down to a crawl. The night air rushed past him as Bess raced away.

The staging room was active in these late hours as Run DMC's "King of Rock" thumped. Nearing midnight now Jack and Hammer were busy calibrating tech that they had painstakingly concealed within the clothing and armoring the Isos would be taking with them on Mission 73. Anything technological had to be well disguised as everyday objects and materials. It was a challenge, but Salazar's contribution helped a great deal. They had lightweight cut and fire resistant fabrics that simulated the look and feel of common silk and cotton. There were panels of super strong lightweight alloys plated in common metals that provided added protection. Padding this metal armoring were leather and leather-like materials that concealed conductive webbing connected to the microcomputers throughout their garb made to look like patches of riveted leather. Everything was the evolution of over seventy missions to strange worlds. Some of these components were still in the process of being fabricated for Nocivo and JP were what Salazar called "Diet Valiants" affectionately.

Salazar's suit would be not be far removed his Generation Five valiants in functionality by contrast. Despite it's period look this valiant would incorporate many of the updates present in other Generation Six valiants still on the drawing board. Each suit though was being fabricated with the individual in mind. After the fallout of Mission 72 Salazar used the experience to update the tactical gear of Nocivo and JP using all his research on them. The best was yet to come. He stood in a lift leading down to the staging room behind a cart with long boxes piled on top of it. The lift came to a stop and Antonio wheeled the cart out into the hallway. The doors slid open and he walked through. The others looked up at him when he entered. More so what he brought. A large clock on the wall displayed the time of departure and a second clock displaying time counting down. Antonio came to a stop near the others and grabbed he long box on top and walked over to Nocivo. Estrello looked at the box as it was being handed over. He already had a positive look on his face, and he hadn't even opened it yet. When he did a grin ran across his face.

"Gladius Hispaniensis," he said and picked up the sword from its box. And unsheathed it from it's scabbard. Antonio set the box back on the cart.

"Forged to your specifications with a half inch extension on the grip with a reinforced pommel. Grip has been modified slightly to maximize edge alignment and blade profile geometry and all that jazz and whatnot. You get the point. You complain I drone on about that kind of thing, so there you have it. Have a name in mind?" he said. Nocivo was deeply impressed with the blade he held.

"You are a true artist with vulcanium Tony. I don't say it enough. What to call her though," he said as he admired the workmanship of the blade. He looked back at Antonio.

"Her name is Xochicalco," he said and slid the blade back into the scabbard. Antonio walked back to the cart and picked up another much larger box. He carried it over to JP.

"The trick is getting the proportions in the alloy right. Too much starcry and the blade doesn't hold its shape. Too little and the properties of the tungsten and chromium otherwise have make the blade brittle. The pitfalls when working with them in other words. Just the right amount though and you mimic the flex of steel but with better edge retention," he said and handed the box to JP. He opened it and pulled out his sword. Antonio took the box back and set it down.

"Up scaled sountaka with a grip to accommodate those bear paws you call hands," he said. JP unsheathed the blade from its scabbard. He too was impressed by the work put into it.

"When the hell did you find time to make these?" he said. Antonio chuckled and picked up a smaller box.

"I can hear the old man's voice right now saying 'Oh, is that right Mijo.' Anyhow, never tell my father that you want to make really cool swords, because the next thing you know, you're spending the entire summer with an angry smith who hates your ricasso, and you're going to get it right even if you have hammer out a thousand swords. It didn't take a thousand but I learned to grind a proper ricasso by the end of the summer. The suontaka doesn't have a ricasso, but it's a beautiful style nonetheless. Got a name for her?" he said. JP slid the blade back in its scabbard and held it up. The leatherwork was humble but well constructed.

"She is Ukko. We had this conversation a few months ago. If you made me a sword, I'd call it Ukko. Your blank stare tells me you forgot we talked about it. That tracks," he said and sighed. Antonio didn't remember the chat. JP wasn't overly shocked. Antonio found his choice curious though. This naming seemed a bit out of character for JP, but Antonio liked the sound of it.

"Interestingly spiritual. Would not have expected that," he said. JP smirked as he attached Ukko to his belt.

"Was going for the cultural angle. Not much for that spiritual stuff. I do like how you have made all our stuff look worn. Jeremy would be impressed," he said sarcastically and looked over at Jeremy who was sitting nearby cutting lengths of leather cord for the mission. He looked up and flipped JP off. JP laughed. Jeremy had passed on a considerable amount of input to Antonio who took it all to heart.

"If we went Mall Ninja we'd stick out like a sore thumb. Pre-distressing the materials was the easy part. Mimicking the scents of the local environment and proper levels of oxidation odors in the materials was far tougher. Going out there smelling like Axe Body spray would probably not be the best idea even though Dark Temptation gives me that extra edge when it counts, and none of you will change my mind about that," he said. Nocivo shook his head.

"Hijole vato. Cállate con that shit man," he said. Antonio smirked and opened the box he was holding. He took out a small parrying dagger. He set the box down and opened the longer box that was sitting next to it. In it sat a blade with a semi-caged grip. He held up the smaller blade to show everyone.

"This is Piña. And the big one is Colada," He said with a grin. JP rolled his eyes and walked off. An alarm went off on Jeremy's table. He picked it up and walked over to the others.

"Okay outer armor fabricators are good to go. I would have gone plain-Jane to blend in better but you guys have your style thing, so travelling mercenary it is," he said and looked over at Antonio who raised a brow.

"What? We're travelling with a 15-foot tall alien robot. I think subtlety isn't in the cards. No offense Strat," he said and looked over at Stratum who was sitting in the corner working on travel calibrations. He looked over at Antonio.

"I wasn't even listening. You guys keep playing with your little swords. I have a lot of mathematics to do," Stratum said dismissively. Antonio shrugged his shoulders and looked back at Jeremy.

"Is the bull taken?" he said. Jeremy sighed and looked over the list of all the family, regional and historical sigils already in use. No instances of the bull came up. He grimaced and looked up at Antonio.

"No, the bull isn't taken. Starting Salazar fabrication sequences," He said. Antonio pumped his fist. Jeremy looked over at Estrello.

"Scorpion wasn't taken either. Went ahead and got yours fabricating. Only available secondary color for dominant blue nobody was using was yellow. I think you'll like what ol' Fate has for you though," He said. Nocivo flipped a thumb up. Jeremy looked over at JP.

"Sorry JP. The ram was taken. Some family named Tolliver. Any backups?" he said. JP thought a few moments and rubbed his chin.

"I'll go with a Snow Goose. My daughter and I share the same birth totem. January babies," he said. Jeremy looked over his list. He didn't see any kind of goose.

"Good to go man. Still thinking about army green?" he said. There really wasn't a question in JP's mind.

"Once Army. Always Army. Hooah!" he yelled. Jeremy rolled his eyes and tapped on his tablet.

"Okay man your stuff is good to go. Fabrication time five hours," he said. This was to be expected. Though sophisticated 25th century machinery, Salazar's materials were still a chore to work with. Nocivo looked over at the direction of the door.

"That will give us time to familiarize ourselves with our long range weaponry with Pauly," he said. The others glanced up at him. The looks on their faces were confused. A few moments later Pauly walked through the door pushing a cart with a pair of bows and quivers of arrows. JP picked up his bow and casually strung it. Pauly looked surprised. He remembered it took two men to barely manage getting it strung before. JP didn't seem to have much trouble. Antonio looked at JP's bow. His brow furrowed.

"Damn Pauly. Did you just put a string on a whole fucking tree. Holy shit!" he said and looked over at Pauly who shrugged his shoulders.

"It's what JP asked for. Challenge was to find a material strong enough for the string. I borrowed the formulation from your valiant Generation Three armor. Soaked the natural material in it for a couple of days. Did the trick," Pauly said. Antonio knew the polymer he was talking about and why it was chosen.

"Dynaleather agent. Spectacular tensile strength. An accidental discovery. I was trying to create a plastic explosive. Works great for bullet resistance, but it breathes like ass. That's why I go with a slightly weaker material now that keeps me cooler," he said. JP pulled the string back most of the way and grinned. The feel of the draw was exactly what he wanted. Nocivo's bow was a fairly modest recurve bow but still a formidable weapon. His arrows were also much shorter. He took one of JP's arrows from its quiver and held it to his side to compare its height to his own.

"A la verga JP!" he mused. JP laughed.

"You didn't think I was going to use those short ass things you have?" he said and laughed again.

The garrison outside the city in Bucklers Bend growled and snarled with the sounds of Marsh soldiers marching and training. New men were being broken in. Lord Addar Marsh and his eldest son Lestor surveyed the progress being made to strengthen Marsh forces. Allies were few that would come to Addar's aid. Many feared opposing Lord Haddock, and all knew Parnell Haddock had his eyes fixed on Buckler's Bend by now.

"How does it stand with our allies now boy?" Lord Addar said. The number in Lestor's head would not be pleasing to his father.

"Between our allies father, roughly two-thousand men. That is Halls Solur, Resty and Fennel combined. Haddock had made cowards from everyone else I petitioned close enough to come to our aid should Parnell

Haddock defy his King's orders. We have only three thousand men if you count the lads holding a sword for the first time today. Our outlook appears grim," Lestor said. Addar shook his head and sighed.

"We must look farther east and north to The Borderlands then," he said. Lestor looked at his father in disbelief.

"Surely not The Borderlands father. There is enough controversy surrounding the north and Hall Marsh as it is. If we start petitioning the north it's as good as admitting to the fantasies Haddock and his ilk have dreamt up," he said. Addar was undeterred.

"We might as well seek allies in a land we are already accused of colluding with lad. If we are handed the cloak, we may as well wear it. Already we train our men into the night to prepare ourselves to fend off Haddock and his growing list of allies. Would you begrudge your Hall seeking to even at least some of the odds lad?" Addar said. The younger Marsh was very much against this. He understood the value of appearances. He knew of what southerners felt about The Borderlands. They were as dubious as The Midlands in their eyes. Support from the Halls already declared may waver.

"I will set out east at daybreak father. I would urge you to reconsider entertaining seeking alliance with northern lords. But I will do as you ask. Regardless of what consequences I fear will follow if we do," Lestor said. Addar admired his son's wisdom. If this were a less desperate situation he would consider fewer options. But a threat like Parnell Haddock could not be underestimated.

"You have a wisdom beyond your years lad. If I could change the wind and where it was blowing I surely would. Haddock is not a rational man. He would see our Hall put in chains or face the hangman. His hatred and suspicion of the north is well known. I wish it were not so, but the man has a sickness that time and hope cannot cure. Our defenses must be ready, and our backers must be more numerous. I wish you all the best in the east lad. Hopefully Haddock has not gotten to them before we have a chance to plead our case," Addar said. Should Lestor be unsuccessful more drastic measures may have to be taken.

"What of our silent ally father?" he said. Addar laid his hand on his son's shoulder and leaned close.

"We do not speak of this outside of confident spaces. Especially not out in the open near any ear that may overhear. Should matters become so dire this hand will be played. But only then. We already tread on dangerous ground even having the knowledge we do. Greater war could sweep over our Hall like a storm of fire. We look for all other options before even considering graver possibilities," Addar said. Lestor lowered his voice and calmed his tone.

"Utmost discretion father. Utmost," he said. Addar patted his son on the shoulder.

"Good lad. Good lad. Another option on the table would of course be expensive. I hate the idea of spending silver we cannot afford to part with on hirelings who celebrate death as much as they do the glint of silver, but we face difficult times and don't have the luxury of certain reservations. I will be sending feathers to those I trust to get the word to these sorts of men. If we get five hundred purchased blades, that will be five hundred more than we have now. Go and get some rest boy. Your ride will not be an easy one," Addar said. Lestor embraced his father.

"Your faith in me will be rewarded father. I swear it by The Wind," Lestor said. Addar smiled proudly and watched his son walk away to his bedchamber. He sighed and looked back at his men training as clouds covered the stars in the sky. He would pray to The Wind his son would find the support he pledged to.

It was late, very late on this very dark night. Clouds covered the sky. With no moon the darkness was great. Attheon and Antimony waited behind a bend in the road while one of his riders scouted ahead from higher ground. The heir to the Southgate was taking as few chances as one could on a night like this and a path like this before him. Having two Princes on this errand stood out as more and more foolish and cavalier in his mind the more miles they put between them and Creendea. He doubted he could have kept Antimony there even if he wanted to.

He was a young but determined man. He would have found a way to ride with him. A sound off in the distance caught Attheon's attention. A chirp in the air came soon after. A false birdcall put Attheon and his men at ease as the scout emerged from the darkness with his report. He slinked over to his Prince quickly.

"My Prince the road is clear for many miles ahead. The gods have blessed us with favorable terrain," he said. Attheon patted the scout on the shoulder.

"Good work soldier," Attheon said and then headed back to where his horse was hitched. Antimony followed close behind. He had grown more and more agitated as the ride had gone on.

"We bargain too boldly brother. We test the gods too readily. I see calamity before the sun chases away this night," Antimony said. Attheon turned and placed his hand on his brother's shoulder.

"I have heard your words Antimony, I feel the dread as you do. They have not been dismissed or disregarded nor has the love behind them been overlooked. I know the forest. She has many things to say. I am her audience and I see the signs she leaves for me. Take heart brother. This night will not prevail against us," Attheon said and smiled. Antimony managed a smile as well. The brothers mounted their horses and the group continued on. Attheon turned back to his squire Stockard who had insisted on joining as well.

"What is our progress?" he said. Stockard had been doing his best to keep track of their travel without the moon or stars. Songs that he had been singing in his head for the entire ride had certain durations, which he selected, based on the speed he reckoned the horses were travelling overall. A practice called song gauging which gave him a rough idea of how far they'd travelled and how much farther they had to ride based on Mayor Runeo's estimation.

"By my reckoning we're still twelve miles or more out from Cotter's Hill. We passed Old Whisperer's Wall a little while ago. That puts us most of the way if we keep a good steady pace my Prince," he said. Attheon grinned.

"Good work. Let's ride," he said and kicked his heels. The men of Southgate were back on the move.

The staging room was filled with the sounds of clanking metal and tightening of leather straps. The clock on the wall read 2:42 AM. The countdown clock expired. The others had cleared out by now so it was just the four Isos. Each one of them was deep in their own thoughts as they prepared. Stratum sat in the corner still, but he now convened with the harmonies around him. He listened to their tales. Every minute fluctuation in the auras from the room itself, the people inside, the ship and the earth around it spoke to him in his meditation. He could feel the dissonance in his friends in this state. He knew each of them had great reservations about this world they were travelling to. Before every mission there was some of this. But his trip seemed to bother them more. Mission 72 revealed much about Antonio Salazar. He'd be a fool if he didn't think that had some influence on what he felt now from the others. Each of them had escaped death many times already. But somehow things had changed. They were young, still learning and still very new to these kinds of changes in course. He would be there to help them as best he could. Estrello looked over at the meditating giant.

"T-minus five minutes Strat," He said. Stratum emerged from his trance and looked over at Nocivo.

"10-4 Skipper," he said acknowledging the time was very near. Antonio was helping JP make adjustments to the fit of his armor. He had thought about the last mission a great deal. He suspected the others would be watching how he watched them from now on. Or for the time being at the very least. He didn't blame them. He did not intend for them to find out they way they did. But things shook out how they did and now the fallout would have to be lived through for however long it was a relevant issue. These things were not under his control. How tight JP's pauldrons fit were however. He pulled the leather binding tightly.

"How is that man?" he said. JP stepped away and rotated his shoulder.

"Much better. I think that'll work. How did you get this stuff smelling so much like wet grass and dirt? I feel like I've had this stuff on for months," he said. Antonio grinned. He enjoyed when his hard work gave others pause.

"That's the idea. Visual camouflage is highly effective at tricking the eye. That's just one of the senses," he said. Nocivo was impressed as well. His nose was difficult to fool. He suspected this olfactory camouflage was another one of Salazar's countermeasures designed with him in mind that he neglected to mention. It would be a discussion for another time. He looked up at the clock. It was almost time. He whistled to get everyone's attention. The group picked up their weapons and other gear. Antonio put his helmet on. The tech inside read his biometrics and came alive. He looked down for a few moments and sighed. He picked his head up and turned to JP.

"Hey man," he said and took off his belt and handed his sword and dagger over to him. JP looked down at them and then at Antonio.

"I'll give them back later," he said and took them. The countdown from five seconds began. The group prepared themselves. The light around them began to distort. Then they were gone.

Epilogue: Hourglass Turns

December 16th 2011. Dry sands blew over the hot dunes outside Cairo, Egypt. The god Sobek stood on a stone wall overlooking the city. He did this often as he enjoyed the way the sun hit the pyramids at this time of day in this time of year, one of the small pleasures. He cherished those the most. Behind him he could feel a powerful presence. He looked over his shoulder with his reptilian eyes. There stood three figures dressed in sand colored robes. One carried a staff. A man of dark complexion had a sword at his hip. The third was a woman with armored gauntlets that reached almost up to her elbow. Sobek was surprised if somewhat alarmed to see any of them. The news they brought was typically grim. He greeted them warmly nonetheless.

"Ezekiel? How long has it been? Why does he send you to me? The Pantheons stood aside and did not interfere in Lucifer's war as he instructed. We also did not meddle with the children of Abraham as instructed. His people chosen. To what end? A book tells the story after a fashion. A book I'm quite fond of. Except the part about the plagues. Pharoah wouldn't listen. Not even to us who cared to try to sway him. Arrogant mortal mired in his own malfeasance. We said as much at the time. Is this the matter that you bring to me after so long? I do not claim to speak for my Pantheon. I only speak for myself. Still, whatever the purpose of your being here, it is pleasing to see all of you again, despite my concern you bring me no glad tidings. I hope you've been well," he said. Ezekiel stepped forward. There was a serious look in his eyes, but there was also warmth.

"Sobek old friend. We seek you out, because you out of your entire Pantheon are the most reasonable and rational. The others would not speak to us even if we tried. We have not visited you to discuss our brother's obsession with power, or old matters with this land. We came to you to discuss another matter," he said solemnly. Sobek looked at each of them with concern.

"If he requires my assistance, I will give it. How may I help him?" he said. Ezekiel leaned forward on his staff and sighed.

"Troubled times have come again old friend. We seek four men who defy the laws of existence. Men who insult him. Insult us. Insult you, with their sins. They must be found. He would like you to ask of the Eyes of The River that reach long into the vast desert sands to watch for these men and the sins they commit," he said. The group talked a bit longer in the blowing sands, and then Sobek nodded.

"It will be done. I would ask why he would choose this method, but I know it is not your place to ask these questions, so I too will refrain. I send my love with you on your journey and hope in my heart you will find those you seek soon. Be well my old friends," he said and held out a hand. Ezekiel shook it and nodded.

"Until we meet again. Under better circumstances I would hope," he said and smiled. Sobek watched as the three angels departed in their craft. The desert sand whipped around him as they rose into the sky. He turned and looked upon The Nile. He sat, and began to pray.